CW00519956

# THE NEEDWOOD DIAMOND

## *The second*
## *Alan Shobnall story*

**By**

**Simon Clark**

## Burton-upon-Trent

*Alan Shobnall and his family are inseparable from
the historic corner of Staffordshire dominated by Burton-on-Trent.
The town and the settlements of its southern hinterland,
especially around Wychnor, are central to this story.
Burtonians and others who know the place will note that,
while many of the local references hold good,
the area, its landmarks and its buildings have
in some measure been re-imagined for their roles.
Neither the author nor Alan Shobnall mean any disrespect.
Quite the contrary.*

*This story is dedicated to the legacy of James Brindley, architect of the Trent & Mersey
Canal.*

# Burton in the County of Staffordshire

*For those unfamiliar with the location of Burton, it sits proudly in the heart of the English Midlands.....*

.....And to its immediate south, we find Alrewas, Fradley, Barton-under-Needwood and – most notably – Wychnor, the Staffordshire communities that set the stage for this story:

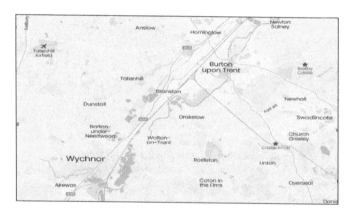

# SUMMER HOLIDAY

"Daddy, help! We have to stop the sea!"

Shobnall snapped out of a light doze, pushed his sunhat off his face, shaded his eyes. Down the beach sat their grandest castle of the week: a majestic crenellated mound decorated with little paper Union Jacks, encircled by a wide moat and a Maginot Line of an outer wall. On its far side, Josephine was scampering hither and thither, spade whirling as she shovelled fresh sand onto the wall where the incoming tide surged, threatening to swamp their defences. He could see, waving in the air, a pair of chubby legs. Alice had obviously toppled into the moat.

Elaine beat him to it – not that he was showing any sign of motion – leaping from her deckchair, tossing her newspaper onto his lap and trotting round the castle to pull the stricken two year-old upright. She bent over Alice, covering the child's hand with her own, helping her pick up her plastic spade and join her sister in the struggle to shore up the wall.

The sun was low but bright still, adding a sparkle to the waves, silhouetting a bobbing crab-boat as it puttered across the view. The beach was almost deserted: one other family, mum, dad and three boys, over the next breakwater, their transistor bleating the tinny sounds of Freddie and the Dreamers; an elderly couple up on the promenade; gulls squabbling over the contents of a waste bin. The crowds who, a few hours ago, had spread themselves like a second skin over the hot sand had packed away their seaside paraphernalia and moseyed off to whichever Sheringham hotel or guest house or bed-and-breakfast they were staying in. The Shobnalls, on the other hand, were intent on making the most of their last day. Friday June 29th was their final night with Mrs Bayliss. Tomorrow they'd set off back to Burton-on-Trent.

Not yet, though. Shobnall unfolded the paper. 'BERLIN SALUTES JFK', 'KHRUSHCHEV MEETS RUSSIAN COSMONAUTS'. He raised his gaze to the castle and his family. *How we need these leaders to get along, that Cuban missile business was scary, days I really thought a nuclear war was on the cards.* The Elaine/Alice combination was fruitlessly piling wet sand into a calamitous breach. Josephine was standing back in the shallows, watching the tide's inexorable advance with a pensive expression on her face, seawater rippling back and forth around her ankles.

He flipped the paper over. 'TEST MATCH ENDS IN DRAMATIC DRAW'. A shirtless Brian Close, his chest a mosaic of livid bruises, the consequence of the Yorkshireman using his body to defy the West Indian fast bowlers as the Second Test clubbed its way to a savage draw. *They call it sport, incredible no bones were broken.* A turret - the product of a bucket, daddy's steady hands and sand of precisely the right moistness - tilted slowly sideways, shed its little flag and slid down the crumbling side of the main rampart. The fastness wasn't going to hold out much longer.

The other family were off, costumes rolled in towels, the boys tasked with the picnic basket and the deckchairs. The man waved: Shobnall responded. Sheringham depended on its visitors. A rural fishing community had, like so many of Britain's coastal settlements, been transformed by the railway late in the nineteenth century. The fishermen found their catch could be in London within four hours, boosting prices and incomes. Then the capital woke up to the attractions of travelling the other way for vacations and second homes in the ozone-laden air of North Norfolk. Mind you, with the Beeching Report slapped on the table back in March, the town was worried about the fate of its railway station. And not at all about its sandcastles.

Elaine and Alice had retreated to dry sand, where Alice was already being distracted by a scattering of sea shells. Josephine, spade at rest, remained tide-side as the deepening surf lapped at her calves, washed over the wreck of the outer wall into the moat and gnawed at the castle's heart. Shobnall threw the paper aside and strode over. He took her free hand as another turret collapsed into the water. The two of them had been the prime architects, working diligently for much of the morning with, of course, the occasional disruptive 'assistance' from Alice. He looked down at his elder daughter. "Well, Jo, shall we call it a day or do you want to wait?"

She was silent for a long moment as the water demolished their day's labours, their best-ever castle. She raised an untroubled face to her father and announced, in a very matter-of-fact tone, "We can go, daddy, you don't argue with an ocean".

The girls led the way, dancing along the promenade, past the brightly-painted beach huts, perfectly aligned like a set of miniature Swiss chalets, up Beach Road and along Cliff Road to their temporary home-from-home. Mrs Bayliss hovered, ready to fuss over the girls and usher them all into the parlour for their final tea. In the morning there would be packing and farewells. A last family wander down to the promenade to make sure that the uniformed attendant, ticket dispenser to hand, was laying out the striped deckchairs; that the donkey-man had his string of mounts in place, harnesses gleaming, ready for the first rides of the day; that the ice cream, candy floss and seafood stallholders were opening up their kiosks; that, down at the Fishermen's Slope, the morning's crab and lobster pots were being heaved ashore. Time for a family to stand together and wave goodbye to an ocean.

They would have Sunday for the post-holiday chores – washing and ironing, brushing all that sand out of the Anglia, sifting through the mountain of post – and preparing for normality. Elaine was only back at school part-time as yet. She would have time in the morning to ferry the girls to her parents in Winshill. Shobnall might have wondered how on earth his in-laws had survived, starved of Jo and Alice for a whole week but he had other matters on his mind. The DI's regular Monday meeting and a run of night shifts.

\* \* \*

Fred Bull, astride his beloved Royal Enfield Bullet, weaved the bike through the Birmingham traffic. Well into evening but there was always a bustle on the roads in Brum. He kept the needle dead on 30mph through Castle Bromwich, past the old Spitfire factory, and on through the heart of Sutton Coldfield, driving within himself; he could cut loose beyond the restricted roads zone. Three days dipping in the Trent for a child's body and the boat engine had misfired. A brand-new starter motor nestled in his pannier. They had to be able to rely on the boat.

He upped the speed on leaving the built-up area, leaned into the curve as he joined the A38 northwards and cranked it up to around 70. At Lichfield he would veer westwards to Stafford where Vern was working late on the boat. Fred never turned down the chance of a burn-up. One day, some over-weaning Transport Minister, like that chump Marples, would decide to make a name for himself by bringing in speed limits on all roads but, for now, anything went out here! He edged up to 75, the air whipping across his leathers. Traffic was sparse now, overtaking was a doddle. Dark clouds were gathering. The land had been basking in a glorious summer but a night of rain wouldn't go amiss. The farmers would be happy.

Fred saw the vehicle in his mirror, angled his head astern. It was overhauling him at a rate of knots. He held his speed, tucked the bike to the nearside. He was doing almost 80 but it swished by nonchalantly. He'd never seen anything quite like it. A long, powerful black limousine with a bonnet that seemed to go on forever and a passenger compartment elongated beyond normality. The windows were obscured. Must be celebrities or suchlike, he thought.

He dragged extra out of the 500cc engine. The manufacturers claimed a max of 87 mph but that was before Fred effected some enhancements of his own. At a smidge over 90 he matched the limousine. The rear profile said American, a Lincoln Continental, but he'd never seen any motor that long. The rear window, too, was curtained. Rain began to spatter down gently. Lichfield hove in view. The limousine driver must have been aware, seen him slow. The big motor flashed its lights twice. Fred raised an arm in salute before turning off for Stafford.

\* \* \*

6

We can follow the limousine as it barrels on up the A38, windscreen wipers sweeping aside the intensifying rain, headlights now on full-beam. Past the sign to Streethay on the right, a disused airfield visible to the left, the Fradley Junction sign. Sweeping past an Ind Coope lorry, the Royal Warrant resplendent on its cab. Decelerating through Alrewas and slowing right down crossing the River Trent, the driver clearly looking for a landmark. Finding it, the left indicator flashing in the gloom brought about by a combination of rainclouds and oncoming night, turning off west at Wychnor Bridges across a humpback over a canal, and trundling a couple of miles along a road barely wide enough to accommodate the vehicle. Beyond the village of Wychnor the road becomes a dirt track but the packed earth is well-maintained and offers easier passage between ranks of poplars.

Abruptly, the trees fall away and the limousine tyres crunch onto a gravel driveway fronting a stately mansion; three storeys, high windows shrouded in burgundy ivy, a forest of ornate white chimney stacks spiked like lofty coronets. The car pulls up at the imposing pillared and canopied entrance. A black transit van is already parked here. The wipers stop, the engine stills. Nothing moves. Lights are on inside. The limousine horn sounds twice, echoing around the building. After a minute or so, the large door beneath the canopy creaks open. A man looks out, descends the steps to the gravel. Tweed shooting jacket, waterproof breeches tucked into wellington boots. A man of the country. He moves easily, comfortably, yet with a hint of wariness. He waits.

The driver clicks open the nearside door and jumps out, stretches his arms, rotates his shoulders. A long drive, muscular tension to be dispelled. A stocky, muscular figure, denim jeans and shirt, brylcreemed hair. He speaks to tweed jacket, who nods, points towards the open door. The driver raps on the roof of the car and out tumble five younger men. Four medium height and slim build, one more of a bear, clutching a beer bottle. All in black jackets, t-shirts and jeans, all with hair almost to their shoulders. They climb the steps in a gaggle and duck inside out of the rain, paying no heed to the house or the scenery or tweed jacket.

The driver and tweed jacket watch them go. The driver opens the car boot, pulls out half-a-dozen hold-alls. He and tweed jacket stare at each other. Eventually the driver spreads his arms in a gesture that says 'what can you do?' Tweed jacket shrugs, walks over and the two men lug the holdalls in through the entrance. As the drizzle washes down, the slam of the great door shudders among the trees like a warning.

\* \* \*

## TWO

He made it by the skin of his teeth. *How was I to know they'd be digging up the road at The Branston Arms?* Lennie Morton looked pointedly at his wristwatch. Gideon Watson grinned; the young DC, not noted for his own punctuality, enjoyed seeing someone else squirm. Shobnall waved a greeting to his fellow-DS, Angela Bracewell, and took up position beside the window. Nobody in the street below apart from a scrum of kids pinch-punching the first day of the month.

The DI went through the list. Much as usual plus a rash of burglaries. Shobnall surveyed the room. Cyril Hendry, Angela, Lennie, Gideon, Eddie Mustard. *No Bob, where's Bob Saxby? He's not due for leave.* Worthington rattled on. "I don't want any repeat of the shenanigans at the 76 Club the other night with that Brian Poole and his Trembeloes. We do not tolerate such behaviour. HQ has issued guidance on these mods and rockers. Here, Gideon, pass these around please." He handed over a stack of pamphlets. "Some bad news, I'm afraid. That missing six year-old from Stapenhill. The divers found the body yesterday. Looks a simple tragedy but we need to make sure. Angela, I'd be grateful if you'd talk to the parents. Take Lennie." *A ticklish assignment but that's the pair you'd want to check everything's kosher.* "And I'd like a word with the sun-tanned prodigal by the window." That lightened the atmosphere, even for Angela and Lennie.

\* \* \*

His pipe firing, the DI relaxed. *Something on his mind, though.* "Good holiday, Alan. Elaine OK? The wee girls?"

"All fine, sir." *He worries about the young, he'll have been troubled by that lad in the Trent.*

"Good." The DI rested his pipe in the big yellow *A Double Diamond Works Wonders* ashtray, rubbed his eyes. "I'm glad you're back. We're still a man down on complement. HQ have at last agreed that Joe Short has been transferred to the new Forensics Unit instead of being on loan but those clowns in admin are taking an age over the paperwork. Saxby's father fell ill. I couldn't not let him go on compassionate. Cyril's side is alright but Heather Wilson's replacement isn't fully up to speed yet. Nevertheless, we were capable of handling a normal workload, even with you at the seaside. Then that little boy went missing. Fred Bull and his mate, er...."

"Vern, sir." *He never remembers Vern's name.*

"Aye, Vern. They pulled the body out yesterday. Sometimes I wonder how that pair stay sane. Next night we cop a string of burglaries. Centre of town. They walked along the roof, breaking in through skylights as they went. Furniture shop, insurance company, machine tool storage, estate agent, haulier, milliners, you name it. Amateurs or vandals. Not much taken but you know the time and paperwork involved. And now I have an extra little job." He paused.

*My cue.* "Is this something *you* have to do, sir, or something nasty you want to hand to someone else?"

"I wish I *could* hand it over." He centred a sheet of paper on the desk. "Are you familiar, if I may put it that way, with Lady Catherine Melinda Ketteridge Montague?" Shobnall looked blank. "What about Lord and Lady Needwood? You consort often with them?"

*What is all this?* "I have no idea who these people are, sir."

Senior eyeballs rolled. "There's me thinking of you perusing Debretts in your deckchair. Right. Lady Catherine Melinda Ketteridge Montague. She likes to be called Melinda and prefers that you address her on bended knee. Daughter and sole heir of the aforementioned Lord and Lady Needwood. You're not the only person who's never heard of them. The word that crops up is 'reclusive'. Back in the mists of time, some bent monarch handed tracts of Staffordshire to a robber-baron lackey, who assumed the title of Lord Needwood. The present title-holder is in his 80s. His wife is somewhat younger. They retain all their marbles, spend time in Switzerland and Bermuda, haven't set foot in Britain for at least two decades. Tax matters.

"Two things you need to appreciate. Firstly, these people are unbelievably rich, among the ten richest people in Britain. Even though they aren't *in* Britain. They own estates, property, lots of it, companies, lots of them, a bank in the City of London, half of Bermuda, probably a sizeable chunk of Switzerland as well. If you asked me how rich, I could write down a 1 but wouldn't know when to stop writing noughts after it."

"And Melinda will inherit all this." *There's a sting in the tail somewhere.*

"Already inheriting. For the past few years his lordship and his highly-remunerated financial advisors have been moving stuff over. A lot of their British wealth, investments, property and land including a swathe between Burton and Lichfield. She has other local interests, shares in several breweries and a major stake in Marmite and Bovril."

"How do you know all this, sir?"

"The right contacts. Frank Mercer at The Burton Daily Mail." He looked sly. "Your mate, Henderson, at Jardines Bank." *Ah, talking to Aitch explains a lot.* "There's not much Henderson can't dig out about someone's wealth. I don't know how he knows some of the things he knows and it's probably better I don't."

Shobnall took a moment to unwind that last sentence. "The second thing?"

"Connections, Alan, connections everywhere. Melinda is a friend of our Chief Constable. Ian Jessop doesn't have much truck with the notion of friendship but it's how Melinda describes the relationship. She has wealth and clout. If she wants something and it ain't illegal then Jessop will let her have it. This is for your ears only, Alan, you and Angela. It's not because muggins thinks there's anything that needs to be kept quiet. It's a condition laid down from on high." The DI tapped out his pipe into the yellow ashtray. "The British Museum is about to launch a major exhibition about India. 'Across the Ganges' or something like that. Ancient times through the Raj to India as an independent country. It's taken years to organise. Exhibits are being pulled in from all over. I'm no expert but Esmée tells me it'll be a monumental show. She wants to go.

"There's politics. It's only sixteen years since Indian independence and there remain some, er, sensitivities. MacMillan or whoever succeeds him will be at the opening. So will Nehru, their PM, and Earl Mountbatten as Governor-General. That side shouldn't affect us. I'm only mentioning it to emphasise how significant an event this will be. All parties will want something, probably none of them will get it and yet they all have to walk away happy. What *will* affect us is that one of the issues winding up India concerns exhibits they think were stolen from them and should be returned. Lord Needwood has – given the circumstances, I am reluctant to say 'owns' – in his possession one such exhibit. The Needwood Diamond."

"Never heard of it, sir."

"Me neither, until last week. Henderson had. Says it's one of the largest, most perfect diamonds ever known. It was one of the eyes in a statue of Vishnu, some god or other, in a temple in north India but it was nicked in the early days of the British Empire. The thief was never identified but who should have been serving out there but the-then Lord Needwood? He got his hands on it, whisked it out of India. Been in their vaults ever since. Henderson says if it went for auction it would carry a reserve tag in the order of fifteen million pounds sterling." Shobnall whistled through his teeth. "Quite. The Museum persuaded Lord Needwood to loan the Diamond for a couple of weeks. They're likely hoping to negotiate an extension. Melinda is in charge, on behalf of the family, of making sure it gets to London and back into Needwood hands safely.

She's playing it low profile. There have been several jewel robberies in London lately. She asked the Chief Constable for the services of a couple of dependable officers for the duration. Jessop decided one of them should be me. I choose the second."

"Hang on, sir. Two people aren't enough for a fifteen million pound jewel."

The DI picked up his dead pipe, sucked on it. "Personally, I think Jessop should have sent her away with a flea in her ear but we are where we are. Melinda is a work of art but not stupid, far from it. The main security load will be shouldered by Pinkertons, the Americans. They'll supply brawn, brain and probably firearms. The Museum has to stump up for them. Melinda is after a second layer, one not beholden to the Museum, someone to watch Pinkertons watch the Diamond. Pinkertons will love that."

*The Chief Constable knows how to pick the right man for a prickly job.* "You'll be taking Cyril, sir?"

The DI smiled approvingly, as if something nice he had been expecting had arrived bang on time and beautifully wrapped. "From Monday next."

"Sir, why are Melinda and Jessop looking this way?" The DI waited. "Ah. Local connections. It's here, isn't it."

"I think so. She's stashed it somewhere but she's giving nothing away until she needs to. Which is what I'd be doing in her place. Frank Mercer's digging around, see if he can get a fix on anything. I prefer to be a step ahead."

"We're losing our DI and station sergeant for two weeks."

"At least. If Lord Needwood lets it stay longer......I don't know, that would be up to Melinda and Jessop. I'm afraid you'll be losing more than that." *Here's the sting in the tail.* I need you on nights while I'm gone, however long that may be. You can pass my apologies to Elaine. I want Angela to take the day shift. I'll be on the end of a telephone if she needs me. I can't guarantee the same after dark and I need to be confident that someone's in charge while the law-abiding are asleep."

\* \* \*

"Well, *I* think it's a compliment. I'm proud of you. Here." Elaine pushed a mug of cocoa across the table. "You've been DS for less than two years and George is leaving you in charge. He's pleased with you."

"I suppose so." *Come on, Shobnall, not only is he trusting you, he let you know.* "A long stretch of nights straight after the holiday."

"You were always going to be on nights this week, it's just being extended. D'you think I can't manage a little short-term re-organisation?"

Shobnall relaxed. "I know you can, love. I'll stop feeling inadequate."

Elaine reached for his hand. "There's no need for my husband to feel inadequate. In any way." Shobnall's pleasure index rose another couple of degrees. "It does seem odd, though, hiring out the police as a favour to rich friends."

"I guess Jessop will claim there's an element of crime prevention."

"Huh! You'll have to tell Corky and Gordon. Now drink up. Tomorrow's going to be busy. School in the morning and Lavinia has arranged a trip to the Odeon."

"What's on?"

"Sink the Bismarck. Kenneth More's stiff upper lip. War films aren't my first choice but Lavinia says it's very good of its kind. She wants to see her god-daughters. After the cinema we'll collect the girls from Winshill."

They paused on the wide landing. They enjoyed the spaciousness of the new house. Elaine had felt a wrench at leaving their first home, in Ash Street, but a growing family needed elbow-room and they had managed to remain in Branston, close to old friends. The door to the girls' room had been left ajar; Elaine pushed it further so the light from the landing fell across the bed. Soon, they would have their own rooms but Elaine and Alan had felt that sharing during Alice's infancy would help them bond. It seemed to be working. Alice lay on her back, breathing softly, clutching Mr. Teddy. Josephine slept on her side, face towards her sister, an arm outstretched, her hand over her sister's and the bear. *I remember Elaine once telling me what a responsibility parenthood would be, she didn't tell me about the joy.*

\* \* \*

12

# THREE

He wedged his heels against the edge of his desk, pushed until he was balanced precariously on the back legs of the chair. *It's so quiet, I'm almost wishing for a crime.* The BBC headlines burbled from the office's Bush radio. 'Kennedy in Wexford, Russians in space.....Buddhist monks setting fire to themselves in Saigon.....The Taylor-Burton "Cleopatra" breaking cinema records.' Wobbling slightly, he extended an arm, clicked it off.

Eddie Mustard was along in the squadroom. *Wonder what he intends to do with those studies.* Downstairs, Charlie Taylor was continuing the induction of the new WPC, Sheila Redpath. Last time Shobnall had looked in they'd been playing cards. Redpath's predecessor, Heather Wilson, had gone off to try her hand as a freelance designer. *Good for her, a talent like hers shouldn't languish in a police station.* Angela had left him a typed summary of the day's events, asterisks against the couple of things she thought he should note. The surface of her desk wasn't arrayed with the mathematical precision that Gideon employed but it spoke of a very orderly mind. *She knows the book off by heart.* He swung his legs off his desk and wandered along the corridor.

\* \* \*

Eddie was on the floor doing press-ups. "Healthy body and all that, Alan." They'd worked together too long for the formalities of 'Sergeant' or 'Sarge'.

"You'll have the healthiest mind in the nick, Eddie. I take it you were at that 76 Club ruckus?"

"Yeah. It was nothing to do with the act, Brian Poole. It's Tremeloes, not Trembeloes. I think the DI does that on purpose. There was one of those mods, trim haircut and parka, sitting on a Vespa scooter right outside the club, smoking. Two more lads, long hair and leather jackets, came round the corner, shoved him and the scooter over. Cashier in the box-office saw everything. The mod didn't hesitate, climbed out from under and went for them."

"Bit of scrapping in the street then?"

"That was for starters. The cashier phoned in and I went down with Charlie and Paul Fraser." He shook his head. "Someone inside got wind and they poured out. Must have been forty or fifty in the scrum. We lined up with the bouncers and waited until it fizzled out. The Burton Daily Mail had a photographer there. I think it was the pictures in the paper that irritated the DI."

"Many hurt?"

"Nah. Handbags at midnight. It didn't look like they knew much about fighting."

"That HQ circular referred to similar incidents in London and on the South coast. Are these gangs?"

"The DI doesn't think so, Alan. His view it's more of a copycat movement. What worries him is if they get properly tooled-up."

"I can see his point. Tell me, did –"

Eddie's telephone shrilled. "Charlie, wotcha got?" Eddie listened intently and, as he did so, shifted round to the map of Staffordshire on the wall. "Where exactly, Charlie?" His forefinger moved across the map. "OK, I've got it. Who called it in?" His free hand found a pen and paper. "By the church. Off the green. OK, I'll have a dekko. Alan's here. He might like a trip out. I'll take a black car........Nah, we can manage, don't need to get there yesterday. I'll ring in later." He turned. "Report of gunshots out in cowboy country, Alan. Fancy it?"

"It would be something to do. Where?"

"Wychnor, a mile this side of Alrewas. Rung in by the local vicar."

"They say travel broadens the mind. Let's go."

* * *

Eddie drove. Shobnall liked to think of himself as a careful driver who knew his way around The Highway Code. He preferred not to think about being driven by Charlie Taylor; Eddie was no slouch behind the wheel but he did like to keep all four tyres on the road. South from Burton and through Barton-under-Needwood on the A38 as far as the turn-off at Wychnor Bridges. The side-road was narrow but deserted and Eddie put on a little more speed than Shobnall would have liked until the road branched around what was clearly a village green, a triangular grassy area with a small stand of trees beside a red telephone kiosk and, beyond, a clutch of buildings. Wychnor village. *More of a hamlet really*. They nosed up to the church and its adjacent rectory.

The vicar was waiting, light spilling from the open door onto the garden path. "Good morning, gentlemen. I am Edwin Bullard, Rector of St Leonard's." The Reverend

14

was well-built, an inch or so shorter than Shobnall but broader across the shoulder and maybe two stone heavier, imposing in his double-breasted black cassock. *Looks the part.* A full head of greying hair, a well-lined face, eyes flicking back and forth between them. *The usual nervousness.* "Will you come in?"

Shobnall let Eddie do the talking. "May not be necessary to intrude on you, vicar. If there's someone out there shooting, then the sooner we get after them the better."

"Oh, there is definitely someone out there, officer. With a 10-guage shotgun, unless I'm very much mistaken."

"You know your guns, sir?"

Bullard laughed, a deep reverberation. "You are surprised that a man of the cloth should be familiar with ordnance. We are in the countryside here. I take a close interest in the habits and hobbies of my flock. Besides, earlier in my calling, I spent time in America where a man feels incomplete without a gun." He laughed again. "I called tonight *because* I identified the 10-guage. It's a heavy instrument with a recoil that most people find hard to handle. The pattern of shots suggested an amateur out of his league. That is not safe."

"Could you tell where the sound was coming from, sir?" *He's like most vicars, always performing.*

"I was in my study when I heard the first shot. A blast, a pause, a second blast. I came out to listen. After a while we had a re-run. That's when I telephoned although there was a third pair of shots." The vicar strode down the path to the gate and pointed. "They came from over there, gentlemen. From the Big House." They looked blank. "Forgive me. We are off the beaten track here. If you go back to the green and continue down the track westwards, you will come to Wychnor Hall. The Big House, we call it. The shots came from there."

\* \* \*

Eddie drove sedately; the possibility of a rogue shotgun demanded circumspection. The headlights illuminated dirt rather than tarmac but the surface was smooth. They had the windows down. Shobnall leaned out. Tall trees on either side. The engine the only sound. No gunfire. Nothing moving aside from them. The Big House loomed suddenly. Shobnall looked down as the gravel crackled, then up and there it was, a dark hulk. The outlines of outhouses off to one side. *Who knew we had a place like this out here?* The doorway showed in the light from the windows to either side; the rest of the façade was in darkness. Their feet were noisy on the gravel. "Feel like I should be on tip-toe," whispered Eddie. "More like I'm intruding than investigating."

"Social class thing, that's what Lennie would say but I know what you mean. It all seems peaceful. What do you make of *that*?" Two vehicles stood by the entrance. A black transit van and something else. They walked over.

Eddie stared. "What the hell is it?"

Shobnall did a circuit. It took a moment. "It's a car, Eddie." *Not the kind of car I've ever seen, looks like a saloon stretched out to twice its normal length.*

"Huh!" Eddie snorted. "It's not the kind of car I've ever seen!"

"It must be American. The steering wheel's on the left. Let's see if we can find the owner."

The door was ajar. A push and it groaned open. They entered the Big House. Lights were on in the lofty entrance hall, wood-panelled, hung with heavy-framed paintings, a staircase, numerous doors leading off, all of them closed. *At least we're spared antlers or suits of armour or crossed swords. Or shotguns. Let's see if anyone's awake.* "HELLO! ANYONE AT HOME!" His shout bounced around the space. "Let's start over there, Eddie." The first room, to the front of the building, was empty of life. Dust sheets covered the furniture. Shobnall couldn't tell from the shapes what function the room served. He tried the light switch. Live. The opposite room was also empty, also shrouded. These drapes suggested a breakfast or dining room. *Place this size probably has a room for every meal.* They came up trumps with the third room.

Here the lamps were lit. A lounge. No dust sheets. More paintings. A magnificent stone fireplace, coals glowing red in the grate, an ornate gilt mirror above. The principal furniture – armchairs and couches – appeared designed to accommodate absurdly large people. The delicately-carved side-tables looked Lilliputian by comparison. One of the couches was occupied. A young man, a *big* young man, long hair, black shirt, jeans and socks, no shoes, unconscious but breathing, arms crossed on his chest like a corpse. *Looks like one of those pop musicians, large hands, strong arms.* He bent over the man, sniffed. *Goodness me.* "What do you make of that, Eddie?"

Eddie did his own snuffling. "Metallic, Alan, oily. Something else though." Eddie lifted the man's shirt, revealing a raw weal by his right armpit. "Recently fired a gun with heavy recoil. Very likely a guage-10 shotgun. Thank you, Reverend. I'm getting another smell though."

16

"I think we're picking up the scent of marijuana."

"No kidding. I've not done HQ's drugs briefing yet but I've heard about that. Makes people go woozy."

They tried to wake the sleeping beauty but whatever spell he slumbered under was too strong. Their consideration of the next step was interrupted by a voice from behind them. "Can I help you gentlemen?"

\*　\*　\*

# FOUR

They followed him down stone stairs to a huge kitchen, typical of the factory-sized space required in the mansions of the privileged rich. *Lennie would say they had to be large to accommodate all the oppressed servants.* "First things first. Can I offer you gentlemen a cuppa or don't you drink on duty?"

"We're allowed tea," growled Eddie. Their host marched the mile or so to the other end of the room and filled an electric kettle. Shobnall, wondering why a basement had a door and windows, peered out. Grass. *The land must fall away behind the house.* The moon illuminated a large expanse of water. *Their own private lake!* The bare walls, the stone flags and the fireplace and oven set into an end wall spoke of long ago but a modern kitchen had been inserted around an outsize Aga where their host was doling leaf tea into a warmed pot. Shobnall recognised the labour-saving devices Elaine pointed out to him from her magazines. *All mod cons, eh?* The table was long enough to seat a regiment. Shobnall studied their host. Denim shirt and jeans, dark hair greased back, work-boots, steel toe-caps. A solid look but light on his feet. *Not flustered to find a pair of coppers in his lounge.*

"Here we go." He laid a tray on the table; three mugs of tea, a jug of milk, a sugar bowl. "Help yourself."

Eddie was warming to the man. "Good brew."

He laughed easily. "One of my main functions, making tea. I'm Gary Stubbs. Call me Gary. Now, I've always rubbed along fine with the Old Bill so how can I help you?"

Eddie led. "Mr Stubbs. We'll get straight to it. We received reports of shots around two o'clock. We have reason to believe these came from the vicinity of this house."

Stubbs raised his arms with a rueful smile. "We surrender. The gun was fired by him upstairs. See, Basher – him on the sofa – he isn't strong on self-restraint. He found the gunroom. Not a good idea to put a notice on the door advertising its contents, not with Basher around. He kicked the lock in and off he went. Woke me up. He was out the back trying to shoot a tree. I took the gun away, parked him in the lounge. I'm sorry if he upset anyone."

"Where's the shotgun now?" Asked Eddie.

"Back in the gunroom. Which I've chained shut. I chucked the used cartridges in the bin."

Shobnall leaned forward. "Gary, what made Mr, er, Basher, decide to shoot at trees at two in the morning?"

Stubbs read a message in Shobnall's eyes. He sighed. "His proper name is Bob Carter. And you know what made him do that. He'd been smoking dope."

"Dope?"

"Marijuana. We brought a small stash with us."

Eddie switched in. "Mr Stubbs, could you explain to us what you and your party are doing here?"

Stubbs drew a packet of Players from his shirt pocket and lit up. "Tobacco only, OK?" They practised looking disapproving. "Sorry. There are six people in the house. Me, Basher and four others who are in their beds. Although their minds are probably in far-off parts of the galaxy. You're looking at a pop group." *Thought so.* "The Reapers. Heard of them?" Eddie nodded.

"See, the start and finish of all this pop is The Beatles. They're turning the music business upside down. Every kid with a guitar wants to be in a group. Anywhere in Britain, you'll find fans flocking to the clubs and halls. Dave Clark, the Searchers, Gerry and the Pacemakers. They're going to be household names. The Beatles are the big wave but these others are rolling in behind them. The boys in this house could be right up there with them." *He's really excited about this.* "It's mainly Steven Lee and Alex Schwarz. I got hooked up with them in South London. They were folksy then, went out as the Campbell Brothers but they expanded into a group, became the Wild Boys."

He dropped his cigarette butt into his mug. "Look at The Beatles. Great image, great personalities, musicianship, fantastic tunes. Tick all the boxes, 'specially those Lennon and McCartney songs. Brian Epstein, their manager, he saw how to package it all. For us, Steven and Alex were producing the songs and the band could play but it wasn't coming together the way it should have."

"How do *you* fit in all this, Gary?" Shobnall was intrigued.

"I was their fixer, hustle gigs, drive them, look after the gear, handle the money, what there was of it. And make the tea. Suddenly things began to move. The drummer fell out with Steven and Basher came in. He has trouble with self-discipline but behind a drum kit he's sensational. He changed our sound. We played the Crawdaddy. It's one

19

of the venues bands want because the audience will be full of industry talent-spotters. The Wild Boys played a cracking set. I was really pleased. That's when Morgan Vetch arrived on the scene."

Eddie interrupted. "Who's he?"

"Good question," muttered Stubbs. "He appeared out of the blue that night, persuaded the band to join what he called his 'management stable'. Turned out they were the only horse but maybe that's sour grapes." *Hello, hello, something bubbling here.* "He changed the name to The Reapers, tarted up the look and got them a one-off record deal that nibbled the Top 50. On the back of that, he sweet-talked Decca into a contract and they've been climbing ever since. Their last single, 'Run to the Dark' made the Top Ten. Their debut LP topped the album chart for three weeks. Everyone's waiting for the next single. Could put them into the stratosphere. Or onto the scrapheap.

"I'll be honest. I don't get on with Morgan. I'm the roadie, the road manager, I do all the workaday stuff but he doesn't like it that I'm closer to them, to Steve and Alex. Even though I know if they really make it there'll come a time when they'll drop me." He lit another cigarette. "I'm not sure why I'm telling you all this." *Possibly because we're from a different world.* "Morgan's American, he's a sharp operator and his number one interest is Morgan. I'd go so far as to say that his *only* interest is Morgan. But he has a finger on the pulse, I'll give him that. He clocked that The Beatles are the nice boys next door with the others queuing to be more nice boys and grab a smaller slice of the same cake. He saw a different market, the big one waiting for the bad lads, the ones who you don't want living next door but who still fascinate you. The Reapers. He's aiming The Reapers at that slot."

Eddie pressed. "What are you bad boys doing here, aside from blasting off shotguns?"

"They needed a break. People think it's non-stop fun in the music business but it's tough spending half your life in the back of a van, going on stage night after night and it's pressurised like you wouldn't believe. It's always the *next* song and the *next* album. They're tired but the machine is ravenous. The next single's in the can but they need more songs. We're here for a fortnight. The gear's set up in the ballroom. The lads are supposed to go in there every day until we have an albums-worth."

Shobnall's turn. "We saw the van outside. And the car."

Stubbs smiled. "The limo. Morgan's. He had it shipped over from the States. I doubt there's another like it in this country. I like a big motor and that Lincoln drives like a dream but what do the lads do? Empty its cocktail cabinet on the way up. Then they break out the dope." He paused. "Look, the shooting was a bit out of order but no harm was done, not even to a tree. Basher missed. Let me take care of it. It won't happen again."

Shobnall caught Eddie's wink. "They call this the Big House. Who normally lives here?"

"Dunno. Morgan and his assistant, Barbara, fixed things. A woman comes in and does the grub. Terrific grub. There's the Estate Manager, Haynes. He's not ecstatic having a pop group here but he's OK. He lives in a cottage near the farm. He showed us round. Dust sheets everywhere. I'm not sure anyone lives here regularly."

"Estate Manager, you say."

"Yeah. From what he said, the estate includes the village, the house here, the lake out back and all the fields and forests you can see in every direction. Morgan said the owner had let it be known the property was available. You could check with Haynes."

"We'll do that." Shobnall relented. "Gary, we'll consider the incident closed. On one condition." Shobnall fished out a card. "No more disturbances. If there are any more incidents or if you have any concerns while you're here, call us. Ask for Alan Shobnall or Eddie Mustard. We're working nights. During the day, ask for – *Who'd be best for this, perhaps not Angela?* "Ask for Lennie Morton. I'll warn him"

\* \* \*

They sat in the car, the sky brightening. An upstairs light went on. After a while, it went off. Eddie wound down his window. Silence. Until broken by the church bell. Shobnall counted. Six. "What do you think, Eddie?" One of the advantages of promotion, Shobnall had discovered, was the right to ask those of lesser rank to hazard an opinion first. He tried not to abuse the privilege. Anyway, he had a fair idea what Eddie would be thinking.

"Straight guy, Alan, I liked him. Don't envy him his job. This pop music business! Lennie was a right call, too, our manual would have trouble with this lot."

*You mean Angela and the manual.* "You heard of these Reapers?"

"Yeah. Friend of mine works at Norman's Records in town. These Beatles are like nothing they've ever seen before. They can't get hold of enough records. They say if you go to a concert you can't hear the group over the screaming. And the money. You wouldn't believe the amounts of money I'm told are at stake. Millions. What Stubbs said is right. The Reapers are on the brink."

"Won't want adverse publicity then. Another reason to trust Stubbs. We should talk to this Haynes."

"Bit early in the morning, Alan?"

"Possibly but an Estate Manager might be sensitive to gunshots."

The track led past a chestnut grove, a jumble of outhouses, a conifer plantation, a sawmill surrounded by pyramids of cut logs, a farmhouse and Dutch barn, a neat terrace of farm labourers' homes. Finally, a thatched cottage next to a meadow that stretched away to distant woodland. A huddle of black and white cows, udders distended, stood expectantly at a gate, breath steaming in the cool air. The cottage boasted a well-tended flower garden dressed brightly in yellows and reds, pinks and blues; a sign above the door, 'Estate Office'; a wooden bench. On the bench, hands clasped atop a sturdy walking stick and watching their approach, a man in a tweed shooting jacket and waterproof trousers tucked into wellington boots. "Mr Haynes?" Shobnall led the way up the path.

"Aye." The man rose, offered his hand. "Albert Haynes, Estate Manager. At your service, officers."

"People can always tell."

"We all have our uniforms. You'll be here about the shooting?" Shobnall nodded. "Woke me up. I went down there but the lad, Stubbs, he looked like he was well on top of things. I didn't butt in." He looked quizzical. "The vicar? Bullard?" Another nod. "Aye, he's a careful chap."

"Does he know there's a pop group staying here?"

"Unlikely. The instructions were to keep it private. Press weren't to know."

"How do *you* feel about them being here?"

Haynes looked squarely at Shobnall. "Not my job to have views on that kind of thing. I'm happy Stubbs is along there with them, though. He can handle himself. Saves me extra trouble."

Eddie had been watching the cattle, seeming to pay little attention. "You look after all this?" The meadow was bathed in early sunlight. Smoke rose from the farmhouse chimney.

"I'm in overall day-to-day charge. We've the farmer, his family and labourers, the sawmill, foresters, of course, carpenters and other trades as we need them, folk to service the house when it's in use. But yes, I look after it all."

A question was nagging at Shobnall. "And who do you oversee it for?"

"These days I take my orders from her ladyship, Lady Melinda. Montague, that is."

They left Haynes with his bench. A farm hand was herding the cows out of the field, the beasts jostling one another for the middle of the track, lowing sonorously. Shobnall was trying to work out what this all meant, if anything. *Is this coincidental or is there a tie in to the Diamond, can't let on to Eddie, should I try George?*

Eddie hadn't noticed anything unusual. "Might be an idea to turn into the village on the way back, Alan? Let the Reverend Bullard know that Staffordshire's finest have matters in hand."

"Why not? I wouldn't mind another look at the shepherd of the parish."

\* \* \*

On impulse, he called Dave Charteris. The big Londoner, also now a DS, was delighted. "Alan, mate, 'ow are yer? Elaine? Them two little angels?"

"Everyone's fine, Dave," laughed Shobnall. "Haven't spoken since the wedding. How was the honeymoon?"

"Wot a place! Never thought I'd spend so much time lookin' at art or sittin' in a caff watchin' the world go by an' feel triffic about it. It 'elps 'ave someone like Frankie, knows 'er way around. You get a chance to visit Paris, Alan, grab it. Bin the regular nightmare since getting back, course. You 'avin' a quiet summer in the country?"

"Not so quiet as I'd like. Our humble backwater is being graced by one of your London pop groups."

"Pop groups! Springin' up by the bucket-load. We try an' keep up. Loadsa money in that business. I mean loads! You know wot big piles of dosh does, attracts the wrong sort, like flies to 'orse manure. Which one you got?"

"The Reapers."

"Yeah, I've 'eard of them. Up-an'-comin', makin' a bit of a stir. Bad boy image, 'f I remember c'rectly."

"That's them. Currently ensconced in a country mansion outside Burton. The chap with them, Stubbs, he seems OK but I'm curious about the manager, an American name of Morgan Vetch. Ring any bells?"

"Not off the top of me 'ead. Want me to ask around, see what gives?"

"I'd be grateful, Dave, thank you. Love to Frankie."

"'An' from us to Elaine an' the girls. Get back to yer."

\* \* \*

# FIVE

By Wednesday 3 July, JFK had reached Rome. *He won't be rolling around in an old Anglia.* Shobnall approached the DI's office at the end of the day. He was unaware of The Central Health Services Council report suggesting that smoking in hospitals was 'inappropriate' but he knew he would have to contend with a full shift's-worth of pipe-fug. Agnes and Betty were cleaning the corridor. Well, Betty was down on her knees, scrubbing away; Agnes, in her customary turban, was rolling a fag.

"'Ullo Alan, nice 'oliday? Kids awright?"

"Yes to both questions, Agnes. The DI in?"

"'E's got someone wiv 'im. Nice lookin' gennelman. I could fancy 'im." *Goodness, who could this lucky man be?*

It was a dapper Frank Mercer, leaning by the window as the DI puffed away in his chair. Frank was The Burton Daily Mail's correspondent for.....well, over the years, Shobnall had seen him under pretty much every label – Crime, Births & Deaths, Gardening, Social Affairs. *What's he doing here, reporting or working for George on the quiet?* Shobnall ran through events at Wychnor Hall in some detail. Frank knew the place. "Means 'village on a bank'. A bit dull but you can't argue the point. The Hall's a grand building, eighteenth century, Queen Anne. I'm told the interior is remarkably well-preserved. If you drove past on the A38 you'd never guess you were so close to such a monument. Private reach of the Swarbourn, acres of grounds, croquet hoops on the lawn, its own lake and all the commercial stuff."

"And she owns it, Melinda?" The DI wanted to know.

"That's what the Estate Manager, Haynes, told me," said Shobnall.

"She owns most of the land you can see down there," Frank confirmed. "She's in London. I have no evidence that she has been at Wychnor at all recently."

The DI turned to Shobnall. "What about signs of extra security?"

"To be honest, sir, there wasn't much sign of security full stop. You've got a stately home with a pop group in it and an estate going about its business. Haynes had to be nudged a bit but he wasn't unhelpful."

The DI drummed his fingers on the desk. "I'd prefer to know more than Melinda wants to tell me. The Diamond is said to be in this country and I'm certain it's not in London. Melinda has it somewhere. Maybe not Wychnor. Perhaps the pop group is designed to draw attention while she holds it quietly someplace else." He sighed. "For all I know, Henderson has it locked in Jardine's safe. You're sure about security, Alan?"

"Absolutely, sir. I can't imagine you'd hide a diamond like this in a place where a musician who's out of his head can break into the gun-room, shoot at a tree and all you have is their roadie to put him back to bed with Haynes watching from afar. If there were Pinkertons about they'd have been swarming all over the place."

\* \* \*

They met before Thursday's shift in The Devonshire, close by Alsopp's New Brewery. The bar was busy, lined with draymen, maltsters and junior managers, but a booth provided a degree of privacy. The sun's late rays beamed through the windows, catching the motes in the air and the curls of smoke from Gordon Crombie's cigarette. Corky wiped his moustache. "Your DI's got a bee in his bonnet over this stone."

"He hates being kept in the dark, especially by someone like this Lady Melinda." Shobnall toyed with his orange juice. *The Bass smells lovely.*

Crombie stubbed out his cigarette. "I've long thought your DI could have fitted in well in local government. This pop group, The Reapers, and their mysterious manager, it all sounds deadly."

"Doesn't have to mean the bony fellow with the scythe, Gordon," countered Corky. "Puts me in mind of summer harvesting. I don't know about Reapers but I like those Beatles, jolly catchy ditties if you ask me."

"Can't argue with you there, Corky." Crombie fiddled with his lighter. "But there are large amounts of money rolling around this music industry and large amounts of money attract the wrong sort of people. What do you make of the Estate Manager, Alan, this Haynes?"

*Typical Gordon, straight to whatever's niggling at me.* "Don't know. Eddie Mustard did some checking. Haynes has been Estate Manager there for nearly twenty years. Prior to that, junior positions elsewhere in the same line of work. He's in with the bricks."

"A new boss. That made any difference to him?"

"No reason to think so. Twenty years service in those circumstances can build a strong sense of loyalty, not necessarily to any individual but to the family."

Crombie nodded. "Indeed it could."

"What about Lord Needwood?" Corky wanted to know. "Why let the Diamond go on display?"

"No idea, Corky. Won over by the Museum? Maybe he'd like to return it but wants to embarrass our government into compensating him. If you had a lump of carbon worth fifteen million would you simply hand it over?"

Crombie again. "Two things strike me. In the first place, Alan's nose. You." He pointed at Shobnall. "Are mulling over all these things – Wychnor Hall, The Reapers, The Needwoods, the Diamond – and smelling something not quite right. If your nose is even tickling slightly then we need to take it seriously."

"The second thing, Gordon?"

Crombie drained his glass, pocketed his cigarettes and lighter. "I need to be off pronto. Lennie and I are bowling tonight. Lady Melinda is moving this stone around. We don't think it's in London yet. Frank Mercer says her ladyship is in London but he's not reporting any news of the Diamond down there. Curiously, Lady Melinda has rented the house, on a short-term let, to an up-and-coming pop group. A group with a dubious reputation deliberately constructed, a motor that looks like nothing else on the roads in Britain, what sounds like a Svengali of a manager and a penchant for drink and drugs and going out in the wee small hours with a shotgun to take pot-shots at trees."

*Come on, Gordon.* "What are you suggesting?"

"These pop people stick out like a sore thumb. Watch David Nixon on television performing his tricks. Smooth voice, smart attire, moving gracefully, shifting things under your very eyes, inviting you to concentrate over HERE when the sleight of hand is actually being conducted over THERE with the cards or a rabbit. You can't imagine how he did that. It must be magic. When it's really about distraction and diversion. Suppose the purpose of having The Reapers there is not about making us look somewhere other than Wychnor but about helping us look at a pop group in the Big House and not at........."

Shobnall nodded. "Something else at Wychnor. Like a big diamond."

\* \* \*

Friday meant family time. The girls seemed to understand instinctively when daddy needed to sleep in the daytime, kept the noise down and forbore from racing around upstairs. Once daddy was up, washed and shaved, normal service was resumed. Elaine's father had taken a day off from work, where construction of the mammoth Drakelow C power station, already dwarfing the A and B stations that had formerly seemed so vast, was absorbing so much of his time. Thus to the gentility of Winshill for afternoon tea and a spot of relaxation as James took the girls on a tour of his garden. Shobnall looked on: Jo's face a study in concentration as she drank in her grandfather's wisdom, Alice's expression of wonder as James parted greenery to reveal another plump fruit. When James herded them back to the table, Josephine trotted ahead. "Grandfather gave me some strawberries. One for you, daddy." She laid a succulent berry on his palm. "One for you, mummy." The child turned, seeking out her sister who, having fallen to the ground three times in her journey across the lawn, now tottered into the group. "Here's one for you, Alice." *Life doesn't get much better.* He popped the strawberry into his mouth, savouring the explosion of sweetness. He glanced at his wife. Her eyes sparkled and she blew him a kiss.

\* \* \*

Home. The girls in bed. Brief time for them before he headed for the station. The BBC news was on in the front room. No JFK anywhere; such a let-down. Chuck McKinley had seen off Fred Stolle in the men's final at Wimbledon. Shobnall was feeling content. "Jo's so protective of Alice. They are a delightful pair, aren't they?" Elaine laughed, leaned over, pecked him on the cheek. "Gordon and Corky send their love. They were on good form, doing what they usually do, making me look anew at Wychnor."

"And have they given you a plan?"

"No, love, to be frank they were more interested in this blessed Diamond. It's intriguing but that's all. Having said that, they did help crystallise my feeling that there is something odd at Wychnor. I'm not happy about the Estate Manager. He's hiding something."

"What are you going to do about it?"

"Nothing in a hurry. George will be off to London on Monday and Lady Melinda will have to produce the Diamond. Once he's out of the way, I might just go and do some leisurely digging. I don't think anything out of the ordinary is about to happen at Wychnor."

It would be over-egging it to say that Shobnall had a reputation for precognition but, as Crombie had implied in The Devonshire, he was considered to have a fairly-refined 'policeman's nose'. If Shobnall wasn't anticipating anything untoward to happen then his colleagues rest easy. Except that, this time, he was completely wrong.

*   *   *

# SIX

Friday's shift panned out largely as anticipated. Utterly uneventful. The same team was on: Eddie Mustard busy studying, Charlie Taylor and Sheila Redpath downstairs at cards. Shobnall dealt with all his paperwork. Tidied his desk, drawers included. Emptied the waste baskets. Checked Angela's report; nothing for him. *Nights can be so isolating, I'm missing the rest of the team, Lennie, Gideon, wonder how Bob's dad is.* He read Lennie's newspaper from the USA banning financial transactions with Cuba on the front page to the darts league results at the back. Around half past two, he gave up, angled his chair, laid his calves on the desk and dozed.

*     *     *

The telephone jolted him awake. The window showed dawn's lightening. The clock: just on five. He grabbed the handset. Listened. "OK, put him on." Waited. "Alan Shobnall."

The voice was distressed. "Alan, Mr Shobnall, you said to call, there's a problem –"

"Hold on, Gary, calm down. Talk slowly."

"Sorry." He could hear Stubbs gathering himself, deep breaths. "Sorry again. Wait." Shobnall heard him speaking to someone else – 'stay there and don't move!' – before he came back fully. "I think he's drowned, in the lake, it –"

*Uh-oh.* Shobnall cut him off. "Gary. Listen to me. Who's there?"

"The band. Running round like headless chickens."

"Call Haynes. Get him up there to help. Round up the others in the kitchen. Keep them there. We're on our way. We'll honk three times and you come out and meet us. OK?"

"Yeah. Thanks. Yeah. OK, I'll do that."

*     *     *

Shobnall rang down to Charlie Taylor. "Charlie, your lucky night. We need to be at Wychnor Hall ten minutes ago. Sheila will have to cope. We'll meet you out front."

He told Eddie what little he knew – "I could hear it in his voice, there's big trouble" – on the way downstairs. That meant he could shut his eyes and stick his fingers metaphorically in his ears as Charlie Taylor ignited the afterburners. The A38 wasn't so bad; a modern, tarmac-surfaced road on which Charlie simply gave it everything. It was even tolerable as the car took to the air over the humpback bridge. The fright kicked in when they screamed onto the side road and then the dirt track on both of which Charlie continued to give it everything. Shobnall was worrying he had issued instructions for an early grave when the car hit the gravel, Charlie hit the brakes and the black car broadsided towards the entrance, miraculously coming to rest perfectly alongside the entrance steps. Shobnall needed a moment to compose himself. Eddie clambered out, unconcerned. Charlie looked in his rear-view mirror. "Want me in with you, Alan?"

He drew breath. "Yes please, Charlie. Give it three toots on the horn, if you wouldn't mind.

*   *   *

The dawn chorus was done. The sky was gloomy. Every window in the building blazed with light. Gary Stubbs ran to meet them. Shobnall read the urgency on his face. "Thanks for coming so quickly. I couldn't sleep. Went round checking and he wasn't in his room." *He's holding it together but it's a near thing.* They sent Charlie in to relieve Haynes in the kitchen and Stubbs led Shobnall and Eddie round the side of the building, down steps to the rear lawn, jabbering all the way. Shobnall was hardly listening, acknowledging Haynes emerging to meet them but concentrating on the lake. Mist drifted here and there but he could make out a pair of small islands far out in the water. A rowing boat sitting between the shore and the first island, an empty rowing boat.

Shobnall put a hand on Stubbs' shoulder. "Who did you say's missing, Gary?" His eyes stayed on the rowing boat.

"Mick. Mick Cox. Guitarist."

"You've been through the house thoroughly?"

"Yeah, checked all the doors were locked, came out and saw the boathouse open."

Haynes intervened. "I went round again after we'd corralled the rest. Checked the outhouses. Nothing."

Shobnall turned to Eddie. "Ring the station will you, Eddie? There's a handset in the entrance hall. Give Sheila the number. We're going to be here a while. Ask her to rouse Fred Bull and Vern and get them out here. And I want Joe Short." Eddie hurried off. "Anyone got binoculars?" Haynes proffered a pair and Shobnall focused them over the lake. "There's nobody else here, Gary?"

"No." *The man could do with a drink.* "I rang Morgan. Bastard hung up on me but he'll be on his way."

The boat was rocking slightly but not drifting. A rope disappearing over the side. *Someone dropped anchor out there.* One oar rested in a rowlock. He panned around, found the other floating. Back to the boat. Nothing else. "Let's get back inside. Thank you." He returned the binoculars. "Show me his room." *I'll not bother the DI yet but I have a notion this particular party is only beginning.*

* * *

Later at Wychnor Hall. Approaching seven o'clock. A grey, cloudy morning, moving from spitting to a light drizzle. Fred Bull and Vern are here. They seem to know the precise location of every drop of surface water in the County. Their Land Rover dragged a tarpaulin-covered trailer straight down the grassy bank beside the house and onto the lawn, swinging around and reversing up to sit the trailer at the lake's edge. They threw back the tarpaulin, manhandled an inflatable into the water. Fred had kitted up while Vern primed the outboard, speaking with Shobnall the while. The inflatable, Vern on board, is roped to the rowing boat. The second oar has been secured. They know where Fred is because there is no sign of him. Albert Haynes is inspecting the gouges made in the manicured lawn by the Land Rover and wondering how much more damage these hooligans will do.

Joe Short is here with his bag of tricks. Shobnall and Gary Stubbs gave him a tour and left him to it. Joe took one look at a lowering sky and got busy photographing the ground surrounding the house, examining all the exits and the boathouse. He was very careful with the boathouse. He has finger-printed everyone on site. He is upstairs dissecting Cox's room molecule by molecule.

Charlie Taylor has not budged from the kitchen, fulfilling his brief to do whatever he considers necessary to keep the other four occupants (a) in the kitchen and (b) quiet. He's happy to be on the scene; the alternative was continuing to lose money to young Sheila. Eddie said they were a pop group. As far as Charlie is concerned, they're a bunch of spoilt layabouts who can't go more than ten minutes without whingeing about being cooped up and who, every now and again, try to leave the room. Charlie has kept his temper. So far. Three of them are pretty much identical: middling height and build, black clothes, long dark hair, pale faces, looking like they don't yet need to shave. The one with the metal around his neck has more metal on his fingers, at least one of the rings featuring a death's head. Eddie said he was called Steven Lee. Charlie's forgotten the names of the other two look-alikes but he knows the fourth is Basher Carter. He remembers because Carter looks different. Like he knows his way around. Like he could grow a beard. Charlie sees a man with possible villain tendencies; that makes him memorable. He is also the only one of the four who seems to have twigged that something bad may have happened outside. He has helped keep the others in order and maintain some semblance of morale. His capacity to do this is being diluted as he swigs from the bottle of vodka he refuses to share. Charlie is weighing up whether he will have to take the bottle away or whether the boy will keel over first.

Gary Stubbs is not cooped up. Shobnall and Eddie trust him. He has spent time on the telephone. Fruitlessly. The people he feels a need to contact are unavailable. Now he is trying to be useful, to keep himself occupied, especially after the divers bulldozed over everything and sailed out onto the lake. He prefers not to watch them. He is looking out at the rain as it starts to fall in earnest.

Shobnall and Eddie stand together on the lawn, close to but a little away from Haynes, who is testing the depth of a tyre-mark with his boot. They are confident Charlie can handle the rest of The Reapers, including the unpredictable Basher. They have absolute faith in Joe Short. Their attention is 100% on the lake. No need of binoculars, even in this gloom. Fred and Vern are accustomed to night-work. The Land Rover is festooned with searchlights aimed at the rowing boat and lamps throwing a circle of light onto the lawn. Vern has lights clamped to the sides of the inflatable. The spectators on the lawn can see more than enough. Fred, down in the cold blackness, presumably has his own illumination.

Stubbs emerges from the house, distributes umbrellas. "I found these in a cupboard." The four men stand there in the grey and the wet, watching Vern, the inflatable raft, the rowing boat. Momentarily, Shobnall is distracted by a distant sound. A mechanical sound, a pulsing, whoop-whoop. It throbs louder. *Coming this way, something in the air?* He turns his head but the sound fades, dies abruptly. He isn't bothered, turns back to the lake. Nothing but the lake. They are all watching, waiting, wondering. Hoping.

A disturbance in the water out there. Fred's rubber-helmeted head pops up with an audible splash. They see Fred detach his breathing tube. He and Vern are speaking. Vern picks up a coil of rope already secured to a cleat in the bottom of the inflatable, passes it to Fred. They see Fred replace his breathing tube, flip over and vanish again, the rope paying out behind him. Haynes and Stubbs stand and watch. Shobnall and Eddie exchange a look. Eddie kicks a divot out of the lawn. "Shit," he hisses quietly.

*   *   *

It took Fred and Vern a while to drag the body to the surface, lever it into the inflatable and bring it ashore. They tented the trailer with the tarpaulin and laid the corpse beneath, out of sight. Stubbs, transfixed, and Haynes, unmoved, looked on. Eddie made for the telephone to call for an ambulance and update the station. Shobnall sought out Joe to let him know they were now beyond a missing person. Joe was back in the boatshed, scanning the walls through a magnifying glass; he grunted over his shoulder. Shobnall went out front for time to think. He stared, unseeing, at the old chestnut tree beside the drive gates. *Should I alert the Old Man? We have a body but no grounds for suspecting dirty work.* That was when Wychnor Hall turned into Piccadilly Circus.

Shobnall was jerked from his reflections by that sound, the pulsing noise he'd heard earlier, a rhythmic whoop-whoop but much louder now, coming closer. Lights in the sky, too low for an aeroplane. A solid roar now. *There!* The helicopter seemed to rise up from behind the trees like a giant bird of prey and hover above the croquet lawn next to the drive before touching down, the din easing but its rotors continuing to whir. Two figures jumped down, ran, crouched under the blades, to the edge of the grass. One of the figures waved. The helicopter roared again, lifted off, swivelling. Within seconds it had gone from sight and gradually the sound died. Shobnall watched the figures tramp across the gravel, waited until they reached the bottom of the steps. "Good morning."

The leading man was tall, athletic, expensively dressed: black fedora and double-breasted trench coat open over a grey pinstripe suit. Shobnall's first impressions were of keen eyes, a mouth that didn't look as if it smiled often and a forcefulness not to be trifled with. The second man hung back, powerfully-built, his undoubted air of menace only marginally undermined by the cheap mac he wore, belted but not buttoned. He looked like an ageing wrestler still capable of inflicting serious pain. The first man leapt up the steps and eyeballed Shobnall. "Who's in charge here?" *Ah, American accent, this will be Morgan, I can already see why Gary hasn't hit it off with him.*

"I am. Detective Sergeant Shobnall. Welcome to Wychnor Hall, Mr Vetch."

The new arrival seemed to be looking right through Shobnall. "I guess Stubbs described me."

*He could be hard to handle.* "I'm glad you're here, Mr Vetch, you and......?"

"This is Preston, my Head of Public Relations." *If he's public relations I'm a Dutchman.*

Eddie had joined them. "This is Detective Constable Mustard. Mr Vetch, I think we should have a quiet word. We can use the lounge. I am afraid we have some bad news for you."

Vetch looked as if he'd have preferred an argument but the conversation – if we can call it that – stalled immediately as headlights blazed, tyres sounded on the gravel as a large dark red motor rolled towards them. They hadn't heard its approach because the engine wasn't making any noise. Vetch seemed to recognise the car and skipped down the steps and over towards the new arrival. "Blimey," said Eddie. "A Bentley Continental."

A uniformed chauffeur climbed out and opened the rear compartment, adroitly blocking Vetch while handing out the passenger. "Eddie," Shobnall murmured. "Get on the blower. Tell the DI he needs to be at Wychnor Hall. Tell him Lady Melinda's here."

\* \* \*

# SEVEN

*She has presence, I'll give her that.* Lady Melinda glided imperiously across the drive and up the stairs, one of those assured individuals who seem more real, more finely delineated, while rendering lesser mortals fuzzily misshapen. As her bow-wave flowed into the house, she snapped over her shoulder. "The lounge." There was only one thing they could do. They obeyed.

They were in the entrance hall when yet another vehicle rattled over the gravel. The ambulance. "Sorry, Eddie, would you show them round?" Eddie didn't seem upset about changing the company he was keeping.

In the lounge, Lady Melinda arranged herself in front of the fireplace and waited for her vassals to stumble into place. *Younger than I expected, maybe fifty, no-nonsense though.* "What is going on here?" Lady Melinda was addressing the room in general. Vetch and his associate had no option but to defer to Shobnall.

"Detective Sergeant Shobnall, ma'am." He figured 'ma'am' was safe enough. "Staffordshire Constabulary. We are investigating a death. We have recovered a body from the lake. It will be taken to Burton for examination. Our forensics officer is combing the property for any evidence that will help us understand what happened, how it happened and why. We need to establish the cause of death. Whether it was an accident, whether the man took his own life or whether a crime has been committed." Out of the corner of his eye he registered Vetch's head swivelling in his direction.

"You mean." Lady Melinda's tone was glacial. "The crime of murder." Shobnall nodded as bravely as he could. "We do not have murders here at Wychnor."

Shobnall held his nerve, returning her stare. "With all due respect, ma'am, that is for us to determine." Vetch continued to watch him.

Unseen wheels revolved. A ratchet clicked, effecting a minor adjustment to aristocratic protocol. "Show me."

Gary Stubbs unlocked the kitchen door. Lady Melinda sailed past Charlie Taylor, three bemused Reapers and a now-unconscious Basher as a Cunard liner steams past a shoal of sardines. Oblivious. They stepped outside. In deference to her ladyship, the weather gods had paused the rain. Lady Melinda was able to survey her demesne in the dry. The lake, steely beneath the grey sky, and the two islands; along the shore, the boathouse, the rowing boat now tethered to the small dock, Fred and Vern packing up, Eddie and the ambulance men carting a blanketed stretcher off the scene. Shobnall was trying to keep tabs on everyone. The PR chap. *Can't remember his name, Presley?* Was doing nothing. Vetch had pulled Gary aside and was talking fast in a low voice.

Eventually Lady Melinda deigned to face them. She gave Vetch an especially regal withering. "One of yours, Morgan." *How is it the nobs make statements instead of asking questions?* Vetch, question or statement, wasn't responding. *They know each other but there's a tension there.*

Lady Melinda surged back through the house, assuming, correctly, that the riff-raff would follow. As she reached the top of the kitchen stars and set foot in the entrance hall, the front door scraped open and the DI faced her at the other end of the hall. "Melinda," he announced, unnecessarily.

"Ah. Worthington. A word." The pair disappeared into the lounge. The rest stayed put, sensing that they remained under orders.

It was probably no more than five minutes but it seemed an age. When they re-emerged, Lady Melinda was already in the process of departing. A flick of the hand to Vetch and he set off after her, followed in turn by his PR man. *No, Preston, that's it.* The chauffeur had the nearside rear door open, assisted Lady Melinda in and shut the door. Vetch climbed in the back; Preston rode shotgun. The Bentley slid away silently, only the crunch of the gravel, then quickly hidden by the trees. That left the DI, Shobnall and Gary Stubbs at the head of the steps. Shobnall introduced Gary. *The DI seems calm, that's good. I think.* The ambulance had departed, leaving the transit and the limousine, the black car Shobnall and Eddie came in, Joe's little van and the DI's smart grey Riley. Eddie was leaning on their black car.

The DI was in affable mode. "She's a piece, isn't she, Alan?"

"Sir, she had no idea what was going on. Morgan did. Gary phoned him and he came to look after his investment. She arrived here for some other reason." The DI looked inscrutable. *He's not disagreeing.*

Eddie joined them. "Where did the Bentley go? I don't mean now, I mean while you were with Lady High & Mighty." They stared at him. "Alan, remember she turned up and went in and we followed her and then you sent me out to direct the ambulance men. When I came out, no sign of it. When we came to load the body the Bentley was back. In a different place because your Riley, sir, was in their original spot."

Shobnall and the DI spoke together. "Where had it been?"

"What I was asking in the first place." Said Eddie, placidly. "And where's Haynes?"

Nobody said anything for a while but, in the clean country air you could hear several sets of cerebral networks whirring. They were distracted by the Land Rover, Vern at the wheel, bumping back over the grassy bank onto the driveway and pulling up. Fred jumped out and made a bee-line for the limousine. Gary trotted over and within seconds the two were deep in conversation and it was 'climb inside and take a look' and 'try the controls' and 'let's peek under the bonnet, or hood as the Yanks call it'. Vern sat, reading a paperback, obviously prepared for this sort of hiatus in life.

"Another thing, sir," said Shobnall. "Lady Melinda and Morgan Vetch. They knew each other. Like you said, she's the lady of the manor and most other folk are peasants but he doesn't act like a peasant and she doesn't treat him like one, gives him a lift, just like that. There's something funny about their relationship."

The Land Rover horn honked. Fred was back on board, waving from the cab as Vern gunned the engine and clattered off. Gary rejoined the three policemen. "I guess I'll leave you to it, you'll have official business to discuss."

He made to move but the DI stopped him. "If Alan and Eddie are happy having you around then it's OK with me." Gary stood taller; he took it as a complement. Alan and Eddie were happy too; they had more questions.

"Morgan bent your ear, Gary. What did he say?" Shobnall wanted to know.

The grin vanished. "What I expected. Keep the band happy and working. 'Happy' means let them have anything they want. He'll send a replacement guitarist, one of the regular session men. And I have to ring Mick's family." His voice tightened. "Morgan's got no idea who they are. The bastard. Mick's mum. She lives in London. Morgan's on his way back to London. He could have asked and had the decency to go and see her or at least send Preston. No, Gary Stubbs has to do it over the telephone."

"That Preston," asked Eddie. "Is he really in PR?" *Eddie smelled the same haddock I did.*

Stubbs was weighing something and coming to a decision. His head came up in determined fashion. "I've never seen any sign of it. Generally our PR is handled by Babs, Morgan's assistant. Preston, he's more of a personal fixer."

"That his first or second name?" Shobnall asked.

"No idea. He was introduced as Preston and that's what everyone calls him"

"Big chap," observed Eddie. "Looks like a bodyguard. His trousers were soaking wet under that mac."

"Yeah, Morgan doesn't go far without him. Listen -" He broke off, studied his boots for a moment, straightened up. "About Mick. He was OK in my book, although I didn't know him like I know Steven and Alex. He was in a group called The Space Cadets, slung together to support The Tornados on tour but he was a good guitarist and when the Cadets folded, he seemed right for us. You need to know, 'cos I heard Alan explaining to Lady Whatsername how you have to work out exactly what happened. Mick wasn't the most stable of people. He had a bit of a breakdown when he was a lad. I know Morgan's had him see a shrink a couple of times lately. Mick found the pressure hard. I mean, if you ask me, it is possible he might have........done something." He stopped.

Shobnall patted him on the shoulder. "Thanks, Gary, it helps to know that sort of thing but we'll be taking a careful look at all the possibilities."

"One other thing. I guess your medical folk will be, um, opening him up. Don't be surprised if they find drugs in his system. I already owned up to the fact we brought a bag of dope with us but that's not what I mean. Mick was using something stronger. I don't know what or where he was getting it from and I've never caught him at it. When you've been in the music business a while, you get to know the signs."

The DI nodded. "We know all about intuition, Gary. That's enough for now. Alan and Eddie, you're over your time. Time you were home. We're not going anywhere until we get the medical and forensic reports but we'll meet in my office at the start of tonight's shift.

"Gary, your boss - yes, I can see you don't like that word but he's the one who hands you orders - told you to stay here. That's fine by us because we don't want any of you going anywhere until we say so. In due course we'll need a formal identification. Meantime, keep Alan and Eddie close. My feeling is that the four of us are on the same side. We just need to work out who the opposition are. Now get along with the three of you. I'm going to grab Joe Short before he begins dismantling Wychnor Hall brick by bloody brick."

* * *

An hour or so to sunset and the air held the stored warmth of a prolonged summer. The night's rain and clouds were a memory. Shobnall paused by the police station steps, savouring the biscuity aroma that lay on the town like a comfort blanket; the maltsters were exercising their craft. Low shafts of sunlight warmed the redness of brewery brickwork. The New Bass, Middle Bass and Ind Coope. The mountain of scaffolding around the burnt-out Number 3 malthouse – what an inferno had raged that night! Shobnall had been there, wincing at the heat. Alsopps on Station Street and, over there, the Old Bass complex, its water tower poking out from behind the spire of St Modwen's. Insects were wafting skywards; martins traced graceful arcs as they soared among the chimneys. *So much change, it's reassuring to see the familiar sights, smell the old scents.* He braced himself.

In the squadroom, he found Eddie in conversation with Lennie Morton. "Alan." Lennie stood and shook hands. "Good to see you. Elaine and the girls alright?"

"They're fine, Lennie. Good to see you too, I miss the team when I'm on nights, no offence Eddie." Eddie smiled; he *loved* nights. Shobnall had noticed something out of place. "What are you doing with a crate of wine?"

"Hands off." Lennie looked down. "That's not a crate of wine, it's evidence."

"Evidence of what?"

Lennie sighed. "Forgery. The secretary at the bowling club bit my ear. He'd bought some wine on the quiet that turned out to contain a liquid worth considerably less than he paid for it. New labels for old vinegar. Bob Saxby and I knocked on a few doors. This crate is from a restaurant in town that would prefer not to be mentioned. These are buyers who know their stuff but the labels are very good."

"Where did they get them?"

"Chap came in and offered them. Guess what? He opened one and it was the real Chateau Neuf du McCoy and a bargain. The rest, of course, contained donkey urine. Someone's at it."

"Should keep you and Bob out of mischief. Anyway, what are you doing still here?" Lennie liked to cultivate an image of laziness, the Macavity who, when the jobs were distributed, was never there. Everyone saw through him. They regarded the DC with his perennial Derby FC tie as their elder statesman.

"Waiting for you, as it happens. Fred Bull called. He meant to speak to you this morning but was distracted by some American car. Trust Fred to be more interested in a carburettor than a corpse. He said to tell you there was a second boat, a skiff he called it, in the boat shed. Something didn't feel right. Its oars were in a rack on the wall." Shobnall and Eddie were looking at each other. "He says they'd been used. He pointed it out to Joe Short but thought he should tell you direct."

"Oh dear." *Don't like the sound of this.* "Thanks, Lennie. We have to see the DI. I'll catch you later."

* * *

Again, the DI had company, this time the Medical Officer, Dr Gordon Roxburgh with his bottom on the window ledge. The martins in the background appeared to be swooping through his head. The DI was not smoking his pipe and the air was transparent. *The window's open, must be the doctor's doing.* "Sit down, lads." The DI wasn't hanging about. *He wants a smoke.* "I have Dr Roxburgh's report." He waved a manila folder. "But I thought it would be as well to consult the horse's mouth, so to speak. Gordon."

"Thank you, George. Alan, Eddie, I'm not sure I can be a lot of help but this is what I can tell you with certainty. We have a male, Michael Cox, 23 years old, five feet nine inches, seven stone nine ounces – that's right, somewhat underweight and, as will become apparent, not in the best of health.

"He drowned. That's the cause of death. Unquestionably. If he hadn't drowned, I doubt he'd have lived much longer. He had the liver and kidneys of a much older man. He had clearly indulged in heavy drinking for a long time. His heart was in poor condition, his veins and arteries furred to a major degree. I would not be surprised if he experienced breathing difficulties.

"His body contained significant traces of cocaine, ingested not long before death. Have you chaps done HQ's drugs briefing? Not you, Eddie. Well, cocaine is a highly addictive stimulant derived from the leaves of coca, a South American plant. It gives the user a high, a feeling of euphoria. The effect is fast but transient. The user needs more and more and there is considerable overdose risk. In exchange for the euphoria, the drug can do serious physical and mental damage. Typically, addicts inject or snort it through the nose. Cox snorted. I found a loss of mucous membrane, destruction of nasal cartilage and incipient septal perforation – basically, the drug eating through the septum, the wall between the nostrils. He'd been on it for a while. Cocaine can cause anxiety, panic, paranoia. Anyone remarked on his mental equilibrium?"

"Yes," said Shobnall. "It seems he was a bit unstable and has recently been seeing a psychiatrist."

41

"Very likely connected to his addiction. Shortly before drowning he also took on board several jiggers of whisky. I can't tell you what brand. You'll need Sherlock Holmes for that. Cocaine and whisky make a perilous cocktail."

"Lastly, Cox had struck his head, not long before death. A concussion of substantial force, I should say, sufficient to render him unconscious. The contusion spans his forehead, midway between hairline and eyebrows. I removed splinters of wood that had been mashed into his flesh and bone. Somewhere there should be a piece of wood with his blood on it. And that, gentlemen, is all I can reliably tell you."

The other three mulled over the doctor's words. *We can get a little more from Gordon.* "Doctor, you know what's on our minds. Accident, suicide or murder?"

Roxburgh removed his spectacles, wiped them with an Omo-white lawn handkerchief. "An accident? Possibly. Full of cocaine and whisky, intoxicated into fancying a moonlight scull, he could have lost his balance, banged his head, gone overboard. I'd be impressed if he'd managed to get himself out there with that cargo on board but cocaine can enhance perception and provide bursts of energy. Suicide? Also possible. In either of these cases I would not have expected an experienced addict to go out on a boat to snort the stuff. He'd do that in privacy, probably where he keeps his supply. If you told me he drank the whisky on the boat, I might lean towards deliberate suicide. If he drank it with the cocaine, I'd think more of misadventure. There must be a bottle somewhere."

Shobnall pressed. "And murder?"

"Murder? As you well know, Alan, it can *always* be murder." He paused. "You're wondering about the blow on his head. Yes, he might have been struck by someone but he might equally have fallen. All I can say is that my examination of the body has revealed no other evidence that tips me towards that conclusion. You'll need to see what Joe Short produces. If the site includes any evidence he'll have found it."

\* \* \*

42

# EIGHT

"Bit of a dog's breakfast, eh lads?" With Roxburgh's departure, the DI had heaved himself up, closed the window and lit up. "What do we think?"

"We need Joe's report," said Eddie.

"We do," agreed Shobnall. "I'll check with Fred about any bottle. We should interview the group again. We spoke to them last night but they were all over the place. Or unconscious. You know, I still can't decide whether The Reapers are a coincidence or a diversion. I get a feeling about Melinda and Morgan Vetch."

"That Morgan's a swine," Eddie exclaimed. "I can see why he needs a bodyguard. Gary Stubbs is OK, though."

Shobnall nodded. "Agreed. I wouldn't want his job."

"I'm with you there." The DI puffed contentedly. "The chauffeur going off. He'll not have done that off his own bat. He'll have been under orders from Melinda."

"Haynes buggered off," said Eddie. "Gary noticed that. Did the Bentley collect something from him or deliver something? At his cottage? There was time, I reckon."

*Eddie doesn't know about the Diamond, I'm going to have to tell him, all of it or certainly enough of it.* The DI had reached the same conclusion and, after extracting a vow of secrecy from Eddie, outlined the Needwood Diamond story. "Fifteen million!" Eddie was impressed. "You're telling me that's small beer to her ladyship." He shook his head in wonderment. "How many years would I have to work to earn that much? Forever, probably."

Shobnall was happier. "Assume it's the Diamond. It has to be in London next week. The Bentley must have been collecting. So how did it get to Haynes?"

The DI had forgotten about his pipe. "Ye gods. Playing pass-the-parcel out there with no security! Risky but utterly unexpected. The insurance people would have a fit if they knew. That's Melinda alright. Mm. You'll need to beard Haynes on that one."

Shobnall went to the window. The sunset was throwing an orange glow over the town. "Sir, what did she say to you in the lounge? Did she mention Vetch?"

"Talked a lot, said little. Nothing about Vetch. She briefed me on the Pinkerton team. Confirmed Diamond duty starts tomorrow. Maybe she was delaying us to make sure the chauffeur had time to get to Haynes and back."

"So was the presence of The Reapers merely chance?" *Gary said Vetch was heading back south.* "That doesn't seem likely if she has the Diamond and now she's off to London with Morgan and his so-called PR man."

The DI grunted. "Ah. But. She hasn't taken them to London. I omitted to mention when I came out to Wychnor, I left Charlie Taylor in a black car at the green with instructions to tail the Bentley. He followed until he was sure it was headed for London. I have no doubt the Diamond was with her. On the way, though, she dropped our friends at Alrewas railway station."

* * *

Shobnall went back to Wychnor, partly for loose ends, partly because he wanted a better 'feel' for the place. He pushed open the front door of the Hall as the village clock tolled ten. Gary Stubbs was in the kitchen, staring out through the open window at the darkness of the lake, a half-drained bottle of beer on the table before him. "Hi Alan, fancy one of these?" His tone was subdued.

Shobnall recognised the plain red-on-white label. "Thanks, Gary, but I'm on duty. Bruntons IPA, I see." *He seems a little flat.*

"Yeah, tasty. Youngs of Wandsworth are my beer of choice but these folk know their business."

"I'll pass your testimonial to the owner. His sister is godmother to my daughters."

That perked Stubbs up. "You got kids?"

"Two girls. Josephine and Alice. Here." He extracted his most recent photograph from his wallet.

Stubbs examined it. "Nice. We forget policeman have families. Like us normal folk." He smiled sadly.

"Not sure the pop business counts as normal, Gary. You got family?"

Stubbs took a swig. "I'd like to, I think. I'm with someone in London. We moved in together a while back and we've been talking. Things have been awkward since The

Reapers went big. Look at us now. She's in London with a regular job. I'm up here, doing.......whatever it is I'm doing. This music business eats you up. Janice isn't sure it can work. I dunno....."

"Gary, if it's any help, me, Eddie and the Old Man, we think you're OK."

Stubbs' face blossomed. "Yeah? Thanks. I liked your boss. Long time since anyone said anything nice to me. But what did you trek out here for? It wasn't to pep up a down-in-the-mouth roadie."

"True. Where's the group, by the way?"

"In the ballroom. Morgan dispatched a new guitarist pronto. They're bonding."

"It's ten o'clock! They must work nearly as long a shift as Eddie and I do."

Stubbs was amused. "Alan, this is pop music. They only got out of bed a few hours ago."

"Ah, right, different world." *How do people survive, living like this? Though Michael Cox didn't.* "I wanted to ask you. When you drove up here in the limousine, you said Haynes was here to meet you."

"Yeah. He came out and gave me a hand with the bags."

"Did you bring anything for him?"

"How did you know? Sorry, you're asking the questions. Yes. A bag. Morgan gave it to me. I was loading the motor. He said 'give this to the Estate Manager, Haynes. He'll be expecting it.' Alan, what's going on?"

"That's what I'm trying to find out, Gary. What did you think you were handing over?"

Stubbs scrutinised the label on his beer bottle. "They need to spruce this up," he muttered. "Alan, all of a sudden, I'm not sure what this conversation is about. I was getting to trust you."

"You can. If I'm going to find out what happened to Cox, I need to understand everyone's movements. Look, there may be something else going on. It doesn't affect you and the group but it is a complication." Shobnall watched as expressions flitted across the other man's face. *Suspicion, fear, uncertainty, determination, admission.*

"Normally, Morgan wants a bagman for one of two reasons. Sometimes both. Money. Drugs. The bag didn't feel lumpy but stuff could have been wrapped up." *Defiance.*

"Thank you. I doubt it was either of those. I'm sorry I have to be a copper."

Stubbs finished his bottle. "Nah, we all have our jobs to do. We all have machines to feed."

"There are more important things." Shobnall held out his hand. With the briefest of hesitations, Stubbs took it.

\* \* \*

*What about Haynes? Not everyone in the countryside goes to bed early.* The sky was clear, stars winked, the moon hung fatly over an idle sawmill and a darkened farm but lights shone from the cottage. In the distance, a train rattled along from somewhere to somewhere else. Haynes was on his bench, smoking a cigarette. *He just lit that, he heard me coming.* "Mr Haynes, I'm sorry to trouble you so late. We're trying to flesh out the picture of what happened at Wychnor Hall from the moment The Reapers arrived. You were there to meet them, I believe?"

"I was. My orders were to prepare the place for a fortnight's residency. Mrs Farlowe, the woman who does the cooking, she'd been in but she'd gone by the time they arrived. I heard the car horn and went out."

"What happened then?"

"Stubbs introduced himself. The rest staggered indoors. I helped Stubbs with the luggage, showed him round. Gave him my telephone number. Left them to it."

"Did Stubbs have anything for you?" He was watching Haynes carefully.

"Yes." *Um, not the answer I was expecting.* "He had a bag for me with a uniform for Mrs Farlowe. According to Lady Melinda, the group had developed a certain, er, image that called for them to dress in black. Anyone else with them in the house had to wear black as well. Mrs Farlowe doesn't mind, long as she gets paid. I told them I'd rather just stay out of the way."

It sounded plausible if a tad strange; the music industry obviously operated on laws of its own. "That was all?" Haynes nodded. "Last night, did you meet Lady Melinda's chauffeur?"

I did not." *A bit brusque.* "I didn't see Porter or his motor last night."

"You're sure? The Bentley is very quiet."

"Officer, there were no cars down here last night." *Irked, a man who doesn't care to have his word doubted.*

Shobnall retreated with as much grace as he could muster. Back into the Anglia and back to the nick. Driving with all due care and attention. All the way pondering that triumphant gleam in Haynes's eyes.

\* \* \*

He parked right outside their house. One thing he did like about working nights was the early morning hush before the town rose and went to work. He was pleased with the house. Like the one in Ash Street, it formed part of a terrace but here they had the end of the row, effectively semi-detached. A good size; a modern design aimed at the young-family market. He crossed the modest front garden and let himself in. Nobody stirring yet. He walked through to the kitchen. He felt, somehow, a little more grown-up now that they had a mortgage, as if he'd passed some test of financial maturity. *We can afford it, could do even if Elaine wasn't working at all.* Out the back door into the long garden. There was a lawn, a vegetable patch, a dilapidated greenhouse and a shed full of hardly-used tools bequeathed by the previous owners. *We'll have to sort this out, not now, though.*

He went to the end wall and gazed over the fields to the wispy morning mist that marked the route of the Trent, concealed in a dip. In the distance, St Modwen's bell rang clear. A skein of geese passed across the scene, honking as they descended to the river and a day's feeding. Further off, the great cooling towers of Drakelow loomed above the trees. *What is going on out at Wychnor, how much is coincidence, how much diversion, like Gordon said?* His musing was interrupted by the sound of the back door opening. He turned to Josephine hurrying down the path and Alice, in her wake, struggling to negotiate the steep step.

"Daddy! Mummy says come in for breakfast." He scooped her up and went to lift Alice back into their home.

\* \* \*

# NINE

Esmée Worthington set breakfast in the dining room, the French windows open wide. The air was warm, laden with sweet garden scents. At this hour, Repton's sounds were limited to the buzzing of early bees, clock chimes, church bells and the far-off crowing of the cockerel on duty. She sipped her coffee. She loved this time of day. She didn't have to share it with anyone but George. The oasis of peace before he rode off to do battle was precious. After all these years, watching him cope with the worst the criminal world and police bureaucracy could fling at him, still, every day as she waved him off, she felt the need to pray for his safe return. "They're going to find out that you and Cyril are off on a sabbatical?"

George scraped up the last curd of scrambled egg, placed knife and fork parallel on the plate. "Some know already. Shobnall and Bainbridge. We had to tell Eddie Mustard because of Wychnor. They'll be fine. I'm a telephone call away most of the time and they're all confident in Alan and Angela. Those two complement each other nicely."

"And the body at Wychnor Hall?"

George Worthington considered his wife. So sharp! "I'll admit to a germ of concern. You know my attitude to coincidences. The Needwood Diamond, fabulously valuable *and* politically sensitive. Her ladyship, loaded and connected. A pop group that by all accounts is on the brink of competing with these Beatles. Lob a corpse into that mix and you have to wonder."

"You have Alan Shobnall on the case." She fished out a Rothman's.

"Alan and Eddie Mustard. The Shobnall nose is twitching. I can tell."

"I know you, George, you don't want to be stuck in London guarding a fifteen million pound egg while there's a possible murder investigation under way."

Worthington burst out laughing. "I'll be keeping an eye on things. When are you coming down?"

"As soon as I can. I've a board meeting on Wednesday. I need to be there to make sure they don't do anything daft. I'll get a ticket for Thursday and turn up at your hotel. It's The Carillion in Bloomsbury, isn't it?"

"Aye, I'll tell them to expect you." The distant cockerel gave voice again. Esmée gave her husband one of those looks, the ones that even now made him squirm with pleasure inside, as if the belle of the ball had told a gauche teenager that, yes, she'd love to dance. He walked around the table, squeezed her shoulders, kissed the top of her head. "I'm away. See you on Thursday, love. Don't be late.

*   *   *

It seemed years since the holiday. *There I was moaning about boredom! I could do with space to work out what I think is going on, here's another Monday night and I'm wondering what's waiting.* Joe Short, that's what, his lanky frame sprawled in Angela's chair. "Thought I'd make a special trip in."

"Hello Joe, we miss you around here, you know. How's Heather doing?"

Joe grinned broadly. "Fantastic. People are starting to call her. She's been asked to go to London and talk to some department store in South Kensington. If she gets any busier, she'll outgrow our spare bedroom. But here, you'll find this interesting." He slapped a pink file on Shobnall's desk. "The rowing boat. Only Cox's prints. I should say the boat hasn't been used in years. No traces anywhere of drugs or alcohol. In the port gunwale, embedded blood, shreds of human skin, consistent with the wound identified by Gordon Roxburgh. He'll run some comparisons but it's going to be Cox.

"The boatshed. Fred was right about the second boat. The oars had been used and put back carefully. No prints but I'd say they'd been wiped down. His room. I found his drugs in a canvas bag on top of the wardrobe. Roxburgh thinks he was a frequent user, in which case there wasn't enough to get him through the rest of the stay at Wychnor. Presumably he was intending to source some more."

"No sign of a whisky bottle or something that could have held whisky?"

"No trace of any alcohol in his room. There was a complete off licence in the ballroom but it looked to me like these musicians are well-organised. Everything had been tidied away after their session and there was no sign of a later entry. Nothing else of any note except for one oddity. The only prints in Cox's room were his own. Fair enough. But the door, handles and finger plates inside and out? No prints at all."

Shobnall thought about that. "Spell it out for me, Joe."

"They'd been wiped. Someone else was on the scene. They took Cox out in the boat. The second boat brought them back to shore, leaving Cox in the lake, the rowing boat out in the rain, washing away evidence. They returned to Cox's room and tidied up. That's what I think."

49

*Yeah, there's more going on here than messing around with a diamond.*

\* \* \*

Shobnall hurried to the squadroom where Eddie was describing Lady Melinda to Lennie Morton and Gideon Watson. "Lennie, Gideon, you doing overtime?" *Lennie's looking fit these days, must be all that bowling.*

"Angela sent us to Wychnor to see your pop music friends. Thought you might appreciate quick feedback. Gideon will summarise. Once he's switched the radio off." Bob Saxby's transistor was, uncharacteristically, burbling out jangly guitar noises. Gideon quelled them.

The young man consulted his notebook. "We interviewed four members of The Reapers pop group. Steven Lee, aged 22, from South London, the singer. He likes to talk about himself. Alex Schwarz, also 22, also from South London. English mother, American father, accounts for the surname." He shot a glance at Lennie, who stared at the ceiling. "He, um, he likes to call himself 'Eternal'. He plays rhythm guitar. Jem Wicks, 21, another from South London. Bass guitar. He only talks about music. Anything else, he looks blank. The fourth one is Bob Carter, 25, from Liverpool. Also known as 'Big' Bob or 'Basher'. Because he's the drummer, I suppose. We talked to Gary Stubbs, 30. He's the road manager and another one from South London. As far as I could make out he does everything the group need done. You want to add anything, Lennie?"

Lennie loosened his Rams tie. "You wonder how this lot manage to rub along as a group of humans. The singer, Lee, he's an ego on legs. I wouldn't put up with him for five minutes. Schwarz is smart and very ambitious when it comes to the music business, totally disinterested in anything else. I quite took to Wicks. The boy's potty about music. His dad was a jazz pianist. When it comes to foul play, you can forget these three. None of them would say boo to a goose. One way or the other they're all about themselves. Basher's different. He's got muscles, for starters, and there's fire in him. Stubbs said Basher's vocabulary doesn't include the word 'restraint'." Shobnall couldn't help smiling. "He isn't daft and he's the only one who gives a toss for his late colleague. Partly for that reason, we don't see him for anything dodgy, apart from drink and probably drugs like the others. We liked Stubbs, solid and straight."

Gideon resumed. "Apparently these people sleep most of the day and start what they call work in the afternoon. Stubbs says he sleeps all morning and cat-naps so he can keep an eye on things through the night. The group are in the ballroom until about six. There's a fridge in the ballroom, full of bottles."

"Don't mention that to your Mam," muttered Eddie.

"Friday night. Around six, Basher, Wicks and Cox adjourn to the kitchen where food is laid out. Lee and Schwarz remain in the ballroom, listening to what they've recorded. About seven, Schwarz comes and fetches them back to the ballroom until midnight. During this time, Stubbs watches TV and periodically checks inside and outside the house. He says everything was normal. At midnight, they pack up. Lee and Schwarz stay behind again. Cox returns to the kitchen; Stubbs confirms that. Basher and Wicks go upstairs to Wicks' room where they drink beer and smoke marijuana. They admitted that." He looked anxiously at Shobnall. "Lennie said not to worry about it, Alan."

"Lennie's right, Gideon, we've enough on our plate."

Gideon looked relieved. "After an hour or so, Basher goes to his own room. Lee and Schwarz leave the ballroom around half past midnight, collect Cox from the kitchen for a walk in the grounds. Stubbs said they probably went out to smoke as well. They come back in at half past one. Neither Lee nor Schwarz could recall anything out of the ordinary but we're not sure how well their senses were functioning. Schwarz and Cox go upstairs. Schwarz sticks his head into Wicks' room. Only Wicks is there and Schwarz says he was out cold. Schwarz goes to his room and sees Cox into his on the way.

"Lee goes to the kitchen for some food, chats with Stubbs for a while, goes to bed. Stubbs checks the ballroom and then each bedroom. They were all in their rooms. He does the rounds, inside and outside every two hours or so. They're sensitive about the press. All quiet by about two. At four, he finds the boathouse doors open, checks the rooms. Cox is missing. He wakes the others, calls you and then the Estate Manager, Haynes. You didn't ask us to talk to him. Lennie?"

"Gideon's covered it." Gideon swelled. "Accident, suicide or – let's say it - murder, these people had nothing to do with it. There's only two worth talking to. Basher. You need to catch him when he's got a clear head. And Stubbs. He must love them. Otherwise can't see why he hangs around."

Shobnall had been making his own notes. "Gideon, Lennie, brilliant. Thank you. And thanks for hanging on here."

Lennie raised a hand. "One more thing. You asked me to call Fred Bull. No bottle. He said they always check roundabouts. Cox's body was beneath the rowing boat, snared in the weeds. The bed was soft mud coated with a layer of slime built up over years. If anything else fresh had gone in he'd have seen it. There was nothing."

"Thanks, Lennie. Talking of bottles, how are you and Bob faring with the fake wine labels?"

Lennie leaned back. "We're learning how busy these boys have been and that people who run hotels and restaurants lose all common sense when faced with a cheap deal. Weston Park shelled out a grand a crate for vino you can buy in your local off licence for three quid a bottle."

"These people are buying outside the law."

"No point going after them. They've paid enough in money and self-respect."

Shobnall conceded the point. "Good hunting, Lennie, I have faith in you."

*   *   *

Eddie pushed his books aside while Shobnall shared Joe Short's findings. "We're talking murder, then?"

"It's an option we have to think about, although we're very short on evidence."

"Nothing to do with the group. Or Stubbs. Can't see Haynes for involvement. What about that business with the Bentley picking up something, maybe the Diamond?"

"The Diamond will be in London now but there's something not right. We know the Bentley moved and I still have a nagging doubt about Haynes but I don't think he's been lying. Forget the Diamond. Concentrate on the corpse."

"It's been all over the press. Gary Stubbs has been fending off photographers. An innocent young man seduced by the evils of the pop music business or a drug-crazed fiend getting his comeuppance, depending on which paper you read."

"They've not been knocking on our door, have they?"

Eddie chuckled. "Angela had Charlie Taylor stand behind her in the doorway while she saw them on their way. From what I hear, she didn't need Charlie. This'll be the first murder case I've been on, you know. You did the Bruntons brewery one."

"That took a year to solve. I hope this isn't going to drag on. We've not much to go on. An unknown person, or persons, entering Wychnor Hall."

"Or meeting Cox outside, could have been arranged."

"I don't think so. Cox took his cocaine indoors, Roxburgh thinks. When it comes to the drink, Joe found nothing in his room, Lennie and Gideon have confirmed that Cox couldn't have gone to the ballroom and there was nothing in the lake. I'm thinking our visitor brought the booze to Cox's room. They take the boat, towing the skiff. Was Cox in a fit state to know what was going on? He bangs his head or is banged on the head, goes in, drowns. Could still be manslaughter, misadventure even."

"Agreed," Eddie continued. "Could be a murder going to plan or a panic. In either case, takes the skiff back to the boathouse, puts everything back to normal. Returns to Cox's room to clean up. Departs with the bottle."

"All between two and four in the morning. The band members are all out for the count but Stubbs is on guard."

"He might have dropped off but I doubt it. How did unknown person get in and out? You can't get over that driveway quietly, even on foot, Stubbs would have been alerted."

"What about motive? We need more. The estate, the village, someone must have noticed something. It'll have to be done during the day. I'll talk to Angela. Is Bob Saxby back, by the way?"

"Can't you tell from the pork pie wrappers? I saw him yesterday. He was on good form, dishing out his usual Test Match bulletins. His dad's fine. The doctors signed him off for a week's rest and now he's as right as rain."

"Good. Nobody should take their parents for granted." *Some of us never really have the chance, do we?*

\* \* \*

# TEN

DS Angela Bainbridge swung into action. *Like she'd been waiting for me to ask.* "A small community, self-contained. We'll include Wychnor Bridges. Any intruders will have come by road and that's where they'd have turned off. Posters. I see no school but we'll do the church, village shop, must be a pub somewhere, public display boards and leaflet throughout. Any other common areas?"

"There's a telephone kiosk up on the green, could be worth a poster."

"Fine. You said you met the vicar?"

"Edwin Bullard. He struck me as a man with his finger on the pulse of the community."

"We'll start the door-stepping with him. I'll send three. Charlie Taylor, only has to stand there and he intimidates; young Sheila Redpath, green but she has a talent for persuading folk to open up; Lennie, because he's capable of seeing right through people. It's unlikely anyone would have approached from the south, over the river, but we'll include Orgreave and Overley in the posters and leafleting. We'll check where the estate workers come in from in case we want to back-track any routes. How's that sound?"

"Perfect, Angela, thank you."

"I'm still the new girl but we all need to pitch in. As soon as we get any results, you'll know!

\*    \*    \*

Came the time when they asked Gary Stubbs for a formal identification. Early one morning, they let Charlie Taylor off the leash to collect him. Shobnall didn't care for parading the limousine in Burton's streets. He was standing at the main door, chatting with Gavin Kennedy, Dr Roxburgh's right-hand man, when the black car skidded to a halt beside the entrance. Charlie gave Shobnall a thumbs-up and settled back to await the return journey.

"He thinks he's Stirling Moss," murmured Kennedy.

"If you were in the car you'd believe he *is* Stirling Moss. I hope Gary kept his eyes shut."

54

It was a moment or two before the rear passenger door opened and Gary Stubbs edged out, an arm on the roof of the car for support, like a drunk late on a Friday night, dislocation in his eyes. Looked about him, saw Shobnall, shook his head to dispel any clear air turbulence, marched over. "Man's a menace."

"I know, Gary, but he got you here safely."

"Safely? Alan, I enjoy driving. That man is insane!"

"I usually close my eyes. Gary, this is Gavin. And thank you for coming to do this, it isn't fun."

As usual, Shobnall was discomfited by the contrast between the clinical white and steel and the messy death represented by the cadaver on the gurney. Gavin did no more than expose the head; pinched, bluish, crunched across the forehead, straggly hair. The *face of someone who died long ago.* Gary took a long, focused look, the one Kennedy called 'the farewell stare'. "That's Mick. Michael Cox. Is that what you need me to say?" Shobnall walked him back along the white corridors, an arm around the man's shoulders. "I rang Mick's mum. She was in tears, Alan. Over the phone. She knew he had problems but you know, mothers and sons." Shobnall tried not to think of his own mother. "I was almost weeping with her. I'll see her when I get back to London. I'll make Morgan do something for her. Jesus! Poor Mick."

"How are the rest of the band doing?"

"The band?" He felt Stubbs' muscles tighten. "Couldn't care less. The replacement is good. They're working well. They've forgotten Mick already. Fame, money, drugs, they leave no room for friends. Christ, Alan, it's all gone bad. I might walk away." They'd reached the exit. "Don't make me get back with him. I'd be happier *walking* back to Wychnor!" Shobnall pressed him into the car. Charlie Taylor took off like a guided missile.

\* \* \*

Seven-thirty, the fag-end of the shift. Rolling back from Tatenhill in the Anglia, responding to complaints about a gang of motorcyclists 'hanging about'. *Getting so anyone in leathers is regarded as a criminal, wonder how Fred Bull feels about that.* Into the fringes of Burton, isolated houses then ranks of substantial villas standing shoulder to shoulder on parade. He slowed as the railway bridge hove in view. *Wonder if he'll be in.* He peered across the low wall and the grassed turning circle. A black

Humber Pullman parked precisely at right angles to the massive building. He spun the wheel, turned through the gates. High above, the outsize brass letters glinted on the redbrick brewhouse, B-R-U-N-T-O-N-S.

The brewery seemed poised for industry, a tiny vibration continuously underfoot. Inside, the air of readiness persisted, a faint hum in the background. Victoria, her vivid red hair piled atop her head, was opening up reception. "Mr Shobnall. How nice to see you." Her smile blinded him every time. "You're up and about early."

"This is late for me, Victoria, I'm on nights at the moment. His car's outside."

"You'll find him in his office. I'll bring some tea in a minute."

Up to the first floor. Mr Salt rose at once, wrapped both hands around Shobnall's right, shook warmly. "You're looking well. Lavinia reported back after seeing Elaine and the girls. She was full of little Josephine, said she's becoming quite the precocious little lady. Sit down, I'll ask Victoria if she can make a pot of tea appear."

"In hand, Reuben. I saw her downstairs and she took charge immediately. You look well yourself. Business good?"

"Very good, Alan, very good indeed. As you know, I detest politicians and their glib catchphrases. 'Never had it so good.' Disgraceful. However, Britain is becoming richer and I am pleased to say the well-off Brit enjoys his beer."

"Brunton's beer?"

"We are punching above our weight. Sending George Galbraith across Europe has turned out to be a far-sighted investment, if I do say so myself. Sales of bottled beer are lifting year by year. Let me show you our next generation." Mr Salt padded over to a pinewood box sitting by the empty fireplace, drew out something wrapped in white tissue paper. "Having plagiarised the best Europe had to offer, George and I felt we could raise the bar. What think you?" He ripped aside the tissue paper.

Shobnall looked at it. Picked it up and rotated it, hefted it. *Hm, tall, slim, stylish, no hard edges, all curves and how have they done that with the glass?* "Reuben, how have they done that with the glass?"

Reuben Salt smiled impishly. "Irresistible, isn't it? We wanted an echo of the sunlight on the brass letters on the brewhouse. "And the label, Alan?"

Shobnall was already there. Brunton's bottles had stuck with a basic label, white background, plain red lettering, Mr Salt claiming their products sold because of the contents, not their packaging. This was different. A graceful oval, the lettering – 'BRUNTON'S BOLD' over 'Beer with Bottle' with 'Brewed in Burton since 1842' below. All in that shiny brass hue but now on a distinctive red background encircled by brass globes edged in a darker red. "The colours are from the brewhouse façade, aren't they?"

Mr Salt beamed. "The staff tell me it's a work of art. I have to remind them it's a beer bottle. Mind you, I've told my marketing chaps I want this entered for design awards. D'you like the name? I hear customers asking for 'a bottle of Bold'! We'll give Double Diamond a run for their money."

"That is *so* clever. Who designed it for you?"

"Oh." Mr Salt feigned surprise. "Did I not say? A local designer, of exceptional flair, as you can see." He sat back. *What's he playing at? No! He can't mean....* The realisation must have shown on his face. "That's right. Your erstwhile colleague, Heather Wilson, principal of HW Designs."

"I only saw Joe the other day and he didn't mention it."

"He won't know. We had Heather sign a confidentiality agreement. Even she doesn't yet know what we think of it. George and I loved it immediately but we wanted to take the views of the troops. Don't you say a word." He wagged a finger. "That will be my privilege. But I am such an inconsiderate host. What brings you here?"

Victoria chose this moment to bustle in with a tea-tray, irradiate the room with a smile and withdraw. Mr Salt, as usual, played mother. It gave Shobnall time. *Where to begin?* "There's been a murder." Mr Salt gave Shobnall his vegetation-searing look. "Reuben, do you know anything about Lady Melinda Montague, daughter of-"

"Lord Needwood." Mr Salt handed him a teacup. "Carry on, Alan, my diary is my own this morning." Shobnall gave him everything, from the moment the Chief Constable assigned the DI to The Needwood Diamond through The Reapers leaving London with a bag destined for Albert Haynes all the way to his and Eddie's conclusion that Michael Cox had not fallen accidentally into the lake or reached the end of his tether and elected to end it all. Someone else had done him in. Someone unknown for reasons unknown.

\* \* \*

Mr Salt sat silent for a minute. "The Needwoods are complicated. Lavinia has known Melinda for some years and does not care for her. She considers the woman arrogant and ruthless. I would not disagree with that but I would place in the opposite scale my perception that she is brave, clever and capable of the unexpected move. She also seems, within the limits of their feudal ways, to engender loyalty in her subordinates.

"I consider her father a friend, although I have not seen him lately. He is in his eighties and spends his time overseas. Billy is as straight as they come and as hard as nails. He came after Brunton's brewery. We weren't having any of it. He has been married three times. Melinda's birth mother was the second wife. Vanessa died early. His current wife is the only one who has lasted; she has been Lady Needwood for over twenty years. She is devoted to her husband, she dotes on him but in every other respect she is devoid of scruples. Moral deficiencies are not unusual among the aristocracy – although I exempt Billy Needwood from that criticism – but she is discreet. There have been whispers but no scandal. I fear she has exerted a negative influence on the daughter.

"I should find the combination of Melinda and shady characters from this new world of pop music perturbing. You say this Diamond is valued at fifteen million. From what my business colleagues tell me, it is nothing in relation to the amounts of money washing around the music business. I enquired of your friend, Henderson, how much these pop groups earn. He said 'for some, not as much as you think, for others, more than you can possibly imagine'".

"I only met her briefly but she seemed very much her own woman."

"That is fair and I will say one more thing in her defence. I believe that, at heart, she remains very much her father's daughter."

\* \* \*

He dandled Alice on his knee, absorbed in her beatific smile. He could hear Elaine in the kitchen. The lounge door nudged open. Josephine hurried in. "Daddy! Mummy wants to take us to see Granny and Grandfather. You have to go to sleep."

He stretched out an arm, looped it about her waist and drew her to him. "Will you help me upstairs, Jo?"

"Yes, daddy. Come along." She tugged his arm. He set Alice down and allowed himself to be tugged, his heart bursting.

\* \* \*

The Brains Trust met in the lounge over tea and coffee cake. Elaine and Shobnall on the sofa, Corky next to the rump of the cake, Crombie over there with his cigarettes and lighter on the arm of his chair. "What baffles me." Corky brushed chocolate from his whiskers. "Is whether the Diamond is tied up in the murder."

"Indeed." Crombie agreed. "Instinct tells me the issue is *how* they connect. The chauffeur was off in the Bentley for some reason at a time when, we surmise, they had no notion of the murder. Haynes denies any rendezvous and Alan thinks he's telling the truth. We know something had been passed to him. Perhaps, by the night of the murder, he'd already passed it on."

"The village." Shobnall looked round the room. "The Bentley wasn't gone long enough for anywhere else but it could be anyone in the village."

"At that time in the morning," Corky took up the thread. "Chances are people are up, some will be on the move, workers arriving. You might strike lucky with the door-stepping."

"Can't we be more specific?" Elaine had up to now been quietly listening. "You don't throw a diamond to any Tom, Dick or Harry."

Crombie approved. "Elaine's right. Wychnor isn't your normal set-up. This is the lady of the manor. Feudalism alive and well in the twentieth century. Her ladyship's favoured servants."

Shobnall nodded. "Of course. The squire, for whom Haynes stands in, the schoolmaster, absent in this case, and the man of god. The Reverend Bullard."

"One more thing," added Crombie. "If Lady Melinda is using her personal network, people bound to her, people she trusts, what was this American, the manager of the pop group, doing handing it to your chum, Stubbs, to stow in their limousine and bring it here? How Is Vetch involved with the Diamond?"

\* \* \*

He made time to walk into town and see Henderson. *Best to consult the oracle.* Half way, the sky blackened, raindrops began to fall and he felt the temperature plummeting. By Market Square, stair-rods were bouncing off the pavements. As he ducked into the alleyway, his trilby was channelling water down his neck. Inside Jardine's Bank, a different, ultimately calm climate prevailed. Aitch was in. And expecting him. "I said you'd be along, knew it as soon as your boss asked for help."

"Am I that predictable, Aitch?"

"No but if I were you, I'd have wanted to see the complete list. That is why you're here?"

The office was lined with photographs of what Aitch liked to call *'familiar forgotten faces'*, deluded dignitaries who had momentarily thought themselves worthy of record but for whom neither Aitch nor history had any time. One – Shobnall thought it might have been a recent mayor now being investigated by the Inland Revenue – had been replaced with a shot of Aitch's family: his wife, Hilary, and their five children. "I see the tribe up on the wall now."

"A Frank Peacock special in case I'm so busy I forget what they look like. They're growing so fast it can be hard to keep track. The twins, Helen and Hilary, they've passed their Eleven Plus so they're joining Hermione. She's doing exceptionally well, university material, we think. Henry's ticking along nicely. Harold's eight and we're putting all our effort into supporting him. But to business. Thomas will join us. He's done the work on the Needwoods. I've appointed him as my deputy."

"Gosh. What happened to Christopher?"

"I'd nothing left to teach him. I persuaded him to put in for the South Midlands job when my opposite number retired. Head office tell me he walked it."

A smart young man carrying a tea-tray strode in. *I remember him as a nervous office boy.* "Hello Mr Shobnall."

"Hello, Thomas. Good to see you. Alan will do. I gather congratulations are in order."

"Thank you." The young man blushed slightly. "I hope I can fill Christopher's shoes."

Aitch was pouring. "Wouldn't have appointed you if you couldn't. Here." He distributed cups. "I told you Alan would come sniffing about. Why don't you lead off?"

"Sure." Thomas plucked a sheet of paper from the tea-tray. "Mr Worthington wanted to know which parts of Lord Needwood's wealth had been or were being transferred to Lady Melinda. Let's start with investments. An interesting portfolio, always buying and selling. Mainly conservative holdings but there are quirky twists. Big in mining. Copper, silver, gold, diamonds, they've had De Beers for decades. Oil companies, Royal Dutch Shell, BP, Kuwait, Standard. A string of insurance holdings – Needwood's a full member of Lloyds of London. Steel stockholders, car manufacturers, a couple of those new commercial television outfits. All in all, current valuation around twenty-five million. Ownership is complicated but it looks like Melinda is becoming the ultimate beneficiary for everything listed in London.

"Then there's land and property. Lady Melinda now owns nearly all they have in Britain and that's almost as much as the Westminsters. Estates and farms, including a huge swathe between Burton and Lichfield, several Scottish forests, much of Dorset, whole streets in London, Charlotte Street near the British Museum. Hotels in the capital and along the south coast. Half of South Kensington, a mansion or two in Belgravia. Oh, and orchards in Kent."

Shobnall was losing track. "How on earth do they manage all this? It must be a full-time job."

Aitch intervened. "They contract the financial management to us and people like us. Needwood is sharp. You only have to look at the timing of disposals. He realised a small fortune out of selling Great Western Railway before nationalisation appeared on the political agenda. Same with his coal mining interests. There's some other wholly-owned companies, are there not, Thomas?"

"Yes, Aitch. The Needwood Shipping Line, operating around the Mediterranean and the Baltic. That's registered in Panama and ownership has stayed with Lord Needwood. However, Lady Melinda now has TransUK Haulage, a nationwide storage and distribution company, a brewery in Stoke, 'Jennings & Joyce', known for its lager, and even a funeral director, based in the South-east but expanding fast. That's called 'HeavenSent', believe it or not. Their private bank in the City of London has a wide range of interests, shares and loans, some large enough that she effectively has temporary control. Like Marmite down the road currently. Her bank's loan funded their expansion."

"She owns *all* this?" Shobnall had given up trying to figure what it might be worth.

Aitch laughed. "Yes and no. Any normal person or, more to the point, the tax authorities would have terrible trouble getting to the bottom of it. The trails vanish and re-appear - or not - in a maze of sophisticated trusts and offshore legal devices. It's all to do with tax of one kind or another, you understand. However, if you wanted a superficial but realistic answer to the question who, at the end of the day, receives the financial benefit by way of revenue income or capital growth then yes, Lady Melinda does."

Shobnall shook his head. It was all too much. "So Lord Needwood has relinquished his fortune?"

Aitch and Thomas looked at one another. Thomas went on. "Not at all. As far as we are aware, he is only clearing out assets connected to this country. He retains his South American estates and oilfields, his land and plantations in Bermuda, tea plantations in India – "

"Enough." Shobnall gave up. "It's a different world. No, it's not that, is it? It's the *whole* world, that's the difference. Could I have a copy of the list, Aitch?"

Henderson reached into a desk drawer. "Thought you'd never ask, old chap. With our compliments. Bring the family over for tea on Sunday, why don't you?"

\* \* \*

The Friday night/Saturday morning shift irritated with trivial call-outs and false alarms. Around six, as Shobnall completed yet another incident report (in triplicate), his thoughts turned to Crombie's question about Vetch. *He slips in and out leaving no trace, how does it all fit together?* He was impatient for feedback from Angela. He wished Dave Chateris would call. *Patience, Shobnall, you've a night off tonight, maybe after that I'll go see Bullard.* Gary Stubbs rang. "Morning, Alan, hope you don't mind me calling, I figured you'd be there, leading the fight against crime."

"Doing my best, Gary. How are things out there?"

"We're done. Steven and Alex are happy they've enough new material for an album. Morgan's given us the go-ahead to make for the Smoke and a recording studio. I'm loading up the limo. Wanted to say so long. And thanks."

"I appreciate that. Good luck, Gary, and look after yourself."

"I'll try, Alan. I'll, er, hang on to your card if that's OK. I value the human face of copperdom, as Eddie put it."

"Call me anytime, Gary, as a copper, as a friend. Whenever you think I can help."

"I will. Cheers, Alan. I'll see you again."

He wouldn't.

*   *   *

# ELEVEN

*Her wardrobe must look like it's full of rainbows.* Today, for afternoon tea with her god-daughters, Lavinia Salt had encased herself in a creation of deep crimson slashed with yellow and studded with sparkles. The girls didn't care. Josephine and Alice doted on her, the former open-mouthed on the floor, the latter transfixed on Corky's lap.

"Jo, darling," crooned Lavinia. "Have an éclair?" She'd arrived with a box of cakes from Birds.

"You'll spoil them," protested Elaine as Josephine obediently pushed the éclair, inch by inch, into her mouth.

"Only now and again." Lavinia's eyes shone with affection. "I think young Jo takes a very balanced view of the world. They are divine! Don't you agree, Corky?"

Corky was helping Alice with a fragment of strawberry tart that was decorating her front more than it was entering her mouth. "You know I do, Lavinia. They are going to be the most remarkable pair of young ladies."

*What a choice of god-parents, I remember we expected an argument but came up with the same names, God forbid......*His memory floated up the indelible scene in which his parents shepherded him and his brother, Neil, to the train. *That last time.* He thrust it aside. *If anything happened they'd be in the best of hands.*

\* \* \*

The platter of cakes had become a scattering of crumbs. Alice was asleep on Corky's lap while Lavinia and Josephine were engaged in a studious game of stone-paper-scissors when there was a rap on the front door. Lavinia started. "Oh! That will be Reuben. Josephine, come here." She knelt in a flashing of crimson and yellow and sparkle and hugged Jo to her. "See you soon, darling."

Josephine beamed up at the kaleidoscopic adult. "Thank you, Aunt Lavinia."

Lavinia regarded the child. "My, my, my," she murmured.

Shobnall ushered in Reuben Salt. Alice slumbered on but Josephine hurled herself at the big figure, extending her arms. Mr Salt swept her up. "Good evening, Josephine."

"Hello Reuben."

"Have you been a good girl?"

The child stared into the eyes of the brewery boss. "Of course I have."

"Then I am proud of you, my dear."

"Thank you, Reuben."

Mr Salt set Josephine down. "Time, Lavinia."

*How good can life be? Almost makes a marathon of nights tolerable but what would help would be a note from Angela that says more than 'no results yet'.*

* * *

The night off and the family time replenished Shobnall's energies. Anyone can cope with the occasional graveyard shift but doing it night after night is wearing (unless you're Eddie Mustard). On Sunday, conscious they'd be hanging on for the Monday morning meeting, he plunged into the paperwork. *You get promoted, they reward you with money and responsibility but they never mention the paper, dunno how Angela disposes of it so effortlessly.* Around the two-hundredth signature, Eddie appeared with two mugs of tea and plonked one in front of him. "Drowning in it."

"Too right but I'll feel better if I catch up before Monday's meeting."

"*Look* better, you mean, can't have Angela outstripping you on the bureaucracy stakes, eh? Hope we get some feedback on Wychnor. We need more than these billet-doux saying nowt. "Look at this." Eddie unrolled a paper. "New Musical Express."

Shobnall took in the headline. 'REAPERS GO TO NUMBER ONE.' Below. '*The latest release from The Reapers, 'Shame' b/w 'Dumb, Dumb, Dum-dum'* "What's b/w mean, Eddie?"

"Backed with. It's a double-sided hit."

"What's that mean?"

"No idea, Alan, I read it somewhere."

He read on. *'which entered the chart at number 15 last week, has surged to Number One, dislodging Elvis Presley's 'Devil in Disguise' and giving the bad boys from South London their first chart-topper. It may not be their last.....'* He skimmed. *"Charts inside."* There it was, The Top Twenty. There *they* were, The Reapers. At the top.

"They were all saying it, Eddie. The next record would make or break them. I guess the publicity around Cox's death hasn't harmed them. Morgan Vetch will be pleased.

Eddie's lip curled in distaste. "He'll be organising his Swiss bank account, I shouldn't wonder."

Shobnall was examining the picture. "They didn't hang about cranking out a new publicity shot. That's not Cox."

"All their Christmases have come at once. That lot will have forgotten about him."

*I don't think everybody's forgotten, Eddie, I wonder if Gary's been round to see Cox's mother.*

\* \* \*

Angela left them with Lennie. "Sorry, Alan, the DI asked me to stand in at the HQ personnel committee."

*So the Old Man has been on, I'll not ask how often.* "Don't worry, Angela, chivvy them about Joe Short's replacement."

Shobnall sought out Bob Saxby, who had returned relieved about his father and shouldering a hamper stuffed with what he fondly referred to as Yorkshire 'delicacies'. "Henderson's Relish, Alan, it puts hairs on the hairs on your chest." Bob peeled back a layer of his sandwich to reveal a viscous brown substance barely recognisable as a northern interpretation of cheese and chutney.

"I, er, think I'll leave that with you, Bob. Your dad OK?"

"He's fine. All a bit of an overreaction but mum was worried. Needed the family about her. Think my sister was glad to see the back of me, house was crowded. You been following the cricket? Those West Indian bowlers –"

"Sorry, Bob, must catch Lennie. Murder case, you know."

Lennie, inevitably, had his nose in the papers. "I don't know why you two are trying to drag me into the sleazy world of modern music. Give me Glenn Miller any day. I see your Reapers have no sooner lost one of their number in a lake than they're hogging the headlines as the future of popular entertainment. That Beatle, McCartney, caught speeding and they let him off with a measly £15 fine. Mrs Dickie Henderson dies of a drug overdose. Drugs! I remember when they were things prescribed by doctors. I quite like the Dickie Henderson Show, must be my age." He folded the paper. "Suppose you want to know what we have for you?" They waited. "Nothing."

Shobnall realised that, for some reason, he wasn't surprised. Eddie couldn't believe it. "Lennie! There must be *something*."

"Trust me, lads. We interviewed anyone moving and if they weren't moving we wanted to know why not. Charlie and Sheila did a great job. That Sheila, by the way, is one smart girl. Nobody saw anything. Everybody heard the helicopter, the dead in the churchyard probably heard *that*. Not a single lead. Angela feels we've failed you but I can't see there's anything else we can do."

Shobnall considered. "What did you make of the vicar, Bullard?"

"Sheila and I saw him. I have to confess, Alan, he made me uneasy."

*Unusual observation from Lennie.* "What do you mean?"

For once, Lennie Morton hesitated. "I'm not sure. You know I don't take to these people who like to style themselves 'of the cloth'. Rubbish, if you ask me." He stroked his tie. "I couldn't read him. I'll own that makes me wonder if he's hiding something but then, I am a copper. He got under my skin, I'll admit that."

"Interesting. We'll not score Bullard off the list yet. Anything else?"

"You seen this? Lennie turned his newspaper so they could read the headline. 'SCHOOLGIRL MISSING. NEVER REACHES DANCE'. "Gave me a shiver, Alan. Reminded me of Brokendown Wood. Pauline Reade, 16 years of age, on her way to a dance in Gorton, Manchester. Know what I mean? There's some lonely moors up there. Policeman's nose. They'll not find her."

\*   \*   \*

He made for the rear exit. The new girl, WPC Sheila Redpath was on the desk. "Sheila, thank you for your help out at Wychnor." The blush was instantaneous. "Hey, don't be embarrassed." *Guess she's still settling in.*

A tall, slim girl, she looked fit, short dark hair, eyes that when they came up from the floor were gray and alert. "Thank you, I mean, thank you, Sergeant."

"Alan will do, no need to be formal." He moved behind the desk, made for the back office. "Cheerio."

"Sergeant, er, Alan...." He half-turned. "I'm sorry we couldn't find anything. Memories are funny. I think the recollections of the helicopter obliterated everything else. It came from Birmingham."

Shobnall came back to the counter. "How do you know that?"

"My brother works at Birmingham Airport. He's in administration, nothing exciting. I asked him what he could find out. The helicopter was chartered to meet a private light plane arriving from Croydon. Mike – that's my brother – said it left Birmingham at 07.15 that morning with the passenger from the private plane and returned with only the pilot at 08.30. If you want to know anything else I can ask Mike."

"Hang on a minute, Sheila." Shobnall ran her words through his brain again. "You said 'the passenger'. A man? One man?"

"Yes, Mike said the manifests for the plane and the helicopter stated one passenger. Do you want me to see if I can get a name?"

"No, your brother's done his bit. I've a good idea who it was but we need proper confirmation. We'll go through the channels. Ask Charlie, he'll show you the drill. Thanks again, Sheila, you've been *very* helpful."

"Oh!" She couldn't restrain the smile. "Golly!"

*Lennie said she was smart.* "Did, er, anything else strike you while you were out at Wychnor?"

She frowned. "Actually, Sergeant, Alan, sir........Could I just call you sir, sir? It feels easier."

He chuckled. "Any of those are fine, Sheila."

"Well, sir, I didn't like the vicar." *Hm, Lennie couldn't read him, she didn't like him, and I thought it was the normal nervousness when faced with the law.* "He was.....courteous in an old-fashioned sort of way and he answered all our questions as far as he had to, if you see what I mean, and he had that distant, um, gravitas you find in older men who've had a professional career, the military, doctors, the church. But he made my skin crawl. I kept thinking 'there's something not right'. Maybe I've let my imagination run away with me, sir. I was keen to do well."

"You *have* done well. Never ignore your instincts. I think I'll pay the Reverend another visit. Now, I must go. Don't forget to talk to Charlie about approaching the airport authorities."

\* \* \*

*Was Angela wrong? Were we all wrong? They came over the river?* He parked at Wychnor green, made his way through the village. An hour of daylight left, crows straggling roost-wards. A distant clock chimed. The clang of the Wychnor bell and the village was quiet, a handful of windows lit, here and there by a flash from a TV screen.

The rectory was in darkness. Not so the church. Candles were burning on the altar. To one side, a door stood ajar, lit within. A small room, wood-panelled, a white sink in one corner. On the far wall, church vestments hung, some full-length and grand, others simpler black and white garments. Bullard was fiddling with them, his back to Shobnall. "Excuse me, Reverend." Bullard froze for several seconds then turned slowly. *Something in the man's eyes.* "I knocked at the rectory."

"You startled me." Bullard was himself once more. "Sergeant Shobnall, isn't it?"

"You have a good memory, Reverend. I merely wanted to complete our picture of movements on the night of the drowning. Did Lady Melinda's chauffeur collect something from you? Around eight o'clock on the Sunday morning?"

*He looks taken aback rather than shifty.* "How did, er.....Yes, he did. Er, a bag. A black hold-all." Shobnall waited. "I don't know what it contained. It was not my place to look inside."

"Was it heavy?"

"Not particularly. It felt well-packed. It might have been a bag of clothing, material, something like that." Shobnall waited some more. "Albert Haynes had given it to me."

69

Bullard seemed untroubled now. "He said Lady Melinda wished me to keep it safe. Porter, her chauffeur, said she was otherwise engaged up at the Hall and he would take it. That's all I can tell you. In our various ways, we here all serve the family." *You do, don't you, without questions, without peeking.* "Is there a problem, Sergeant?"

"No, Reverend, as I said, we like to have a comprehensive picture. I'm sorry to have troubled you again. I hadn't intended to divert you from your.....labours." *You don't need to know you held a fifteen million pound gemstone in your hands but I see the reason for the look in Haynes' eyes, he thought he'd put one over on the plods.*

\* \* \*

*Lennie's right, Sheila's right, there's something off-kilter there, when he saw me, he was frightened about something.* He drove along the track, parked on the driveway. Walked round the side of the Hall, over the lawn, still scarred by the tracks of Fred and Vern's Land Rover. The lake was hardly moving. He checked the boatshed. Both craft present and correct. Back to the car. Thinking. *The vicar said he'd been in America, must look into that.* He started up, checked his rear mirror even though he was the only vehicle for a mile, aside maybe for a tractor or two. Stopped, switched off. *What did I say? Maybe we were all wrong?*

He set off for the river, across the croquet lawn, little used to judge by the rust on the hoops and the dandelions peppering the green, the neatly-tended gardens and an ancient orchard, tree trunks layered with moss and lichen; past the jumble of sheds and compost heaps, through a scattering of trees and bushes down to the Swarbourn.

It wasn't much of a river but it wasn't a channel you could leap over. Smooth waters running swiftly, free of surface weed, thick grass at the bank, willows arching out to brush the surface. Shobnall edged down the bank. Nothing out of the ordinary. As he turned back, light flashed among the roots. He bent, parted the leaves. *What do we have here?* An empty bottle, clear glass, minus its cap. He cast about, snapped off a length of branch, inserted it in the neck of the bottle and rolled it over. A white label featuring a red rosette with a 'B' at its heart. 'Jim Beam Kentucky Straight Bourbon Whiskey'.

\* \* \*

## TWELVE

Shobnall waited at the entrance to the Big House but the Land Rover and – he realised as it bounced over the drive – empty trailer headed straight for the rear of the house. He trotted after them. By the time he caught up, they'd drilled a fresh set of furrows across what was coming to look more like the Somme than a lawn. "You haven't bought a boat, Fred."

Fred and Vern looked at each other. "Why he's a detective and we've not evolved out of the water yet," rumbled Vern.

"We'll take the skiff," said Fred. "You give Vern a hand getting it onto the trailer." He opened the rear of the Land Rover. "We've brought the outboard, clip it on the stern."

Once they had the skiff in the Swarbourn, Shobnall had second thoughts about the whole thing. *We'll never manage three people in that, none of us are small and Vern's a big bloke.* The big bloke read his thoughts. "Just you and Fred. He likes a summer evening boat trip in the countryside."

"What about you, Vern, what are you going to do?"

"It's a lovely evening, couple of hours sunshine yet. I'm going to sit and enjoy the river. If I get tired of that, I've me book."

\* \* \*

They made good speed. Shobnall was surprised how quiet the outboard motor was. *People wouldn't give it a second thought, if they heard it at all over the telly.* The Swarbourn surrendered to the Trent, no more than 15 or 20 feet wide but a full weight of water surging along. *A proper river!* Fred trailed a hand in the water. "They used to catch eels along here, you know." He no longer noticed the putter-putter of the outboard. Here and there a coot or moorhen scuttled into the reeds in alarm. Then the Trent swung eastwards, towards the A38.

"Fred, not this way. We drew a complete blank in Wychnor Bridges."

"Glad to hear that, don't want to be cursing James Brindley as we tumble over Alrewas Weir."

"Who's James Brindley?"

"Don't you know anything about local history? Eighteenth century engineer, lived up Leek-way. Look around you. He built this." Fred pushed the tiller over and angled them back westwards into the entrance to a canal, hidden until now. "The Trent & Mersey. This is where anyone in a small boat is likely to head." *This feels right.* Within a few hundred yards, his heart sank. *Oh no, lock gates, Fred's going to make me do all that paddle and windlass stuff.* He wasn't. "Why we took the skiff, Alan, light as a feather, even with the outboard." Fred tilted the motor inboard, they hoisted the skiff out of the water, marched and re-launched. "Easy-peasy." On they went. A stretch of open countryside, a curve through Alrewas, back to fields. Two more sets of locks, the drill with the boat now pretty slick. All the time, Shobnall was scanning the banks, the fields, the woods, the tracks and bridges, the possible means of exit as they passed Alrewas – imagining he was making the journey at three in the morning having just killed someone. *You'd have a light, it's feasible but where to?*

It came to him as they neared a bridge over the canal and a fourth set of locks. "Hold it, Fred." The engine was slipped into neutral, the boat lost way. "This is Fradley Junction, isn't it?"

"Uh-huh."

*What better place to put a helicopter down? Here's a bundle of notes, pick up a second passenger, keep your mouth shut.* "OK, Fred, I've seen what I need to see, let's rejoin Vern"

*  *  *

Fradley Junction. They'd be on time; they always were. He parked at The Swan, crossed the canal, waited by the workshop. Two minutes to eight and here they were. A short man, talking ten to the dozen; a taller, younger man, a toolbag in each hand.

"Alan Shobnall!" The shorter man threw his arms wide. "How are you, my friend?"

"I'm well, thank you, Ernest, as you obviously are. Hello, Ernie."

The Waterhouses were delighted and curious. "Not another murder?" Ernest wanted to know.

"A dead body, certainly."

Ernie, the younger, paused unlocking the workshop. "Wychnor Hall? The pop group?"

"I can't say much, Ernie, too early."

The two men gave him a knowing look, nodded simultaneously and Ernest spoke. "How can we help?"

"I suspect someone made a trip along the canal the night that young man drowned and came ashore hereabouts. If they did, what happened to the boat they came in?"

The Waterhouses stared at each other and with one voice exclaimed "Told yer so!"

They walked Shobnall to the junction with The Coventry Canal and a short distance along it. Moored at the bank was a rubber dinghy, a one-person job. Complete with Evinrude. "What's it doing here?" Shobnall demanded.

"What we asked," said Ernest.

"No, I mean why is it tied up here?"

Ernest looked up at him. "Oh, it wasn't like that. When we arrived that morning it were floating out in the middle of the junction, like it had been abandoned. Ernie hauled it in."

"We thought," added Ernie. "It might have drifted so we made it fast. Odd no-one's come for it. Nice motor, that. Bit fishy, we thought."

"I told 'im so!" Ernest exclaimed.

"Ernest, Ernie, thank you again. Our divers will come for it." *Floating out in the middle? I wonder if he fell in?* In his memory, Shobnall heard Eddie saying that Preston's trousers had been soaking wet under his mac.

\* \* \*

The old aerodrome could have been the set for a film – a frontier western through which the tumbleweed tumbles forever. A redundant facility the Air Ministry had forgotten it owned. The runways crumbling, thistles sprouting where Wellington bombers once loaded up, grass tangling everywhere. *Why bother, no-one's ever going to fly from here again.* The high perimeter fence was decaying, rust devouring the wire.

Yet someone *did* bother. The padlock on the gate was shiny and new. The glass in the guardhouse window was cracked but smoke was rising from its chimney and an old bicycle leant against its wooden slats.

Shobnall called out. No response. He leaned in the car window, pressed his hand on the horn. The guardhouse door sprang back and a short, tubby man in uniform stomped out and stood, hands on hips, glaring. Shobnall brandished his warrant card through the gate and the man's officiousness gave way to caution. "I'm not allowed to let anyone in unless they're from the Ministry."

"It's OK. I don't want to come in. I just need some information. This aerodrome is no longer operational, is it?"

The guard guffawed. "Hasn't seen a plane since the war. Not sure anyone at The Ministry remembers it's here apart from whoever pays my wages." His manner was softening. "Don't you go saying nothing, neither."

Shobnall laughed. "Don't worry. I don't want to have to deal with Ministry bureaucrats any more than you do. Is there someone here all the time?"

"No." The man glanced around as if he expected Air Ministry spies. "Always thought it was rum. I come in for nine, stay until four, every weekday. I come in early to get the stove going. They only kept the electric for the perimeter lights. Only way of brewing a cuppa is the stove. Overnight and at weekends, the Ministry don't seem bothered."

"At night then, there's no-one here but the lights are on?"

"Them that still work, yes. Not my job to fiddle with 'em. One by one they're failing. I notify the Ministry but nothing ever happens."

"The lights go on and off automatically?"

"Seven to seven."

"I see. You cycle in. Where from?"

"Orgreave. Me and the missus live in Orgreave. It's not far. The cycling helps keep me fit."

*He has to be joking.* "July 6, Saturday morning, early. You hear anything?"

The guard eyed Shobnall with renewed interest. "The dead kid up at the Big House."

"Routine enquiries." The guard's eyebrows lifted. *More shrewd than I first gave him credit for.* "You know how these things work. Maybe not entirely routine. I can't say more than that."

The eyebrows fell. "I told my missus there was summat up. Maybe nothing to do with that poor boy and I'll be honest, we were in The Crown in Alrewas Friday night." He wiped his face with a red-spotted handkerchief. "It woke me, the noise. These helicopters, they ain't quiet. Strange thing was, it woke me and then it stopped. I turned over for some more kip but it started over, real loud, then faded. I got up for a jimmy riddle and decided on a cup of tea. I was boiling the kettle when I heard it again, going in the other direction, one long noise this time, getting louder and after a bit disappearing again."

\* \* \*

July sweltered, the mercury stuck in the 80s. Bob Charles of New Zealand lifted the 92nd Open Golf Championship at Royal Lytham & St Anne's. Lavinia Salt, Elaine and Hilary Henderson saw "Day of the Triffids" at the Gaumont; Elaine had preferred the book but she didn't say anything – the film had been surprisingly good fun. The Government proposed merging The Admiralty, The War Office and the Air Ministry into a unified Ministry of Defence and upset a host of admirals, generals and air marshals who saw their sinecures vanishing. DI George Worthington phoned to say he and Cyril would be doing an extra week in London with 'this bloody stone'.

\* \* \*

"Makes that Diamond seem inconsequential, eh?" Gordon Crombie lounged against the kitchen wall. Smiling. He had a view into the hallway-cum-circus-ring where Corky was performing his popular elephant rides for little girls, Alice on board but inexorably sliding forward over Corky's head while Josephine looked on, hands to her mouth. "Is that in the godparent job description, Alan?"

Shobnall was pouring Brunton's IPA. "Here you go, Gordon. There seem to be no limits to the duties; if the post is offered to you, think *very* carefully. I agree, murder trumps all. And I'm not making much progress."

Crombie sipped his beer. "You've a reasonable case shaping up. You found that whiskey bottle."

"Clean. Nobody's prepared to swear its contents were what Roxburgh found in young Cox's stomach."

"OK, circumstantial, but what about this helicopter?" Corky, with Josephine's assistance, was replacing his miniature *mahout* on what passed for the *howdah*.

"There *is* something in that. The bottle was clumsy. They should have chucked it in the river. I think they abandoned that dinghy at Fradley Junction and marched up to the old aerodrome. We know Vetch flew to Birmingham and transferred to the helicopter. By the time it reached Wychnor Hall, the pilot had two passengers. Fits with what I heard and what the Ministry guard heard."

"That places Vetch's associate well and truly in the frame."

"Yes and no, Gordon. It won't be enough to pin the murder on him. All it will do is put him in the grounds. You can bet he'll have a story of his own. Vetch knew to collect Preston and where he'd been. Question is how much did he know about what his associate had been up to. My money's on everything but what I think doesn't constitute proof. I need more. We're tracking down the pilot."

The only known British elephant in captivity had collapsed in a heap in the hall. Josephine was disentangling her sister from the spread-eagled beast while kicking its leg. "Come on, Uncle Corky, my turn now."

The stricken animal lifted its head from the carpet, looked towards the kitchen door. "Please, a beer, for the love of retired policemen!"

Crombie and Shobnall raised their glasses. Shobnall was relishing that glow of affection that comes from being surrounded by friends when Gordon Crombie, whose thoughts were anchored at Wychnor Hall, posed a question that really ought to have occurred to Shobnall by now. "So how did this Preston get to Wychnor in the first place?"

* * *

The nights had become busier. Burton was seeing a lot of housebuilding these days as the rising middle class sought new houses to accommodate the stylish furniture and shiny gadgets they could now afford. The builders were suddenly reporting a rash of

76

thefts – materials, equipment, even a steamroller. As Eddie remarked, "the Japanese could build a house with the paperwork these construction sites have generated."

Shobnall paused about five, tired of it all. *How can there be such a black market in cement?* He needed some movement on Wychnor. Sheila Redpath was mining airport bureaucracy in search of a helicopter pilot; Gideon was plumbing layers of ecclesiastical administration for the Reverend Bullard's history. He simply had to wait on them. But Crombie had a point. He went downstairs.

Nobody in. The Marie Celeste. A pack of cards on the table. He could tell by the relative size of two piles of pennies who sat where. The toilet flushed out back and Charlie appeared. "Hello, Alan, Sheila's out. Little old lady lost her cat."

"Charlie, a question about when the DI had you tail Lady Melinda's Bentley."

"Oh yeah! That was good fun. I'd have liked to chase 'em the whole way. Some car, that Continental."

"The DI said she dropped her two passengers at Alrewas railway station. That right?"

Charlie nodded. "Yes. I thought that was odd. I mean, there's not that many trains go through Alrewas in the week and here we are early on a weekend morning, for goodness' sake."

"Did you see them go into the station?"

"'Fraid not, Alan, the DI was very specific. Don't lose the Bentley."

"Oh well, it was just a thought."

"If it helps your thinking," said Charlie, grinning. "I went back. Once it was obvious her motor was headed for London, I turned round but I was curious. I went into Alrewas station. Between the time she dropped them and me getting back, there was not a single stopping train through there. And no sign of those two blokes. None of the staff had seen anyone answering their description."

In that moment, Shobnall forgave Charlie Taylor for every helter-skelter ride he had ever had to sweat through.

\* \* \*

His telephone rang. "Hello, Charlie......Dave Charteris? Yes please, put him on."
*Wonder if he's managed to find something on Vetch.*

The Londoner didn't hang about. "Alan, sorry mate, know you'll be thinkin' I've got the goods on that Yank. Ain't that but it is yer Reapers group." *Dave sounds agitated, not like him.* Chateris gabbled on. "The good guy you said was wiv 'em, what was 'is name?"

"You mean Stubbs, Gary Stubbs, their roadie. Yes, I liked him."

"You give 'im yer card?"

"What? Yes, I gave it to him that first time we went to investigate a disturbance, told him to call me if there was any more trouble. How did you know?" A cold sensation was prickling Shobnall's spine. *Oh no.*

"Lissen, Alan, you need to get darn 'ere, I think. Found yer card in 'is pocket when we fished 'im art the Thames. 'E ain't ringin' no-one ever again."

\* \* \*

# THIRTEEN

We are all creatures of habit to some extent. Given a long solo train journey, Shobnall would buy a copy of The Times from Smith's on the platform. Late afternoon on this occasion but he was lucky, the last copy. He'd survey his surroundings until departure. Quiet today, few people on the platform, two porters chatting, an old man asleep on a bench. A heat haze lifting from the 'up' line. The whistle would blow and the train would begin to move. *Hardly noticeable in these diesels, you don't feel that sense of power straining at the load.* He'd unfold the paper, ignore the front page of small ads, turn to the headlines within. 'YUGOSLAVIA EARTHQUAKE DEATH TOLL OVER 1,000'. 'KIM PHILBY IN MOSCOW'. A shot of Christine Keeler leaving court, arms across her face as egg yolk splashed her jacket. Beside the weather chart, the Manchester Chief Constable confirming no progress on the missing girl, Pauline Reade.

At this point, he'd glance out of the window. And that would be that. The newspaper forgotten while Shobnall stared out, over the industrial sprawl of the Black Country, on to Rugby and through a patchwork of fields, hedges, trees and woods, over rivers and roads and canals, past level crossings and signal boxes and small stations where only the slow trains halted. A parish spire peeping from behind the trees, a farmer manoeuvring his bales of golden corn, a postman leaning on his bicycle. On towards the capital. The Old Man had been unequivocal: 'get down here as quickly as you can.' As towns and villages and hamlets whirled by, his thoughts ricocheted around his head. *Is this coincidence? Are The Reapers jinxed? Do we have linked murders? Wait for facts, Shobnall, wait till you get there.*

On the DI's instruction, he took a taxi. "The Carillion Hotel, please, Charlotte Street." He saw the cabbie giving him a look in the rear-view mirror. *Probably marking me as a copper, as usual.* The traffic was heavy and it was after six when they pulled under the stylish *porte cochere* fronting a tall, graceful building of slate-coloured brick. Shobnall became a tad flustered as, while trying to decide how large a tip to offer, the door was yanked open by a man in a grey top hat and matching coat festooned with yards of gold braid who swept up his bag and virtually frog-marched him inside. The DI was loitering in the lobby; he and the commissionaire seemed to know each other. "Hello, sir, this is all a bit, um......" He wasn't sure what.

"Fast, Alan, everything is faster. You'll catch up." He turned. "Thank you, Stan, I'll take him from here." The bag changed hands. Shobnall had the distinct impression that a coin went the other way. The DI shepherded him to the lift, up several floors, and into a thick-carpeted corridor before handing him a room key. "Freshen up, Alan. In the lobby for seven, we're taking you out. Cyril's working but we may bump into some friends. Hurry along now."

*A far cry from Mrs Bayliss in Sheringham.* The room was huge. Plush. It looked pristine, as if the space and contents had sprung into existence a split-second before he opened the door. It was decorated and furnished in subtle shades of grey in a way that created a sense of stillness, an oasis of calm amidst an outside world so frenetic as to have put him off his stroke. *Even a radio, a grey radio.* He punched a button and it spat out one of those twangy American pop tunes, a nasal voice whining about a brown-eyed handsome man. He switched it off. *Come on, get a move on.* The bathroom wasn't much smaller than the bedroom. Smooth white porcelain, a full-length mirror, towels over a warm rail. *Warm at this time of year?* He laid out his pyjamas. *Wonder where we're going to eat, hope it's not too formal.* He changed his tie. *The DI would have said something.* He peered out of the window at a Victorian office block opposite. *The something Mutual Association, can't make it out.* The street was a flux of vehicles, cars, vans, lorries, black cabs, red buses rolling north and south in silence. *Double glazing.* He checked his watch. Five to. *Shoulders back, Shobnall, best foot forward.*

* * *

Worthington was waiting. "Bang on time, Alan. Esmée's exercising a woman's prerogative. Room alright?"

"It's awful posh, sir. Is, um, Lady Melinda stumping up for it?"

"Don't worry, lad, she owns the bloody building. And half the rest of the street. Convenient for the British Museum, though. She'll be staying here. She's in and out of the Museum, keeping an eye on the you-know-what and pestering me and Cyril. Luckily, she seems to have plenty of other business to keep her out of our hair. Ah! Here's Esmée."

Esmée Worthington contrived to look as if she had stepped straight from the pages of Vogue magazine and, simultaneously, as though she had, without thinking, flung on whatever had happened to be lying around. "Alan, it's been a long time."

Her handshake was  firm, cool. "Mrs Worthington." They'd met before but for the life of him he couldn't recall the circumstances.

"Esmée, please." She read his mind. "Christmas drinks at the police station in 1957. George invited spouses that year. You came with Elaine, your first Christmas as a detective, I think." *One of these people who never forget a thing, better watch what I say.* Stanley the commissionaire had organised a cab. As Shobnall took one of the fold-down seats, he heard the DI request 'Soho Square please, driver.' Stanley unobtrusively palmed his tithe.

As night enfolded the city, London simply turned on the lights and switched from work to play. The pavements were bustling with sharp-suited executives, high-spirited youngsters, society couples, all manner of folk clutching guide-books. Every nationality in the world was here. The DI sat contentedly while Esmée entertained Shobnall with a running commentary. "Large slabs of University here, George's friend, Lord Needwood, I know, George, don't give me that look, likely made oodles out of the land he sold them, Bloomsbury, home to Virginia Woolf and her circle, too arch for my taste, I don't suppose you're a great reader are you, Alan? No, these days policemen rarely are, you spend so much time filling out forms that your fingers rebel at the prospect of picking up more paper, a pity as we're not far from Foyle's in Charing Cross Road, quite the most wonderful bookshop. Ah, this is Wardour Street, an odd route our driver is taking but there always seem to be roads closed, all manner of film enterprises here, that's Film House, home of Gaumont-British and over there." She pointed. "Novello & Co, the music dealers. Chinatown isn't far but chopsticks are not for us tonight, look, Manor House, home of the GPO Film Unit and once a brothel, I believe, as well as the headquarters of Crosse & Blackwell, makes you wonder about salad cream, doesn't it?"

Shobnall let it wash over him. The monologue formed a mellifluous counterpoint to the constant movement outside. The DI leaned towards the driver. "Top end of Greek Street if you don't mind" and something rustled into the front compartment. *It must be expensive to live like this but I don't suppose all of London does live like this.*

Suddenly they were tumbling onto a narrow pavement full of people heading determinedly in all directions. Tall, grimy buildings transformed by the light shining from pubs and bars and clubs and restaurants, flashing neon bestowing a garish tone on the street. Shobnall instinctively put a hand on his wallet but the Worthingtons, ignoring the bright lights, steered him through a shadowy doorway beneath a blue neon sign, '*Paolo's*, and down a shabby set of stairs. At the bottom, a door was flung back as if someone within had sensed their approach and a hubbub of chatter and lilting music spilled out. A tall man in a white tuxedo, sallow-skinned and with a saturnine expression, held the door open with one arm, waved them in with the other and abruptly blessed them with a smile that totally changed his look, a smile of the warmest sincerity that seemed to well up from deep within his being. "*Signora* Worthington, *Padrone, buona sera.*"

Esmée visibly basked as the man took her hand and raised it to his lips. "Evening, Paolo," said the DI. "This is our friend, Alan Shobnall."

"*Benvenuto, Signore* Shobnall, welcome to my humble trattoria." Paolo released Esmée's hand and shook Shobnall's. *An Italian restaurant, I hope the menu's in English.* "*Padrone*, your other guests are already here. I have taken the liberty of placing you beside the kitchen." He gave Esmée another smile. "I know the *Signora* enjoys the *spettacolo*. Please, follow me."

Esmée nudged Shobnall. "This will be fun. I do like to see the shop-floor." Shobnall had other issues on his mind. *Think I'll get by, mostly ties, don't see any dinner jackets, mind you, some of the women look awful glamorous, hope George's other guests aren't too stuffy.* Esmée Worthington's ability to divine his thoughts was beginning to concern him. As Paolo led them to a sheltered space containing two tables, one to the left and one to the right and both with a view over the half-height barrier into the kitchen, she whispered. "As if we'd make you *work* for your supper, Alan."

The moment he saw the couple already seated at their table grinning back, he understood. "Mr and Mrs Charteris," he cried. Frankie threw her arms around him, slapped big kisses on each cheek. Dave wasn't settling for a handshake either, a bear-hug was in order. Frankie was kissing and hugging everyone. Paolo withdrew, fearful, perhaps, for his tuxedo.

Shobnall forgot about Gary Stubbs, Cox, Vetch, The Reapers, Wychnor Hall. He was out for a special meal with dear friends, *four* dear friends. George Worthington had parked the professional relationship outside. They sat in a Soho basement filled with Mediterranean culture, at a table covered with a red-and-white checked cloth, a candle stuck in a Chianti *fiasco*, they sat and talked about everything and about nothing. "Your guv'nor knows everyone," remarked Charteris. *Yes, he does, who they are, how they work and what they need.* He observed his companions. *Esmée, cultured and stylish, George, bluff but wise, and Dave, no frills, no nonsense, he'll never let you down and Franc oise, delightful Frankie, film star looks, a heart of gold and an expert on French art, as couples they have a lot in common.* He wished Elaine could have been there but he refused to allow the thought to spoil anything.

There was only one area of risk. As he had feared, the menu was in Italian and he couldn't make head nor tail of it. *I think that's spaghetti bolognaise, I'll play safe.* Again it was the prescient Esmée, asking, before Paolo came to take their order, "What's everyone having? Alan?" When, a touch shyly, he told her, she reached over and patted his hand. "I don't think so. Frankie, what do you think? The Alfredo? Aglio e olio?"

Frankie demurred. "Oh no, Esmée, for his first visit, surely Trenette col Pesto, from Genoa, Paolo's home, he will say it is the best pasta dish in all of Italy. Then Bistecca because Alan must build his strength for more children, no?" The women collapsed in a mutual fit of the giggles.

When he recounted the evening to Elaine, he couldn't remember what he ate, only that it tasted delicious, nor the name of the sumptuous red wine selected by Paolo. On the other hand, he was able to recall every layer of the experience – the vibrancy of the restaurant, the excitement of watching the chefs and waiters in action, Paolo's composed stage-management, the warmth of friendship, the perfect satisfaction. Back in his room at The Carillion, still a fraction dazed by culture shock, he stood at the window, brushing his teeth. *Past eleven, the streets and pavements are as busy as when I arrived, this place never sleeps, better set the alarm, it's an early start.*

* * *

Grisly. That was the word. He'd never liked the Burton morgue but now, here, he was growing fonder of its cosiness by the minute. *I suppose it's only a question of scale but this isn't a morgue, it's an abattoir.* As in Burton and morgues across the nation, it was all white and steel and harsh lights that left you in no doubt which innards you were looking at even if you couldn't tell whose they were. Here, the rank of gurneys stretched away, twenty, thirty of them, the majority occupied but, thankfully, draped, the tell-tale labels dangling. At the far end, curtains had been pulled across to mask whatever was causing the drainage channels to stain red. Shobnall could hear the low but articulate sound of someone speaking for the tape recorder.

"Fresh in, that one, Alan." Dave Chateris plucked his sleeve. "Lemme introduce you. My gaffer, DI Keith Conway. Sir, DS Alan Shobnall."

"Morning, Shobnall, no need to stand on ceremony." Shobnall initially pitched him as Worthington's vintage; the belted trench coat, the pipe and the regulation haircut created that impression but the face was younger, the hair less flecked with gray. *Definitely from the same mould, though.* "You're George Worthington's chap?"

"Yes, sir."

"Good enough for me. They call me Russ, by the way. Our man's over here." He indicated one of the loaded gurneys. "And no, I don't play the piano. I understand you knew him so we can rely on you for identification. I'd rather not drag in his nearest and dearest if I can avoid it. Ready?" Shobnall nodded. Charteris was standing closer. *This isn't going to be pretty.*

It wasn't. Identification was easy. It was Gary Stubbs but...........*I guess the tides bash a body against all kind of obstacles.* The skull had been shaved to reveal lumpy contusions all over. Shobnall was reasonably OK with that but the gaping scar right across the face and through the bridge of the nose, not-quite-closed with large looping stitches, that was something else. "That's Stubbs, no question. I can see why you don't want family in. Is this typical of people who drown in the Thames?"

Conway was sombre. "Depending on when it went in, how the tides were running and how long it's been in, the typical body will be bashed about. Bridge piers are the main thing but there's walls, wharves, ships, all sorts. That slash across the face is another matter. I'd say that's a propeller. The body might have been sucked in or he went in close to a moving screw." The three men stood in silence around the corpse for a long interval. "I'm not entirely happy with this. Nor is Dave and he has a good nose. You're looking at another drowning up your way?"

"That's right, sir." He summarised the story of Cox's death, belatedly realising Conway already knew all about it. "My gut feeling is that Cox's death was no accident. Now Stubbs. Sir, can I ask if you've had any reaction from The Reapers." Conway pointed to Charteris.

"The Reapers are in America. On tour. Vetch is wiv 'em. We're told they're on the move an' 'ard to get 'old of. All our gen comes from 'is assistant, Barbara Ellison. Babs, she calls 'erself. Way she tells it, they come back from your neck of the woods, into the studio an' crank out an album. 'Cording to Babs, fings come to an 'ead. The Cox business got to Stubbs, 'e couldn't 'andle it, 'ad a fight wiv the group an' a real humdinger wiv Vetch. Resigned, walked art juss when they needed 'im, left 'em in the lurch. Now, of course, shocked an' 'orrified."

"You interviewed her, Dave," said Conway. "What did you think?"

"I don't think she 'as a clue. She's spinnin' the line she was fed to spin. Might all be true, might all be fiction."

It sounded like a circular saw was in use at the end of the room and meeting some resistance. Shobnall tried to ignore it. Conway was unmoved. "You met Stubbs, Alan, knew him a bit. How does this spin sound to you?"

"Plausible, sir, up to a point." *Like all good lies.* "What happened at Wychnor and the way the group and Vetch handled it left Gary disillusioned so the walking-out, I could buy that. Less sure about a bust-up with the band and definitely not chucking himself in the river. He'd have gone to his girlfriend, Janice."

"Janice North," said Charteris in a low, throaty voice. "I seen 'er. The Ellison woman gave me 'er address in Tooting Bec. Poor girl's shattered. Says Stubbs weren't 'appy when 'e got back to London, talked about doin' somethin' else an' what it might mean for them, 'im an' Janice. Reckon at the time that lifted 'er. Stubbs 'ad arranged to treat 'er to dinner art at the weekend. She was in tears, poor little thing. She thought 'e were going to propose. Instead she gets the boys in blue knockin' on 'er door wiv the bad news."

*I'm getting a sense of how Vetch operates, if this Ellison is handing out Janice's name and address, then he knows all about it, there'll be nothing there.* "Did he have anything with him?"

"Personal possessions are over here." Conway walked to the side counter. "Help yourself."

The usual array of plastic bags. A neatly folded handkerchief. Sunglasses. Packet of aspirin, unopened. Assorted coins. A key ring, each key tagged with a police label – 'car', 'flat', 'office 1', 'office 2' and so on. Shobnall took out the leather wallet. The contents had been dried and replaced. A wad of notes. He riffled through them, fives and tens, at least a couple of hundred. Driving licence. A photograph of a woman. "Janice?" Charteris nodded. A folded sheet of paper, a list of dates and American cities. *The Reapers itinerary.* "I'd like a copy of that." Some business cards; 'Gary Stubbs. The Reapers. Tour Manager'. Absently, he spread them like a hand of cards. Turned them over. Picked one out. Someone had written on it. 'Jenny Cox, 34B Camberwell Grove'. "Let's go there."

* * *

# FOURTEEN

Camberwell Grove. Not exactly leafy suburbia but a pleasant street in a pleasant residential area; semi-detached houses, plenty of greenery. Shobnall's experience of London had tended to oscillate between the glitter of the centre and the unease of less salubrious districts. It was re-assuring to encounter an ordinary, *nice* section of the city. A drape-twitching zone. As Bill, Charteris's long-term mucker, slowed the car towards 34B, a net curtain wave surfed alongside. "Weird, innit? The Brits are so nosy but 'ate yer seein' 'em nosin'. OK Bill, won't be long."

Mrs Cox was waiting on the doorstop. A slight figure, silver-grey hair in a pony-tail, she stood straight but, as she led them into the house, leaned on a stick. The parlour was for visitors: it looked like a showroom. It was Charteris's patch. Shobnall let him open. "Mrs Cox."

"Please call me Jenny."

"Jenny." Charteris gave her one of his disarming smiles. "I apologise for us intrudin' so soon after Michael's death. I'm Dave Charteris....." *Grey hair but she's not old, forty, maybe less, Michael was twenty-three, she had him early.* He saw suffering and pain but also fortitude. *Life hasn't dealt this woman a great hand but she's not one for giving in.* ".....and Mr Stubbs 'ad your address in 'his wallet. This is Alan Shobnall, from-" But Jenny Cox had turned her attention to Shobnall, wherever he was from.

"I've been expecting you."

"Expecting *me*?"

"Gary told me you might come."

Charteris leaned back in his chair. Shobnall leaned forward in his. Like the weather man and woman signalling a change of pressure. Her eyes were on them but Shobnall knew she was seeing other people, other places. "Michael bought this house for me, you know." *Leave her, in her own time.* "We rented a flat in Brixton, near the council offices. Me and my husband, Mark, and then.........Michael. There was an accident one night. A car went out of control. The driver didn't stop. They never found him. Mark died in the ambulance. I was in hospital for a long time. They didn't think I'd walk again but I wasn't having that. The council said they'd look after Michael. They put him in one of those homes. Afterwards he had changed." She halted a moment. "I'm not going to give you my life history. I want you to understand."

"Jenny, darlin'," said Charteris. "You take all the time you need."

"I got him back, I wasn't going to lose him as well. I tried my best. Our neighbours helped but none of them had far to look for troubles of their own. These last days, I've thought back over those years. The times Michael and me nearly got him sorted. Always he slipped again. Three steps forward, three steps back, sometimes four.

"He loved his music. I encouraged him, bought him his first guitar. When he started playing for money I hoped that was it, he'd found his gift and people appreciated it. But it brought the drugs. Yes, I knew about the drugs." There was defiance in her voice. "Ever since being in that home, whatever happened there, he'd lost something. Strength. He couldn't resist.

"He was so excited when he joined The Reapers. Then they began to do well. I didn't realise how well but one day he turned up in Brixton with the keys to this house. I didn't know what to say. He was trying to say thank you. He believed he was going places. It wasn't Michael's idea, though. Don't mistake me, he was so anxious I should be happy here, he was so sweet, but it came from Gary. The only person who cared anything for him was Gary. He knew something was wrong with my boy. One evening he came and asked me about it. I should have told him everything but I felt that would have been a betrayal.

"The rest of them, I don't think they know I exist but Gary, he was a good man. He did his best to help a fellow human being who was finding life hard. When Michael died.........." She faltered. "When Michael died, in the Midlands somewhere, Gary phoned me the next day. He was almost as shocked as I was. He came round to see if I needed anything. All I wanted was Michael back. Gary made the funeral arrangements. I told him to make it simple, keep all those vultures away. He brought me home afterwards, made me a cup of tea." She stared into space. "Now he's dead, drowned, like Michael. I read it in the paper. I wasn't surprised."

*What did she just say?* "What makes you say that, Jenny?" Charteris's voice was soft but tense.

"He was here one more time, maybe four days ago, said he wanted to check I was alright. I made the tea this time. He said he was getting out of the music business but he had something he had to settle first. I'm sure it was something to do with Michael. He said he hoped to see me again but he had doubts. I could hear it in his voice, see it in his face." She rose, moved to the sideboard and opened a drawer. Shobnall noticed the framed photograph of her son, a recent photograph.

"Gary said, depending on how things panned out, somebody else might come." She smiled wryly. "I don't get many visitors. I thought it was Gary trying to cheer me up; he was always doing that. He said it would be someone I could trust and anyone else with him I could trust them too. I was to give you this envelope. He wrote your name on it. That's how I'm expecting you, Alan Shobnall. Here, this is from Gary."

\* \* \*

Dear Alan,

Letters aren't my strong point. At school it was one of those things you had to learn but I could never remember which side you wrote the address. You won't mind. I knew you were a good bloke from the moment you and me and Eddie sat down for a cup of tea at Wychnor. I hope you don't have to read this. If you do it means things haven't gone well for me. I'm going to leave it with Mick's mum, Jenny. She's a soldier and she's nothing to do with The Reapers or Morgan or any of that. If I'm not around you'll find your way to her. Mick kept quiet about his home background. I don't think he was protecting his mum, more like there was something in his past he wanted to keep private. I asked Jenny once but she wasn't letting on.

It's been all go since I saw you. I think I told you the group's next single would take them to the stratosphere or the scrap-heap. It's the stars. They're taking off in the States. Over there the single is selling like fresh doughnuts. So are tickets for the concerts. They'll launch the new album over there. I've had enough. Janice and me are heading off together, at least I'm hoping she'll come with me. I talked with Steven and Alex. I owed it to them, we've been mates a long time. They're OK with it. I mean Steven is. Alex doesn't really care. Steven listened but I guess it doesn't bother him too much either, if I'm honest. He's busy imagining himself on stage at the Shea Stadium. I wish them well, I didn't want to part on bad terms.

Charteris grunted. "Don't tally wiv the line the Ellison woman was spinnin' but I'm puttin' my money on Stubbs."

Back in London, I helped an old pal with a gig. American outfit, doesn't matter who. After, we had a drink with their manager, Channing Brooks, he's been in the trade for yonks. Turns out he knew Morgan from way back and he had some things to say. Warnings.

He said Morgan had connections in bad places over the pond. You'll know how to check it out. The way Channing told it, these weren't links you could break when you felt like it, you joined this club, you were a member until death, his words. The second thing was that Morgan always seemed to have something on people. That reminded me I once overheard Morgan saying to Preston *'everyone has a secret, something they don't want made public'*. I've been wondering if Morgan had discovered what it was Mick was hiding in his past and was leaning on him.

The third thing. I remember Channing's words. *'For Morgan, whatever he's doing, however much he's earning, it's never enough.'* I asked him if he knew how much Morgan would make out of The Reapers. He laughed, said pop was a new business and big bucks were on offer now but the money would attract more and more people like blood draws piranha and the money would be spread around more and the accountants and the corporations would get it all organised. Everyone would do fine but not like before. That made me think. Morgan's real smart. If Channing could see that then so could Morgan. So he wasn't about the music. He must be into something more lucrative.

I'm ducking out, but suddenly Morgan wasn't someone I didn't hit it off with, he was dangerous. I told you Mick was on something but I had no idea where he was getting it from. I never saw him off to meet the man. Talking to Channing made me wonder if I never saw him going out because the man was already in the house.

What I mean is, maybe Morgan was supplying Mick. With drugs. Then I thought hang on, Morgan's a man who takes. Relationships are complicated. I don't suppose I've ever really understood one but if Morgan's got something on Mick and yet he's giving something to Mick why would that be? Did Mick know something about Morgan?

I spoke to Basher. He's the only one with a heart. He's from Liverpool and he's smart when he's sober. He said Mick was definitely hooked on coke and his money was on Preston and that meant it came from Morgan. Preston cornered Basher with one of those *'can I help you with anything, anything you'd like?'* lines. Basher's heard it all before and saw him off. Maybe Preston tried them all. It made me uneasy. Too many odd things. I've been worrying about Morgan and what role he played in Mick's death.

I'm going to have it out with him. He trades in other people's secrets but I think he has a lot to hide. I'm doing it for Mick. And Jenny. He's agreed to meet but wants it away from the others so we're meeting at The Prospect of Whitby in Wapping tonight. It scares me. I don't know what Morgan's limits are any more. I have to do it. Maybe I'll get some answers or maybe you'll be reading this.

Thanks for your help and friendship, if I can say that, even if it wasn't long. Give my best to Eddie and your boss (I don't remember his name but he was very decent to me).

Gary
PS. I almost forgot. I don't know if it's worth anything but I was in the office late the other night, checking on the US itinerary. Morgan had a visit from that nob lady who turned up at

Wychnor. They were in his office with the door closed for one hell of a long time.

* * *

Charteris went to the window and stared down at the Thames. "Swingin' London my arse. Strewth, Alan, this is a smelly box of whelks, innit? Brave boy. Left you the signpost in 'is wallet. Left 'is last will 'an testament. Poor bugger!"

They were in Charteris' office in New Scotland Yard. Shobnall had recognised the pair of oddly-classical buildings with their bands of red brick and white Portland stone but this was his first venture inside. *A let-down really, no different from an old school building except more storeys.* They would have liked to do something for Jenny Cox but she had wanted nothing more than to get on with what was left of her life. It left a nasty taste. DI Conway had looked in, sampled the atmosphere and effected a tactical withdrawal.

"Does anyone dare to call him 'Russ' to his face?"

"'Is own team an' then 'is peers and the brass and when they do we reckon 'e marks it in a secret ledger." Charteris was still watching the river. "Tryin' to work out the time-line. The letter says he was to rendayvoo that night. Jenny says he called round four days ago, Tuesday. He writes, delivers, goes to meet Morgan in Wapping. Wednesday afternoon, The Reapers depart 'Eathrow. Small hours of Friday we fish 'im out, I call you, darn you come." His teeth flashed. "We have the most brilliant blow-out. Today, Saturday, 'ere we are."

"Where did you fish him out?"

"Woolwich. Drifted ashore by Royal Arsenal. Look." He pointed to the map on the wall, the Thames wriggling across it like a giant blue worm. "Wapping. Woolwich. Not a lot of help. The doc says 'e's bin in the water 36-48 hours. Could be from when 'e met Morgan. If 'e did meet Morgan. Until we found 'im. Could be less. If 'e was chucked in, we dunno where it was. I've asked our boffins to work out the tides but it'll not help any. Me an' Bill need to get down to The Prospect of Whitby and sniff around. You?"

"I'm leaning more and more to Michael Cox as murder with Preston in the frame and Morgan in the background, maybe accessory. Morgan booked a one-way helicopter trip. He knew he wouldn't need it to get back. I think Preston had driven up and left a car in Alrewas while he went down the canal. Then it all went belly-up.

Preston had to go all the way to Fradley on his return journey. That's why they had Melinda drop them at Alrewas station, to collect Preston's motor.

"I'm surmising. Gary's pointing a finger but I still need proof. He says Morgan has form back in the US. I need to speak to George about that. Then there's those comments about Morgan and money. Gary told me Morgan wanted The Reapers for his 'stable' but in reality there wasn't anyone else. Are The Reapers a stepping stone? To what? And Morgan and Lady Melinda. I told George there was something odd there." He looked down at Stubbs' letter. "Dave, I'll come down for his funeral. He deserves a decent send-off."

Charteris turned from the window. "Yeah." His voice was tinged with melancholy. "'E does." He shook his shoulders as if dislodging an invisible daemon from his back. "Time we was out of 'ere. Your DI wants you to cop an eyeful of what 'es bin up to. Me an' Bill gonna drop you at the British Museum. Be ready first thing on Sunday. We'll collect you. I've arranged breakfast with some, er, knowledgeable people. Sort of people might not restore yer faith in 'uman nature."

\* \* \*

## FIFTEEN

Roasting was not confined to the maltsters. The mercury rose so high on Saturday that the tarmac on the streets began to melt. Sir Keith Joseph, the Minister for Housing & Local Government, proposed that Burton should lose its County Borough status. Digby Cooper MP vented his spleen in The Burton Daily Mail while the Council leader, Joel Goode, quietly phoned a contact in Westminster to see whether this might be turned to his own advantage. England toiled at Headingly as they forlornly sought to stave off defeat; the gates were closed an hour after the start on a capacity crowd – 30,000 knotted handkerchiefs and straw hats.

Inside the police station, even DS Angela Bainbridge acknowledged the heat. Not only had she opened the window, she had removed her jacket and hung it on the back of the door. Expediency mattered more than the look of things. She liked it here. The DI ran a good ship; they were a nice bunch and very capable. She felt she had acquitted herself well during the DI's absence; his oversight had required no more than what you might call 'maintenance' calls. With Alan now also down in London, she really felt in charge – and she intended to make a success of it. She knew the manual by heart but she wasn't driven by it. She appreciated you didn't manage Lennie Morton in the same way as young Gideon Watson and that Cyril Hendry blithely went on running the station whatever anyone else said. She decided to see how the battle over the radio was going; would it be Saxby and his obsession with cricket or Watson with his youthful penchant for pop tunes? She slid her jacket from its hanger; you could only take the comfort issue so far.

The troops were, in one way or the other, absorbed in their work. PC Paul Fraser was filling out the forms for an accident at the Derby Turn. Each successive incident seemed to add a layer of paper and Paul's infuriation levels were on the rise. Sheila Redpath was having the time of her life. This was how she'd hoped policing would be! Under Charlie Taylor's tutelage, she had submitted an application to Birmingham Corporation for information on flight activity on the night of Michael Cox's death. All at once her telephone was ringing, the facsimile machine spewing out copies of requisitions and manifests 'FAO WPC Sheila Redpath'. She stood, bubbling inside, by the machine, scooping up each sheet. She'd decided Mr Worthington looked like Inspector Maigret – or was it the other way around? Vetch. Was that the name Sergeant Shobnall was anticipating? 'CalMart Air'. The helicopter operators, based at Birmingham airport. Nathan Callaghan, the pilot. 'Calmart', she mused, 'Callaghan.' She dialled her brother's number.

\*   \*   \*

Gideon Watson wasn't in the station. He wasn't even in Burton. He was having a day out in Lichfield. Somehow, being a policeman bearing a warrant card in a different city made him feel more adult although he'd have preferred an afternoon's trainspotting to sweltering in a dusty ecclesiastical office. In reality, there wasn't a speck of dust to be seen but the room, dark panelling, antique furniture and ceiling-high bookshelves, left Gideon *feeling* it was laden with the powdered dross of centuries. His Mam, he thought, would be at home here.

His preparation had been scrupulous; he had the requisite papers and signatures. It had been time well spent. The Secretary to the Diocese, a spare, wrinkled man who stared unblinkingly through beer-mug lenses, had been unable to fault them. The little man had scuttled off like an insect to fetch the file. Gideon stared out of the window. St Mary's House overlooked The Close, the green space forming a buffer around the cathedral. A constant flow of visitors in and out, cameras at the ready, the occasional cassock among them. Gideon couldn't see the attraction of looking at buildings, inside or out. They didn't *do* anything. Not like locomotives.

His reverie was interrupted by the rustling of the Secretary returning and dropping a large ledger onto the desk. The thud displaced no dust, Gideon noticed. The Secretary located a page, thumbed through several more, inserted a red marker ribbon behind the batch, left the ledger open "These pages." Before stepping back, he flicked slowly through the subsequent pages. If Gideon had been a betting man – as if his Mam would have allowed it! – he would have said the man was unhappy about something but he couldn't tell if it was the presence of a policeman or something else. The Secretary turned the ledger towards Gideon. "Before my time here, you understand."

Gideon heard the alibi, the sound of a man putting distance between himself and..........and what? He began reading, his brain on red alert. He reached the marker ribbon, went back and leafed through again. There was no doubt about it. This, he thought, will interest Mr Shobnall. The Secretary waited, radiating unease. When Gideon stood back, he immediately slapped the ledger closed and left a protective hand on it, as if he feared a stray cherub might essay an escape. Gideon took his time checking his notes. "Thank you, Mr Secretary."

The Secretary snatched up the ledger, hugged it to his chest. "Come, I'll show you out."

* * *

At about the same time, a short distance north of Burton, the sun poured its balm onto Rolleston-on-Dove and onto the Salt estate. The mansion's brickwork glowed a rich red. The drapes had been closed behind the tall windows. If you had driven up the long driveway, parked your motor on the shady side of the house, alongside the big black Humber and the racy Triumph Herald, and passed across the frontage, the house would have seemed suspended in hibernation. Yet you would have heard voices, murmurs, laughter and yelps of excitement underpinned by the sound of falling water and punctuated by chinking, clattering and rattling. If, curious, you had turned the corner into the well-groomed gardens, cordoned by a row of beech trees, neat lawns and flower beds around a pond notable for the stylish statue of a young maiden channelling an arc of water into the air from her outstretched arms, you would have joined the family party.

A wrought-iron table and chairs, shaded by an outsize umbrella, had been set on the flagstones by the lawn. The remains of lunch. Lolling in the chairs, Elaine Shobnall, laughing, her children's god-parents, Lavinia Salt – dressed conservatively today in a vermillion robe – and Corky, plus Mr Salt, this last not lolling, of course, but sitting erect. On the lawn an inflated paddling pool, abandoned toys strewn around. Josephine Shobnall had hooked her arms over the edge of the pool to support her in rapidly scissoring her legs and showering water over her sister. Alice was responding with gleeful whoops and by slamming her arms randomly into the water and adding to the spray. Mr Salt was feeling smug; it had been his decision to position the pool well away from their table.

After a while, Lavinia and Corky went to intervene, lest the pool be completely emptied. The right to a soaking is, after all, in the godparent job description. "Any news from Alan?" Mr Salt enquired.

"He called this morning. He had a wonderful meal last night with the Worthingtons and Dave and Frankie Charteris. I made him promise he'd take me there soon. He'll have been to the morgue with Dave by now and then, um, I've no idea, depends what he finds."

"Hold him to his promise. London is entering a period of change and it is going to be very exciting."

"Not just London I hope, Reuben, the whole country deserves some excitement."

Mr Salt patted Elaine's hand. "Do not mistake me, my dear. London is inevitably in the vanguard but we will all benefit or have the opportunity so to do. Now, I think we need to fetch some towels and bring succour to Lavinia and Corky. I fear they are losing the battle with the Rhine maidens."

* * *

He had to admit, if you wanted a building that looked like the storehouse of history, the British Museum would at least be on the short list. As he walked the short distance from the Great Russell Street pavement to the entrance hall, the classical pillars seemed to rear up through huge to gigantic, the mythic figures on the friezes holding at bay the clamour of a city savouring its burgeoning reputation as the epicentre of pop culture and whose every second citizen seemed to be carrying a transistor radio belting electric chords into the air. Inside was different, calm and urbane, commanding that visitors tread quietly and with respect for the past.

It was easy to find the exhibition. Had Shobnall missed the signs or passed by the enormous gilt figure with multiple arms, he would surely have spotted the sentries. One on each side, clad in immaculate white turbans, blue tunics with gold buttons, white knee britches and yellow stockings, leather sandals. They topped Shobnall by a good six inches and held lethal-looking three-pronged spears in an 'at rest' position. Statuesque. Shobnall was reminded of being lifted as a child to view the sentries at Buckingham Palace. *Noble features.* Although they stared straight ahead over his head, he sensed every detail of his being was being logged as he edged past.

At first, he strove to take in as much as possible, conscious that Elaine would give him a grilling. *Or Mrs Worthington.* However, the scope of the display and the quality of exhibits were overwhelming. An endless army of statues in stone and every metal under the sun; a procession of domestic, decorative, celebratory, religious and military artefacts large and small; a blood-curdling arsenal of daggers, spears, bows and arrows, axes and maces, intricately engraved and inlaid with precious metals and stones, cutting edges and bludgeoning surfaces offset with gorgeous ornamentation; mannequins arrayed in all manner of sumptuous fabrics, robes, saris, tunics in the colours of the rainbow; paintings, models of buildings and settlements, photographs; jewelry everywhere, rubies, diamonds, sapphires, pearls, emeralds, you name it.

After a while, he lost track of which multi-limbed deity was which. Many of the items had come from Britain and America, some on loan from public institutions, many more from private collections. *No wonder they want stuff returned, we do seem to have helped ourselves liberally.* He became more selective in where he lingered. A scale model of the Taj Mahal's Mughal architecture didn't detain him but the blown-up photograph of a Vishnu temple in North India did. *The Diamond must have been taken from a temple like that.* He scrutinised the fantastic carving, the distinctively bulbous dome. *All crammed with jewels.* He found it hard to balance the pervasive spirituality – the devotion, the meditation, the asceticism – with the intensity of the wealth and the cultured viciousness of the weaponry. *I'm not seeing any of these 'gurus' or 'yogis' but*

96

*that's a round dozen of those guards with three-pronged spears so far.* He felt intimidated - *no, daunted is a better word* - in the face of a culture about which he had been largely ignorant but which demonstrated with each successive display cabinet the intelligence, dedication, artistry and wisdom of a great people. Then he reached the Diamond.

Sir Robert Smirke, the architect, had fashioned a wide circular space at the junction of two corridors, each quadrant equipped with a seating ledge, a large glass cupola overhead. Shobnall stopped on the threshold. Nothing on the walls, no statues. A single display case in the centre, a pair of English matrons huddled over it. Another woman shepherding four small children was leaving the area; a uniformed attendant was drifting through in the opposite direction. To Shobnall's left, a bulky man in a grey suit sat on the ledge, legs spread, feet firmly planted. *Pinkertons, must be.* Directly on the other side, a duplicate. *They might as well wear a uniform.* Another attendant floated past. *At least they are maintaining a watch.*

The matrons were moving on, enthusing over Fanny Craddock's latest recipes. Shobnall took their place. It took his breath away. *They shower you with stuff then back off and hit you with this, it's beautiful.* The Needwood Diamond sat alone on a bed of black velvet. It was......indescribable. He had no idea a diamond could be so big. This was no engagement ring toy. It seemed alive; its myriad facets shimmering and shifting with the light as if the perfect angles framed some elemental essence. *How could those women look at this and talk recipes?* He couldn't take his eyes off it. *How could you make this one eye of one statue in one temple?* He rocked his head from side to side and the Diamond responded, flushing and shining, or so he imagined. *No wonder India wants it back.* He rocked his head again.

"Sir, I must ask you not to become intoxicated by this exhibit." The voice was right beside him; he had been so absorbed he had totally failed to hear the attendant's approach. "It's the rocking of the head gives folk away."

"Excuse me, I –" He turned, disoriented, saw past the uniform and cap. "The uniform suits you, Cyril. How are you?"

"Tickety-boo, Alan, tickety-boo, though I can't wait to get back home. Mrs H is going to take some placating, let me tell you. Good fun, though, something different. Today I'm an attendant, tomorrow I might be a visitor."

"The Pinkertons are transparent."

"Of course. Any villain interested in the Diamond would expect to see security. Tip of an iceberg, son."

*Should have had more faith.* "Sorry, Cyril. You're getting on alright with the Pinkertons, then? I remember the DI thought they might not be happy being watched."

"Time I was on my rounds. Man on the way to answer your questions. Cheerio, Alan." Cyril sauntered off.

'Man on the way' proved to be George Worthington accompanied by an ordinary-looking chap in a natty double-breasted dark suit. *Stepped right out of a Whitehall department.*

"Afternoon, Alan, everything in order?"

"Yes, sir, at least I think so. I bumped into Cyril a moment ago – or he crept upon me."

"Ah yes, the Museum attendant, he's quite taken to that role. Let me introduce you. Detective Sergeant Alan Shobnall, this is Hank Walker. Hank runs the Pinkerton's team." Walker handed over a business card.

"I get you British and politeness," said Walker. "You call me Hank, OK?" Shobnall shot a glance at Worthington. *How does the land lie?* "Oh, I know." The transatlantic twang wasn't strong. "British police and American detective agency, they'll never get along. We've been delighted to work with George and Cyril. You know how it is, Alan, professionals like nothing better than to work with other professionals."

Worthington gestured. "Let's keep moving. If we hang about, the security will be on us like a ton of bricks. Alan, I believe Dave Charteris will be looking after you tomorrow morning. Anything you need from Hank or me?"

"Now that you ask, sir, there is. Hank, I wonder if you could check a couple of names for me faster than if I went through the normal channels with the US authorities?"

"No trouble, partner. Who do you want to know what about? We can access any law and order facility over the pond short of National Security. And even then...." He spread his hands.

"Morgan Vetch, manager of The Reapers pop group. And a vicar, Edwin Bullard. They both have history in your country. I need to find out what they were up to there. I'll get the details faxed."

"Contact details on the card. Get me the information and I'll set the Pinkerton wheels in motion."

The DI and the American wandered off. Shobnall had another few minutes at the Diamond. He felt encouraged. *We might be making progress here.* When he re-emerged onto Great Russell Street, he exchanged an ancient calm for the shock of a modern maelstrom. The motion was incessant, people and vehicles, hooting, revving, shouting, the air full of petrol fumes and pop music; the colours kaleidoscopic, every nation in their robes, tunics, kaftans, turbans, garments he'd never seen before, the babble of foreign accents. It was comforting to see, at the nearby crossroads, a British bobby, his arm raised, imperturbably escorting a woman with a pram through the traffic.

\* \* \*

## SIXTEEN

Next day, Sunday morning, approaching eight o'clock. The lobby of The Carillion Hotel was hushed. The blinds over the high windows had not yet been raised but sunlight was filtering round the edges, stippling the varnished floor. The couches and armchairs provided for the comfort of residents and visitors were empty. To the rear, a pair of dapper, moustachioed receptionists were preparing for the day. The only others present were Shobnall and Stanley, gazing out at a street deserted except for a street-sweeper and, huddled in the doorway of the Mutual Association of Whatever, a man wrapped in flattened cardboard.

"Have you always worked here, Stanley?"

"I have, Mr Shobnall. Started in the kitchens as a boy. Course, it wasn't The Carillion then, it was The Raglan. When Lord Needwood took the place, he said he wasn't having a hotel commemorating the man who failed at Balaclava. His lordship brought in fresh management, much better management, I have to say, and they offered me a junior position out front. I love it, Mr Shobnall. Look at all this." He spread his arms like a peacock fanning its tail for the world to marvel at. "All this braid and finery. It's a performance, Mr Shobnall, and I do enjoy the show and-" He broke off and looked round. "What the blazes is *he* doing *there*?"

Shobnall spun to catch a figure hurrying from the lift, back past the reception desk and through a small door. An after-image of a floor-length blue robe or tunic and a bright white turban. Stanley continued to glare at the closed-again door. "Did you see that, Mr Shobnall?"

"I did, Stanley. Exotic dress. Indian. Where does that door lead?"

"Service area. The back entrance. That door says 'Staff Only' and he ain't staff. Guests aren't supposed to use our back-stairs. But then he's no guest."

"You recognised him?"

"In a manner of speaking. He's an Indian prince but I couldn't give you a name or a kingdom. This exhibition Mr and Mrs Worthington are down for, there's a party of Indian nobs over for it as well. They have the penthouse at The Cathay Majestic. My cousin's head commissionaire there, like me but his costume is dark red. I was visiting him for a jar and he pointed out the Indians. Our back-door man was one of their party."

"What on earth is he doing here at this hour?" Shobnall asked without thinking. Stanley looked at him. "Oh," said Shobnall. "I see." Shobnall switched approach. "Stanley, does *this* hotel have a penthouse?"

"Certainly does but at The Carillion it's reserved for the owners."

"Anyone staying there at the moment?"

Stanley put a finger to his lips. "Can't say, Mr Shobnall. Commissionaires are like the clergy, bound by the rules of the confessional. Lord Needwood would not be at all happy." His expression brightened; he was hearing the hoof beats of the Seventh Cavalry. "This looks like your transportation. Mr Charteris, unless I am very much mistaken."

* * *

The streets were as empty as Shobnall had seen them. *Maybe London isn't quite round-the-clock.* Bill didn't need to deploy his knowledge of the back-ways. Or slow down much. Buildings and signs whizzed by – Kings Cross, Old Street Underground Station, Hackney, Shoreditch, Bethnal Green Road. The further East, the more it seemed they were entering a different London, one that had changed little since the war. The new swinging-ness hadn't reached this far. The garish posters pasted on blank brick walls advertising concerts - The Tornados, Heinz, Billy J Kramer – seemed out of place, splashes of false colour. *Maybe that stuff is all surface glitter.* Along Bethnal Green Road, Bill slowed and came to a halt a few yards before a crossroads. Shops and cafes on the other side, a street sign, Vallance Street, for the road running off south.

"'Ere we go," announced Charteris. "Right across the road. Two of them, two of us, that's the deal. Stay close, Bill. Please." They walked, not slow, not fast. A stationer. A jewellers. Charteris halted at a double-fronted cafe, the lower portion of its glass frosted. Shobnall looked up: a custard-coloured fascia, 'E.Pellici' in steel letters, and a low white trellis with greenery overflowing in a carefully-pruned fashion. Charteris put a hand on the door. "Probly should 'ave briefed yer better. Juss keep yer cool, mate."

A single space, basic tables and chairs, sauce bottles, cruets, laminated menus. To the rear, the kitchen; to the left, a formica counter with a striking sunburst design. A radio was on somewhere; the ubiquitous electric guitars. Shobnall looked around; art deco designs repeated in the wooden panels and in the mirrors placed one to a wall. It had a homely but stylish feel, as though the place had been here like this forever.

There were only two other customers, seated at a corner table. Twins, Shobnall saw that at once, they had to be. Side by side. Big, handy, dressed expensively but not looking as though they were comfortable in the togs, the one hemmed in the corner in cream linen. *Something odd about his face.* The one on the aisle wore black, matching his hair and prominent eyebrows. Crude, brutal features, pasty skin. *What stone did this pair crawl out from under?* Empty plates on the table, smeared with grease, egg, tomato pips, coffee cup in front of black suit, milk shake for the other.

"Mornin' Dave." The one in black was the spokesman. "This your mate from the Midlands?"

"That's right, Ronnie. This is DS Alan Shobnall. Alan, this is Ronnie an' 'is brother, Reggie."

Ronnie extended a large paw across the table, gripped Shobnall's. A boxer's knuckles, the shake was firm, very firm, but not threatening. *Calculated, likes to dominate, never seen eyes so blank.* "Pleasure to make your acquaintance, Alan. We don't worry about rank and that here, not on a Sunday, anyhow. Welcome to our local gaff. Me and Reggie, we live round the corner."

Reggie leaned over. His handshake was cursory. *Not really interested.* He was the spitting image of Ronnie, the same sense of a face assembled by someone unfamiliar with the human physiognomy. It was the eyes that unnerved Shobnall. Ronnie's were devoid of expression but they belonged to the body. Reggie's eyes were hooded and constantly mobile. Shobnall had the uncomfortable sense that an alien being was peering out of a human body whose workings were foreign to it. "Nice to meet you," said Reggie, looking past Shobnall's left ear. "Best breakfast in London, this place."

"Yeah." Ronnie resumed control. "You want breakfast, Dave? Alan? Have whatever you like, our shout."

Charteris had taken the seat opposite Reggie. He moved the sauce bottles to the side. "Thanks, Ronnie, don't want to take up your time, just a cuppa, thanks."

"Same for you, Alan?" Ronnie bellowed towards the kitchen. "Nevio! Two teas if you don't mind. So what part of the Midlands you from, Alan?"

"Burton-on-Trent."

Ronnie's low forehead furrowed. "Never 'eard of it. No matter." He leaned towards Shobnall. "Dave 'ere tells us you're interested in a certain American citizen, a Mr Morgan Vetch. Am I right?"

"Yes." *At this moment, I do wish Dave had given me a bit more warning.* "He manages The Reapers, the pop group. One of them drowned on our patch and I've been investigating the, er, the death. Then last week their Tour Manager was pulled out of the Thames. I'm very curious about Vetch."

"His little pop group." Reggie was toying with the cutlery. "They come in our club in Knightsbridge."

Ronnie turned. "No, Reggie, you're thinking about that Dave Clark lot. Vetch wouldn't let his boys anywhere near our clubs. Now listen, Alan, you won't find many folk who'll talk about Morgan Vetch." He presented a grin that contained not a single degree centigrade. "We don't like him."

"We don't like him one bit." Reggie was using a knife to clean his fingernails.

"Vetch." Ronnie continued. "Works with the Richardsons. Ah. Ta very much, Nevio." Shobnall identified another Italian, an older man with a neat pencil moustache and glasses. Cups of tea were positioned, milk and sugar indicated. Like Paolo, this Nevio was assured in his movements, not a jot abashed by his customers, though he likely knew what manner of guest he was hosting. "What you have to understand, Alan, is that me and Reggie, we're businessmen. Our firm is in the entertainment business. We could have breakfast anywhere we wanted."

"Anywhere," said Reggie. "But we like it here."

"Right, Reggie, we like it here." Shobnall was trying to focus on Ronnie but out of the corner of his eye he could see Reggie's fingers dancing over the table, as if the intelligence within were experimenting with those spindly extensions on the end of the arm-thing. "Our firm." Ronnie emphasised the word. "Our *firm* has business interests all over London. Our establishments are the haunt of celebrities, Alan." *Where did he pick that phrase up from?*

"Like Diana Dors." Reggie was still listening. "I like Diana Dors."

Ronnie ignored his twin. "The Richardsons, the people what Vetch chooses to associate with, they're a bunch of thugs. Some geezer said you can tell a lot about

103

someone from the company they keep. Man wants to hang around Mad Frankie Fraser, tells you all you need to know."

"Any idea why Morgan chose to associate himself with these Richardsons, Ronnie?"

Ronnie gave Shobnall the blank stare. *This is not a man to underestimate.* "You don't know the Richardsons, do you?" Shobnall shook his head. "Me and Reggie, we own nightclubs, casinos, gyms, snooker halls, boxing clubs, pubs, all that. Couldn't tell you how many, need to ask our accountant. Dave will back me up on this. When you're running an empire, an *empire*, you can't swear nothing illegal happens on the premises. Me and Reggie can't be everywhere at once. But I guarantee you one thing. No drugs. "He wagged a large finger. "Our mother wouldn't have allowed it, ain't that so, Reggie?"

Reggie was emptying the salt cellar onto his plate, studying the growing pyramid. "Right, Ronnie, no drugs."

"You interested in drugs, Alan, you go see the Richardsons and their boy, George Cornell. That's what you do."

Shobnall thought he understood. "So Morgan gets the drugs for his pop group from these people?"

The twins, for the first time, looked one another in the eye. Reggie paused emptying the pepper pot onto his salt pyramid. "He don't get it, do 'e Ronnie?"

"Nah, Reggie, he don't, but he's from north of Watford so we have to excuse him. See, Alan, Vetch's group, what they called again?"

"The Reapers."

"Yeah, Reapers. They don't matter a toss to Vetch. Window-dressing, that's what they are."

"But they're going to be big stars!"

Reggie cut in. "Then they'll need to come to our clubs, hang about with me and Diana Dors."

Ronnie carried on. "This is London. Eight million people. One of the biggest cities in Europe. Swingin' London, pop music capital, Beatles and all. One of the biggest markets. For whatever you got to sell. Vetch, 'e's a foreigner, a Yank. He needs cover for what he's selling. See what I mean? But British business don't like Americans horning in. They been seen off before, we'll see 'em off again."

Reggie was stirring his pile of salt and pepper with a fork. "This Vetch, you want us to whack him?" Charteris spluttered into his tea and Shobnall wasn't sure he'd heard what he thought he'd heard.

Ronnie sailed on. "Reggie never said that, Dave, by the way. What he said was we've been racking our brains what to do about Morgan Vetch. I think we've given you enough, Alan, if you've been listening properly, but I'll tell you one more thing for nothing. That bloke with him, supposed to do public relations. Preston." Reggie giggled, positioned the refilled salt and pepper on the cruet. Ronnie paid him no attention. "That's not his given name. He was *born* in Preston, somewhere up north. He's Terry Carpenter and he's one of Richardson's lot. Over the river they call him 'Cutter' Carpenter."

"Why Cutter?"

"On account of how he likes to cut corners sharp, know what I mean?"

"Not just corners he cuts!" Reggie giggled again.

Ronnie lumbered to his feet. "You'll need to excuse us. Nevio will want to clean up and sort out the salt and pepper again and me and Reggie got to trot. Nice talking to you, Alan. Our apologies but that's the way it goes in the entertainment business."

\* \* \*

Round about the same time, WPC Redpath, in jacket and pressed denim jeans, met her brother in the concourse at Birmingham airport. Mike was five years older, five inches shorter and five degrees more conventional; he wore a suit and tie – but then this was his place of work and you never knew who might be 'in the office'. He took her behind the scenes, along corridors, down staircases and out onto the tarmac. Sheila had expected rows of airliners, not a couple of four-propeller craft and a Tiger Moth. She figured Sunday must be a quiet day.

They meandered along the service road chatting of this and that – parents' health, their respective careers – to a small hangar with a board advertising 'CalMart Air'. Inside were a helicopter, crouched like a giant spider, and a partitioned office area. The young man at the desk wore flying overalls and a scarf around his neck. He looked like one of those too-young fighter-pilots you see in films about The Battle of Britain. He did a double-take, grinned broadly, vaulted the desk. "Sheila!" He hugged her, lifting her off the ground. "Sorry, I'm probably guilty of assaulting a policewoman."

"I'm off duty, Nat, you're safe. How are you? Haven't seen you since school."

"I'm great." He pointed at the helicopter. "You know I was always mad about flying."

"I remember only too well, especially when we were going out and you kept dragging me on plane-spotting expeditions. But it looks like you're doing well. Mike says you're busy."

"It's going OK. My uncle put up the money and he's already getting it back. Air travel is the future, I'm sure of it."

Sheila gave him the look, the one that had been so effective a million years ago when they had been teenagers dating. "I want a favour, Nat."

"For you, Sheila, anything." Nat, too, was thinking back fondly.

"You picked up a passenger from Croydon and flew him to Wychnor Hall."

\*   \*   \*

# SEVENTEEN

Charteris made no move to leave the cafe. The radio in the kitchen was crooning about being 'bad to me' but it was the jingling guitars behind the voice that took the ear. After a couple of minutes, Bill came in and slipped into the chair Ronnie had vacated. "Saw them go. One of the firm's motor's been waiting."

"Who. Are. They?" Shobnall spoke with feeling. "I want to wash my hands."

"Tell 'im, Bill," said Charteris.

"You've had the pleasure of meeting the Kray twins, Ronnie and Reggie." Bill always spoke softly, the same measured tone for telling you the time of day or that a ton weight had just dropped on his foot. "This is neutral ground, convenient for the twins. They really do live round the corner. See, on one level, they are legit businessmen. They own nightclubs, sports venues, pubs, casino or two. Nobody these days wants to ask where they got the money to get started. When they talk about their 'firm', they don't mean their business, they mean their gang. Protection, extortion, fencing goods, illegal gambling and worse, much worse."

"Can't you nick them?"

"It's hard to persuade witnesses, even victims, to step forward. They tend to worry about the health of their families more than justice and the law. We got Reggie eighteen months for leaning on a few folk. Ronnie kept the machine moving. 'Sides, when you get near, you find they got friends in high places."

Shobnall nodded. "Like Diana Dors."

Bill ignored the flippancy. "In London, all sorts with cash in their pocket or on the arm of someone with a fat wallet swan around nightclubs, visit casinos, run up debts they can't afford, dip into things they ought to keep clear of."

"Bill's right." Charteris stretched. "the twins see the Cabinet more often than the Prime Minister does. We juss 'ave to live wiv 'em. You want a cuppa, Bill?"

"No ta, Dave. I checked in while you were in conference. Russ wants to see us as soon as."

"Not about this?"

"Uh-uh. He's got a situation up in Notting Hill. It's the usual."

Charteris groaned. "'E finks I'm the only copper who can talk to West Indians. What you make of Reggie?"

"One scary man."

"Yeah. Gives us the willies, don't 'e, Bill?"

Bill looked thoughtful. "Ask me, Reggie's off his chump. I'm not claiming Ronnie's normal. There's different kinds of nutcase. Least Ronnie can control himself. Don't take much for Reggie to flip his wig."

"So when he asked if we wanted Morgan whacked, he was serious?"

"Christ, he never?" Bill's equable tone didn't change. "The Richardsons are different. They're more traditional." Charteris laughed. "No, Dave, they are. None of this pretending to be in business, no rubbing shoulders with the great and the good. They're villains pure and simple but they've gone extreme. It's not beating people up or knifing or even shooters. They like nailing folk to the floor with six-inch nails or do-it-yourself dentistry with a pair of pliers or electrodes on your gonads. The Krays and the Richardsons hate each other."

Charteris joined in. "The river keeps 'em apart. There's skirmishes but the nightmare is they go to war."

*It's a different world.* "I must be a country boy at heart. Now I've met the Krays, I know Burton's my kind of town."

"You got a family to bring up." Charteris slapped him on the back. "This was meant to 'elp."

"Dave, it did. I'm closer to Morgan Vetch. I *thought* he was in the music business. Now it seems he's about drugs. Don't worry, though, I've got the message. If Morgan is tied in with these Richardsons then I need to take great care where I put my feet."

Bill nodded. "And any other sensitive parts of your body, Alan."

Charteris stood. "We gotta run and make Russ feel important. C'mon, we'll drop yer back at The Carillion."

108

The vagrant had departed. He'd either taken his cardboard sheets with him or the street-sweeper had waited until he could turn chambermaid. Bloomsbury was waking lethargically; hackneys and buses. Out of curiosity, Shobnall wandered into the warren of lanes and alley-ways that served the working zones behind the hotel and its neighbours. At the rear of The Carillion, he came to a row of large, wheeled metal bins, material fluttering from one, unidentifiable stains around several. *No matter how posh the frontage, round the back is where the waste comes out, ugh!* The stench of rotting food hung in the air, flies buzzed continuously.

He was on the point of retreating when he heard a voice raised in anger. He recognised it. He crept past the bins, side-stepping the pools of liquid, peered into the yard at the rear of The Carillion. At the far end, a 'George Chalmers & Sons, Quality Butchers' van sat next to a large steel door, wedged open. *The kitchens.* Nearer this end was a normal-sized door with a 'FIRE EXIT' sign over it. *The service corridor from reception.* There were two people. The one with his back to Shobnall wore a white turban and a long blue robe. *Our friend from earlier this morning.* Facing him was Lady Melinda Montague.

*She owns the bloody place, what's she doing at the bins having a shouting match?* He was too far away to make out the words but tone and body language confirmed this was not a friendly conversation. Lady Melinda was rapping out sentences like bursts of machine-gun fire, rapid, authoritative. *Is she accusing him or upbraiding him?* The Crown Prince wasn't ducking for cover but retaliating, finger jabbing. *Not acting like friends, I wonder who he is.* He wasn't going to learn more. When George Chalmers' driver banged his van into gear and revved up for departure, distracting the disputants, Shobnall retraced his steps back to Charlotte Street.

In reception, not a scintilla of waste in sight, he thought the area was empty until a motion caught his eye and he realised it was Esmée Worthington in the corner waving to him. To his surprise, not only was the DI with her but Cyril Hendry as well, the debris of morning coffee on the table. "Sir, I thought the arrangement was that one of you and Cyril was at the Museum all the time."

"So it was, lad, but all of a sudden we're surplus to requirements."

"What! Is Lord Needwood withdrawing his Diamond then?"

"Seems not. The Diamond stays. Only Worthington and Hendry are leaving."

"Now, George." Esmée laid a hand on her husband's arm. "You and Cyril can't wait to get back and see what a mess has been made of the station." *He blushed, the Old Man bloody well went pink.*

"You're right, Esmée. Not used to being fired, that's all. You can imagine, Alan, that Melinda doesn't major in care and compassion. She did manage a 'thank you' but it was more short than sweet and mainly 'you may go now'."

"What about the Pinkertons?"

"Still on the job. Hank will be in touch about your enquiries. Odd thing, Melinda didn't mention it, Hank told me, there's to be a bigger role for those Indian chaps."

"The tall blokes with the nasty three-pronged spears?"

"We were told they were part of the decor, turns out they're some elite Presidential Guard. Huh! We'll be back Wednesday, bit of clearing-up needed." *A certain trattoria, I think.* "I'll telephone Angela later. You on your way?"

"Yes, sir, I'm intending to catch the early afternoon train."

"Have a good journey. Thank you for your help while we've been living it up down here."

They said their goodbyes. Shobnall's mind was whirling with questions about the Indians and India and the Diamond and Melinda. As he semi-distractedly shook hands, he looked into Esmée Worthington's eyes and again had the uncomfortable sense that she was sifting through his thoughts to make sure he hadn't missed anything.

\* \* \*

Stanley organised a taxi. Shobnall hesitated before clambering in. "Stanley, can I ask a favour of you?"

"Ask, Mr Shobnall, and I shall see if it is possible."

"That chap we saw leaving by the back door this morning. I need to know who he is. For work reasons. Your cousin identified him as a prince. Could you find out his full title?"

"Not a problem, sir. How shall I pass the information to you?"

"Give it to George Worthington, if you would. He and his wife will be here until Wednesday. And thank you."

He tried to tip the commissionaire but Stanley wasn't having any of it. "Very nice of you, Mr Shobnall, but your Mr Worthington has treated me handsomely and it has been a pleasure looking after you all. In you get, sir." Stanley slammed the door shut with a flourish and a wave of his grey hat, a top-of-the-bill performer bidding his matinee audience farewell.

*  *  *

By the time he was lugging his case down the St Pancras platform, fatigue was kicking in. He'd packed a lot into his stay; corpses, dear friends, gangsters the like of which he'd never conceived. A city of limitless wealth and people sleeping on the street while he slumbered in luxury. He wasn't sorry to be leaving the hurly-burly. *Always on the move, always going somewhere but I'm blowed if there's any notion of destination, pop music everywhere in shops and pubs and cafes, all those guitars.* Wearily, he changed hands with his case. Ahead of him were a pair of teenagers with that necessary appendage, a tranny. The music floated back to him and he found the pounding rhythm strangely hypnotic, the timbre of the singer's voice attractive and unsettling at the same time. "Excuse me. What's that you're listening to?"

The teenagers looked him up and down as if they had never seen anything like it outside a museum, sniggered and turned away, but one threw him a dismissive response. "Man, that's The Reapers."

He hurried to the train. *Steam!* He shared the British indulgence in nostalgia, a world-view investing steam with memories of an idyllic heritage. He toyed with going to the head of the train for a look at the locomotive. It was a long train and his feet hurt. *I don't need to traipse up there to evoke childhood memories.* He climbed into the nearest carriage, found he'd blundered into First Class and had to trek further. Luckily, the public had little enthusiasm for Sunday travel in British Railways carriages that, while the heating had signally failed through one of the worst winters ever, would assuredly be blasting hot air into the oven of summer. He found an empty compartment, levered his case onto the rack and dropped onto the window seat facing forwards. On the dot, the whistle blew. *And a flag is being waved.* The starting jerk pulsed through the train, the carriages experiencing that initial jostle, the rattle of the bogeys, before power took over and the ensemble launched out from under the station canopy. Shobnall settled down to immerse himself in the passing landscape.

111

"Alan, can I join you?"

He jumped. "Heather! What are you doing here? Of course!" He leapt up, hugged her. "Come, sit down."

Shobnall hadn't seen Heather Wilson since she'd left the Force. *She's completely different.* The woman who had looked short, a tad portly and reluctant to impose herself when in uniform had been transformed into the epitome of the modern, fashion-conscious era. She'd had her hair done, tinted, he thought, and she was sharply-dressed in black flared trousers and a rainbow jacket that made Lavinia Salt's dresses seem dull and boring.

"Heather, where did you get that jacket?"

She giggled. "I made it, Alan, designed and made it. Like it?"

"It's sensational!" He meant it. Heather looked terrific. "I'm glad you spotted me."

"I saw you go past in First Class."

"You're travelling First Class? HW Designs must be doing well!"

"I'm not paying for it. Gosh, Alan, it's all happening so fast. I sent some designs to the buyer at Derry & Toms on Kensington High Street. They asked me to come down, sent me the train ticket and put me up in a local hotel. I felt like royalty. I haven't told Joe all this yet, you won't say anything, will you?"

"Huh! We never see him, he's that in demand."

"I took samples I'd been working on but on the way down I thought I'm not totally into these. Since I had time I went to the British Museum. They've an exhibition on about India." *Now there's a coincidence.* "Their patterns are so inspiring, I stayed up half the night sketching. Derry & Toms took me up to their roof garden and I showed them the original stuff I'd brought down and they liked those but the Indian ideas really grabbed them. They're going to send me a contract! It's not only Derry & Toms."

"There wouldn't be a beer bottle involved by any chance?"

Heather pointed a finger. "You know Reuben Salt. What an angel he is. Mind you, he's got a business head on him. If you know about the bottle, you'll know I'm not allowed to talk about it."

112

Shobnall was trying to imagine Reuben Salt as an angel. "He swore me to secrecy too."

"It's a bit frightening." Shobnall raised an eyebrow. "I'm so up about these successes and I need to deliver on them but already I'm worried about what comes next. Can I do it again?"

Shobnall considered the woman opposite, once a colleague, now a budding fashion entrepreneur. He thought about The Reapers, a bunch of young lads headed for the stars. "I know what you mean. The world is changing. No time to rest on our laurels any more. Clients, bosses, London, the world, all wanting the next thing, a new thing, a better thing. The next design, the next sale, the next case, the next hit record. Pressure all the way. You have the skills, Heather, you can do it."

The countryside flashed by, traces of steam flicking across the window, reminding him of the past and how the present was accelerating into the future. Heather sat opposite in her rainbow jacket, still rather stunned by the velocity of change. *I'm all for this new future, the freedom, the opportunities but I worry about the pressure and anxiety and what they can do to people.* They powered on towards the Midlands, home and the re-assurance that comes with familiarity.

\* \* \*

113

## EIGHTEEN

"I feel like the pistons are going full-tilt but we're hardly moving. The Wychnor drowning looks more like murder by the day. All my instincts tell me Preston, whose name it turns out isn't Preston, he did it but at the moment I can't even prove he was in there at the time. I'm certain his boss was a party to it. But why? I've no idea what game they're playing. In any case, they're out of the country. We're checking out a country parson and chasing down a helicopter pilot and Pinkertons are in and about American security for us. Now the group's roadie is dragged from the Thames. We're waiting on the autopsy report. The supporting cast only makes things worse. British aristocracy, Indian royalty, London gangsters."

They were in the Shobnalls' back garden with the late afternoon sun. He'd found in the shed a fold-down wooden table and chairs, now set out on the grass. Shobnall and Gordon Crombie were seated; Corky was assessing the ramshackle greenhouse. Elaine, 'assisted' by Josephine and Alice, was making a fresh pot of tea. "The Reapers sail on. Eddie Mustard passed me the latest New Musical Express, or NME, as I gather people call it."

Corky harrumphed. "This the new language, eh, initials instead of names?"

"The Reapers are all over it. Still in the Top Twenty. In America, there was a near-riot at their latest concert in Boston. And they're rocketing up the Billboard Hot 100. With a bullet. Whatever that means."

"All going swimmingly," observed Crombie. "At least you no longer need to worry about the Diamond."

"Even that's not certain, Gordon. It's sitting there in the British Museum, only the guardians have changed. The Diamond comes with Melinda attached and she's connected to Vetch *and* to this Indian."

"Talking of the Indian," remarked Corky. "Any news on his identity?"

"Yes. The DI brought back the message. Hang on." Shobnall fished out his notebook. "Crown Prince of Saharanpur. I can't vouch for my pronunciation."

"Where the hell's that?" Corky demanded.

"North of Delhi. Where he's ruler of matters less than the fact he's a Minister in the Indian government-"

Crombie interrupted. "Minister for what?"

"Nobody seems to know for sure. There's an awful lot of ministers and no-one can explain what they all do. What makes him significant is that he's married into the Prime Minister's family."

"Ah." Crombie sat back. "Not much to do except enjoy a spot of nepotism. Sounds like here."

Corky laughed. "Gordon, you're such a cynic. How do you manage inside the bent system we call Town Hall?"

Crombie spread his arms wide. "Try to remember why we're there in the first place, Corky. Avoid getting upset about things. Put my faith in young folk and a regular game of bowls. Hang about decent people."

Corky, en route from the greenhouse to his seat, gave Crombie's shoulder a squeeze in passing. "Know what you mean, old man."

"Thanks, Corky," said Crombie. "Talking of young folk, here they come."

And come they did, Elaine carrying the refreshed tea-tray, Jo helping her sister down the kitchen step, then dragging her over to the adults. "Hello Uncle Corky, hello Uncle Gordon, look at us, we're helping mummy."

\* \* \*

It was good to be back on days. He preferred the buzz of a station full of people and being able to walk outside into a bright, wakeful world. He had resolved regularly to be in early to cross over with Eddie. *He's still on the case, it's only fair to keep him in the picture.* This morning, WPC Redpath, ready to leave, was still at the public counter. Joe Short was using the telephone in the corner. He waved to Joe. "Morning, Sheila, had a quiet night?"

"Yes, sir. I won another pound off Charlie. Here's my report on the helicopter." She proffered a buff folder.

*She hasn't hung about.* "That was fast work. No trouble, I hope?"

"No, sir, he remembered alright. He said it was a wet night and he had to clean up the cabin afterwards."

Shobnall tapped the edge of the folder against his free hand. "Thanks, Sheila. I'll read the full report this morning." He could feel the excitement emanating from her. "Give me the headlines."

"The helicopter pilot did pick up a second passenger at Alrewas aerodrome, a man. Nat – the pilot - never saw his face but he said he was dripping water all over the cabin. He dug out an old mac and made him put it on. He didn't get it back, said the man wasn't the sort you wanted to upset. The two passengers didn't say a word for the rest of the flight. The other thing you asked, sir, the Croydon flight, that was booked for one-way carriage only. One other thing, sir," she blurted. "I know the pilot. We went to the same school. He was a couple of years ahead of me and he was always mad about flying. When I saw his name......"

"That's absolutely fine, Sheila. Now, off you go." She pranced out happily. Joe had vanished. Shobnall made his way upstairs. *I remember what it's like when you're starting out, hm, sounds like an old boyfriend.*

\* \* \*

Viewed from today, the sixties present a tumultuous picture. That week, for example, General De Gaulle declined the USA's offer of nuclear support – La France would have her own, *merci beaucoup*! ITV launched 'Ready Steady Go!' as The Searchers went to Number One with 'Sweets for My Sweet'. Beryl Burton crashed while leading the World Cycling Championships. A Newton Solney man died in a car crash. Arthur Ashe became the first African American to be named in the US Davis Cup team. Another young Buddhist monk knelt in a square in far-off Saigon and set fire to himself. None of these news items made the front pages or the radio and TV headlines.

Shobnall found Lennie with what looked like the entire output of Fleet Street *and* in possession of Bob Saxby's radio, for once tuned to neither cricket nor pop music but to the Home Service. "Alan! You seen the news?"

*What's going on?* "No, Lennie, in our household first thing in the morning is all about kids. What's up?" Gideon was at his desk. Bob Saxby couldn't be far away; a steaming mug of tea sat among his papers.

"They've only robbed a train and got away with two and a half million quid."

"You're kidding me! A train robbery?"

"Yup. Two and a half million!"

"What's that much money doing on a train?"

"It's a Royal Mail train," said Gideon. Shobnall and Lennie stared at him. "A TPO."

After a short silence, Shobnall asked. "Gideon, what's a TPO?"

"Sorry, Travelling Post Office. It'll have departed Glasgow about seven last night, scheduled for London four-ish. A dozen carriages, seventy Post Office staff. It's probably hauled by an English Electric Type 4 locomotive-"

"Yes, thank you, Gideon." Shobnall cut the train spotter short. "They won't have stopped the train to steal Jock's letters. What about the money?"

Gideon built steam again. "That will have been in the HVP, sorry again. High Value Package carriage. Second one behind the locomotive, where they deal with registered mail and cash. There's not usually that much money, though. Normally it's only a couple of hundred thousand."

"Bank holiday," said Lennie. "Takings will have been up. But there must be security. They don't use ordinary coaches, do they?"

"Well, no." Gideon scratched his head. "They have carriages with bars and bolts and alarms for HVP work. I've seen them go through Crewe when we've been over for some late-night spotting."

Another pause while Gideon's colleagues pondered the attractions of a cold midnight on a Crewe platform. *Blowed if I can think of any.* Lennie went on. "Fascinating, Gideon. Love of money is the root of all evil, eh?"

Gideon made a face. "'The wages of sin is death' into the bargain. Romans, chapter 6, by the way."

"Of course." Lennie nodded. "The gang was well-prepared. A bit of violence, mind you. The train driver was banged on the head with a metal bar. He's not too good."

*Scotland Yard will be scrambling on this one.* "Where did it happen?"

117

"Buckinghamshire. Just a mo." Lennie riffled through the pile of papers. "Here we are. Bridego Railway Bridge, Ledburn, near Mentmore. Early hours of the morning. They rigged the signals."

"They knew about the signals," Gideon pointed out. "They knew about the train, they had someone to drive the locomotive, they probably knew about the money and it seems they knew how to get into the HVP carriage. They must have had inside information. There's too many people involved, there'll be loose ends."

Lennie regarded Gideon appreciatively. "You're right, Gideon. A lot may depend on how fast the gang and our brother officers move. My goodness, Buckinghamshire will be crawling with reporters."

"Scotland Yard will be all over everything," said Shobnall. "I don't envy the locals. If it goes well, the Yard will be taking the press conference. If it goes badly then guess who'll be carrying the can."

* * *

Joe Short burst in like a man in a hurry. "I'm in a hurry, Alan, I've made time to squeeze you in. Did I tell you Heather's winning contracts left right and centre? Let's get a move on."

Shobnall lifted his arms in a slow-down gesture. "Whoa there, where's the fire?"

"Wychnor Hall. I overheard you talking with Wendy the other day. I read your report."

"How did you get hold of that?"

Joe looked arch. "Forensics Unit wants report, Forensics Unit gets report. Don't sulk, it's why HQ gets copies of everything."

Shobnall chuckled. "Wouldn't get sulky with you, Joe. Heather would never speak to me again. What are we in a hurry about?"

"Wendy told you the helicopter pilot had to clean up. Gave me an idea so I stopped off at the airport to see young Bleriot. See, it was raining that night but this needed more than a rub with a chamois leather. The passenger up from London was well wrapped-up, nice and dry. The second bloke. I think he fell. Show me where you found that bottle."

They went in convoy, Shobnall in the Anglia, Joe in his little van. Conkers, bursting from their shells, lay beneath the mighty chestnut tree. The Big House was posturing, its cloak of ivy shimmering a deep crimson. There was no-one else around to admire it. The only sound was a regular screech from the sawmill. He walked Joe across the croquet lawn, through the gardens and orchards and down towards the river. Joe was carrying his usual case but also had a long, slim canvas bag slung over his shoulder. *Looks like a thin golf bag.* "Here, this is it. The bottle was under those bushes." He made to step forward but Joe stopped him.

"Stay back, Alan. I know you've walked over the patch but I'm hoping it's only been you and chummy. I may be able to make sense of it." He snapped open the lid of his tool-case and gloved up, unzipped the canvas bag and withdrew a metal rod about four feet long with a handle at one end and what looked like a steel dinner plate at the other, the whole thing laden with switches and different coloured wires.

Shobnall was fascinated. "What is that? Some new toy?"

Joe held the dinner plate hovering above the surface of the bank. "Metal detector. Look." Joe moved the dinner plate close to his tool case; a series of staccato burps burbled from somewhere in the contraption. "See? Now hop it. Give me half an hour here, that should be enough. I'll meet you back at the house."

Shobnall strolled back, musing. *Amazing the impact of science on policing.* He walked round to the rear of the Hall. Someone had placed a wooden bench outside the kitchen door. He sat and watched the lake, following the infinitesimal movements of the water as breaths of air played across it. It was hypnotic. He was still there when Joe re-appeared, looking abundantly smug.

"Have a look at these." He dangled a couple of clear plastic envelopes. "Exhibit A, m'lud, approximately fifteen shillings in assorted loose change. Exhibit B, your honour, one Yale-type key, door for the insertion into."

Shobnall snatched at the bag containing the key but Joe whisked it out of reach. "No touching! It's not the front, I checked. Let's try the kitchen." Joe's gloved fingers inserted the key. It clicked over smoothly. Joe opened the door an inch or two, closed it and re-locked it. "Now you know how he might have entered the house."

"Joe, you're a genius. Now if – no, *when* you find a print, get in touch with Dave Charteris, ask him to run it through their system. If we have him inside the building then it's game on!"

* * *

"Do you have a moment, Alan?" *My, you do make me feel old.* Gideon laid a folder on his desk, depositing it delicately, as though it were Holy Writ. "The Reverend Bullard."

Shobnall leaned back and linked his hands behind his neck. "Tell me."

"Most of this is straightforward but there is a question mark. Edwin Parker Bullard. Born 1901 in Eastbourne. Makes him 62 now. Third and youngest son. His father owned a gents' outfitters, well-to-do, respectable, C of E. Edwin decides it's church for him. Cambridge, gets a third – I don't think that's a great result but it is Cambridge – and theological college. 1923 he's curate at a village outside Sheffield, five years later he's vicar at a church in Northamptonshire. After seven years there he goes off for some missionary work in Africa, Kenya, still a British colony then. Well, it is now but Lennie says independence is on the cards. While he's out there he gets to know someone called Lady Needwood." Gideon paused.

"I see." Shobnall calculated. "That's going to be the second wife, Melinda's mother. Any mention of a daughter?"

"No. Lady Needwood was apparently out doing good works. Whatever that means."

"Melinda would have been a young woman then, probably packed off to some finishing school. Carry on."

"With war on the way, he moves to Bermuda." *Oh surely not.* "Where the Needwoods own a large estate. They have a vacancy for a chaplain." *How very convenient.* "Bullard is there for ten years and then he moves to a teaching post in a college in Boston, in Massachusetts. In case you think he's parted company with the aristocracy, his position at the college was endowed by Lord Needwood. I don't like all this wealth washing around the church. 'Ye cannot serve God and Mammon', Matthew 6, 24."

"But your mother's a stalwart of the church, isn't she?"

"Mam's chapel. She doesn't hold with gold and finery. She says 'wisdom is better than rubies'. Proverbs, 8, 11."

"Sorry, Gideon, let's get back to our friend, Bullard."

"There's not much more. He teaches in Boston until 1955. Mam says it's been a sinful city ever since the Salem witch trials. Then Wychnor."

"Which is, presumably, in the gift of the Needwoods?"

"When it comes down to it, yes. I managed to talk to several of the church elders. Nothing useful. All that seems to matter to them is that he delivers sermons that keep them awake." He stopped.

"You mentioned a question mark, Gideon."

Gideon assumed his most earnest expression. "Yes. I went to Lichfield. Over by the cathedral is where the Diocese has its administration. Wychnor parish may belong to Lord Needwood but the church does have its procedures. I met the Secretary. Creepy place and a creepy bloke but he let me see the papers concerning Bullard's appointment. Application, CV, the reference from Lord Needwood, copies of certificates and stuff. Thing is, there were papers missing."

"How could you tell?" Shobnall's tone was sharper than he had intended. ""Sorry, didn't mean to sound snappy."

"Simple. Whoever put the papers together had numbered them. Pages 8 and 9 weren't there."

"Did this Secretary know?"

"That's the funny thing. He was very careful to separate out the pages I had asked to see. I had the feeling he did know. He made a point of telling me that he hadn't been in post at the time. I didn't let on I'd spotted the gap."

"Any idea what might have been missing?"

Gideon wet his lips. "Someone had been very thorough in their research. The chronology suggests it's to do with Bullard leaving a comfortable position in a big American city for a sinecure in the back of beyond."

*Interesting.* "Could Bullard have removed it?"

"No. The Diocese is like the Bank of England. If you want to poke around in their personnel files then first you need enough authority and a pile of signatures. Took me over a week to get them. Even then they don't leave you alone with anything."

"No use asking the Secretary what it was that's not there anymore?"

"I'm not sure he knew. He wasn't surprised some pages were missing but what exercised him was whether I'd noticed. I'm not explaining that very well."

"You are, Gideon, you've done a fine job." Gideon's chest swelled. *He'll repeat that to his mother, I hope she appreciates it.* "There's a chance we can track down whatever it was now we know where and when to look." *And see why the Reverend is seeming a key player in all this.*

\*   \*   \*

# NINETEEN

"Mornin' Alan, all kosher up there?"

"Hello Dave. Yes, all well here. Quiet really. I expect you're rushed off your feet with this train robbery."

"Tell me! I've managed to steer clear but the brass 'ave stripped art 'alf the building. Us what's left are 'avin' to cover everything. Any road, got the autopsy report on Gary Stubbs in me 'and. I'll send a copy but I knew you'd be keen. Ready?"

"Fire away, Dave."

"OK. Screeds on all the stuff what we already know. Bangs on the 'ead an' body. Nothin' much to add aside from a couple broken ribs. Doc says that scar might well be a propeller. Bloke strong, fit, general good condition but a bit of a smoker, some cloggin' of 'is arteries. Tidy chap, finger an' toenails neat an' trimmed. Strewth, Alan, this doc fancies isself as a Sherlock, don't 'e? Appendix scar, metal plate in 'is left forearm, broke it maybe three, four years ago. Some bruisin' of 'is right ankle. Doc says no trace of any drugs, e's 'ad bodies art the music business before, knows the signs."

"Hm. Any comment on the ankle bruising?"

"Nah. The doc's thorough, nuthin' on the left one, nuthin' on 'is wrists neither, all part of the bashin' in the water."

"He's not flagging up anything suspicious."

"Well." Charteris sounded apologetic. "Cos I knew about yer other case I was on the lookout but the doc ain't soundin' any warnin's and it ain't lookin' bad. Bill an' me went darn The Prospect. Nuffink. They said they was busy that night an' nobody remembers a thing. We're that short-'anded Russ ain't lookin' for more work, although 'e ain't closed the file yet."

"I understand, Dave. Not every drowning is a murder. I mustn't go looking for them. Listen, thanks for that and don't over-work. Remember you're a married man! Love to Frankie."

"Cheers, mate." Charteris sounded happier now. "An' to Elaine an' the girls. See you all soon, I 'ope."

Shobnall replaced the handset gently, stared thoughtfully out of the window. *I wonder, they don't always know.........*

* * *

Gary Stubbs was buried in London, south of the river in which he had died. Lambeth Cemetery in the Borough of Tooting. He had no surviving family and it was left to Janice, who had thought herself on the verge of a new life, to say that she wanted to hold him close. Dave Charteris had a quiet word in the appropriate corporation shell-like. To Shobnall's surprise, the DI confided that he would be attending the funeral. *I realised he took to Gary when we all met but taking a day out seems a bit excessive, I wonder if he has another agenda.* Lambeth Cemetery was the largest graveyard Shobnall had ever seen, a vast green tract in the middle of South London's industrialised suburbs and multiracial communities. This was no 'Swinging London', nor was it the 'old London' he'd seen in the East End. The cemetery was a green oasis among the shifting grey dunes of successive new settlements bound by networks of legal and illicit trading.

The taxi dropped them at the Victorian chapel. Shobnall read the nearby plaque while the DI paid the fare. *1854, they've been burying Londoners here for over a century, someone had the foresight to set aside so much land.* In the distance, through the clumps of trees, he could see a more modern construction. *The crematorium, I wonder what it's like, I've never been in one.* The chapel was chock-a-block for the short service. Dave Chateris and Bill were standing at the back. Shobnall joined them. DI Conway was in the last pew, clearly holding a space for Worthington. Shobnall remembered meeting Conway; 'you're George Worthington's chap, good enough for me.' *How well do they know each other?*

Charteris leaned over. "Me and Bill fetched Janice North. Jenny Cox said she wanted to come so we picked 'er up an' all. They're darn the front. We'll take 'em 'ome after but Russ will run you back."

"Who are all these people?" Shobnall felt obliged to whisper even though proceedings had not yet got under way.

"Music business, mostly. Stubbs was well-respected. Blokes from the clubs, I seen Crawdaddy staff, Ronnie Scott's, The Roundhouse. Promoters, musicians I couldn't put a name to. And some conspicuous by their absence, as they say."

"The Reapers?"

"In one. You'd 'ave thought the Ellison woman."

"I think, Dave, that Morgan Vetch considers Gary to be history."

The service passed off as these events always do – slowly, accentuating the bass notes and with a hesitancy in the air as if someone with an important part to play was missing, not to say late. Outside, the mourners trailed behind the coffin, the policemen again bringing up the rear. The final words at the graveside, the controlled lowering of the casket, the slithering noise as the ropes were withdrawn. Shobnall had stopped following the ceremony. He'd turned up to pay his respects but Gary Stubbs simply wasn't here anymore. He ran his eyes back and forward over the crowd. Their black clothes were a uniform, distinguishing only men from women.

*Where's Jenny Cox, that doughty lady.* He could see Janice North with her back to him and he guessed, from the way she periodically looked down to her right, that Jenny was alongside. Janice's left hand rested on the arm of a man. Long black hair. *Loads of people with long hair here.* A tall, a big man. *The only man here without a jacket, something familiar about him.* The man turned towards Janice. *It can't be.* The man spoke to Janice. *It bloody is, it's Basher. Bob Carter.*

\* \* \*

As last words were aired and handfuls of earth lobbed into the grave, the party fragmented, some heading for the wake organised in a nearby pub, others heading home or back to work. Shobnall made a bee-line for Basher, still with Janice and Jenny. "Basher. You're supposed to be in America."

Basher surveyed him equably for a long moment. "Got it. Policeman from when Mick died."

"That's right. Why aren't you with The Reapers?"

That tickled Basher. "Group I used to be in. Look, nice to see you again but I'm helping Janice and Jenny. We need to find the coppers who promised them a lift."

"Basher. Bob." Shobnall held out a card. "I need to talk to you. Can we meet? Talk on the phone?"

Basher took the card, studied Shobnall afresh. "Burton, eh? Railway station?" Shobnall nodded. ""I'll come see you. Day after tomorrow."

"Terrific. You won't forget, will you?"

Basher smiled. "I'm here. I'll be there."

* * *

The long hot summer was showing no sign of relenting as August dragged its charred carcass towards September. Shade was at a premium. Shobnall and the DI sheltered in the lee of the station, watching Gideon park his moped and unbuckle his crash helmet. The DI shook his head in wonder. "He must be melting under that."

"Imagine what his mother would say if he came a cropper and he wasn't wearing it, sir."

"I know, she'd be after my hide. Any movement on the Wychnor business?"

"'Fraid not, sir. I'm treading water. I've my fingers crossed that Hank will come up with something. It's all moving so slowly."

"Relax, Alan. The race is not to the swift. Isn't that right, young Gideon?"

"Gideon came up to them. "Nor the battle to the strong, Ecclesiastes 9, 11."

Shobnall wasn't satisfied. "If speed and strength aren't enough, then what else do we need, sir?"

The DI turned, shading his eyes. "Stamina. Imagination. And a large dollop of good fortune."

* * *

## TWENTY

Basher wanted a drink so they walked along to the Devi. The man had marched into the station around noon and asked for Shobnall. Sheila Redpath, taking a stint at confronting the public, had no idea who he was but kept her cool as Basher became persistently curious as to whether she was busy that evening. She was grateful for the solid counter between them, thankful when Shobnall whisked the Liverpool Lothario away.

Basher liked the Devi. "Nice. Good feel. That the landlady? Woman knows her trade, I can tell."

*A man who knows his pubs.* "What'll you have, Basher?"

"This is the capital of beer, yeah? I'd like a pint made here. Food, whatever you're having."

Shobnall ordered two shepherd's pies with a pint and a half of Bass. Normally, he'd not take alcohol during a shift but he felt obliged to show some degree of solidarity. He had been surprised that Basher still wore his funeral rig but then he twigged it was the other way around; this was Reapers gear, what he was used to. He hadn't dressed up for the funeral. He set the glasses down. "So, Basher – is that what you like to be called?

Basher had drained his glass. "That's real good. Basher will do. I'll have another."

With the second pint, Shobnall tried in earnest. "Right, Basher. Where are we? You and The Reapers?"

Basher stared at him. "What's the name of that lass in your nick? The one behind the desk?"

Shobnall was taken off-guard. "You mean Sheila Redpath?"

"Sheila. Sheila." Basher tested the sound, tasted it. "Aye, Suits her. She's cute. Capable, too. You wouldn't have her phone number?"

The situation was eased by the arrival of their lunch; a digestive hiatus ensued, broken only by Shobnall fetching a third pint of Bass. Basher was showing not the slightest deviation from stone-cold sobriety and, once he'd finished eating and had his fist round a fourth drink, was ready to talk. "I'd had enough of Morgan Vetch. That man is bad news. We should never have signed with him."

"You left? Walked out?"

Basher grinned. He looked like a mischievous schoolboy. *Gary said he lacked self-restraint but he's simply irrepressible.* "Yeah." He emptied his glass yet again. "This is really good beer, y'know." Another pause while Shobnall secured pint number five and tried to quell concerns about his expenses claim. *Is he going to drink the place dry?* "You're police but Gary trusted you. Mick's mum likes you. Janice was nice about your mate, the big London copper. I'll talk. We blew America away. That's the truth. But the longer the tour went on the less happy I was. I know, you're thinking he's on his fifth pint. Don't worry, I can handle this. Believe it or not, I don't drink at all on tour. I'm drumming and that's what I'm all about. I'm seeing a Morgan I don't want any truck with. I don't say nothing 'cos I'm doing what I love, getting up in front of thousands screaming and showing 'em why drums were invented.

"By the time we hit Boston, you couldn't buy a ticket. We tore the house down. Steven had them in the palm of his hand. What Morgan wanted, his master-plan, the stage painted black for death and red for blood, the fans in a frenzy, loving us but frightened at the same time, the cash registers tinkling, the honourable citizens up on their high horses." He frowned. "Morgan started needling Jem – Jem Wicks, our bass player. They'll tell you it's all about Steven and Alex and their songs. They got a point. No songs you're not at first base. Then they look at the lead guitar. Mick was good but there's hundreds of good guitarists out there. What a group really needs, 'specially one like The Reapers, is a powerhouse rhythm section. Drums and bass. Me and Jem. We were the rock the cissies could strut about on. Jem was my mate. And Morgan was at him. I saw what he was up to. Like Mick. Morgan took against Mick and then he was in the water. Like Gary. Now he doesn't like Jem.

"No way for me to stop him." Basher studied his beer which, for now, he was not sluicing down his throat. "I'm not just a big Scouser, y'know. I'm into some of this eastern stuff. I like to explore my limitations. When I'm drumming I want to go beyond them. When I'm not drumming, OK, I can go over the top. Gary said I stole a shotgun and went shooting at trees in the middle of the night when we were up here. Was he winding me up?"

"No, Basher, you did. That was my introduction to The Reapers."

Basher shrugged. "Don't remember a thing. I told Morgan I was leaving. He didn't seem bothered, brought in some pick-up guy for the New York shows. Wanker! He'll not scoop up another drummer like me in a hurry."

"But you need to live, Basher, you need some work, surely."

Basher gave him a pitying glance. "You don't know the music business, do you? I'm worth a pile. Probably I don't never need to work again. But I will. I'm one of the best drummers around. Long as Morgan lets me go."

"You said Morgan wasn't bothered."

Basher swilled his remaining half pint around his glass. "Gary. He'd left. Mick was ready to leave, wasn't he?"

"Was he? No-one's mentioned that before."

"He told me. I don't know the ins and outs of it. People weren't drowning back then. You got a river here?"

"The Trent. Third longest river in England. Sorry. Habit. My wife's a teacher."

Basher nodded as if Shobnall had just revealed the true purpose of the universe. "The Trent. What would you think if, let's say, you pulled me out of it next week?"

*He's not going to say it but he's frightened of Morgan.* "I might start by checking the alibis of Morgan Vetch and his henchman."

"Ah." Basher disposed of the last of his pint but halted Shobnall in mid-rise. "Enough, I think. That Preston. He isn't in PR. Y'know, before turning pro, I worked on the Liverpool docks. I met men like him. It's in their eyes. Emptiness. Slit your throat as soon as look at you. And enjoy it! I ask myself why Morgan needs a man like that."

*I'll not reveal his real name.* "Do you get an answer?"

"I can see why Gary trusted you." Basher leaned back in the booth. "In this business – touring, recording, publicity, all the bits in between – you watch a lot of telly. I like police dramas, mainly American. I know how it works. The police got to have proof. Right?"

"Right." *You must have something, Basher.* "I don't have enough. I haven't even worked out exactly what has been going on here. All contributions gratefully received."

"Morgan scares me but he's clever. He knows the business and he understands how the money works. There's more, though. Drugs. I'm sure he was supplying Mick. Preston once offered to fix me up."

"Yes, Gary told me about that." *Posthumously, that is.*

"Pop music and drugs, it's getting so they go together naturally. I like a joint for relaxation but mostly I'll take alcohol, it's more traditional, if you like. In the States, it's all five-star hotels, limos, police escorts, sirens, pampering and anything you fancy by way of flesh or narcotics, anything at all. You got to watch for the hangers-on. There's the cringers begging for scraps or tempting you with something in exchange for a favour. Best thing is look away like they're beggars on the streets. Then there's the handful who don't even notice you 'cos they control everything. To see a man like Morgan fawning, nervy, blows your mind in a bad way."

"Organised crime, that's what you mean?"

Basher gazed into space. "Yeah. The Yanks call it The Mob. Pop music plus drugs plus the Mob. All of a sudden, the solid ground under your feet starts to wobble." Basher returned to Planet Burton. "No way can I see Gary choosing the Thames over Janice. I can't take Mick as an accident either. I'll tell you something. Mick Cox was terrified of the water. Twenty-three years old, he couldn't swim and I never knew him climb in a boat." Basher leaned close, lowered his voice. "He was in a home when he was a boy, while his mum was recovering in hospital." Shobnall nodded. "Something happened to him there. I don't know for sure but if you were talking and chat went that way then he made sure it changed direction. I know about those places and some of the people work in 'em. Creeps! The kids can't handle it and it fucks them up. I saw the signs in Mick. What was the name of that palace in the countryside?"

"Wychnor Hall."

"Yeah. I liked that place. Brilliant grub. Morning after we got there, me and Jem and Mick went for a walk and when Mick saw the lake he freaked. He was sweating and shivering. Jem never noticed. Jem never sees anything if it isn't the music." He looked hard into Shobnall's eyes. "See what I'm saying? Never mind drink or drugs. Mick Cox would never, *could* never have gone out on the water. Not voluntarily." *Implying drink, drugs and incapacity in his room with someone taking him out and returning to clean up.*

They went out into the sunlight. "What are you going to do now, Basher?"

"Keep my head down. London's good for that. Check on who's drumming. Burton produced one of the great drummers, you know. Phil Seamen. Jazzman but what a player, way ahead of me. I saw him at Ronnie Scott's last year and I'm still trying to work out how he did some of those things. Maybe I'll try me hand at some jazz. But what are *you* going to do now, Mr Policeman?"

Shobnall was becoming fond of the Liverpudlian. "I'm going to plug on, Basher. That's my way, keep on going. I'm not happy with either death and I intend to get to the bottom of them."

They'd reached the police station. Basher surveyed the array of maltings and breweries congregated in the middle of the town. "I love all this brickwork. Reminds me of home. Don't have all these railway lines, mind" He turned. "Those telly programmes, the coppers always win. Do that for me. Win. For Gary and Mick and Jenny and Janice." He put out his hand and they shook. "I'll hang on to your card if that's OK."

*Oh, Basher, that's the last thing Gary said to me.* "Do. Call me anytime. And Basher. Be very careful." He watched Basher walk away. *What a world we live in. There's a young man who has no memory of a night-time blasting away with a shotgun, who has an eye out for the weak and the vulnerable, who may have upset this Svengali figure knee-deep in music and drugs and possibly organised crime. And with Lady Melinda. What is it all about?*

\* \* \*

# TWENTY-ONE

He drove out to Wychnor. *Several weeks since I was here, maybe I'll pick up some of that luck the DI says is so important.* The village was simmering in the mid-afternoon heat. He left his car at the green, in the shadow cast by the clump of trees, and walked through the somnolent village. The locals were sweating at work or sunning themselves in back gardens. Towards the rectory, he saw the black-clad figure of the Reverend Bullard making his way into the church, bent beneath something over his shoulder.

Shobnall caught up with the priest in the nave. Bullard was in jovial mood. "Good afternoon, Sergeant. You catch me on repair and maintenance duties." He had rope coiled over his shoulder. "Your arrival is most timely. Might I impose on you for some assistance?" Shobnall could hardly refuse. "Would you carry one of these?" Bullard separated the rope into two coils and handed one to Shobnall. "New bell ropes. I have already removed the old ones. Mind your head. It is a bit of a climb."

Five minutes later, Shobnall could only agree, having climbed, sweated and silently cursed his way up a series of ladders, Bullard mounting steadily ahead of him. *Maybe a bit more regular exercise wouldn't be a bad idea.* They emerged through a trap-door into the belfry. Home to the two bells, it was open on all sides with a narrow wooden bench – more of a plank, really – around the edge. Bullard sat to get his breath. Shobnall dropped the rope, balanced with one hand on the nearest corner pillar and took in the view. *Must be what a bird sees, or that young man up in his helicopter.*

The world seemed spread at his feet. The village immediately to the north, huddled around the church, backed by a chequer-board of fields, hedges and woodland, groups of cattle lying in whatever shade they could find and, in the distance, the towers and chimneys of Burton quivering in the haze. Eastwards, the A38, miniature vehicles crawling in both directions, then the railway at Wychnor Sidings and the main line splitting at Wychnor Junction, the Lichfield branch empty but a diesel locomotive tugging carriages across the Tamworth viaduct spanning the Trent and Tame rivers. To the south, more countryside, sunlight bouncing off the Trent & Mersey Canal, Alrewas, the old aerodrome and a far hint of Lichfield. Looking westwards, he could see down to the River Swarbourn, a heron motionless in its shallows, and through the trees to Wychnor Hall. He couldn't quite see the entrance. *Something on the gravel.* He moved for a better angle. *There's a car parked there.*

"Have you been up a bell tower before, Sergeant?" Bullard cracked a knuckle.

*Wish he wouldn't do that.* "Not that I can remember. Everything looks unreal, like a model."

132

Bullard laughed. "I know what you mean. One feels removed from it all. I like to come up here for the sunset or to take in the marvels of the Milky Way."

*Not to be closer to the Good Lord, eh?* "No such leisurely purpose today, by the look of it." Shobnall focused on what Bullard was doing. Each bell was suspended from a wooden frame and joined to a side-mounted wheel into one of which Bullard was feeding a rope. After a few minutes of tapping and wrenching and tut-tutting, Bullard gave the rope several tugs, "That seems secure." He fed the rope down through the hole beneath the bell, rhythmically, ensuring it met no obstacles. "These ropes are good for fifteen to twenty years but eventually they begin to fray. I splice them for as long as possible but there comes a time when we have to ask the Diocese for new ones."

"That looks like quite a skill."

"I suppose it is." He slapped the wooden frame over the bell. "The headstocks are in good condition. As are the wheels, good solid elm."

"What's the fluffy bit?"

Bullard uncoiled the second rope and lifted a padded section, ringed in green, yellow and white, like a smaller version of the bollards Shobnall had seen on narrowboat hulls. "This? It's called a Sally and please don't ask for I have no idea. The ringer will hold this and pull down to move the wheel and thus the bell." He stretched the rope and displayed the loop at the end. "As the bell swings the other way, it drags the rope upwards and the Sally will rise too high to hold. It is important to hang on to this, the tail-end. That, I think, is self-explanatory." His hands moved deftly with the second rope. "Have you completed your investigations into the fate of that unfortunate young man?"

*Curiosity and the cat, vicar.* "The lad from The Reapers? We haven't closed that book yet."

"Really? That does seem a long delay for what one hears was either an accident or suicide."

"You know how it is, sir. Loose ends we need to tie up. The group are touring America and we are finding it hard to contact them." *A little push, I think.* "They've lately been in Boston and stirred up quite a furore. You've been in America, haven't

133

you, where you got to know shotguns? Do you know Boston?" He tried for nonchalance while watching Bullard's expression.

The vicar leaned down, ostensibly to check the play in the second rope. *Or to hide his face.* "I have sojourned in many parts of the globe. Boston, of course, is in New England, in the state of Massachusetts. America is a land of contradictions, so modern in some aspects, so primitive in others. I heard that speech by Mr King at the Lincoln Memorial the other week, the one about having a dream. In America it can sometimes be hard to distinguish a dream from a nightmare." He glanced at his watch. "My goodness! I must be on the move. Please follow me down."

Which meant slow single file descent in silence and the effective termination of the conversation. Shobnall wasn't bothered. He filed the vicar's obfuscation for the time being. There was somewhere else he wanted to be.

\* \* \*

He left the car and set off, jacket over his shoulder, along the track towards the Big House. The rows of poplars shielded him from the sun, their slender trunks holding the protective green canopy high above. At the gate posts he halted beside the chestnut, reviewed the scene; anyone who was around would hear his footsteps on the drive. Even in full sunlight, the Hall retained a mystique. It seemed.....What? Respectful? Reserved? No, secretive, as though the swathes of burgundy ivy were concealing forbidden knowledge. The curtains had been drawn across every window; there was neither sign nor sound of occupation. The only noises were a drone from the sawmill and the far-off keening of an invisible buzzard. The plum-red Bentley sat in the shade of a sycamore tree beside the croquet lawn. Only the machine; no driver, no passengers.

He crunched over the gravel to the far end of the building. No challenge, no welcome. *Just because there's a car sat there doesn't mean there's someone in the house.* Down the grass bank to the rear. The gouges made by Fred and Vern's Land Rover had dried out. The police seals on the boathouse were unbroken. The lake was placid, the islands fuzzy in the hot air. He returned to the front and the car. Peered in. Luxurious fittings. An Automobile Association Members Handbook for the current year lay on the passenger seat. He tried the door. To his surprise it opened. He leaned in. *Nothing, no, maybe, yes, a faint perfume, something flowery.*

He set his back against the motor, faced the house. The sawmill whined on but the buzzard had moved away. The longer he stared, the more the ivy leaves seemed to blur into a bloody smear across the brickwork. *Places like this tend to hide a dark history, I don't suppose young Cox was the first to meet an untimely death here.* The church bell tolled. Five o'clock. The buzzing of the saw fell silent. He felt like the house was awaiting his next move. *Am I going back to the green for the car?* He levered himself off the Bentley, walked up the steps and tried the handle. Secretive or not, Wychnor Hall admitted him.

He stood in the hallway. He'd been in the building three times – that first call-out for Basher taking pot-shots at trees, the night of the drowning, the last visit to see Gary – and only in a handful of its rooms yet he felt he knew the house as well as his own home. There were no sounds but it wasn't silent, it was..... suppressed. *Strange atmosphere, pressured, holding its breath, I don't like it.*

It was cooler inside and shadier, the drapes performing efficiently. He went from room to room, listening, opening doors, checking, withdrawing, leaving as he had found. The reception rooms. Downstairs, the kitchen, the old servants' quarters, pantries, a butler's room, the famous gun room, its new lock gleaming, store rooms, cupboards and presses as large as small warehouses. Back upstairs to a dining room, a vast library and the ballroom, a lofty space decorated in scarlet flock with ornate white cornicing and a majestic chandelier high above the wooden dance-floor. *Lavinia would love this.* It was largely bare; a few chairs against the wall, a long table perched on what would be the musicians' podium. On the table, a small lamp with a plain shade. The equipment The Reapers had brought in had been removed. He recalled Gideon's comment. *Including the fridge and the bottles.*

The first floor. More reception rooms and lounges, spaces with no identifiable purpose. A room full of stuffed creatures in glass cabinets and under glass domes. He shut that door quickly; every dead bird, mammal and reptile seemed to be staring accusingly at him. To the top floor, the sleeping area, bedrooms laid out pristine, ready and deserted. *They must have needed an army of servants to manage all this in the old days.*

He finished up on the top floor at the end of a corridor running to the rear of the building. He should surely have been looking at a window with a view over the lake or simply a continuation of the varnished panelling. Not another door. He opened it to a spiral staircase. *An attic?* In here it was dusty, be-strung with cobwebs. Every other room in the house was spotless. Nobody cleaned here. *Because no-one ever comes in here, so why has the dust on the stairs been disturbed?*

He trod carefully, avoiding the foot-marks already there. It was, indeed, the attic. No-one had been here for a long time. Trunks, boxes and tea-chests lined the full depth of the roof space, every inch covered in dust and spiders' webs, the floor littered with dead flies and bees and wasps which had wandered in forever. Old furniture stuffed in gaps. Framed paintings leaning here and there. Centuries of families storing away items for which they had no further use, for which they had no space, superseded items, things they wanted to hide. The secret history of the building and its ruling families, hundreds of years of lives and of childhoods, squirreled away here in case they were ever wanted anew. And someone had wanted something.

*   *   *

## TWENTY-TWO

She was on the chair. An old, old-fashioned wing-back armchair. The fabric had once been damson red, ripe as fresh blood, but age and decades in the shadows had drained life from the colour; it was stained and threadbare, stuffing oozing from every seam, here and there exposing the bones of the wooden skeleton within. Spores of dust drifted through the shafts of sunlight jabbing into the attic and settled on the floorboards, on the chair, her dress, her hands, her face. She didn't care. Lady Catherine Melinda Ketteridge Montagu no longer gave a damn about anything.

Her posture was as upright in death as it had been in life, her forearms resting on the sides of the chair, her feet firmly on the floor. Her eyes were closed, her features calm. She might have been dozing were it not for the lack of breathing. Shobnall leaned in and felt for a pulse, stepped back. *Had to be certain, Melinda.* A summer dress covered with purple and red flowers that somehow blended contritely into the sombre scene. Beside her, an inverted cardboard box with an empty glass, smudged with lipstick and, on the floor, a handbag. He edged closer again, gingerly lifted a forearm. *Stiff alright, she could have been here most of the day.* Leaning over, he saw, in the gap between her thigh and the arm of the chair - *it must have rolled off* – lying supine, arms and legs pointing straight up in the air, black eyes wide and expressionless, a child's teddy bear.

Shobnall resisted the urge to touch it. Or anything else. *Leave it for Joe Short, the DI isn't going to want anybody else on this.* He walked the length of the attic and back, skirting the smudges betokening footsteps, presumably hers. Chests, boxes and cases, secured and placed in line except for one. A brown leather trunk, the sort that comes with clasps and a pair of encircling leather belts. It had been pulled out of position and lay open, its contents spilled in all directions. Toys. Dolls of every size, all girls as far as he could see. Stuffed toys in the shape of animals. A carved wooden horse. Ornaments. Imitation jewelry, coloured beads, packs of cards, rubber balls, picture books. *A childhood left behind, a girl's childhood.*

He returned to the chair and studied Melinda's body. He rotated slowly, concentrating. *I can see my footsteps, I can see hers.* He was happy to wait on Joe Short but he couldn't for the life of him see, in this secluded and self-contained space, any evidence of foul play. Nor any clue as to why she had done it.

He made his way back to the entrance lobby and the telephone. "Cyril, put me through to the DI, would you, whatever he's doing?" Cyril Hendry heard the tone and asked no questions. After he replaced the handset, the strangest sensation arose in him. His mind released a scene from a past Remembrance Day, a time when the family

137

had sheltered in the old, shattered cathedral as a choir of monks solemnly intoned Gregorian chants. He had been a youth and indelibly touched by the loss and acceptance and resolution enshrined in the sound. He felt the same mix of absence and certainty now.

He went out to the top of the steps. Albert Haynes was staring at the Bentley. Even in this high summer he wore his tweed shooting jacket and a deerstalker. A shotgun under his arm, its breech broken. Shobnall hailed him sharply. "Mr Haynes! How many entrances to the house are there apart from this one?"

Haynes, like Cyril, caught the undertone of command. "Six. Seven if you count an ancient tunnel to the chapel."

*Didn't realise they had a chapel.* "How many are locked at the moment?"

"This is the only one that's open. I go in every morning, close up in the evening."

"Anyone else been in since you today?"

"Not so far as I know."

Shobnall could hear the curiosity in the man's voice, ignored it. "Do you have the keys to the house?" Haynes licked his lips, selected a key ring from several clipped to his belt. "Let me have those, please." Haynes walked over to the steps and tossed the keys up. "Thank you." There were two keys. It was obvious which he needed.

Haynes watched Shobnall swing the big door shut and lock it. He watched as Shobnall slipped the keys into his own jacket pocket and turned to face him again. He looked at the Bentley, then back at Shobnall. He took a deep breath, turned on his heel and marched off in the direction of the sawmill, the workers cottages and his own house. Shobnall stood until the figure vanished among the trees. He sat on the top step, made himself as comfortable as possible. *It shouldn't take too long.* He settled down to wait for the circus.

* * *

At the family's request, HQ pulled down the publicity shutters. All the press knew was 'a woman's body found near Wychnor, police enquiries continuing' and a lot of stonewalling until interest faded. Word circulated locally, however, and it was like having someone proficient – Henry Cooper, say - deliver a blow to Burton's collective solar plexus. Individuals and organisations struggled for breath and for agency, unable

138

to comprehend. A woman. A lady. Not young but not old, either. Unmarried. A life cut short. Unfulfilled. By her own hand. Here. In our Staffordshire. Just down the road, in fact. And what's all that about a teddy-bear? Many of Shobnall's colleagues had been touched by Wychnor and Lady Melinda; the mood in the station ranged from sombre to depressed and no-one was exhibiting enthusiasm for anything. The DI cancelled a Monday meeting and no-one said a dickey-bird. The profanity of a suicide can do this. Some, however, were immune to the gloom.

"Mummy! Can we play in the garden? Please, mummy."

The adults looked at the children. Josephine to the fore as spokesperson. *Wonder how I'd feel if she grew up to be a trades union steward.* Behind Jo, keenly attentive, cousins Paul Victor and his sister Kate. Alice, one hand clutching PV's pullover, was staring about as though she had already forgotten their mission. As the silence lengthened, the rest of the adults joined the children in looking to mummy. Elaine was up to the challenge. "Do you promise to be careful and not damage grandfather's plants?"

"Yes, mummy."

"Will you and PV look after Kate and Alice?"

"Yes, mummy, we will. Won't we?" She looked round at PV, who nodded vigorously.

"Then yes, you may play in the garden but make sure —" The audience had already departed in a rush of whoops and whirring arms and legs. Alice's sense of purpose had been restored.

They left behind a deal of chortling. James resumed his sommelier duties, passing a sweet sherry to Helen, enthroned in her favourite armchair, Alan and Elaine on a sofa to one side, Alan's brother, Neil, and his wife, Catherine, on the other. The queen finished laughing. "She has such a way with her, always the one in the lead."

"I do wonder," said Catherine. "If PV has worked out that the female of the species can be more persuasive."

James was still distributing drinks. "You mean, behind any successful woman....."

Neil grunted. "Wait until Kate and Alice get going. With all four of them at it, we won't stand a chance."

"Well," rejoined Helen. "I see four bright children who are a credit to their parents. We're very lucky to have them." She raised her glass. The others followed suit.

Conversation inevitably turned to Lady Melinda. They had all heard the rumours and hearsay. They all wanted the inside story. "No question." Shobnall spoke quietly but authoritatively. "Our top forensics man went over the whole place. Nothing untoward. She went up there and swallowed a pharmacy-ful of tablets. The autopsy said barbiturates, Librium and Valium, more than enough to put her to sleep. Washed down with an expensive malt. She must have poured herself a generous shot, screwed the cap back on the flask and put it back in her bag before she got on with it."

"It's so desperately sad." Catherine's expression was woeful. Neil patted her shoulder.

"That's what everyone feels, Catherine." Shobnall resumed. "Melinda didn't necessarily go out of her way to be friendly towards people but you can't help but be saddened that she was able to sit there like that....."

James was replenishing glasses. "With all hope gone. She must have been dreadfully unhappy."

"We'll never know," said Shobnall. "The coroner's verdict is on the record. Her body is to be flown back to Switzerland for burial. It may have gone already."

Neil Shobnall, his arm around his wife's shoulders, had been watching his younger brother, listening to his words and taking in the way in which they were delivered. *Was a time he'd have been backward about coming forward about having his work the centre of family attention. Now he's self-assured, more confident, in charge. Yes, my little brother's in charge.*

They were assembled in Winshill, in the house they all regarded as the family home and the mood was subdued, not only because of Melinda's suicide. Each Remembrance Day since the war, the family had sought to join what amounted to a pilgrimage to Coventry where they would together honour the memory of Shobnall's parents. Vic and Josie Shobnall had perished as the Luftwaffe turned the city into a fireball. Some years, family responsibilities or work requirements reduced the party. This year, next week, 11 November fell on a Monday. Shobnall had used up all available favours and couldn't get away; Neil's presence had been demanded at negotiations with the car workers unions. It would be left to Helen and James to represent them all. The children, naturally, were relatively unaffected but for the adults it was impossible to escape the sense of letting others down.

James, as host today and clan chief, took it upon himself to lift the mood. Which, axiomatically, meant Frank Sinatra on the radiogram and a notably elegant dance involving James and wee Josephine, who demonstrated a natural rhythm as she swayed in tune with Ol' Blue Eyes. With PV and Kate cuddling Alice in a ring, there was only one way it could end. Laughter. A peal that followed the guests as they departed for their various homes.

*  *  *

Jo and Alice were too excited to settle into bed swiftly but, at last, the house was silent. Alan and Elaine relaxed in the kitchen. Mugs of chocolate. "Darling," said Elaine. "You're not too upset about missing the trip to Coventry, are you?"

Shobnall met her eyes. "No. Maybe. Well, yes and no. It's become such a family ritual.....but it's only one day in the year. Memories last forever. Anyway, it's only this year. I'll make a point of fixing it next time. There are more important matters than a drive to Coventry."

Elaine held his gaze. "Good. While we're on bleak things, I don't like to mention Melinda again. Her name puts a dampener on things. Nothing to do with the person. It's what she did. What she obviously felt she had to do."

"Like she felt she had no alternative."

"Exactly!" Elaine frowned. "What does it mean for your investigation?"

"I'm not sure. There was a time when I thought Melinda and the Diamond was a story all on its own, nothing at all to do with the murder at Wychnor. Or Gary's death, for that matter."

"Now you think differently?"

Shobnall blew his wife a kiss across the table. "You should be the detective. You and Gordon. He always thought they were connected. Yup. Now I think the threads are related. Trouble is, I can't fathom how. I don't know enough about Melinda."

"Why don't you talk to Esmée Worthington?"

Shobnall scrutinised the chocolate scum in the bottom of his mug. "What makes you suggest that?"

Elaine swept up the mugs and headed for the sink. "She knows these people. She's a very intelligent woman with her feet on the ground and she's outside the Force so she gives you a different view. Which is what you need." She rinsed the mugs. "Maybe it is a woman thing. We can tell."

"Tell what?"

Elaine rested the mugs on the drainer. "She wants you to ask her what she thinks."

\* \* \*

# TWENTY-THREE

He wasn't sure how to handle it if the Old Man proved sticky. *Plan B then.* Cyril Hendry was in his customary position, leaning on the public counter. The general view was that his presence deterred the public from entering and thus damped down the figures for reported crime. Shobnall had long ago decided that Cyril connected through the counter to the very fabric of the building and was able to monitor what everyone was up to. *The only way to account for his foreknowledge.* He opened with the weather and moved on to families but he took too long. Wariness shaded Cyril's eyes. *I've overdone the trivia.* "Something I can do for you, Alan?" Cyril knew exactly when chit-chat edged into the red.

"Sorry, Cyril, I should have come straight out with it. You know Mrs Worthington, don't you? Esmée?"

Cyril treated him to a lugubrious look. "One in a million. You want to talk to her?"

*How did he know that?* "Yes, Cyril, I need to talk to her about Lady Melinda." *Probably read the headlines printed on my forehead.*

"Smart move." Cyril scribbled. "Mrs Worthington's business number. Which is to say she's the only person who'll answer it." He winked. "No need to worry about George."

"Thanks, Cyril. Another one I owe you. I hope she'll be prepared to speak to me."

The station sergeant was re-connecting to the building. "Oh, she will, Alan. She likes you. But take my advice and don't say anything about it being National Hoover Week."

He could only stare. "You're pulling my leg, Cyril."

"Not a bit of it. The hunt is on for the Hoover Housewife of the Year. Mrs H is up for it but I can't see Mrs Worthington embracing that particular challenge."

\* \* \*

'She likes you.' That didn't help. The collywobbles kicked in as he entered Melbourne. He parked short of the house; he didn't want to be observed. He'd rehearsed his opening gambit during the journey but now it crumbled to incoherence in his head. Fully five minutes he sat there, trying to organise his thoughts, until he caught sight of his face in the rear-view mirror. *How ridiculous!* He climbed out, marched briskly up the garden path. He rapped the door-knocker and Mrs Worthington opened it and regarded him with that all-too-familiar expression. *The one that reads my mind.* "Come in, Alan. I know you'll smell George all over the place but do try and deal with that until we get into my little sanctum. Tea or coffee?"

It was an office and she was right; there was no trace of her husband. "Er, tea please, milk but no sugar."

"I'll be right back." A tidy desk at one end, black handset and high-backed swivel chair. A pair of angular but surprisingly comfortable modern armchairs at the other, a full wall of books – law, business, art, a shelf of Penguins, Braine, Sillitoe, Wain, Amis, they didn't mean anything to Shobnall. A large print on the wall that he recognised as Claude Monet's Water Lilies. He was admiring the print when Mrs Worthington returned.

"You like it?" She set about the teapot.

"Yes, I do. I've only seen photographs of it in magazines."

"Frankie brought it back from Paris for me. Terribly sweet of her. It would be better hung in a larger space but I wanted it in *my* room!" By the second cup, his nerves had vanished. It was 'Esmée' without a shred of embarrassment. "You wanted to talk about Melinda?"

"Yes. Everyone is stunned by her death. Any suicide is hard to grasp but when it's someone you thought had everything, it's impossible."

"Nonetheless, Alan, there will be some rationale underpinning the destructive urge."

Shobnall paused. "I found her. It didn't look like impulse. It looked.....very orderly. As if she was following a schedule she had thought through to the last detail."

"That would have been very much in character."

"That's the impression I'm getting. We know she was handling the loan of the Diamond. I'm working on the Wychnor case and I figured she only had a role in that because she owned the place. Then – did you know the group's tour manager was drowned? In London?"

"Yes. George said you weren't happy about it."

"No, I'm not. It's made me question what the manager of The Reapers is up to. And why Melinda was mixed up with him – and she was, in some way. I believe she was personally involved with someone in the Indian delegation. All this is going on and then she kills herself. It gets murkier and murkier."

"How can I help, Alan?"

"I've been trying to understand the people involved, what makes them tick, how they relate. Melinda has a bigger role than I thought but she's a total blank to me. I only met her once, in circumstances you could hardly describe as normal. I need to understand what might have been going on in her head."

Esmée Worthington pondered. "You will have spoken with Reuben Salt. Reuben knows the Needwoods. He will have told you that Melinda was close to her father?" Shobnall nodded. "And that she inspires tremendous loyalty in her people?" Another nod. "Neither of these qualities would suggest themselves upon encountering Melinda for the first time."

Shobnall smiled ruefully. "True. First meetings with her could be rough."

"Indeed. She was a more complicated, more subtle, deeper personality than many gave her credit for. I have seen her in action regularly in recent years. We have been co-directors of several organisations, including a significant charity and a national distribution firm."

"TransUK Haulage."

"You've done your homework. Melinda was effectively the owner but she did not in any way act dictatorially. I would say she was a model of sound governance – a rarity these days, I can tell you. Her language could be direct but it was always to the point. She was a far better listener than the average board director. Perceptive. Thoughtful. And she delivered. I have wondered why, after so long, the Needwoods allowed the Diamond to go on show but, having so decided, I can see why they put Melinda in charge."

"This sounds like a woman in control, not one approaching the end of her tether."

"Something changed. I saw Melinda twice while we were in London. Most of the time she was off at the exhibition or on other business but we had time for a coffee once and an aperitif another time. I will confess that I was concerned."

"About what?"

"She was hardly the same woman. The first time I thought she was distracted, most unlike her but not so significant. The second time I thought she looked dreadful. You can do a lot with make-up but it's hard for one middle-aged woman to fool another. She looked like she wasn't getting enough sleep. She was having to work too hard on her eyes. She was nervous, couldn't keep her hands still and she'd developed a tic in a cheek muscle. She kept looking around the way people do when they're expecting someone they don't want to meet. She had three drinks to my one. Hers hardly touched the sides, as they say."

"But she didn't want to talk to you about whatever might have been bothering her."

Esmée sighed. "She did not. I tried but she locked me out. She seemed, I'm not sure, haunted? No. Stretched. Stretched to the point of tearing. Given what has happened since, I may be remembering too starkly but she seemed a woman being torn apart."

"By what? Who?"

"The answer to that must lie somewhere in the bundle of issues you have identified – the Diamond negotiations, the pop music business, possibly an affair. And yet, even taken together, they do not seem sufficient to overwhelm such a woman. Are we missing something?"

\* \* \*

It was only a couple of days after Remembrance Day and the missed trip to Coventry but the comfort of family and friends was more than enough to assuage Shobnall's mix of regret and longing. Josephine and Alice were huddled by the electric fire arranging Dolly and Mr Teddy at a miniature tea-table. Corky was lying back in an armchair, lips pursed in thought, watching Jo let her sister take the lead in pouring imaginary tea; he was thinking 'she knows it's not real'. Elaine on the sofa, bent forward, hugging her knees, examining the carpet. Shobnall was at the window; he had just drawn the curtains against a darkening evening. Not a word. Alice brushed against Mr Teddy; he started to slide and Corky tensed but Jo was fast. Alice never noticed.

Elaine eased upright. "I never met her but I feel the loss. When you discussed her before she sounded like another one of those toffee-nosed rich people. Suddenly she's more of a tragic heroine."

"More Desdemona than Juliet, I think," offered Corky.

"Goodness, Corky," exclaimed Elaine. "I had no idea you were a Shakespeare scholar."

Corky chuckled. "I wouldn't go that far but I do like my Bard. This feels like Othello; there are malicious machinations in play and Melinda has proved the victim."

Shobnall turned. "You're right. And from what Esmée Worthington had to say, it seems these machinations came into in play relatively recently. I wonder what Gordon would have to say."

"Huh!" Corky snorted. "He'd remind us he said Melinda, the Diamond and the Wychnor malarkey were connected somehow and that the pop group's manager was involved. Where is he, by the way?"

"Bowling," replied Shobnall. "He and Lennie Morton are in the semi-finals of some cup or other."

Elaine knelt beside her daughters. "Bedtime." The three females put Dolly and Teddy to rest in their box along with the tea things. Jo and Alice did the round of goodnight kisses and Elaine shepherded them upstairs.

"Jolly good fun, this godparent business," said Corky. "I get all the joy and none of the chores."

"Depends." Shobnall turned the fire down. "I recall some elephant rides in the hallway not so long ago."

"Ah! *Few* of the chores then. But what do you intend to do next on this, whatever you call it, this Wychnor-Diamond-Melinda case?"

"I need a talk with Reuben Salt. Then I'm going to wait. Sooner or later, America is going to deliver two things. Pinkertons will provide information on the Wychnor vicar and the manager of The Reapers and we'll get The Reapers back with Morgan Vetch and his sidekick. At which point I can ask some pointed questions."

147

Corky rose, ready to leave. "Well, things are a bit of a shambles over here currently what with Macmillan's resignation and the Tories wheeling out another toff to take over, this Lord Home. I'd like to see him calm things down. These mods and rockers are bad enough. They're now talking about 'Beatlemania'. Did you see the police had to use high-pressure hoses on fans the other night? Amazing. I can't see America producing anything to compare with our shenanigans."

Corky was serious. He had no way of knowing that, within the week, America would produce the news item of the century, overshadowing anything to do with pop music and political parties. Courtesy of Lee Harvey Oswald on a grassy knoll in Dallas.

\* \* \*

# TWENTY-FOUR

Wychnor Hall with a pink dawn dissolving under the first rays of wan autumn sunshine. Tranquillity. A mid-November stillness heralding the advance of winter. The trees, the chestnut sycamore and poplar, are skeletal. Traces of gold and russet in the hedgerows. A veneer of frost everywhere. Rime clouds the windows. The Anglia trundles onto the gravel, draws up on the far side, facing the building. A limpid moon is reluctant to depart. *Feels unnatural seeing sun and moon together, hope that's not an omen.* The ivy has shrivelled with the season, its wiry tendrils coiled about the brickwork. The Big House appears.....withdrawn, hesitant, self-protective, like a woman of a certain age shying from a stranger, gathering about her the garments she knows constitute an inadequate defence.

"What are we doing here, Alan?"

"You keep asking me that, Eddie, and I keep giving you the same answer. I don't know. The DI said I should be here by 06.30 and I could bring you if I wanted. When the DI gives you that sort of choice, he means *do it*! Let's check the house."

"Let's wait here. It's freezing out there."

Shobnall opens his door. "Haynes looks after the place. He'll have had the heating on. Like that word? Heating?"

Eddie opens his door and shivers. "It's probably locked."

"I've got the keys I took from Haynes when I found her. Come on."

Shobnall is right; the air inside is warm, relatively; neither man sheds coat, scarf or gloves. The day is brightening and from the hallway they can monitor incoming traffic. They are not anticipating an approach by water. As the church clock registers the half-hour, another vehicle emerges from the trees. A black police car. The driver stops close to the steps. Passengers who don't walk unnecessary distances. Driver and front passenger spring out, uniformed constables, move smartly to open the rear doors. Stand to attention.

"Servants Division," mutters Eddie.

"We better back them up," says Shobnall, opening the door.

On the far side, the DI clambers out, sees them across the car roof, flutters a hand surreptitiously. The nearside passenger has to duck his head and manoeuvre his legs in order to exit, stands and looks around.

"Bloody hell!" Eddie hisses. "It's bloody Jessop."

"Eddie!" Shobnall keeps his voice down but he, too, is nervous. *The Chief Constable at this time of day?*

The DI is swaddled in a bulky overcoat and woollen scarf; Esmée won't risk his catching cold. Ian Jessop, on the other hand, makes do with uniform and cap. There are those on the force who argue he has no need of warmth since he has been of 'the undead' for years. Jessop is aware of these sentiments. He is happy to allow them currency. "First time I've seen him in the flesh," whispers Eddie. "If it is flesh."

"Shut up," says Shobnall. "He is gaunt, isn't he? Looks more like a priest than a policeman."

The DI and the Chief Constable move towards the steps. Shobnall and Eddie both take a deep breath. All four turn their gaze as a third vehicle crunches onto the gravel. Shobnall knows it. The new arrival circles and stops head-to-head with the police black. *I don't believe it!* He and Eddie are stock-still at the top of the steps in front of the entrance. The DI and Jessop are motionless but relaxed; they know more. The uniformed constables are content to have been discarded.

Reuben Salt, resplendent in dark green tweed, climbs out from behind the wheel of the Humber, waves expansively and bellows "Morning everyone!" No one replies. Mr Salt walks round to the passenger door, opens it. No-one sees his conspiratorial wink to whomever is within.

Mr Salt's passenger is neither tall nor short. Stocky would be a good word. Most people stood beside Mr Salt would be shorter but this man doesn't look *small*. He is of that ilk that is larger on the inside and imposes that scale on the outside world. A top dresser, immaculate in a dark gray three-piece, gold watch chain across the waistcoat. Ramrod straight. A stick but his tread is firm. *It has to be.* Mr Salt and his companion reach Jessop and Worthington. Hands are shaken. They can hear Salt. "Gentlemen, thank you for coming. We apologise for any inconvenience but the situation is, you will agree, unusual. Allow me to introduce my long-time sparring partner and friend, Billy, more commonly known as Lord Needwood."

'Oh bugger,' says Eddie, but only in his head as Salt guides Lord Needwood past the senior officers and up the steps. "Billy, this is Detective Sergeant Alan Shobnall. And Detective Constable Edward Mustard." *Oh Reuben, nobody, but nobody, calls him Edward.*

\*  \*  \*

George Worthington *knew* the Chief Constable wasn't happy. Jessop took most events in his stride but not this one. It wasn't the mixing of police and civilians, only partly the presence of extreme wealth and high nobility. Mainly it was the way the terms laid down by Lord Needwood upset protocol. *That* shifted the ground. Reuben Salt wasn't helping, frankly, waltzing his lordship up the steps to meet Shobnall and Mustard without properly passing the time of day with the man at the top of their pyramid. He sighed inwardly. *I suppose Salt is looking after his pal, leaving yours truly in the exclusive and unenviable company of the aforementioned Chief Constable.* He saw no point in seeking to placate Jessop. It would only make the man grind his teeth harder. He concentrated on keeping step, beside but half a pace behind his chief. At least he had slipped Shobnall the fax.

Inside, Salt seemed to regain a sense of proportion, wheeling Needwood toward Jessop. Worthington quietly separated himself from the group, shifted back to the door. *As close as I can be to the escape route.* He'd forgotten how tall Salt was; Jessop usually had several inches over anyone but he and Salt were level eye-to-eye, locked in a quiet but, apparently and hopefully, amicable dialogue.

Needwood had turned away. Worthington wondered if it was possible to buy a suit like that anywhere in Britain. Savile Row? Maybe but maybe not. The old boy didn't look in his eighties. He radiated assurance. A man who had spent his life getting what he wanted. Aside, that is - if what he had heard was true - from Bruntons Brewery. Worthington couldn't help smiling at the notion. Needwood had button-holed Shobnall. Mustard had drifted into the background somewhere. Worthington was curious about the conversation between Salt and Jessop; it was impossible to tell if they were discussing affairs of state or swapping jokes. Out of the corner of his eye he saw Needwood and Shobnall starting up the stairs. He glanced at Jessop, found the look returned. His chief *really* wasn't happy. In such situations it was usually the next available in seniority who took the flak. Precisely the moment for Salt to produce his rabbit. From somewhere in that capacious tweed suit, the man conjured a pewter flask and a handful of shot glasses.

\*  \*  \*

Eddie Mustard wanted to be somewhere else. *Anywhere* else. Jessop *and* a bloody nob! Who must be a top man given how he's treating Jessop like he's any old copper on the beat. And that suit! He'd considered staying outside, cold as it was, but the nob had insisted on shaking his hand and somehow he was inside. Seemed a decent cove, the nob, father of the woman who topped herself upstairs. To be fair, he decided, the old chap's behaving with a lot of dignity.

Still, he hated being there. Bit by bit, he sidled away from the rest. One reason why he'd never make a copper long-term, he knew that. The hierarchies! It was bearable in the station but that was down to the DI. He ran it like a big family. He looked at Jessop. Buttons shining, trouser creases razor-edged, shoes gleaming. Eddie's tie rarely covered his top button. Without thinking, he rubbed the toes of his shoes on his calves. *Not to worry, a couple more qualifications and then we'll see!*

The others were, one way or another, absorbed in each other. Eddie made it to the far side of the staircase, screened by the newel post but with a reasonable field of vision. He saw the DI ease to the sanctuary of the doorway, sensed him relaxing. He saw the brewer, Salt, occupying Jessop's attention and the nob moving towards Shobnall, like it had been choreographed. He saw the look that flashed between the DI and Jessop. He'd missed something. Then the nob came into view with Alan and they mounted the stairs. Alan had said the nob was over eighty but he was sprightly enough. He craned his neck to keep them in sight but heard his name being called. Salt was extending a hand, proffering a glass of what looked very much like Scotch. Jessop and the DI were already holding glasses. The DI's expression said it was extremely palatable. Eddie didn't fancy the close-quarters stuff but it wasn't that warm in here, was it? Besides, be rude to refuse, wouldn't it?

\* \* \*

152

# TWENTY-FIVE

The old boy was easily agile enough for the winding stairs to the attic. As far as Shobnall could see, the stick was a prop, part of the image. *A nice manner, not pushy or dismissive.* He'd said 'young man, I'd like to see where you found her.' Not much had been moved; the chair, the upturned box, now without glass – Joe Short had taken that. The teddy was here, propped in a sitting position. The main difference was the absence of the body.

Lord Needwood looked around for a moment. "She was in the chair."

"With the toy. There was a glass on the box, she'd filled it from a flask. Her handbag was beside the chair."

Needwood tested the nearest packing chest, found it stable and settled himself, half-sitting, half-leaning, placed his stick before him, both hands on it. "Tell me, what do *you* think about it?"

*I'm not a hundred per cent sure what he means.* "This must be very painful, sir, but I have no doubt that she committed suicide. I could see no sign anything suspicious. The forensics officer is one of our best ; if there were anything untoward he'd have found it." Needwood said nothing. "And I think it's terribly sad." *He's going to have to help me here.* "Do you, sir, do you have questions about her death?"

Needwood met Shobnall's gaze head-on. "My friend, Reuben Salt, tells me that you are unusually persistent."

*Thanks, Reuben.* "It rather goes with the job, sir, but I don't like giving up early."

Needwood nodded, as if Shobnall had confirmed something significant. "Your Detective Inspector, Worthington, has given me to understand that *you* may have questions about Melinda and her death."

"That's a broader question, sir."

Needwood smiled. "Reuben and Worthington agreed you are no pushover. I do not question Melinda's suicide. I have questions, shall we say, *around* her death, beginning with 'why?' I would like to know what you think."

Shobnall stared. *Can I trust him or should I play it by the book?* "Would it be possible, sir, to reach an accommodation? If I share my thoughts with you, will you then tell me what Melinda was doing for you with the Diamond?"

There, in the dusty attic his daughter had chosen for her last moments on earth, Lord Needwood grinned, a genuine grin with a flash of white teeth and laughter lines about his eyes. He rapped his stick on the boards. "Young man, we have a deal."

*In for a penny, in for a pound.* He laid out the story as far as he had so far discerned it. Not the whole story, of course; he held back names, skipped over one or two incidents. "A young man, a member of a pop group, drowned in the lake behind this house. I believe it was murder and I am close to being able to prove it. Subsequently, the same pop group's roadie drowned in London. I'm suspicious about that, too, but evidence is in short supply. The management of this group is up to something. It may well be drugs. These people are connected with major gangs in London. This matters because Melinda had become involved with these people."

"Do you know how?"

"No, sir, I don't. Whatever was going on there was happening by the time I came on the scene. The first time I saw her was in this house the night of the drowning. The parties knew each other. The relationship included the Diamond but there was more to it than that. There was also something going on between Melinda and the Indian delegation to the exhibition. I don't want to offend....."

"The truth has never scared me, young man!"

"There was something personal between Melinda and a member of that delegation. There also came a point when Melinda withdrew the protection she had sought from us and those Indian guards took over." He paused.

Needwood was taking in every word. "Why do you consider that important?"

"My gut tells me it stemmed from the spot she found herself in. I don't have a clearer answer. On that first occasion, downstairs, I met an intelligent, balanced woman who was very much in control. She might have been thrown momentarily by the death –"

"Why was she here, do you think?"

"Oh, to collect the Diamond. We'd advised her of the spate of jewel robberies in London and she was using her own networks to smuggle it around until it was time for it to go to the museum. It all seemed like a bit of a game back then. More recently she had become agitated. People who knew her say she was showing signs of distress. I think your daughter was subject to unyielding pressures, opposing pressures that couldn't be resolved, a situation so unanswerable as to drive her up here." He fell silent.

Needwood rolled the head of his stick between the palms of his hands. "Do you mind if I call you 'Alan'? I don't feel I can properly refer to the man who found my daughter dead as 'young man'."

"Of course not, sir."

"Thank you. The Diamond has a clouded history. I presume you know?" Shobnall's nodded. "I have never been happy with its presence in our vaults. Some have wondered why I chose to allow it to feature in the exhibition. You see, ever since independence, India has wanted it back, restored to the temple from whence it was stolen. Not only would that be a major signal of the strength of the new nation, it would coincidentally cement the position of the current Indian government in a province on which its grip is not secure. Then we have a second issue. Our two governments are wrangling over the ownership of a range of assets - tea plantations, textile mills and the like. Britain wants India to accept ownership by British interests. India is not playing ball. There was a deal to be done and releasing the Diamond to public view helped focus minds."

"And you, sir, how would you benefit from the deal?"

Needwood grinned again. "You mean aside from proving myself a jolly good chap all round? Reuben did tell me you caught on fast. One of those plantations is mine but that is nothing. It's simple, Alan. India regains the Diamond. India is happy and settles on British ownership of the outstanding assets. Thus Britain is happy. So happy and grateful that it rewards me by waiving tax laws and regulations and allowing me to live out howsoever many years are left to me in this country. Perhaps here at Wychnor Hall."

The two men faced each other. One squatting against a tea-chest, the other standing by the armchair. One waiting, the other going through the mental gears. "I see. Melinda was looking after the Diamond. That other business occupying her during the exhibition, she was haggling with HMG. She was negotiating your get-out-of-jail card."

"Nicely put."

"Except the deal was at risk. The relationship with India was under threat, partly because of her liaison with one of them. Publicity around that could have been explosive. The transfer to India is in jeopardy, creating a scenario in which the governments remain at loggerheads and you don't get to come home. And it's Melinda's fault." Shobnall walked back and forth across the width of the attic. "Or maybe not her fault."

"Meaning?" Needwood's tone was peremptory.

"That wasn't enough to light a fuse. Neither Melinda nor her – whatever we call him – want publicity. Back to the pop group. Their manager is a villain for whom blackmail is a standard currency. Melinda had become involved with him in some way. Suppose he had uncovered her liaison and was holding it over her."

Needwood stood slowly, stretched his spine, strode away between the rows of storage. *That really is some suit he's wearing, I've never seen a fabric so rich.* He walked back. "A personal  liaison such as you describe would not have been out of character for Melinda. Yet for your speculation to hold water, we require a better understanding of the relationship between Melinda and your villain. Why would he apply pressure? What did he want in return?"

"I don't know." Shobnall rolled his neck to ease the tension. His companion waited. "Lord Needwood. There is no way I can leave this case alone. I'm close to making one murder charge stick but there is more to it. I'm going to get to the truth of what was going on."

"I *want* you to get to the bottom of it. I loved Melinda. I loved her mother deeply. Vanessa was my second wife and I fancied I had made the choice of a lifetime. Vanessa's final years were terribly troubled and I suppose I have never completely got over that period. Not many know this but Melinda was not my only child. She was the first of twins but her sister survived barely a fortnight. Vanessa took it mortally but one consequence was that Melinda and I grew very close." He stared at the chair. "And close to this place, this childhood home. She has left me physically but she lives on in here." He tapped his chest. "Who can be sure, Alan, whether or not there is a hereafter? If there is then it may not be too long before I join with her again. But I prefer to hedge my bets. I want the corporeal world dealt with. I want to know what and who drove my daughter to her death. Find out for me, Alan, please."

"I'll do my best, sir."

Lord Needwood extended his hand. "I know you will. My card. Day or night, you may call any of these numbers if you need anything. Whoever answers will know you. Is there anything I can help with immediately?"

Shobnall was taken aback by all this but tried not to show it. "I don't think so, sir, although I may shortly be in need of accommodation in London."

"By this evening The Carillion will have set aside a complimentary room for whenever you need it. Anything else?"

*How quickly money can fix things, no, that's unfair, he's a man who gets things done.* "Not just now, sir." They stood in silence for a moment, both looking at the chair and the teddy bear.

"We stayed here during Melinda's childhood, Melinda and I at any rate. Vanessa took to spending time in Africa and then...." His voice tailed off. "That teddy bear went everywhere with her."

"There must be some natural affinity. My younger daughter dotes on Mister Teddy."

"Ah, little Alice." *Does he know ALL about me?* "We must look to our children. It is they who will inherit the earth. Our task is to bequeath a legacy that is worth inheriting. Now, we should join the others. I rather like your Detective Inspector and I fancy he will be fretting over whether Reuben's blend of malt and charm can hold down the Chief Constable's blood pressure." Shobnall couldn't help it. He burst out laughing.

\* \* \*

The assembly ended with a plangent coda. Mr Salt had held the ring with ease, having teased from the Chief Constable his secret passion for Richard Wagner; the pair argued the merits of this and that recording of The Ring cycle while Eddie and the DI eked out their scotch. With the return of Lord Needwood, the reverse-protocols of gratitude and preparation for departure began. Mr Salt went ahead to his Humber while Jessop accompanied the Duke. Except that word had, who knows how, been noised abroad. As the party broached the crisp morning, they found the driveway crowded. To the fore, Albert Haynes, in tweed jacket and wellington boots, clutching his cap. Behind him, the foreman and hands from the sawmill, the farmer and his

157

family and workers. The foresters. Others Shobnall couldn't identify. *Folk from the village, maybe.* All standing in silence, bare-headed, paying tribute to him. And to her.

Lord Needwood placed a staying arm on Jessop and strode across the gravel. Straight to Haynes, grasping his hand, clapping him on the shoulder, speaking briefly, moving on. Shobnall could see that Haynes was close to tears. Needwood went round every soul gathered there, shaking hands, offering a few words. He seemed to know every one of them. A sense of ritual hung in the air. Eddie nudged Shobnall, pointed. On the edge of the driveway, sheltered by the great chestnut, the Reverend Bullard. *Not quite joining the congregation, Needwood must have seen him but he's not getting a handshake.* Ultimately, it was done. The gathering dispersed, the cars moved slowly away until only Shobnall and Eddie remained.

"Our job to lock up," said Eddie. "Think we can cut it as janitors?"

"Jacks-of-all-trades, Eddie, that's us. Tell you what though, I can go home and see my daughters. That bloke can't."

"I know. The old boy isn't just a nob, is he? He's a parent who's lost a child."

* * *

158

# TWENTY-SIX

Gordon Crombie was impressed. "Not every day you hob-nob with one of the wealthiest men in the country. You should have asked him along for a pint."

"You know, I think he'd have come. He might have tried to buy the Devi."

"So long as he kept the landlady I wouldn't mind. Can I tell Councillor Goode my friends move in these circles? He'd go green!"

Shobnall smiled at the thought. "Gordon, Corky reminded me that ages ago you said Vetch was linked to the Diamond. How did you cotton on?"

Crombie launched a perfect smoke-ring up into The Devonshire's rafters. "It felt too odd for Vetch to have a hand in transporting the stone. That didn't fit with an aristocrat using her personal networks. In local government, we like things neat and tidy. When something doesn't fit a bell goes off."

*I felt a bit like that but heard no bell.* "You see the big picture while I'm assembling the facts. You're the Sherlock. I'm the plod, Lestrade."

Crombie grunted. "You're no Lestrade, Alan, that's for sure. And it isn't you who needs facts, it's your occupation that demands them. You're strong on intuition. It's what makes you such an effective detective." He stubbed out his cigarette. "You said Worthington slipped you a fax."

"He did." Shobnall pulled out a swatch of paper. "From Hank Walker, the Pinkerton chief the DI got friendly with at the British Museum." He spread the flimsies on the table. "An article from The Boston Globe. January 1955. Shortly before the Reverend Bullard returned to England and Wychnor. He was teaching at a college there. It seems there were financial irregularities in Bullard's department. Fingers were pointed and the mud stuck."

"There's normally a reason for the adhesion of mud."

"The claim was that Bullard had siphoned off funds to buy gifts for a lad singing in the local choir."

Crombie groaned. "Don't tell me. Under age. Evidence?"

Shobnall picked up a second sheet. "Not a lot. An extract from an FBI report. Repetition looks to have clinched it for the authorities. Bullard had spent time in Kenya. The FBI said there was a similar furore, funds missing from the mission, Bullard gifting a young boy. Matters were settled by the owner of a local coffee plantation."

"A pay-off, eh? I know. The Needwoods. Why would they dig Bullard out of a sleazy mess like that?"

"Because the then-Lady Needwood was out there. Vanessa. It's clear from his lordship that she suffered from depression. Sounds like she had some kind of breakdown, took to spending time out in Kenya where I think Bullard was able to help her in some way. Needwood felt in his debt, paid off the locals and dropped him into a chaplaincy on their Bermuda estates." The landlady was staring hard, willing them, the last customers, to leave. "When Boston found out there was a precedent, it got too hot."

"And Needwood helped again. No real choice this time."

Shobnall leaned back and, as he did so, looked straight at the landlady. *I think we are outstaying our welcome.* "When I chanced upon him in the vestry with those fancy robes, there was something off about his reaction. Our WPC said he made her skin crawl. Lennie found him odd - and there isn't a better nose than Lennie's. We all sensed something. It may help explain why Lord Needwood, out at Wychnor, attended to every one of his workers but made no move to go to Bullard. Then there's this."

He swivelled the Boston Globe flimsy towards Crombie. "Look at the photograph. The police arriving at the college to deal with a stand-off between Bullard and local residents." He moved his finger. "*That* is Bullard, shielded by college staff. And *this*" He indicated a face in the surrounding crowd, a face turned towards the camera. "*This* is Morgan Vetch, today manager of The Reapers."

"Oh-Ho! The plot thickens!" Crombie was oblivious to the light but insistent thrum of the landlady's fingers on the bar. "What's next?"

Shobnall stood. "Next, we are going to leave the pub giving mine hostess the best smiles we can muster. We may be treading close to the point of being barred."

\* \* \*

He walked Crombie back to the Town Hall. They didn't hang about. Winter was arriving: not yet out of November but already Scotland and the North-east were battling gales and blizzards. Along the South coast six counties were under water. Burton was merely cold but the sky was full of that pallid blue-white promising snow.

"I'm expecting more from Hank Walker, about Vetch. I'll wait. I need to understand Melinda's role. Another talk with Reuben. Dave Charteris is fixing for us to see this Indian prince. Then there's the vicar. I want to know how he plays in but I don't want to scare him off. Before all of that, it's a quiet afternoon and home on time! Lavinia will be there. The film buffs are at the New Empire in Swadlincote this afternoon. Lavinia likes tea with her god-daughters afterwards."

"She's such a sweetie. What's showing?"

"New Alfred Hitchcock thriller, Elaine said. 'Psycho'. Not a clever title for a piece of entertainment!"

Crombie turned away. "Grabs your attention, though. Say hello to them all!"

\* \* \*

Cyril was at the public desk. "Afternoon, Alan. Joe Short said to tell you he's here."

"Thanks, Cyril." *Has Joe come up with something? That's fast if he has.* He hurried upstairs, almost tripping over a mop and bucket in the corridor; he could hear Agnes' raised voice emanating from the ladies' toilet.

Joe was in the main office with Lennie, Gideon and Bob Saxby but he broke off at once and hustled Shobnall to the DS' office. "Sit down," he said. Shobnall sat. Rank had no bearing; they were in Joe's field of expertise. "My report." He laid a folder on the desk, flicked over typed pages to a set of photographs of a fingerprint, virtually complete. "I managed to lift this from the key, a right index. He must have held the key between thumb and index, probably easing it into the lock as quietly as possible." He rehearsed the motion. "Without gloves. Must be an idiot."

"Amazing job, Joe. Um, I don't want to push my luck....."

Joe laughed. "Yeah, we have a match. That print, that index finger and the bone, muscle and nerve that carry it around. They all belong to a chap name of Terry Carpenter, also known, the Met tell me, as 'Cutter' Carpenter."

\* \* \*

He was in a good mood when he got home. As expected, Lavinia was there, swathed in a pink-and-white number that made her look like a seaside rock confection. She, Josephine and Alice, accompanied by Dolly and Mr Teddy, were grouped on the living room carpet where Lavinia was tutoring in the finer points of afternoon tea. Elaine was sprawled on the sofa, looking totally relaxed. *Maybe 'Psycho' didn't live up to its name.* What he had not anticipated was the presence of Reuben Salt. As far as Shobnall could tell, one of Burton's most prominent brewers was currently in charge of the cake knife. Now Mr Salt sought to pass the responsibility to his sister. Not everyone was happy.

"Reuben! Where are you going?" Josephine was on her feet.

"I must speak with your father, my dear. Lavinia will be queen of cake."

"She can't," insisted Jo. "She's mistress of the teapot. She can't be everything." A short silence during which three of the four adults in the room conscientiously suppressed the urge to laugh; Lavinia clearly sided with Jo.

"Don't worry, darling." Elaine to the rescue. "I am qualified on cake."

Jo looked at her mother, then at Reuben Salt. "Thank you, mummy. Reuben, you may go and talk to daddy."

Mr Salt delivered a low bow. He and Shobnall withdrew to the kitchen. "Delightful," opined Mr Salt.

"You're good at it, Reuben. Now, what are you doing here? You haven't been to the cinema."

"No, I simply thought in the wake of developments you might want a further word about Wychnor and associated matters."

*Is he curious after chaperoning Lord Needwood or has Esmée been at him?* "As it happens, I would." Mr Salt rubbed his hands. "For goodness' sake, Reuben, I know you love being involved in these things." Mr Salt did his best to look sheepish. "Lord Needwood. He seems a decent old boy. He wants to know why Melinda took her own life and he's offering me virtually unlimited assistance. What do you think of that?"

"Billy is as straight as they come. He loved his daughter. His only daughter. Did he tell you....?"

"About the twin, yes, he was very gracious about it. That was when I started to like him."

"If I did not have complete faith in him I would not have helped him to private time with you at the Big House."

"I understand. Now, what about Melinda? Any further thoughts?"

Mr Salt's expression darkened. "That is more difficult. I am aware that you have spoken with Esmée Worthington. *I thought so.* "She told me nothing of your conversation; Esmée is always discreet but she and I had discussed Melinda previously. I know Esmée felt the woman to have come under severe pressure. Your chat with Billy will have given you an idea of the importance of the mission with which her father had entrusted her. According to Billy, everything was proceeding smoothly until a week or so before the exhibition opened."

Shobnall tutted. "I wish he'd told me that. The timing of events might be significant. What happened?"

"Nothing specific. Melinda wanted to keep the stone's whereabouts under the radar. She had arranged to transport it privately from Switzerland and hold it safe until it went on show. Then she went quiet. Telegrams and telephone calls ceased. Billy didn't worry. He had confidence in Melinda. Now he's looking back and wondering."

"The pressure wasn't coming from HMG," said Shobnall. "While there have been sporadic discussions with India over a number of years and we have no reason to suppose she couldn't handle them. There has to be a third party. Maybe, as the exhibition looms, Melinda finds out what this third party was up to."

A short silence before Mr Salt spoke again. "Alan, do you have an identity for this possible third party."

A longer silence. "Between you and me, Reuben, I suspect Morgan Vetch, the manager of The Reapers. I'm certain he was holding something over her. But I can't see why."

"Melinda was an extremely strong personality. I doubt her susceptibility to blackmail to the extent of suicide."

"Let's assume Melinda is armour-plated when it comes to being blackmailed on her own account. But what if someone had something over her that would harm her father?"

Mr Salt recoiled. "I see. Yes. If Melinda saw a threat to her father, that would be different. But what could this chap want from her?"

Shobnall placed a hand on the older man's arm. "That's what I need to find out. When I have more of an answer, we'll talk again. Meantime, let's get you back to the cake knife."

\* \* \*

## TWENTY-SEVEN

The local mood of sadness and regret was rudely subsumed beneath a nation's stunned disbelief at events in Dealey Plaza on 22 November. America assassinated its president, an act so shocking that the BBC interrupted its normal programming. Pictures of Kennedy slumped, bloodstained, in the back seat of his open-top flashed round the globe. Politicians scanned their itineraries nervously, checking their exposure. Many citizens, Shobnall's in-laws among them, winced under a blow to their faith in humanity. The Reapers' Dallas concert was cancelled.

The US threatened social meltdown until the sight of LBJ directing the aftermath reminded the world that there is always succession. Nonetheless, to many it seemed another nail in common decency when Jack Ruby stepped forward – in circumstances that Shobnall and his police colleagues thought over-casual given what had occurred a mere two days earlier – and shot dead the assassin, Lee Harvey Oswald. 'She Loves You' by the Beatles returned for a second stint at Number One.

*　*　*

Shobnall and Angela Bracewell worried about morale but found the troops in resilient mood. Nothing, but nothing, wobbled Cyril Hendry, of course, and nobody in the squadroom seemed remotely in need of a lift. Not as far as events in American were concerned anyway.

"You missed Eddie," said Lennie, picking up a newspaper as if it were infested. "He left this for you."

The Melody Maker. Eddie had ringed the main article. 'REAPERS GO GOLD IN FIRST WEEK'. *That's right, they planned to release the album over there, the stuff from Wychnor.* The album had barged straight to the top of the Billboard chart, outselling even The Beatles. Due for release in the UK next month. *Basher will benefit, he'll have played on those tracks.* Then he took it in. The album was entitled 'DROWNING'.

"That is sick!"

"Wait till you see the cover," said Lennie.

"People we have to deal with," said Bob Saxby through a mouthful of chocolate cake.

"Who is like unto the beast," said Gideon. "Revelations."

165

"Too many folk," muttered Lennie. "Notably in Dallas but life goes on. Our wine label merchants have moved into spirits. Better margins, I guess."

"How are they doing business?"

"Call at the back door or a stall at the market. They're canny, never attempt repeat business. We keep turning up labels but no leads. You getting anywhere with Lady Melinda and all that?"

Shobnall stared at his colleagues. "Yeah, I think I'm about to make some serious progress and if you lot don't need anything from me I'll set about it."

"Have a spangle before you go," said Gideon, proffering a pack.

"Thank you, Gideon." He popped one in his mouth and turned but Lennie stopped him.

"A moment, Alan. I don't want to spoil the taste of your sweet but, well, people go into politics they know trouble may come their way even if being assassinated is pretty rare. There's darker forces at work in the sewers we have to slosh around in. Remember that Manchester schoolgirl who went missing?"

"Yeah, you mentioned the moors up there, said you doubted they'd ever find her."

"Aye." Lennie sighed. "They haven't found a thing." He pulled a daily newspaper towards him. "This is yesterday's. Ashton-under-Lyme. The Lancashire police. Investigating the disappearance of twelve year-old John Kilbride. Twelve years! Same neck of the woods. I get the same shivers. They'll not find that lad either. There's something rotten abroad up there."

\*   \*   \*

He and Elaine lingered late over hot chocolate in the kitchen with The Home Service. The usual run of items but as the Lancashire Chief constable solemnly reported a blank on the missing boy, he couldn't help wincing. Elaine interpreted the expression acutely. "The one Lennie pointed out?"

"He reckons it's the second, after that lass in Gorton."

166

"Lennie's like one of those people who have a nose for wine or perfume. He can sniff out certain kinds of evil, the only word for it." She reached out and placed her hand over Shobnall's. Elaine had wanted to listen to the news on the radio. "The journalists are better. On the telly, they know they can be seen. They become more interested in themselves. Funny, isn't it, since we got a TV we've stopped listening to the radio. When The Radio Times comes in, I tend to pass over the radio and see what's on to watch."

"Well, the box is in the most comfortable room."

"I blame the Coronation. The country wanted to watch and television took root in the front room. Now, people spend too much time sitting in front of it, if you ask me."

"There's a teacher speaking. I don't think you can blame the Queen for what you consider a decline in standards. The availability of hire purchase probably has a lot more to do with it."

Elaine switched the radio off. "I'm sure you're right. Reuben has always held that Britain would grasp affluence with both hands. He *also* said we'd want to travel. When are we off to London?"

"Are you sure you can get time off from school? You're back to more than half-time now."

"I've already cleared it with the boss. No need to worry about the girls. Mum's on stand-by. Lavinia and Corky are champing at the bit."

"Well, I don't know –"

"Alan! It's a couple of nights. You and I haven't had that much time to ourselves since Jo was born."

*She is, of course, correct.* "Darling, it's just.....I don't want to seem to be taking advantage of Lord Needwood."

Elaine threw up her arms. "The poor man has lost his daughter and he wants to know why. He thinks you can help. You are going to London to see this Indian gentleman and you will stay at The Carillion. I will not get in the way. I have no intention of having you tut-tutting over my shoulder in Harrod's or Liberty's. But I hope that having me there, instead of a hundred miles away wondering how you are, would – " a coquettish smile "-ease your time down there?"

Shobnall surrendered with an intense inner delight.

*  *  *

"Oh my goodness!" Elaine set her handbag on the corner of a bed that looked wide enough to accommodate Sleeping Beauty and all seven dwarves. "I wasn't expecting this." She looked around. "Alan, where are you?"

Her husband appeared in one of the doorways leading off the bedroom. "I was, um, exploring."

They looked at each other and simultaneously folded into the giggles. "You said he'd arranged for a *room*, not half the building."

He put his arm around her shoulders. "The hotel refers to it as a suite. Come and have a look." The spaces were decorated and furnished in the same soft greys and creams and whites as the room Shobnall had occupied on his first visit.

Elaine was beside herself. "It's gorgeous. Can we come and live here?"

Shobnall let that pass. "Through there is a kind or reception room, more official. Have you seen this?" He took her back to the bedroom and opened another door. "What about that?"

Elaine eased past him. "Golly! I didn't know they made baths that size. And look at all those bottles of oils and scents." She fingered the containers. "We don't have anything we have to do tonight, do we? No-one to see?"

"No, this evening is our own. Tomorrow is shopping for you, work for me and dinner with Dave and Frankie at Paolo's. I thought we could just get a bite to eat in the hotel and have an early night. Why?"

"Well, I was thinking that this bath is easily big enough for two."

*  *  *

168

# TWENTY-EIGHT

Stanley the commissionaire had been delighted to see Shobnall again and doubly-delighted to meet Elaine, doffing his topper with aplomb and turning up the charm dial to eleven. As he watched the young couple checking in over at the reception desk, he thought 'I know you're here to help his lordship so all power to your elbow'. He knew that because Dave Charteris had enlisted him in securing the agreement of the Crown Prince of Saharanpur to an unofficial, secret meeting. The Crown Prince was already familiar with the clandestine routes in and out of The Carillion; Stanley would clear those routes when required. And so it was that they sat together in the suite's reception room, Shobnall, Charteris and the Prince, dressed crisply in what seemed to be his regular blue robes and white turban. Over here, a pot of English breakfast, over there a pot of something altogether more aromatic, its pungent scents hanging in the air.

"Please call me Vijay." The Prince's English was perfect, utterly free of accent. *No airs and graces, seems a decent sort.* "In the circumstances, I see no value in being formal."

"That suits us, Vijay." The Prince sipped his scented tea, cradled his cup in the palm of his hand. "We understand the diplomatic niceties of the situation and we appreciate your help. We would like this to be off-the-record. It's my investigation but I'm making my presence here as unofficial as I can. Lord Needwood is being a great help in that respect. Are you comfortable with this?"

The Prince nodded. "I must help. I have not had the pleasure of meeting Lord Needwood in person but I sent a card and received a most gracious handwritten reply. Like him, I wish to understand what drove Melinda to such extreme action and help him achieve some peace."

"Thank you. You knew Melinda's role in relation to the Diamond?"

"She explained it to me." He placed his cup on the occasional table beside him. "She was, as you say in your City of London, broking a deal. The Indian Government has been seeking the repatriation of the Diamond from the moment we secured independence. We must modernise our industry but we must also look to our heritage. Since I was appointed to the Ministry, I have been a party to the discussions when they have been active. Melinda and I became close friends." He paused, his face showing no change in expression. "No. Let us not beat about the bushes. We became *very* close friends and in the months preceding the exhibition, we entered into what you would call an affair." Dave Charteris coughed. "No need for embarrassment," continued the

Prince. "If we are to make progress then we must be honest. You will be aware that I am a married man?"

"Yes, Vijay," replied Shobnall. "And that you are married into the family of your Prime Minister."

The Prince smiled. "I need not labour the sensitivity of the situation. The plans for this exhibition have been a long time in the preparation. It was a surprise to us when suddenly the Diamond was on the table; our delegation would have been here anyway, for the political show, but now the stakes rose. Lord Needwood used the exhibition as a vehicle to say 'I am placing this Diamond within your sight. If you wish, you may take it home'. At a price. Melinda was responsible for negotiating that price."

Shobnall leaned forward. "Negotiating between who?"

"Between our two governments. We have been haggling over the legal ownership of a range of economic assets in my country. These assets are claimed by British interests. Ownership was not settled at independence, has still not been brought to a resolution. Lord Needwood was offering to return the Diamond in exchange for our agreement that those assets should remain in British hands. That is what, naturally, the British Government wants."

Dave Charteris had been listening carefully. "Why did 'e step in with that offer then?"

"Melinda told me that her father had never been content in his ownership of the Diamond. She said he had a soft heart and would have preferred to return it. He had no need of its monetary worth. But she said he was a complex man with an adamantine sense of business which would not allow him to release it *gratis*. Now he had a means of resolving his soft and hard selves."

Shobnall tried for casual. "So if Melinda clinched that deal, the governments would be satisfied – or at least as satisfied as might be possible in a trade like this – and Lord Needwood's personal conscience would be cleared?"

"Precisely. It would have been very satisfactory all round and Melinda would have emerged with great credit."

"And these negotiations were going on around the exhibition."

"That is correct. Lord Needwood had set a deadline. We had a fortnight to reach agreement, otherwise the Diamond was to be returned to the family vaults.

Negotiations went well but not fast enough. Melinda secured an extension from her father."

"I see. What else was Melinda doing in the vicinity of the exhibition?"

"What do you mean?" *Seems a straight reaction, not startled, not dissembling.*

"My colleagues were here for that first fortnight. We know that Melinda was away from the exhibition a lot. She can't have been dealing with the negotiations the whole time."

The Prince's gaze didn't waver. "She had much business to occupy her. The Needwoods are in the process of transferring certain of their assets. Perhaps I might mention the word 'tax'."

"Bit of a swearie word in this country," offered Charteris.

"Quite," said the Prince. "On top of all that, gentlemen." He glanced between them. "There had to be time for Melinda and me."

*You don't know about the deal between Needwood and HMG, do you? She kept that from you.* "Vijay, I need to ask a sensitive question. The day you and Melinda stood outside the rear of this hotel, arguing. What about?"

Now a flicker crossed the Prince's face. "How do you know about that?"

"I was there. Purely by chance. I could tell you were having a row but I couldn't make out any words."

The Prince nodded again. "I see. It was a dangerous thing to do. When I agreed to meet you, I feared that we might come to this. Whether or not I suffer for what I am about to say is up to you. We were lovers. They say love is blind. Maybe. *Lovers* are definitely blind. You think no-one can see. My religion does not smile on adultery. My Prime Minister would not have smiled either." He bowed his head. *This is hurting him.* "If the fact that Melinda and I had been lovers became public, the political consequences in India would have been seismic. We could have lost control in significant areas. My being crushed underfoot by Juggernaut would have been the least of it. My Government would have been forced to break off negotiations on the Diamond. The deal would have been dead." The Prince fell silent.

Shobnall spoke gently. "And on the rear steps of The Carillion?"

The Prince refocused with a visible effort. "We were continuing a discussion from more private premises." *Up in the penthouse.* "Melinda had confided to me that a third party knew of our relationship and was threatening to expose her. To expose *us*. We were being blackmailed."

"Vijay, I am sorry but this is one of the key areas in this case. Do you know the identity of this third party?"

"She would not say. Melinda hoarded information. She once spoke most disparagingly of 'that impudent colonial'." He spread his arms. "It was a term she might have used to refer to me, after all. I should not have considered it a compliment."

*Bingo! Stay calm.* "From what I have learned about Melinda and her family, I cannot see Melinda referring to you or any of your countrymen and women in that way. I have a better target for her insult - and no, I am not prepared to reveal a name. Vijay, we don't know what the blackmailer wanted from Melinda. Can you help us there?"

The prince looked blank. "She wouldn't tell me. What you saw in the service area of the hotel, out among the tanks of rotting rubbish, was a proud member of the Indian cabinet begging his lover to give this person what he wanted. All she would say was 'I can't'. She was shouting. There was something that for her meant more than all the harm that would be unleashed by exposure. I thought I knew her but it now seems I did not know her as well as I imagined. As well as I wished."

Shobnall caught Charteris' eye. Agreement flashed between them. *Poor guy.* "Vijay, we are grateful for the opportunity to talk with you. There is no question but that Melinda took her own life but her death is connected to other crimes. You have been very helpful in unravelling some of this. I see no reason why we should need to involve you further."

The Prince stood. "Gentlemen," said the Prince. "Please, as you say, get to the bottom of this. Greater beings will decide my fate. You must provide justice for Melinda and salvation for her father. In due course, I should like to know the result of your investigation."

* * *

Around this time, Fred Bull and Vern sailed into view once more. Late afternoon, an hour before knocking-off time. They'd been up all night, summoned in the small hours after a Ford Cortina went off the Swarkestone Bridge into a Trent swollen by a week's rain. Fred and Vern had to drag out all four – driver, passenger, vehicle and the dog in

172

the back seat. Now they were cleaning up and packing away, Fred returning kit and tackle to storage, Vern out on the slipway hosing down the inflatable. A dank November mist hung over the River Sow as it eddied sluggishly past. The big northerner was absorbed in his task. 'Cleanliness is next to godliness,' he thought. 'What my mother used to say. If there was a god, he wouldn't allow folk to take their pets to a lock-in, be unfit to drive and send a harmless animal to canine heaven'. He switched off the water, lugged the inflatable inside and positioned it to drain, went to join his mate in the partitioned area at the front of their unit. 'The office' they called it.

"Pass us the log-book, Vern, would you? It's on the shelf there. Better write this up while we've a moment."

"Shame about that dog, Fred." Vern reached for the book. His voice was doleful.

"I know," said Fred. There was nothing to be done when Vern went mournful, just make sympathetic noises. As Vern passed the log-book over, a half-sheet of paper fluttered to the floor. Fred bent. "Oh bugger!"

Vern knew that tone. "What have we missed, Fred?"

Fred smiled to himself; that was Vern, always ready to take a share in anything they got wrong. "My fault, Vern. Message from Alan Shobnall. I forgot all about it. He wanted us to collect a dinghy abandoned at Fradley Junction."

Vern stood up. "We better go now then."

Fred looked out at the dark and misty evening, more rain in the offing. "As ever in these situations, Vern, you are absolutely right. Come on. We can shove it in the back of the Land Rover. No need for the trailer."

*   *   *

They arrived at the Junction shortly before five, although it could as well have been midnight. Vern swivelled the Landover's searchlight around the surface of the water. "He did say it was on the Coventry?" Fred grunted. "Can't see owt. Let's get down there."

They patrolled the canalsides. "What's that?" Vern's torch-beam settled on a murky shape secured to a bollard. Beneath a waterproof tarpaulin sat a one-man inflatable with an Evinrude outboard. "Gotta be it, Fred, surely?"

"Reckon so. Wonder who belayed it, don't look like Alan's work."

"Would that be Alan Shobnall you was referring to?" They jumped. "Sorry, never meant to frighten. We was just finishing up."

Fred and Vern were confronted by another pair, workmen; one older, shorter, somewhat tubby, the other tall and carrying two workbags. The shorter figure continued. "Only Alan said someone would be along for it. We work in there." He pointed. "Waterway carpenters. I'm Ernest, this is Ernie. We found this boat."

"Aha," said Vern. "The Waterhouses. Pleased to meet you. Alan spoke of you. We're the police divers. Anything to do with water, crime, accidents and whatever. I'm Vern and this is Fred. He's in charge." Vern then went quiet.

The taller Waterhouse explained. "After a while we thought we should cover the boat. It looked a good outboard."

"My fault," said Fred. "Alan asked, I made a note and got distracted. Found the note this afternoon."

"Need any help?" The younger Waterhouse.

"Thanks but we can manage. We'll fetch it over to the Land Rover there. You can have your tarpaulin back."

"Leave it on the bank," said the elder. "We can't hang about. I need my tea."

"If you want anything," said the younger. "You'll find us in the works most days. Alan knows." The Waterhouses made off down the track into the night; more gossip for the table.

Fred and Vern made short work of it. Folded the tarpaulin, hauled the inflatable to the Land Rover. Fred detached the outboard, laid it on sacks in the back. "They were right, nice motor, who'd leave that lying around?"

"It'll not quite go in flat," said Vern. "Need to prop it at an angle. They lifted the inflatable, tilted and slid it in and, as they did so, something slithered out from under the raised bulwark and fetched up under the lower. Fred and Vern looked at each other, finished loading.

Fred put his gloves on and pulled the object from where it had wedged, held it gingerly. A transparent plastic bag. Inside, a white powder. "Tell you what, Vern." Fred spoke flatly.

"We give that to Joe Short."

"Spot on, Vern," said Fred in the same tone.

*　*　*

Dinner at Paolo's was an event in itself, back at the same table close by the cauldron of a kitchen and with Paulo in alert attendance. Shobnall and Chateris agreed that the man ran a top-notch establishment but did seem to have an eye for the ladies. Not that these women noticed. Elaine was bubbling with her day, spent criss-crossing London from Dickens & Jones to the Tate Gallery, from Selfridges to Carnaby Street. Prompted by Frankie wanting to know what she had thought of *that* and demanding whether she had managed *there*, she couldn't stop marvelling at the speed, the bustle, the colours, the wonders! Leaving the boys free for a modicum of shop-talk over the pasta and primitivo.

"Yer gettin' an 'andle on the 'ole picture, yeah?"

"I think so, Dave. We can see everybody, but *everybody*, coming down on Melinda. The Indian Government, our lot, the Crown Prince, even her father and then Vetch."

"Must 'ave seemed that way to 'er. Poor thing. All in balance an' then Morgan upsets the apple cart."

"I still don't know what he wanted from Melinda. Something she wasn't prepared to give. Gary Stubbs says they were closeted for an age that night in their office. They must have been haggling over something and she wasn't budging. The Prince met the same resistance. Except then it all got too much."

"Don't matter, do it? Not if yer got enough to finger 'im?"

"That's the problem, Dave, I don't think I do. There's almost too much going on. I mean, I *could* get him for blackmail."

The forkful of spaghetti travelling towards Charteris' mouth paused in mid-air. "But that would bring trouble for our new pal, Vijay, an' we'd rather avoid that."

"Quite. Besides, I'm convinced Morgan's guilty of more than blackmail."

Charteris chased the spaghetti with a mouthful of wine. "So 'ow close you got 'im to the Wychnor murder?"

Shobnall frowned. "Close but nowhere near the line. I might have enough now to pin the murder on his side-kick but there's wiggle-room for Vetch."

"I 'ad another chat with my gaffer about Gary Stubbs. Russ ain't happy, I can tell. I reckon if you 'ad a case on Wychnor then 'e could be persuaded to take a proper look."

"Good to know, Dave. I feel bad about Gary. He did a lot to help, pity he did it posthumously."

"Russ thinks drugs are in here somewhere. I know." He raised his hand in a pacifying gesture, inadvertently threatening to shower pesto and pasta everywhere. "It's got so any mention of pop music an' we all look aroun' for the drugs but 'e could be right. Those Reapers are buildin' more than a *musical* reputation."

"I can believe it. These rumours don't always settle but we know Cox was hooked and Basher was certain Morgan was supplying him. Even so-"

"Enough! If you *pleeze*." Frankie's accent came through more strongly when she raised her voice. "At this end of the table, Elaine and Françoise have finished and we are waiting on the fantasies of Paolo's desserts, *merci beaucoup*, while you bad boys are not eating the perfect pasta, you are busy with police business. Again I say enough!" Her face bore a huge smile.

"Awright, awright, mamselle!" Charteris leaned over and planted a smacker on her cheek. "'Ere comes Paolo, grab the menus off 'im while Alan an' me catch up." Shobnall looked across at Elaine; her face seemed to be glowing. He caught her eye and she smiled, slid her hand sideways. His hand met it, squeezed gently. Four happy people. *'All you need is love.'* As someone would in due course chant.

\* \* \*

## TWENTY-NINE

On the last day of November, 1963, a Saturday, The Beatles swapped a grasp on youthful emotion for a stranglehold on modern culture. For the previous thirty weeks, their first long player, 'Please Please Me' had defied all challengers at the top of the album charts. Within one week of its release the second, 'With The Beatles', had taken over. It would sit there through to the following April, even make the Top Twenty singles list. They had become a global phenomenon, set on a trajectory that would change popular music forever. For the tabloid press they were henceforth 'the Fab Four' and a national institution. For the broadsheets they were a serious force; William Mann, music critic for The Times, reviewed and analysed their work on the grounds of its cultural significance. Most of us couldn't stop humming the tunes.

Eddie Mustard, slumped in the passenger seat, was whistling 'All My Loving'. Shobnall recognised the melody. *Their tunes creep in while you're not looking.* "What is it about these Beatles songs, Eddie, you hear folk everywhere singing them?"

"Don't you just! They sound fresh and we can all share in them. They've got the common touch, bring people together. Not like our pals, The Reapers."

"No, I've heard some of their music, strikes me as dark."

"Everybody loves The Beatles. Well, maybe not everybody but you don't find people hating them. Even fuddy-duddies who say it's not really music, they still think they're a lovable bunch of mop-tops. With The Reapers, you love or hate 'em. But they're going like a train. My mate at Norman's says when the first Reapers album came out, for its first five or six weeks it sold as fast as 'Please Please Me' had when it was released. I mean, what's the population of Burton?"

"Not sure, fifty thousand, a bit less?"

"Not a large town.  Norman's don't usually order more than a handful of any album, except for people like Elvis or Cliff, they'll maybe go fifty or sixty. My mate reckons they've sold about twelve hundred of 'Please Please Me'. That tells you how things have changed. They've ordered five hundred for the next Reapers album. Multiply that round the country."

"Round the globe, more like." He braked behind a lorry. *No point in overtaking so close to the turn-off.* "How do you find time to chat with your mates, Eddie, when you're on nights all the time?"

"The full English, Alan. I'm coming off shift, they're on their way to work. You want to know where to get a good breakfast in Burton, I'm your man."

*   *   *

He'd collared Eddie at the end of his night shift and Eddie invited himself along at once. Which was what Shobnall had hoped for. They both wore every warm garment they'd been able to lay hands on. It was beyond the Anglia's dodgy heating. During the night – as Eddie well knew – the mercury had fallen to minus eleven on the centigrade scale the Met Office insisted on using these days. With nine o'clock looming, it remained below zero; the windows of the diesel scuttling over the Wychnor viaduct were blurred with frost, those British Railways heaters on the blink again! Its hooter wailed mournfully. Forget the cold, though, and it was glorious, the sun bright, the sky a pellucid blue, the air so clear you could see all the way to Cannock Chase.

There were few people about. A pair stamping their feet at a bus stop, a milk float on its rounds, a van leaving the village. On the weekend, the estate was on a skeleton staff, the sawmill silent but cows still to be milked. The village was comatose, smoke rising from a few chimneys. Shobnall flexed his fingers inside his gloves, drove up to the manse. In darkness. "Lights in the church," said Eddie. Their breath fizzed in the frigid air, the first intake rasping their throats. "I should have gone for breakfast and then bed."

"You'd have hated to miss it."

Mustard grinned, not something he did often. "True." He opened the church door slowly. Tall white candles burned piously on the altar. The pews were deserted but for a figure in the front row, head bent, hands in his lap. The Reverend Bullard. They moved down the aisle to face him, each slightly to one side. The vicar raised his head, considered them. *Like his mind has been somewhere else.* "Mr Shobnall and......" He looked at Eddie, delved into his memory. "Mr Mustard. You came together that first night. I.....I am not surprised to see you again."

There was something so desperately resigned in the tone that Shobnall couldn't suppress a wave of sympathy. *As far as we know he hasn't actually done anything wrong but he's feeling a failure, a sinner.*" In that case, sir, you'll understand that we would like to talk to you."

Bullard breathed deeply. "Can I ask that we do not converse here in the church? I prefer to talk in the open air, cold as it is. Might we ascend the bell tower?"

Shobnall looked at Eddie, who nodded. *He's feeling the same.* "Of course." Bullard plucked a black greatcoat from beneath his seat and wrestled it over his vestments. He led the way.

*   *   *

Despite being wide to the elements, the bell tower provided shelter from the weather's bite. The wind was sticking to low levels and it was a stimulating rather than aggressive cold. Staffordshire stretched on all sides, fields of frost populated only by sheep; cattle had been taken indoors. "You are not surprised to see us again," said Shobnall.

Bullard settled on the bench. "As I told you before, Mr Shobnall, I like to spend time up here, to reflect on the landscape and how it was wrought. I feel at home here. I have discovered, after a life of travel, that I am something of a home-bird at heart and this feels more like it than anywhere else I have been. I should hate to have to leave this place."

"That's a matter for Lord Needwood. We're here because we think you can help us understand what has been going on."

Bullard straightened his shoulders. "I recall that night I telephoned about the shooting and you gentlemen came to the manse. Men of my calling minister over many years in many places. We develop the ability, as it were, to 'read' people. I had no idea what had taken place over at the Big House but I knew I had a pair of bloodhounds on my doorstep. Later, I found out what had passed. We had the.....drowning and the arrival of Morgan Vetch-"

"How did you know?" Eddie cut in. "About Vetch turning up."

"Albert Haynes told me. You may think me mad but the presence of Vetch signalled that evil was abroad. No!" He waved a hand. "Let me finish. Gentlemen, I can assure you Morgan Vetch sits at Satan's right hand. Once I knew he was involved, I was sure the death had not been accidental. You, Mr Shobnall, called a second time and I found myself evading your questions about Boston, seeking to fend off the inevitable. You must have laughed. I knew you bloodhounds would sniff out my past. You will have been in touch with the FBI?"

"Not directly, sir, but we have our connections." *We need him to feel on our side.* "I wonder if we can agree to treat this as an off-the-record discussion?"

Bullard looked askance but asked no questions and went on. "I erred in Boston. No. You will have dug thoroughly. I *repeated* an error. I did no wrong!" He looked at each of them in turn. "I do not wish to sound Jesuitical. I harmed no-one but I did take a step too far on a wrong path. I.....admired a boy and I.....sought to attract him with gifts. I dipped my hand in college funds. I told myself I would pay it back but matters became difficult and turned into disaster because of *him*." Bullard bowed his head. They could see that he was wiping his eyes. "That creature cannot resist picking on someone who is down when the opportunity arises to stamp harder on them. I don't know how but he found out about my..... fascination. He made noise in the right places and fanned the flames and after ten years of excellent work I was doomed! If it hadn't been for Lord Needwood and Wychnor....I genuinely believe I learned my lesson. I learned control. Until Vetch came again."

"The night of the murder?" Shobnall spoke gently, temptingly.

"Before. I don't know how he found me. He has Satan's reach. Suddenly he is at my door, threatening to tell."

Eddie was quick. "What did he want?" *Sometimes Eddie takes no prisoners.*

Bullard was uncomfortable now. "Lady Melinda. He demanded I put him in contact with her, effect an introduction. I knew not why but I complied. You have to believe I had no idea where it would lead."

The tower was silent, the policemen recognising that Bullard *must* have expected *some* harmful fall-out. They said nothing; there was no point. Shobnall's gaze raked abstractedly over the Big House. *Its roof-slates are free of frost.* He turned. "What do you think, Eddie?"

"That we have no reason to link the vicar to any crime. That he has helped advance our enquiries. I'm inclined to see us working together."

A long pause. Bullard stood and again stared at the view. "Thank you." He tugged his coat tight about him. "Thank you. This is hard. I have spent a life-time fighting my own worst impulses. I believe I have never once lost the battle. The Lord says it is enough to fight and I hope that it is. I shall find out in due course." He turned to them. "But He also demands forgiveness and I am not sure I have it in me to forgive Morgan Vetch."

\* \* \*

The wind had slackened. It remained cold, right enough, but it felt too bright and sprightly a day to rush back to an office. A look, a nod and off they went to the Big House. "Looks all closed up, doesn't it?" said Shobnall. Wooden shutters blocked the ground-floor windows, curtains and blinds masked the upper floors.

"Almost." Eddie craned his neck. "Not only is the roof clear, now there's smoke coming out of a chimney."

"Haynes said he goes in every day. In this weather, he'll give the central heating a burst but who needs a fire?"

"Did you ever return those keys, Alan?" Shobnall raised an arm, twirled the keys on their ring.

Inside was warmer than might have been expected from a background heat intended to keep the fabric breathing. Shobnall fingered the hall radiator. Hot. No lights on, only the sun's rays infiltrating around the shutters. They waited while senses adjusted to the gloom. No sounds. All as on that first night when this same pair had entered the building to investigate reports of shooting. Aside from the temperature. And a feeling. *There's someone in this building.*

They went directly to the steps down to the kitchen. A bright line along the gap at the base of the door. Shobnall pushed it open. It took a moment for their eyes to re-adjust. The ceiling lamps were on, the drapes pulled together and a fire crackled merrily in the grate near the Aga. The chair placed beside the fire held only a ruffled newspaper but a figure lounged at the long table, contemplating them with a grin.

"Morning gents. Nice to see you again, Mr Shobnall. Don't think I've met your companion."

Shobnall stared. Eddie looked to Shobnall, then at the figure, then back to Shobnall. Who gave up trying to work it out. "This is Eddie Mustard, my colleague. You won't remember meeting him because you were unconscious both times, if I recall correctly. What on earth are you doing here, Basher?"

\* \* \*

## THIRTY

Basher made a pot of tea. "I'm renting the place." He moved gracefully, sure and spare in his movements. "I know, you're thinking it's not cheap but what with recent happenings it's not been easy to get tenants. They were glad to have someone in. We settled on a very fair price." He lifted an unopened gold-top from the fridge, spun it high in the air, caught it while seeming to be looking the other way. "First few days I rattled around a bit but I soon got used to it. Dunno if you keep tabs on the music press but The Reapers' new album is selling by the truckload in the States. I'm on that. I'm thinking of buying a little place and wallpapering it with Bank of England notes. Only I haven't found the right place yet so I thought I'd hunker down here for a bit. Here you go." He poured out three mugs. "No biscuits. Mrs Farlowe don't approve of nibbles."

"Basher!" Shobnall's tone was firm. Basher tried to look contrite.

Eddie was taking to the drummer. "That's Alan's voice of command, Basher. You better come clean."

Basher laughed. "Are you really police? Coppers aren't noted for a sense of humour."

"We're the human face of copperdom," said Eddie. "We'll stay human if you tell us what you're doing here – and don't say it's nothing to do with Cox and Gary Stubbs and all that. We didn't come up the Trent in a banana boat."

"Fair do's." He downed half his tea. "I reckon he'll be back here." Silence.

Shobnall broke it. "Morgan Vetch."

"Don't ask me why I think that. It's lovely here. Lovely spot, lovely countryside. I don't have to do nothing. Albert pops in every morning. He's a good lad, you know, him and me are getting to be such pals he might even forgive me for blasting off at his trees. Mrs. Farlowe comes in to take care of me grub. What a cook she is! I've told her when I've found my little place, I'll want her to come and live with me."

"Shocking." Eddie mocked. "Propositioning a married woman!"

"Mrs Farlowe's a widow!" Basher looked straight at Eddie. "Not so old, neither. Wonderful woman."

"And Morgan?" Shobnall sought to refocus the conversation.

182

"Yeah, he's bad. Worse than I thought. He had a hand in Mick's death. And Gary's, you ask me. Gary was making noises about what happened to Mick. Albert says Morgan was here the night Mick drowned. I must have been out of it again. He says Lady Thing, the one who topped herself upstairs, she was here too. Albert thinks they knew each other. Blokes at the sawmill clocked Morgan's stretch-limo ages ago. Mrs Farlowe saw the car in the village."

Shobnall stopped him. "When was that?"

"Well before we arrived. She said it was parked on the road by the church. You can't hide that motor."

"We agree Morgan's implicated in Cox's death but we can't prove it. Nor have we come up with a motive."

"I've talked to his mum and his girl and thought about it," said Basher. "Mick *must* have had something on Morgan. Mick saw him more than the rest of us 'cos of the drug supply. Mick saw something, heard something, I don't know what but the fact he knew it was a problem for Morgan."

*Always the drugs.* "OK. Go on."

"Not much else to say. As you pointed out" – a grin - "early in our stay here I tended to be unconscious. Since Mick's death, I've been keeping a clearer head." He went to the window, tugged back the curtain, looked out over the lake. "Morgan was here before and he arrived straight after Mick died. The woman, she lived here as a child. There's history here. Morgan likes history, it's full of stuff from your past you'd rather stayed there. Better than money for Morgan, more flexible. Gives him power. That's what turns him on! He arrives here to dig something up and that means people are going to suffer – whoever he's got something on, Mick, Gary, the Lady."

"You should change career," said Shobnall. "Become a detective."

Basher beamed. "I told you working in the 'Pool docks taught you about bad men." He tapped the table. "A lot has happened *here*. Whatever is going on hasn't done with *here*, I feel it. The tour finishes after Christmas, four straight nights at Madison Square Gardens. Then Morgan will be back."

"What for?" Eddie demanded.

Basher havered. "I'm not sure. He started something here. Maybe he wants to keep it moving and the button he needs to press is here. Or it's all gone tits-up and he needs to close down. I'm following instinct."

Shobnall was intrigued. "What do you do while you're here?"

Basher fiddled with his teaspoon. "I'm being careful. If Morgan returns I don't want him to know I'm here. I get out and about, see what people know."

"What," asked Shobnall. "Do you intend to do if and when Morgan re-appears?"

Basher looked startled. "Er, dunno." He paused. "I guess I imagined bashing him." His face lit up. "What else would a Basher do? Although I might think twice if Preston was with him. I wouldn't trust that slime-ball to fight fair. I see what you're thinking. It's true, I don't have enough of a handle on what this is all about. I just didn't think anyone else was taking it seriously enough."

The three men sat at the long table in the kitchen of the Big House. The fire continued to crackle. Shobnall was revising his estimation of Basher up another notch. Eddie finished his tea, walked over to the kitchen area and placed his mug in the sink. Basher twiddled his teaspoon some more. "I was wrong, wasn't I?"

"Yes, Basher." Shobnall rose, went around and put a hand on Basher's shoulder. "You were. Eddie and I never give up. We know more than you. We have a lot but not enough. We'd like your help."

Basher visibly glowed. "What can I do?"

Eddie stood alongside Shobnall. "Alan is about to ask you to carry on."

"Exactly," continued Shobnall. "Carry on talking to people, making friends, looking for signs. You're here. You can do this. We can't. Are you up for it?"

Basher chuckled. "You bet!"

"Good. But listen. One thing you are right about is steering clear of Preston. That's not his name. It's Carpenter and he's a thug. In London's gangland they call him 'Cutter'. You can guess why. We don't want to be fishing pieces of you out of the river."

*   *   *

He dropped Eddie at the corner of Wetmore Road, watched in the rear-view as his colleague entered a shabby cafe frontage he'd never noticed before. Angela had hung on for him to deal with the November expenses before she, too, clocked off. *Wonder if she's going for breakfast, can't see her in a greasy spoon.* He was still wondering when the DI poked his head round the door. "Hank's on my phone."

As Shobnall slipped into the guest chair and picked up the handset loose on the desk, the DI produced a second telephone from a drawer. *Never knew he had an extension.* The DI got started. "You hearing alright, Hank?"

"Sure thing, George." The transatlantic twang. "Our boy there?"

"I certainly am, Hank. How are you?"

"Alan, nice to speak with you again. I'm well, thank you, still patrolling your British Museum."

"Money for old rope," said the DI.

"Not going to disagree with you there, George, but everyone deserves an easy beat once in a while. It's good to have something extra to fill in the time. You've seen the material I sent about your Reverend Bullard, Alan?"

"I did. Thank you very much for that, Hank. It's already been put to good use."

"No kidding! You saw the photograph?"

*He spotted Morgan too.* "With Vetch in the crowd."

"Yup. I don't have much for you on that guy. The FBI wouldn't say diddly-squat about him."

Shobnall was conscious of the DI's eyes on him. *Why won't the Feds talk?* "Is there something live, something happening now?"

"Attaboy." Hank's tone was warm. "I know the agent on the case. I was able to press him some. They have something in play and it must be big. I told him where I was and how I was doing a favour and he chewed a while and then he gave me coupla things. Whatever is going down, it's international. Your Scotland Yard are in on it. Get on to your friends in there but tell them to tread carefully, this sounds dicey, know what I mean? They need to find Operation White Horse. Upper case first letters."

"White Horse? What's that mean?" Shobnall couldn't help himself.

"Ask your guys, partner, done all I can. Good hunting, Alan. Hope to see you both again before I'm sent back stateside."

"Many thanks, Hank. Try and stay out of trouble." The DI settled his phone back on its cradle and returned the unit to its hiding place. "You know what to do?"

Shobnall rose. "Set Dave Charteris on it." The DI nodded, picked up his pipe. Shobnall had already left.

*   *   *

It took Charteris a week. "Sorry, mate, yer did tell me ter walk on tippy-toe. Remind me 'ow yer got onto this White 'Orse?"

*I didn't tell him and he knows I'm not going to reveal my sources.* "Is that your DI asking?"

"Yeah, I 'ad to bring 'im in on it. I mean, I know me way around 'ere but I wasn't gettin' a whisper. I said to Russ it involved Vetch. I told you 'e was never 'appy wiv Gary Stubbs an' Vetch's name was enough. Russ is good at bein' diplomatic but I fink even 'e may 'ave put someone's nose out of joint. 'E was a bit narked. Cost me more than one pint, I'm tellin' you."

"Did he find out anything?"

That deep gurgling laugh. "Did 'e? I should say so. 'E said it was long an' slow squeezin' blood out the proverbial. No detail but it's summat big, though. The Met workin' wiv the FBI. Drugs, that's what it's about, hence the 'orse. An' our friend, Mr Vetch 'as a starrin' role. How's about that then?"

Shobnall paused a beat. "That fits, Dave. The signs were pointing to drugs. I wasn't sure, though, and it's brilliant to have confirmation. The Americans, though. That's serious."

"Yer not kiddin'. Well, 'ere's a bit more, sort of garnish courtesy of Russ. 'E reads a situation like it's an open book an' there ain't many books in 'ere what 'e 'asn't read before." He paused. "If yer see what I mean. Any road, 'e reckons summat's gone wrong."

"Does he have any idea what?"

186

"Nah, juss 'is impression. Gone wrong or gone wonky, like summat should 'ave 'appened an' it 'asn't an' they got no idea why. Russ says they're actin' edgy. 'E thinks the Yanks are leanin' 'ard."

"So whatever has gone awry is over here."

"'Cisely. Our blokes' fault. Lissen. Russ don't wanna commit hisself but the way 'e's readin' it, they got someone on the inside in their pocket"

"On the inside? Who?"

"Well, mate, fink about it. 'Oo is there in Morgan's set-up the Yard might be able to get their claws into?"

Shobnall was already there. "Dave, unless there's someone we don't know about, there's only one candidate."

"S'right."

"Carpenter. Cutter."

"Yeah. They must 'ave found a way to cut 'im a deal."

"This is too complicated. Here's little old me investigating a local drowning. We haven't used the word murder in public so far but we're not far away and now the man in the frame is a grass. I'll get a rocket if I cut across the Met, never mind the Americans. Thank goodness you and Russ came up trumps before I put my foot in it."

There followed a lengthy silence, the two friends connected only by the rustling hiss of the telephone wires. "Yer gonna sit an' wait?"

"Only thing I can do, Dave. Actually, the next step depends on Morgan Vetch."

* * *

# THIRTY-ONE

He hardly saw the room; Angela's spick-and-span desk, the HQ Bulletins pinned to the wall, the grey filing cabinets, all the familiar paraphernalia was a million miles away. His mind was in Boston, in Scotland Yard with Operation White Horse, with the FBI wherever they were, in gangland London with the Krays and the Richardsons, with The Reapers, Wychnor and the Big House. Unasked, his brain offered direction. He scrabbled through the file. The list of Melinda's assets. Aitch had given him a copy. *Here we are!* He ran his finger down the typed rows, ran the finger back. He strode along to the squadroom. Only Lennie was in but it was Lennie he needed. Bob Saxby's transistor was pumping out the voice of a woman whose voice you couldn't ignore and whose hidden passion was out – '*my secret love's no secret any more*'.

"Blimey, Lennie, that's a bit in-your-face, isn't it?"

Lennie put his newspaper aside. "Kathy Kirby, she's got a real voice on her."

"Come on, I've seen your record collection, your secret love is jazz."

"I like to keep in touch, Alan. On the Derby County terraces there's more chat about what's in the pop charts than which classical composer is being jazzed up by Dave Brubeck. It's young Gideon likes this stuff. He just nipped out. What can I do you for?"

"I wanted your advice. You've done HQ's drugs briefing, haven't you?"

"I have. Not greatly useful, if you ask me. Too much on the narcotics and what they do to users. We need to know about the buggers punting the stuff."

"I *knew* you'd have thought about that. Let's you and I go into the drugs business. I don't mean flogging a few reefers round the back of the Old Bass Brewery. We want to be the number one supplier of drugs in the United Kingdom. Crudely, what do we need?"

Lennie didn't prevaricate; if Alan Shobnall asked a question, however odd it sounded, there would be a reason. "Any particular markets? This music business where every guitar seems to bring drugs with it? The smart sets in Swinging London? Young folk, they like marijuana? The older, long-term addicts? Pain-killers?"

"All of them, Lennie. You want drugs, you get them from Morton & Shobnall, purveyors of drugs to the nation. What do we need?"

"Same as any business. Course, our advertising will have to be lower-key than most. We need customers. HQ's figures show that's not a problem. Any urban area will do. We need the product, products plural, rather. Those HQ statistics were depressing from a policeman's point of view. Steady increases in heroin and cocaine use, vibrant market in uppers and downers and dope going through the roof. Good news for us in our new enterprise." He pursed his lips. "I assume we're a selling operation, we ain't going in for manufacture and processing?"

"Agreed. We're retail. We're buying in from elsewhere."

"In that case, America's fine but we probably need to speak Italian. Then it gets trickier. I doubt these manufacturers are in the credit game. We need cash up front, that's problem *numero uno*. We can't toddle down to your pal, Henderson, at Jardines and ask for a loan so we can purchase a large quantity of illegal substances."

"OK." Shobnall pondered. "Money's changing and there's plenty of it about. Clean and not-so-clean. Let's say we can get dirty money. Our wholesalers are prepared to bankroll us in exchange for a share in the retail profits."

Lennie walked across the room and turned the radio off. "Jesus, Alan, mayhem beckons. Yeah, they could do that but if I was them I'd as soon think about controlling the whole chain. Out go Morton & Shobnall. How we exit don't bear thinking about." He ran his hands through his hair.

"It's not enough though, is it?"

"No. Assume products, customers, finance in place. Now we have a practical hurdle, logistics." He thought for a moment. "Burton is our main depot. An old factory on an out-of-the-way estate or maybe a redundant maltings, somewhere inconspicuous where we can hold our stock. We have customers in Bristol, Birmingham, Bognor Regis. We have reps in all these places. One thing I *did* learn from that HQ briefing was that drugs customers want their goods when they need them. If you can't deliver on time there'll be someone else who will; it's a cut-throat trade. Our problem is how we keep the flow of stock to our reps. Distribution."

Shobnall rose. "Thanks, Lennie. You have, as usual, clarified things for me."

Lennie feigned anguish. "You waltz in here and pick my brains. Don't cut me out of this money-spinner just when I'm wanting to augment my pension. What are you up to?"

"Not yet, I'm still fumbling. Before I commit myself, I need to speak to a lady.

* * *

Esmée Worthington was as sophisticated, attentive and intimidating as ever but, for once, her audience was proving impervious. Now he had reached what he felt was crunch-point, Shobnall was so wound-up he forgot how impressionable he was supposed to be. He paced her office, oblivious to the glorious Monet print. Esmée was not in the slightest put out; she knew all about the inside of policemen's heads. Purely as a precaution, she took refuge behind her desk and a Rothman's.

"Take a deep breath, Alan, and exhale slowly. Repeat." Shobnall grinned and did as he was told. He is an extremely attractive man, thought Esmée, in the sense that others would be prepared to follow. "Now, no rigmarole."

"Sorry, Esmée, I feel on the edge of cracking a problem. When we talked before about Melinda's mental deterioration, you referred to board meetings at TransUK Haulage."

"Yes, and I told you about meeting her at The Carillion."

Shobnall paced again but with a measured tread. "You said you knew Melinda from your participation in *several* boards, not only TransUK. There was a charity?"

Goodness, thought Esmée, a *man* with listening skills! "That is correct." She crushed the last inch of cigarette into the ashtray. "Soon after I joined TransUK, Melinda invited me onto the board of a London charity, established by her grandfather, a previous Lord Needwood. We support clergymen who have fallen on hard times, men of any denomination."

*The Reverend Bullard is lucky, he hasn't slipped that far.* "Is that the only other shared board?"

"No. We have also been non-executive directors of a medium-sized but well-established Birmingham engineering firm. Chamberlain & Company."

Shobnall shot her a glance. "Manufacturers of safes, locks and keys and so forth?"

"You are well-informed." She paused, thinking. "Aitch told you."

"Elaine and Hilary Henderson are Lavinia Salt's regular cinema companions. I think whatever was damaging Melinda started well before London and the exhibition. What I

190

need to know is whether her behaviour on those other boards mirrored the way she was at TransUK?"

Esmée reached for another cigarette, her brow creased. "Let me think. Why are you asking?"

"Please, Esmée."

Ah, the iron hand in the velvet glove. She heaved a sigh. "No. I ought to have realised. With TransUK, Melinda was effectively the owner but not chair of the board and I was a non-exec. At Chamberlain, we were both non-execs with notional shareholdings. I could get George a cheap lock for his shed. At the charity, she was in the chair and I was a director but I was also Treasurer. That made me *primus inter pares* there." She met his gaze.

"I know what that means," said Shobnall. His tone was not soft.

My goodness, she thought, I on the back foot with this young man! "Over the period in question, she sailed on as usual at the charity and Chamberlains. Utterly unflappable." She was talking to herself now. "How could I not have noticed the contrast?" The cigarette in her hand remained unlit. She returned it to the packet.

Shobnall had stopped before the Monet print. "You could lose yourself in that. He must have been happy painting it. Of these three enterprises, TransUK was the most substantial? With all due respect to security and hard-up clergymen?"

"Yes. So the question is why was her behaviour there different." Esmée halted, hesitating. "Alan, I'm not sure where to go with this."

"Can you put a timescale on when her behaviour started to deteriorate at TransUK?"

Esmée leafed through the desk diary in front of her. "The May board. My notes say Melinda was 'a bit on edge'. I remember that. I wondered what had upset her. By June and July I gained the sense that she was increasingly having difficulty holding it together. I thought it was the pressure of succession. Taking over from your parents can be a challenge, you know?"

*Chance would have been a fine thing.* "TransUK Transport. From May onwards, did she bring to the board anything out of the ordinary?"

Esmée was glad of the desk's shelter; she was feeling pressed. "Now that you ask, yes, she did, although it wasn't *that* unusual. At the start of June she did ask us how we would feel about a takeover. Such approaches occur from time to time; there was no reason to think it untoward. What did strike me was that Melinda did not make it an up-front agenda item; she raised it under AOCB, as if she wanted it low-profile. The transport sector is rife with amalgamations and takeovers. It should have been at the top of the agenda or even the subject of an extraordinary meeting."

"Does that mean someone wanted to buy the company?"

"Or take a major stake. Or.....Well, there's no knowing. But there is no doubt that Melinda was taking the board's temperature. The board, by the way, was open-minded."

"Would that have meant money coming in?"

"Of course."

"And what would someone want in exchange?"

"Hard to be specific, Alan, but a degree of control, undoubtedly."

"In situations like that, is it simply the money and new faces in the boardroom? The business grinds on as before?"

"It can be like that but for a business like ours I would say unlikely. If it were an amalgamation, there would likely be changes throughout the company because the new parent would be looking for increased efficiency. If it were an independent investor taking a controlling interest then that investor may well want their own people in the senior executive positions and after that, well, who knows?"

Shobnall was silent, staring at and through the Monet. To Esmée, the young policeman seemed to disappear within himself, as if communing with some inner spirit. She wanted to know the nature of the communion but, for once, couldn't tell and daren't ask. All he said was "Thank you, Esmée."

\* \* \*

192

## THIRTY-TWO

Time to fill in some blanks. Dave Charteris had provided a selection of six-by-ten black and whites drawn from the Met's fast-expanding gallery of pop music 'personalities'. Shobnall chose two full-frontals and added a third portrait he had cut from a society magazine. He had considered going himself. *Not fair, the lad can handle it.* He handed over the photographs with instructions as to how they were to be shown.

Gideon was maturing. Not that long ago he'd have been puffed up with pride at being entrusted with the mission. Now he took it in his stride as he brought a whiff of the late twentieth century into the crepuscular gloom of the Diocese. He felt sufficiently in charge to take, uninvited, a seat at the antique table and to toss his folder onto said table. He hadn't bothered with any paperwork or signatures this time.

He didn't budge when the Secretary scuttled in, half-man, half-nocturnal rodent, the thick lenses magnifying his bug-eyes. "Good morning, Secretary." Mr Shobnall had suggested turning up early, before they settled into the day, looked like that was a good idea. In the office, of course, it was 'Alan', like everyone else; in public, Gideon considered 'Mr Shobnall' more fitting, even in his thoughts.

"You, er, haven't an appointment. I've seen no authorisation. I can't –"

"I don't need to see any papers. I am here to ask you some questions." Gideon stood. He wasn't especially tall but he towered over the Secretary. "On a confidential basis." *That* worried the little man. "When I was here before, you gave me access to certain papers."

"Concerning the most recent appointment to Wychnor parish."

"There were pages missing." The Secretary swallowed, said nothing. "Given the security procedures the Diocese has in place, we are certain that you know who removed them." The Secretary was sagging, like a prize-fighter swaying on his feet who knows that the next blow will finish him. Gideon allowed a lengthy pause. "We have reason to believe that this person was in possession of knowledge that left you unable to resist the removal." Mr Shobnall had been most precise in the wording of that sentence. His precision seemed effective as the Secretary folded himself into a chair and buried his head in his hands.

A small part of Gideon was worrying about the wrath that would flame around him if his mother ever found out he'd harassed a man of the cloth like this but most of him was becoming a touch irritated by the man. "Mr Secretary, we have no interest in

193

whatever leverage this person had or has over you. There is no need for you to speak, a nod will do." He extracted the photographs from his folder and laid one on the table. "Was it this man?" The Secretary stared at the glossy, shook his head. Gideon set down a second shot. "This one? "

The Secretary's eyes bulged behind the industrial lenses, spittle flecked his lips. He wiped it away. "Him."

"Thank you." Gideon returned the photographs to the folder and picked up his coat. "That's all I wanted to know."

The Secretary looked up at him. Gideon noted how sickly his complexion had become. "Will you be coming back?"

"Not if I have anything to do with it," replied Gideon. It's not for me to judge, he thought, let he who is without sin and all that. John, 8, 7. "I can assure you, sir, that you are not part of our enquiries." He sailed back to the twentieth century, leaving a bedraggled Secretary shaking over who knew what.

\*   \*   \*

Gideon spread the photographs on Shobnall's desk. "Can I ask, who was your money on?"

Shobnall placed his index finger on the old chap, the picture snipped from a magazine. "Not him. I could imagine him thinking he ought to but he had no need. He owns the parish. That's Lord Needwood." He shifted his finger. "Not his cup of tea. He normally gets sent in when something more final is required." He moved to the third shot. "My choice. Morgan Vetch. He has something on our Reverend Bullard and he would have wanted exclusive rights to it. He would have won those rights by having something on the Secretary."

Gideon looked somewhat in awe. "You've hit the jackpot, Alan."

"Gideon!" Shobnall's tone was mock-sharp. "Is your mother aware your vocabulary extends to betting terms?"

\*   \*   \*

194

He had to make do with a telephone conversation with Joe Short. "Sorry, Alan, no way I can get anywhere near Burton at the moment. I'm up in Leek and then I'm being sent to Matlock."

"I keep forgetting you cover a wider region now. How's Heather doing?"

"Heather who? She won that contract with Derry & Toms and they keep giving her more work. She's in London more than she's here. She's getting noticed. We're both busy right now but, hey, life is good."

"You both deserve it. Now, what have you got for me?"

"Another goodie. One bag of cocaine, the powder Fred and Vern found in the dinghy. Roxburgh said the body at Wychnor was riddled with the stuff."

"He did. That's good, strengthens the link to the owner of the dinghy."

"Oh I can fix that securely. Someone had put their hand inside the bag. I took a good print off the inside. It's the same chap, Carpenter. I went down to Fred and Vern's lock-up and checked over the inflatable. Interesting. The outboard had been wiped clean but maybe Carpenter isn't that comfortable around boats. I reckon he had trouble keeping his balance when he clambered out. He left a full print of his right hand on the rim."

"Ha! We think he fell in so that fits. Joe, that's brilliant. I may have enough now to convince a jury."

"Let me know if you need anything else. Always happy to do a turn as an expert witness."

"Thanks, Joe. Enjoy the Peak District. You and Heather must come around for mince pies at Christmas."

* * *

At the very moment Joe and Shobnall were signing off, a man and a woman in a comfortably-arranged home in the comfortable village of Melbourne were lancing a boil. Or, rather, the woman was; the man was starting from a state of ignorance and his customary assumption that he must have done something wrong.

"George! It's not you, it's me!" Esmée Worthington waved her cigarette in the air. "I made a fool of myself."

"I'm sure you're being over-sensitive, dear." Worthington was in the dark; wrack his brains as he might, he couldn't recall any previous such claim by Esmée." What happened?"

Esmée's posture – cigarette poised, free arm wrapped around her body, legs crossed, shoulders hunched – screamed tension. "Alan Shobnall paid me another visit. I had formed an opinion of a very likeable, very capable young man. Last time, I was pleased, flattered even, that he should approach me for advice. I fear I over-estimated my position and I certainly under-estimated *him*. He returned to subject me to a painfully subtle grilling and to show me that I'm not as clever as I thought I was."

"Surely not." Worthington was trying to work out what therapy was needed here. "That's not Alan's style."

"Oh he didn't *mean* to do that." She leaned back, seemingly a little mollified, drew on her cigarette. "No. You're right, I am over-compensating."

Worthington was feeling happier; it wasn't anything he'd done. "Was this about Melinda?"

"Yes. Alan had listened carefully to what I told him before. He went away, conducted some thorough research sand put his finger on a key issue. My responses did not surprise him, George, they were what he was expecting, probably what he was hoping for."

"Well then, everyone should be happy with the result!"

Esmée sighed theatrically. "Yes, George, but I should not have needed a prod from Alan Shobnall to spur my brain to action. I should have been more on the ball first time around."

"Sounds to me, Esmée," Worthington was on the move round the room. "As if your liking for Alan caused you to want him to think well of you."

"For goodness' sake, George!" She stopped. "You're right. How ridiculous. Me! Acting like some callow lassie."

"You'll be on your guard in future." Worthington was at the cabinet, assembling his tools. "Back to your old self."

"Less of the 'old', George!" Worthington, his back to his wife, smiled to himself. "Yes, I will. It might have been easier if he'd rubbed it in but he was *too* nice. He'll have your job one day."

There was a subdued pouring sound. "Oh, I expect Alan to go well beyond DI level. There was a time, three or four years ago, when I wondered if Shobnall and the police were right for each other. No doubts now."

"Quite. The more you look, the more clearly you can see the man emerging from the youth. You know, George, I think I could manage a G&T now."

But George was already beside her chair, a glass in each hand.

\* \* \*

## THIRTY-THREE

Late afternoon. A crowded office. Shobnall and Angela Bracewell at the notice-board, arranging the duty roster for the looming festive season. Lennie was poking half-heartedly at a typewriter while Gideon Watson was in and out as if engaged on important business. Only Bob Saxby was absent, called out to a disturbance at Tutbury's post office; he'd gone with Charlie Taylor since he wanted to travel quickly. His absence meant Gideon had re-tuned his radio, now emitting the jangliest guitars Shobnall had yet heard in the British beat boom. The vocals seemed to rest on a children's nursery rhyme, 'sugar and spice and all things nice'. He had no intention of risking ridicule by asking Gideon.

Cyril Hendry joined the two sergeants. "All sorted?" He studied the roster. "That looks fair. Only needs you two to divvy up the season."

Always a little sensitive. Who works nights over Christmas. Angela jumped in. "I see no problem. The DI is volunteering to be in on Christmas Day and Boxing Day."

"He does that every year," said Cyril. "I do likewise. Me and Mrs H, we're happy to work around that."

"Since," continued Angela. "Christmas is a time for families, I propose to take the night shift through to the end of the first week in January."

*That would be fantastic but I can't, can I?* "Angela, that's too long."

"Not at all. I prefer a decent stretch. Alan, your kids are of an age when you need to enjoy the magic of Christmas with them."

"But surely you have people to see?" *She doesn't talk much about her private life.*

"Not at Christmas. In January, I intend to book some leave and go somewhere warm and sunny, make you all jealous. Furthermore, Alan, it'll help make up for your missing out on Remembrance Day."

Shobnall looked at Cyril. "All sorted then," said Cyril, inking their names in the appropriate boxes.

"Goodnight, everyone." They turned. Gideon was poised in the door, jacketed and belted, crash helmet in hand. "Excuse me leaving bang on time. I've to take Mam to the doctors."

198

"Nothing serious, I hope," said Shobnall.

"I shouldn't imagine so. When Mam gets her Readers Digest delivered, she reads the health articles and most months she finds something she's suffering from. The doctor will be expecting her. 'Night." He went off down the stairs.

"Young Gideon's become a real asset." The words came from Lennie, who had pushed the typewriter aside.

"I don't know him as well as you do, Lennie," from Angela. "But I can see the potential becoming reality."

"The boy is coming along very nicely." *Gosh, from Cyril, that's fulsome praise.* "I'll be off downstairs myself if we're all done. Don't forget to remind everyone the DI's Christmas drink will be on the Monday before Christmas Eve. Usual time."

Angela went with him. "I want a word with you about the filing, Cyril. Good night Alan, Lennie."

The radio tinkled on. 'She loves you, yeah, yeah, yeah.' *Everybody knows who that is.* "Beatlemania rolls on," observed Lennie. "It's getting hard to remember a time when we didn't have The Beatles. Where are your pop friends, still over in America?"

"Yes, I think it's Detroit and then Pittsburgh."

"Are they going to rival Mr Lennon and company or are they merely one among the scores of guitar-wielding groups in the charts these days?"

"You're asking the wrong person, Lennie. I rely on Eddie and his pal in Normans Records. Last week, he said in view of how well The Reapers were doing in the US, Normans had doubled their order for the new album so, you know, they could be genuine competition."

"I don't care for their music. No, no." Lennie made a placatory gesture. "That's not a stick-in-the-mud jazzer speaking. I was curious. Went down to Normans and sat in one of those booths, like being on 'Double Your Money'. It's too dark for me and I say that as someone well able to see life's glass as half-empty. There's no joy in their music, no compassion. Compare that with 'She Loves You' which is quite ecstatic."

"Eddie thinks The Beatles write songs for everyone and anyone."

199

"He's right. But I'll tell you this. The Reapers' songs are cleverly constructed and they have a real knack for a tune. Whichever of 'em are producing the material are top class. I was impressed." *So, Lennie's estimation is similar to Gary Stubbs, it's Steven and Alex who really count.* "Anyhow, when are you going to finger someone for the boy who drowned at Wychnor?"

"Soon, I hope. Joe Short has done me proud. I still need to carry out a formal interview with the key players. If they'd been in this country I'd have done it by now."

"How long before they get back?"

"New Year. The tour ends late December with four nights in New York then they fly home. I've arranged to meet Elizabeth Helm to see how she thinks the case would stand up in court."

"You got doubts, Alan?"

"Not about guilt but, notwithstanding Joe's sterling work, a tiny voice at the back of my head keeps telling me it might not be quite enough."

"You'll get a straight answer from Mrs Helm. And with Angela's generosity, you can have a relaxing Christmas."

"True. I am so looking forward to that. Angela was very sporting. It's Jo's fourth birthday next week and end of term and that means Elaine can take on the preparation for Christmas. Don't forget we expect you for Boxing Day."

"Wouldn't miss it for the world. It's a magical time for children. I'm really looking forward to seeing yours enjoy it."

"You sound in need of a boost."

"Oh, it's not so bad. The world is taking on a more humane shape. This month will see Kenya and Zanzibar casting off the oppressive shackles of British imperialism, excuse my hyperbole."

"That should cheer you up."

"It does but on the other hand we're coming to the last-ever edition of 'That was The Week That Was'. That'll leave a hole in my weekend. Then there's this." Lennie reached for his newspaper. "This morning's London Times. Lancashire Chief Constable. No progress on that twelve year-old, John Kilbride, nor on Pauline Reade. She vanished back in July. It says 'The Chief Constable declined to be drawn on the question of whether these cases were linked'. My nerve-ends are twitching. There's cruelty out there. It'll be a bleak New Year for some, Alan."

\* \* \*

Saturday 14 December and 'I Wanna hold Your Hand' by you-know-who went straight to Number One as if in honour of the birthday girl. Josephine Shobnall was a-bubble with excitement but also at her most gracious, greeting each new arrival and seating them in the front room. Alice was demonstrating unusual powers of concentration, assiduously topping up the tea-cups set before Dolly and Mr Teddy. Elaine, who worried a little about her younger daughter, told herself that Alice was showing improved physical balance as well as mental focus. Shobnall, aware of Elaine's concern, whispered in her ear as he passed on his way to the kitchen "she's doing fine, we can't expect development as fast as Jo".

Corky, first in, had been placed next to Mr Teddy. He had given his elder god-daughter a miniature xylophone. The child had unwrapped it carefully, folded and set aside the gaudy paper. Her eyes widened as she examined the instrument, weighed one of the hammers in her hand; a first tap and she sat back as the sound glowed and faded. She tapped up and down the instrument, paused, then tapped out half a dozen notes. Shobnall and Elaine looked sharply at each other. *On my, she loves you yeah yeah yeah.*

Reuben Salt had dropped his sister off as Helen and James arrived. Lavinia had selected a matching robe and turban in a deep sea-green; she flowed about the house with the excited children surfing in her wake. Esther Osborne, their former neighbour and the District Nurse who had helped at deliver Josephine, brought a practical hand to the whole affair. Josephine's grandparents gave her an appropriately-sized satchel. The child, visibly bursting with pride, slung it across her body and paraded round the room – 'I'm going to school, just like mummy'. Helen had thoughtfully included a little bag for Alice, who strutted alongside her sister. As befitting a child's birthday party, the menu featured cake with candles, red jelly, more cake, ice cream and jam tarts and yet more cake. It was easy to see that Mr Teddy had been partial to the ice cream. After the food came games, balloons – humans large and small entranced by Corky's ability to twist them into the shape of a dog (or a cat or horse but definitely a quadruped) - jokes, laughter and a refill of cake. Throughout, Josephine at the centre, radiating happiness but continuously attentive to her guests.

Lavinia and Elaine paused at the margin of the mayhem. "Your daughter is a remarkable young lady."

Elaine draped an arm about Lavinia's shoulders. "She is. I mean, I'm her mother but that's what I think when I stand back. I feel a bit guilty about it."

"Don't. She is a wonderful child. It seems to me that you and Alan have set her fair for life. She is going to be more than a match for anything."

"Oh, Lavinia, I only want for her to be happy!"

"Of course you do and she will be. Elaine, you need some diversion. We have 'Dr No' at Swadlincote next week."

"That's Ian Fleming, isn't it? I read one of his, 'Goldfinger'. It was kind of high-living cartoonish. I can't believe the secret service is anything like that."

"I doubt you'll find the film any more realistic but it does star a young Scottish actor named Connery. Don't let Alan see a picture of him. I'll speak to Hilary and see if we can manage a date before Christmas."

Late afternoon and Reuben Salt's black Humber pulled up outside, here to ferry Lavinia away. Josephine wasn't in a rush and neither, it transpired, was Mr Salt. Josephine dragged him to a chair beside the fire. Mr Salt bent forward, reached his right hand to her ear and withdrew it holding.....a red carnation. Josephine stared. "Where did that come from, Reuben?"

"From within your ear, my dear. Your head contains beautiful flowers."

"I didn't know that," said Josephine, contorting her eyes in an effort to look within herself. "Can you show me another one?" Mr Salt repeated the trick, this time producing an orange bloom. "How do you do that, Reuben?"

"That is a secret. If I told you I would no longer be able to do it."

"Is that magic, Reuben?"

"The magic is holding flowers in your head, Josephine, I merely perform the trick of drawing them out."

Josephine seemed content with that. "Can you do any other tricks?"

One of Burton's most prominent businessmen preened at the approbation from the princess of the day. "Perhaps. Do you have a coin?"

Josephine waved her arms. "Daddy! Please may I have a coin?" Shobnall handed over a shilling. Elaine walked Alice over to watch.

"Thank you," said the prestigigateur. He did something intricate and fast, lodging the coin between his first and second knuckles and weaving it in and out across his hand.

Josephine's eyes never left it. "That's very clever, Reuben, but it's not magic."

"Mere preparation, my dear." Mr Salt placed the shilling in his palm, closed his fist, waggled it in a mystical way and opened his fingers. No coin!

Josephine gasped.   "Where has it gone?" Alice's eyes were as round as dinner plates, her mouth a perfect 'O'. Mr Salt brushed his hand against Josephine's other ear, withdrew it and there lay the shilling. Josephine lifted it from his palm and inspected both sides. "Oh Reuben," she breathed. "My head contains silver as well as flowers."

"Life is magic, my dear. Remember that."

The four year-old gazed into Mr Salt's eyes. "I will. Thank you, Reuben."

"My pleasure. Now, Lavinia informs me that you play like an angel on Corky's present. I should like to hear that because music is another kind of magic."

Josephine lifted the xylophone. "It's lovely." She grasped a hammer, addressed the instrument for a moment and then slowly tapped out the opening bars of 'All My Loving'.

\* \* \*

# THIRTY-FOUR

Elizabeth Helm had squeezed him in on the Saturday morning before Christmas, citing a crammed diary and the ongoing crumbling of a Victorian justice system. Shobnall was off-duty but the appointment suited the family. Elaine handed him a list of Christmas requirements – 'don't let the girls see them when you get back'. Privately, she was relieved; who wanted to brave the pre-Christmas shops?

*Business before shopping.* Mrs Helm was using an office in the upper reaches of the courts adjacent to the police station. It was little more than a cubby-hole. "It suits me, Alan. Nobody bothers me up here." He had sent over his file in advance and she was right on it. "You want to know whether I think we have enough to go to court. Let me first put a couple of questions to you about your suspect, the man now called Cutter or Carpenter. Can you put him on the lake at Wychnor?"

Shobnall had known how this would go but it still felt like he was on trial. "He was in the boat at Fradley and I can show an intruder was on site and out on the lake."

Mrs Helm was unmoved. "That's a no." She steepled her fingers. "Can you put him inside the house?"

Shobnall groaned. "We have his fingerprints on the whiskey bottle. Cox's body contained a large amount of Scotch as well as the drugs." *I don't think this is going to wash.*

"Dr Roxburgh identified the Scotch but he couldn't vouch for it being Jim Beam. Nor can we prove that Cox drank from *that* bottle. A judge would object but we might get away with giving it an airing and a jury might like it."

"We have his dabs on the house key, too. Why else would he have the key in his possession at all?"

"Having it in his possession does *not* mean he used it to enter the house."

"Surely all the pieces add up? He's a villain with a record as long as my arm."

"Indeed. We would table his record. He is undoubtedly a nasty piece of work but remember that in court he would be accompanied by the smoothest of silks, capable of diminishing what seems to us the clearest of evidence. Let that wait. How might he have laid hands on this key?"

"All the other keys are accounted for and it's not a copy. It's one of the set handed over as part of the hire contract. The only place Carpenter could have obtained it was from Vetch."

Mrs Helm gave no quarter. "Did Vetch hand them over to Carpenter or did Carpenter steal them?"

*You can go off people.* "Ah. Well. Vetch knew what was afoot. Carpenter needed to get in quietly which is why he approached and left via water and Vetch was on hand to pick him up in the helicopter." Mrs Helm waited. "I believe Vetch gave him the keys."

"You believe. Vetch will have a different story. Vetch was only there because Stubbs called him. That doesn't look like a planned event. Depending on which judge we are landed with and on the composition of the jury, the case you have assembled could be enough but it would be a risk. I am happy with risk but I would prefer to shave the odds further in our favour." A warm smile. "Plus I suspect you want both men, not Carpenter alone."

*I'm not clever enough to fool this woman.* "You see right through me. From the moment we began to see this as murder, The Reapers have been in America. We have been unable to interview Vetch and Carpenter. They'll be back in this country at the start of January and I was planning formal interviews then."

She stood. "We will hold back for now on a warrant but I shall reflect further. Here." She returned his file. "I have memorised what I need. We will review the situation following your interviews. Carpenter and his silk will have a superficially plausible explanation for why he was in the vicinity but argue that he never entered the house and wasn't on the lake. That could leave us in the lap of the justice gods." She sat again. "But there may be another way for us to augment our weaponry. What will be critical is the line this Vetch chooses to take." Shobnall smiled. *I'm not so daft after all.* "Now, young man, be off about your Christmas shopping. I have more paperwork to wade through. I shall be in the South of France for the festivities but I wish you and Elaine and your children a very happy Christmas."

* * *

Shobnall was feeling chipper. *More work required but she's up for it.* It helped anaesthetise the blend of tedium and angst infecting the queues in Ordish & Hall, in Becknell's, Redmayne & Todd's and sundry other retail emporia. *This list has extended itself since Elaine gave it to me.* It was late afternoon by the time he staggered home. Elaine had been listening out for the car and helped him in the door. "Whisk the bags up into our bedroom, they're watching the telly." When he came down again, Elaine was by the front room door. "They're watching that Dr Who programme."

"Is that OK?" They were careful about what their daughters watched on TV but Alan hadn't a clue who Who was.

"Oh, it's fine, a bit of fantasy. Actually, I quite enjoy it myself. It involves time travel."

"Time travel?"

"Yes, there's a blue police box....Alan, I'll talk to you about it later. Something to keep an eye out for, they didn't come and ask. Jo switched on and the two of them have been glued to it ever since."

He padded into the lounge. Josephine and Alice were propped up against the sofa base, eyes on the television screen. He tried to interpret what was happening in TV-land. A white-haired old man with a child and a couple of adults who looked like Elaine's teacher colleagues, a stone forest, strange buildings, a police box – *Really? And is that a sink plunger?* - funny music and the credits rolling. "What's all this, Jo?"

"We are on Skaro, daddy." Josephine's eyes didn't budge from the screen.

"Skaro, eh? Where's Skaro then?"

"In another galaxy, daddy."

*Does she understand 'galaxy'?* "Yes, so your mother said. What was that at the end?"

"Daddy, that's a Dalek."

"A Dalek?"

Josephine turned her head to look at her father. "Yes. The most intelligent beings in the universe but they are bad." Shobnall contemplated his daughters for a moment. He decided to go and make a cup of tea.

\* \* \*

It was a Burton tradition. Close to Christmas, at the interface between day and night shifts, everyone would gather in the squadroom for a celebratory drink. The DI would make a little speech, peppered with the same seasonal jokes. The term 'team-bonding' had not yet been coined but the event always managed to leave people feeling good about everyone else and themselves. Not only detectives and uniforms but colleagues and associates and, naturally, Agnes and Betty. All strictly against the regulations, of course, but after the initial two or three years without any comment, the event had shifted into that 'grey area' in which no-one was completely sure if it was allowed or not. Which meant no-one from HQ ever turned up and that suited Burton down to the ground. There had been that one time, five or six years ago, when the DI had thought it might be a nice idea to invite spouses. It hadn't really worked and hadn't been repeated. Tradition should stick to being traditional was the general view. This year, of course, Joe Short would be missing and that would leave a gap.

So there was a flurry of activity and telephone calls around lunchtime on Monday 23rd when the message came through that the event had been re-scheduled for the following day. The DI had, out of the blue, been summoned to HQ. Shobnall spoke with Cyril about it. "Doesn't matter to the troops, Cyril, any day before Christmas will do but what the blazes have HQ found for a senior get-together in Christmas week?"

Cyril was displaying his most lugubrious expression, the one that reminded Shobnall of a bloodhound. "I don't think Mr Jessop does Christmas."

"Jessop? The DI's being hauled in for a meeting with Jessop?"

"Who knows, Alan? The big-wigs don't confide in station sergeants. Although it was Jessop's personal secretary who telephoned."

"Blimey! Wonder what that's all about."

"You and me both," said Cyril, slipping a further degree into dog-ness. "I see that tart Christine Keeler got away with six months."

*  *  *

Tuesday went well, at least from the moment the DI breezed in on the stroke of nine through to the end of the drinks event. It proved a quiet day with few call-outs, the DI was round and about, all seemed fine with the world. Late in the afternoon, Shobnall went along to help clear furniture. Cyril and the DI set out glasses and bottles. When Angela Bracewell arrived, she re-positioned them more neatly.

The DI delivered his customary mix of professional counsel, homilies on life, reflections on the past year and a handful of witticisms, some of them nearly good enough for a cracker. Woven into it was a good word for every member of staff. The DI made his eulogy to the success of 'our late Joe Short' sound like a compliment to all Joe's erstwhile colleagues. Gordon Roxburgh added his own endorsement. *We're all pleased for him, pity he isn't here.* Right on cue, Heather Wilson entered the room. Heads turned. A brief silence. Then a cheer. "Hello everybody," cried Heather. "Joe wanted me to come for both of us and wish you all a Merry Christmas."

She was mobbed, hugged, kissed, handed a beer. The Di walked over and gave her a peck on the cheek and there was a soft gasp when Cyril Hendry did the same. The warmth was for a former colleague and, by extension, also for Joe, for was she not his, er, well, not wife, obviously, but, um.....No-one was quite sure in this freewheeling modern day and age what the right word was but Heather and Joe, they're a couple, aren't they, so what the hell! That momentary silence when she entered the room had been for the fashion designer. Shobnall looked across the room. *She's all about style, bet she made that.* A midnight-black trouser suit with subtly flared legs and an extravagant collar that took the eye to her face. *I don't think her hair was that colour on the train, wonder how Elaine would look in one of those suits.*

It was some scene, he thought. As the wave of welcome subsided, Heather remained surrounded by the women – Angela, Sheila Redpath, Agnes and Betty – clearly discussing what she was wearing. *I wonder if it's an exclusive for Derry & Toms.* He stifled a giggle. Over there, one of Swinging London's up-and-coming designers was modelling a trendy haute couture outfit and being ogled by Betty, as broad in the beam as a British trawler, and Agnes, spruce in her Christmas turban and with two inches of ash hanging off the fag stuck in the corner of her mouth. *And why not, eh, why not?*

They all knew how it would go. At some point the DI would bellow for silence, wish them all a happy Christmas, absorb the applause and good wishes and depart. There would be handshakes and hugs all round and within a few minutes there would only be the night shift – Eddie Mustard and Angela and whoever was on downstairs – clearing the decks and washing up. It was therefore a surprise when, half a minute before that phase kicked in, the DI placed a forefinger on Shobnall's sternum and said, quietly, "Before you go. My office. Please" and went to close the event. *The DI's face, this is not good.*

\* \* \*

The DI had cast aside all festive bonhomie. He scowled as he stuffed a knot of dark shag into his pipe. "Sit down, Alan. You're not going to like this. I don't."

Shobnall's brain shoved Christmas aside. "I had the sense there was something, sir."

The DI lit up. "I'll not beat about the bush. I did not have a good afternoon at HQ. I had a meeting with the Chief Constable about Wychnor."

"Just you?"

"Just me and just Ian Jessop. He wasn't happy either. I can hear your mind whirring from here. He had orders for me. I have to pass them to you. We are to lay off Morgan Vetch."

*Why am I not surprised?* "For some reason, sir, I don't feel shocked. Does the instruction apply only to Vetch or does it include his associate, Cutter Carpenter? The villain I have in the frame for Wychnor?"

"I know, Alan, I know. I told Jessop we were on the verge of clinching a case and that, at a minimum, Vetch would be in for accessory." He puffed a couple more times. "These are Jessop's words: nothing is to happen to either of them. For the time being. Got that?"

Shobnall considered the floor. "I'm with you, sir, but.....This message from Mr Jessop-"

"No." The DI chopped him off. "The Chief Constable made it clear to me that the message, the *instruction*, doesn't come *from* Jessop. It comes *through* him. Its source is much higher up."

"You mean The Met?

"No, Alan, not The Met. Higher up."

"Oh," said Shobnall.

The DI leaned forward, pointed his pipe, stem first, at Shobnall. "I want you to go straight home *now*. Enjoy Christmas Day and Boxing Day. Don't fret over this. Put Wychnor out of your mind. Focus on your family. We will return to this when you get back."

"But I better-"

"No! There is nothing you need to do here. I'll speak to Eddie."

*  *  *

He was packing his briefcase when the telephone rang. *Am I here? Shall I ignore it?* He answered and Cyril's voice said "Dave Chateris on the line for you."

"Hello Dave, you and Frankie all set for Christmas?"

"Yeah but never mind that, Alan, lissen." The Londoner's voice was taut. "There's a message gonna come darn. You're gonna get-"

Shobnall's turn to do the cutting-off. "Dave. It's already landed."

"Bollocks," said Charteris. "I wanted to get to you first."

"Don't worry, Dave, my DI told me. He said it comes from high up, higher than your place."

"Too bloody right. Russ got the same message. Politics. The worst. We don't know 'ow it's worked but White 'Orse 'ave to be involved. Favours 'ave bin called in an' that means reputations an' necks are on the line. Christ, we probly shouldn't even be 'avin' this conversation."

"Too late now. Anyway, we're not on the chopping-block yet. I've been told nothing has to happen to Vetch or Carpenter....Cutter. Preston. Oh, let's call him Cutter, it suits him somehow. Before the word came down, did you manage to pick up anything else?"

Chateris laughed but it was a hollow sound. "Yeah. Russ 'as bin pokin' around 'ere an' there before they upped the ante. 'E says the operation 'as to be lookin' at a chunky criminal set-up an' 'e still feels that White 'Orse or the Yanks 'ave cracked someone on the inside an' that's where the problem is. Somethin' 'as 'appened to their man."

"Well, that ties in with the conversation you and I had about Cutter. Maybe Morgan found out and has fixed him?"

"Maybe but we really 'ave no idea."

"Sit tight, Dave. We'll see. Meantime, you and Frankie do what my DI told me to do – focus on Christmas. Have a good time and I'll get back to you."

Somehow, Shobnall felt free of anxiety. He finished packing, put on his coat, paused. *Very well, they want me to back off, no problem for Christmas, a day or three won't matter to Cox, Gary Stubbs or Melinda, then we'll see what it means to make sure nothing happens to a pair of villains.*

* * *

# THIRTY-FIVE

Christmas, eh? What's not to like? Invented by pagans as 'Yuletide' to celebrate the winter solstice, remodelled for Christianity and now, as 1963 drew to a close, passing into the stewardship of commerce. Not entirely, to be fair. Alan and Elaine sat up late on Christmas Eve wrapping the last presents, laying some beneath the tree in the lounge and piling others to be handed out on Christmas day, adding to the mantelpiece display the latest delivery of cards – including the usual offering from Shobnall's Polish pen-friend, Inspector Christian Stasik and his wife, Anna, depicting a stained glass window. Shobnall harboured notions of a visit one day. On the more conventional tack, Elaine's parents were in their usual pews for the carol service. The church could still manage a sizeable congregation although James grumbled that, for another year, there had been more empty places.

Whatever its guiding spirit, Christmas remained a time for children, for families, for your friends and for those you didn't know; a time of giving, of light, of love. And for eating and drinking and laughing and playing silly games. If Shobnall had thought the edict on Wychnor and Vetch would prey on his mind, he was much mistaken. The time was so crammed with people and excitement that all thought of work was pushed out of his head. Despite driving through a landscape edged with frost but free of snow to Wychnor House to insist that Basher joined them. "I've told my mother-in-law to set an extra place. Pack an overnight bag." Basher didn't take a lot of persuasion.

Christmas Day meant Winshill with Helen and James hosting the entire tribe – Alan's family together with Neil, Catherine, Paul Victor and Kate. Plus Basher. *I hope this works alright.* That was something else that he needn't have worried about. The adults were, initially, polite but a tad circumspect. The children saw an outsize cuddly bear disguised as a man and smuggled Basher into everyone's hearts.

The usual. Socks, hankies, pullovers – some in the right size, some in good taste and one or two in both – perfume, selection boxes, chocolate oranges, a Sinatra album for James, Airfix models for PV, assorted dolls and board games....the piles of discarded paper and coloured string grew and grew. Turkey, bacon, chipolatas, stuffing, bread sauce, Helen's 'secret recipe' roast potatoes, Brussels sprouts, Christmas pudding – to the children's and his own delight it was Basher who pulled out the silver three-penny bit – with crackers, novelties, ridiculous paper hats and jokes. In past years there had been a wee glass of Asti for the toast; the family had expanded to the extent that two bottles of bubbly were required and this year PV was allowed a half-glass of his own.

All of which made for what people who probably shouldn't have any more to eat or drink like to call a state of well-being. Shobnall, lying back in an armchair while the company waited on Her Majesty, felt *very* comfortable, *very* warm and *very* close to a little doze. He suspected the others were in much the same state. Brother Neil's eyes were already closed and the regular movement of his chest indicated sleep. Shobnall yawned. *What's that noise?* He rubbed his eyes and struggled into an upright position. In the conservatory at the rear of the house. The four children were in a row, Kate, PV and Josephine sitting cross-legged and Alice kneeling, before an assortment of objects; upturned bowls, kitchen pans, flower pots, a metal waste bin, several boxes that had a while ago contained presents. He went to the doorway, captivated.

The children's attention was on Basher. The big man raised his arms like a musical conductor, pointing to one child, a second, engaging all four; they responded, each wielding a pair of pudding spoons except for Alice who was armed with teaspoons. *He's teaching them percussion.* There was a distinct rhythm. Josephine's eyes were locked on Basher as he brought them together, waving for softness, then gradually increasing the volume. Elaine's arm went around Shobnall's waist. "That is so clever," she whispered. "It's the theme to 'Summer Holiday'. I saw it with Lavinia and Hilary." Helen and Catherine, then James, all came to the doorway. Josephine's expression was ecstatic. Shobnall heard someone humming along and realised it was him. The adults looked at each other as Basher's hands called for a crescendo and a close, signs that even Alice managed to follow. The house was filled with affection, awe and more than a dab or two of sheer wonderment. Basher went pink.

As with everything, the day, its import, the entertainment, the gathering and, yes, the re-confirmation of humanity all had to come to a close. Departures meant a tear for Helen but they all stood together to wave off Neil and Catherine and their children, PV hanging out of the rear window waving until the car was out of sight. Shobnall felt a fumbling at his hand and found Josephine beckoning him down. "Daddy," she whispered. "Can Basher come home with us?"

"Of course," he whispered back. "It may be a bit cramped in the car but I'm sure you and Alice can cope." Their turn to leave. Helen gave everyone a hug; she gave Basher a long one and a wet kiss on each cheek. James shook his hand so long that Shobnall wondered if there were some kind of macho competition in process. Basher was in a permanent blush by now. *You see a big, powerful man and you make assumptions about his character, hope he fits into the spare bedroom.*

*  *  *

Boxing Day was an altogether more.....diverse day. Shobnall was up in good time and twitched the curtains open on a light dressing of snow, a piercing white sky and icicles hanging from the roof. *I may be going soft but I do appreciate having central heating.*

The girls had been over-tired by the previous day. This morning they were manic, racing through the house pretending to be cars, then horses, then aeroplanes and generally getting in the way, especially in the kitchen where Elaine was organising a late breakfast and a buffet for the afternoon. She marched through to the front room where Alan was keeping his head down by sorting the drinks cabinet very slowly. "Alan. Please. Could you quieten that pair down? They won't listen to me." Shobnall was equally ineffective as his daughters ducked his finger-waving and chugged off as farm tractors. Basher, bright-eyed, freshly-shaven and clad in his customary black with a t-shirt that read *'a drum is not a symbol'*, came to the rescue. Within fifteen minutes he had the girls sitting in the downstairs utility room wrestling with the intricacies of the castanets he drew from who knows where. Shobnall went to help Elaine in the kitchen. Calm had been restored. Another day of consumption could begin

Corky and Lavinia arrived in the middle of the day in Corky's Triumph Herald. Lavinia had mixed and mismatched a scarlet turban, a full-length dress of deep green and a white silk shawl. She twirled in front of the girls. "Inspired by the festive holly tree, my dears. Corky has been staying with us over Christmas. Reuben will be along later." Shobnall glanced at Elaine; she lifted an interrogative eyebrow. "And who is this magnificent addition to our company?" Lavinia was tiny next to Basher, who knelt, took her dainty hand in his huge paw and kissed it. "Obviously a gentleman."

Basher roared. "That's a first!"

Shobnall had wondered whether the array of sandwiches, vol-au-vents, sausages on sticks, buns, cakes and other pastries might not – even taking Basher into account – be over the top. Things looked different after Gordon Crombie and Lennie rolled up, claiming to have been for a long hike and to be more than a little peckish. *OK, I was wrong, I've a house full of gannets.* Joe Short and Heather Wilson dropped in, Heather in a stunning dress that left the company breathless. After they had gone, Crombie shook his head and settled into the comfy chair in the corner, Elaine proffered a large ashtray proclaiming itself *'A Present from Sheringham'*. To their surprise, he raised a hand to ward it off. "New Year's Resolution. I'm giving up and I'm starting early."

Lavinia looked pleased. "Good for you, Gordon. Was this prompted by anything special?"

"Sort of. I've long known it's a meaningless habit but I actually read one of the hundreds of reports that cross my desk at work. Most of them I pass on in seconds.

214

This one was from the US Surgeon-General, the splendidly-named Luther Terry. He claims smoking may be bad for your health. I thought, OK, maybe it is and maybe it isn't but why take the risk?"

"I think you're being very sensible, Gordon," said Lavinia.

"Surely," queried Elaine. "The tobacco companies wouldn't sell us something that did us harm? They're always advertising cigarettes as socially-desirable accessories."

"Elaine." Lennie spoke through a mouthful of ham sandwich. "They're advertising something that makes them a lot of money. They won't like this Luther going public."

"I'm sure you're right, Lennie. I've had my last puff." Crombie turned to his plate.

Basher was making a sofa look more like an armchair, especially with the two girls on his lap. "So long as it's only tobacco we have to stop smoking then that's fine by me." A ripple of laughter. *Basher's quite uninhibited, it breaks down barriers, I do like that.*

The afternoon went by at a gallop, an invigorating and educational gallop with dollops of fun. Lennie treated them to his impressions of the Prime Minister and Harold Wilson, the Leader of the Opposition. Shobnall decided to forewarn Basher that Mr Salt would be joining the party and that he might be someone with whom Basher might want to, um, tread carefully. *If you do 'carefully' that is.* Basher laughed, said that Jo had already told him about Reuben and that anyone Jo vouched for was alright in his, Basher's, book.

Ah, the educational aspect. Basher reprised his drumming class, at their request, with Josephine and Alice and they delivered a very respectable percussive version of 'Hark the Herald Angels Sing'. Maybe he felt the applause was too condescending or maybe he loved a challenge but before they knew what was happening, Basher had adults and children alike kneeling on the floor tapping on household objects with items of cutlery. It took a while but in due course they reeled off 'Jingle Bells' before collapsing in gales of laughter. Mr Salt was the final scheduled guest. The Hendersons would have been in but they were abroad. *Funny how so many are choosing to take Christmas in France while Frankie, the only French person we know, is here in Britain. Hope she and Dave are having a great time.*

Reuben Salt, as we know, was essentially unpredictable. To the astonishment of all – except Lavinia – he and Basher struck an instant rapport. It dawned on Shobnall that, as was known, Basher knew about beer and when it emerged that Mr Salt had been in

Liverpool during the war and retained a soft spot for the city, they became bosom buddies, a brotherhood cemented by their shared devotion to Josephine and Alice. *I note there has been no question of Reuben banging on a waste bin.*

* * *

There was an unexpected caller. As well that Shobnall was nearest the door. It was Eddie Mustard, wrapped in dark brown overcoat, scarf and cloth cap. "Eddie! Happy Christmas!" Seeing Eddie reminded him of everything that had been set aside for the break.

Eddie shuffled his feet. "Happy Christmas, Alan. Look, I'm sorry to turn up on your doorstep like this but I needed a word. The DI spoke to me on Christmas Eve-"

"Come in, man. I'm not chatting on the doorstep." He led Eddie through to the kitchen. "We'll go outside, otherwise we'll get interrupted." He grabbed his own coat and they stepped into the back garden, down to the end wall. "The DI spoke to me. I would have come to you but the Old Man wanted to do it personally."

"I understand that, Alan. It feels like we've been dumped on. What exactly did the DI say to you?"

"That nothing is to happen to Morgan or Cutter for the time being."

Eddie looked relieved. "Good. I've been chivvying at the words, running them around my head until I'm no longer sure I'm remembering them right. I need to know what it means. What about Basher? I like him. He's straight up and we invited him onto our team. But he threatened harm to Morgan and that kind of thing can easily get out of hand. I don't want to see a good guy step over the mark."

"I know. We also have the Reverend Bullard to consider. It seems to me." He gazed over the field towards the dip hiding the Trent. "That the DI will have shaped the message carefully. He likely wouldn't be surprised if he could hear this conversation. He took pains *not* to tell us to stay away from the villains. Since you're asking me, I would say we need to protect Morgan and Cutter as much as Basher and Bullard."

"So we don't sit back? We stay active?"

"We do."

"Thanks, Alan, again I'm sorry to barge in. I simply needed to hear you say it out loud."

"He's inside, you know."

"Who? Basher?"

"Yes. It didn't seem right leaving him alone at the Hall over Christmas. He charmed my in-laws yesterday. My girls adore him. Are you any good at drumming?"

"What? Drumming? I've no idea."

"Basher could soon find out. I suppose I didn't think a drummer was really a proper musician but what did I know?

Eddie looked lost for a second but gathered himself. "We definitely look after him then."

"We do but we don't tell him about our instructions."

"What about Jessop and wherever the pressure is coming from?"

Shobnall sighed. "My responsibility, Eddie. When it comes to it, I'll back Basher before any political games the Chief Constable is enmeshed in. Look at it this way. We have to live with ourselves."

* * *

# THIRTY-SIX

Ian Jessop was nettled. There's no other word for it. He never looked forward to the lunch on the last day of the year but neither did he shy away from it; another duty, that's all it was but, as with all duties, he preferred to execute it *his* way. The Chief Constable was forever on duty. His staff would say they couldn't remember seeing him in a good mood but nor had they seen him in a bad one, come to think of it. Always neutral, alert and fair, always fair and that is why, despite everything else, he commanded the unwavering respect of his people.

He had known this would be awkward. This lunch had dealt with many a minor embarrassment or ticklish issue but the Wychnor business was problematic, not least because he had no idea what was behind it all. He couldn't ignore it; one of them would raise it otherwise. Bull by the horns, take charge. Except he wasn't in charge. Turning up at the crack of dawn so Lord Needwood could hold private conclave with young Shobnall had been bad enough but that telephone call had been the bitter end. While it was going on – and he had been doing most of the listening and hardly any of the talking – he had to repress an urge to stand to attention. He hadn't enjoyed transmitting the message to Worthington and he doubted Worthington enjoyed passing it on. As he paced along the corridor towards their private room, he reflected on how fortuitous it was that Shobnall had kept his murder suspicions under wraps. He hoped the other two would be drawn more to the sensationalism of the suicide.

He always came early. He liked to be first in, effectively the host. It bestowed a degree of *primus inter pares*. Thus he was annoyed that Councillor Goode had beaten him to it. The man had obviously done it deliberately, to make the point that he understood the rules of the game and could break them if he so wished. Not so *primus*. The Councillor had a reputation as a fixer and there had been times when Jessop had needed something fixed. However, while their relationship hinged on a kind of mutual reliance, trust was something of a stranger. The two men sparred constantly. This was the Councillor's ninth year at this lunch and he would likely remain Council Leader as long as he wanted. Until one or other of them opted for retirement, the sparring would go on. Jessop was fine with that. Sparring was acceptable. Fighting was not.

The third participant was a younger man, today attending his third of these gatherings. Digby Cooper had succeeded his father as local Member of Parliament when Maurice had retired. Retaining the seat bought him a ticket to the Weston Park lunch. He *did* look forward to it; the food was top-notch, the wine superb and he believed he had established his credentials with the other two, thus placing him among the County's elite, a position he craved. He knew he was still learning the ropes but he was working hard around the constituency - something he thought his father had latterly allowed to slip – and was confident he'd win another term at the next election. He anticipated being a part of this grouping for some time to come.

The Councillor was content with that. He rated Digby a considerable improvement as MP and lunch companion. The lad was conscientious, had so far done what he said he'd do and knew when to stop drinking. The Councillor had spotted that Digby was adrift in his self-awareness; he was brighter than his father but not as bright as he thought and he tended to over-rate what others' opinion of him might be. The Councillor had no difficulty navigating around someone like that. It meant he could give more of his attention to the Chief Constable. He had a thorough respect for Ian Jessop; the man was as straight as a die – albeit you often had to squeeze the *whole* truth from him – an excellent manager, intellectually acute. Turning up first had delivered a most satisfactory result. Jessop had said nothing but that tightening of his shoulder muscles, the clench in his jaw, oh yes, the policeman had been needled successfully. Now the Councillor would concentrate on soothing matters.

It was an excellent lunch; the usual quality of fare served by the usual Italian waiter and the usual French sommelier, both of whom were mentally rubbing their hands in expectation of the usual generous tip. Conversation chuntered along, the implications of the loss of Borough status, the outbreak of hooliganism during the Statutes Fair – shop windows kicked in, the lights out on the Ferry Bridge – what to do about these mods and rockers, the slackening of standards especially among young people and the effect of the contraceptive pill, all that kind of thing. On all of which the MP had a view, one or two of them actually sounding like they might be his own, and in all of which the Councillor was careful to respect the opinions of the Chief Constable.

By the time they were left with the brandy, the Chief Constable was soothed, the Councillor was pleased with himself and the MP was sure he had successfully impressed his companions. Jessop sniffed appreciatively at his brandy (although sniffing was a close as he would get). "Of course, during the year we have also had to endure the unfortunate events out at Wychnor Hall."

"Ah yes," said the MP. "Up at the Big House. Dreadfully sad about Lady Melinda. I didn't know her well but she was a decent sort by all accounts."

You didn't know her at all, thought the Councillor. "Plus the drowning that preceded her suicide. They did not make good publicity for the town. I presume the two incidents were unconnected?"

Jessop had expected the enquiry. "Naturally, where loss of life is involved we investigate with maximum care. It is regrettable that we should have had two in such a

219

short space of time and in the same location. The drowning, as you will be aware, involved a popular music group. This activity appears to go hand-in-hand with alcohol, drugs and outrageous behaviour. I can assure you that we are not anticipating any verdict other than death by misadventure."

Digby Cooper felt the need to chip in. "Looks straightforward to me. A bunch of outsiders breaking all sorts of rules and something went too far." He had become conscious that his opinion had not been sought on anything for a while. Somewhere in his head a small voice was asking whether his father had similarly felt like a spectator at this lunch. He didn't care for the thought but he wasn't daft enough to ignore it.

The Councillor had not finished. "But the case has not yet been closed? No report by the Coroner? I'm not suspecting any hanky-panky here, Ian, I only want to be sure the matter can be put to bed."

Typical Goode, thought Jessop; any departure from the norm and he was nibbling at it, *just in case* there was leverage or privileged information to be had. "A procedural issue, Joel. Because the group left for America so soon afterwards, we have been unable to complete the necessary interviews. They are expected back in this country within the next few days and we should then be able to draw a line." Although I have my doubts, he thought, after that telephone call.

The Councillor nodded. That sounded plausible. He hadn't been prospecting for gold dust there; it all looked like the seamy side of the Swinging Sixties. "And Lady Melinda. I don't know how to put this graciously. There is no question about the suicide verdict? There are always rumours and there has been little public statement. Not a lot said at the Police Committee either, if I may say so."

Jessop made an effort not to bristle. "From the moment her body was discovered, we have been in close touch with Lord Needwood. He accepted that an announcement would have to be made but he expressly asked that publicity should be as low-key as we could manage. I thought it right and proper to respect the father's wishes."

"Hear, hear," said Digby.

Jessop continued. "As you are aware, we now have a specialist Forensic Unit at regional level. We had one of their best men on it. I am comfortable saying to you, as I did to Lord Needwood recently, there is no question but that Lady Melinda took her own life."

"Tragic," said the Councillor, in the same tone, it seemed to Jessop, as the man would have asked you to pass the mustard. "As a matter of interest, who did find her body? Your chaps?"

"Yes. We have been regularly in Wychnor since the drowning, dotting i's and crossing t's. DS Shobnall happened upon her empty car. He searched the building and found her."

"Shobnall again?" The Councillor looked quizzical. "We spoke of him a few years ago."

"Who's this Shobnall?" Digby was feeling out of the loop. The Councillor let Jessop respond.

"A Detective Sergeant in our Burton station. I'm surprised you haven't come across him, Digby. Your father knew him. An excellent policeman. Some years ago we had to deal with another sensitive murder. Shobnall had a central part in unravelling it." The MP made a mental note to speak to his father about this Shobnall.

The Councillor moved smoothly on. "And the year in prospect, Ian, what do you foresee? More of the same? New challenges?"

And new solutions, thought Jessop, whose book club had supplied him with 'A Clockwork Orange' and who was coming to the view that modern criminals might, indeed, call for modern treatment. "I expect more of the same but it is not a same that we want more of. Our society is changing, gentlemen, I am sure we can all see that. From Westminster, Digby, you will perhaps see this more sharply. There is more money about. Love of money and so forth. No, don't take me for a puritan. Greater affluence brings benefits but they do not bring them for everyone. Envy, greed, resentment, they all fuel crime. And when there is more money, there are more things to buy, not all of them legal. Drugs have been with us for decades but the combination of youth, music, money and drugs is going to be a headache for all of us. And then we have the pill and we all know where that is leading." The Councillor and the MP raised their glasses to the Chief Constable. Jessop was right. This drugs thing was creeping in all over the place and society was engaged in a sexual revolution. Who knew where this cocktail might lead?

Around half-past two, they departed Weston Park. As Councillor Goode drove off with a jaunty wave, Ian Jessop buttonholed Digby Cooper. Jessop had been soothed but he hadn't forgotten the Councillor's transgression of the rules. Jessop hadn't survived so long by being careless of all those – friends and enemies – close to him. The MP was blatantly flattered by the attention. And it cost nothing.

* * *

# THIRTY-SEVEN

The turn of the year. We throw out the old calendars and replace them with fresh views of seasonal landscapes or stately homes or cockily-posed British birds of the hedgerow. The days lengthen, the light brightens and those persistently-nagging worries shrink in importance. We straighten our shoulders and resolve to do better this year in the belief that things will be clearer and fairer. If not necessarily warmer. Winter continues relentlessly. Unless you are with the England cricket team sweating the Madras test to a draw in thirty-plus degrees. Which escalates the tussle for Bob Saxby's radio up through skirmishing to a tense cold war that makes the stand-off between America and Russia look like child's play. Saxby, arguing owner's rights, wants his sports coverage. Gideon Watson had become accustomed to a diet of music and doesn't feel like giving up. Lennie tries to block out the bickering but eventually shouts at them.

The ensuing silence is absolute; no-one can remember Lennie shouting at anyone before. Ever. The ensuing silence is also short-lived. The next time Saxby leaves the room, Gideon – with a covert glance in Lennie's direction – switches to pop. Whispers are had. Lennie ostentatiously thumps a file on his desk. A pause. More whispers. So it goes on. Lennie marches out of the station bang on time.

He takes his elder statesman role seriously, more seriously than he would admit. The following day he is late in and, when he does arrive, presents Gideon with a transistor radio little bigger than a paperback and with a thin wire dangling free. "Stick it in your ear, Gideon." The lad will worship Lennie the more for this. So, for that matter, will Bob Saxby. Lennie is pleased; a problem solved and he absolved from shouting. He had welcomed in the New Year with 'Top Of The Pops', the Beeb's latest attempt at modernisation, and he is reconsidering his attitude to this 'pop stuff'. It might be a lot of fun.

* * *

Almost a fortnight into 1964 with the weather, intensely cold and well below zero overnight, deteriorating into blizzards and freezing fog nation-wide. Shobnall is back on nights with Eddie Mustard. They are camped together in the DS' office; it's smaller and holds the heat from the radiators and the single available extra plug-in two-bar. Downstairs, Charlie Taylor has already broken his resolution to stop playing cards with Sheila Redpath. All four are thankful that the weather is keeping villains, minor criminals, accidental law-breakers and clumsy drivers indoors. Not a single call-out in five nights. Boredom can have a warm lining.

The Reapers have returned to Britain. They saw the pictures on the news, youths dressed in black and chanting their heroes' name, saluting in unison. It wasn't the frenzied declaration of passion generated by The Beatles. This was more regimented. Shobnall thought it rather sinister, all these young men in black. It took Eddie to point out that if you looked past the uniform, there were as many females as males. "Even scarier," he opined.

No sign of Morgan or Cutter. Dave Chateris had reported back. "Russ sent a DC to the airport, 'e figured the White 'Orse team would be there an' 'im or me would 'ave bin clocked. No sign of them two. Maybe wasn't on the flight, seems unlikely, or they 'ad themselves smuggled off. Russ gave it twenty-four an' no complaints about our DC an' 'e put the lad on surveillance of The Reapers office, told 'im to keep 'is 'ead right darn 'cos there was probly other surveillance goin' on." He paused.

*Come on, Dave, stop milking it.* "And?"

"Tell yer what." Shobnall heard pride in Chateris' voice. "We employ smart coppers in this Division. Our lad sussed their surveillance. Made 'is job a lot easier knowin' where they was an' it showed us they ain't as good as they think they are." He paused again. "Vetch is here. Our lad got a shot of 'im, Russ an' me confirmed it. No sightin' of Cutter, not so far anyway. Want us to do anythin' else?"

"No, Dave, please, nothing. We need to tread carefully. It's too risky to tail Morgan but it helps to know he's around. Presumably, Cutter isn't far away. You could keep a weather eye open for him. I have every right and reason to haul him in for a chat. Can't do anything until I know where he is, obviously."

So they watched down there. DI 'Russ' Conway and DS Charteris and their team prowled the streets of London with one eye cocked for the spoor of Vetch and Cutter, the other alert for signs of White Horse surveillance. And up here they waited, huddled indoors as much as possible. Eddie had plenty of time for his studies. Shobnall brought his admin chores up to date and made inroads into Angela's. Then, one freezing dawn in the second half of the month, black ice thick on the roads, drifts of snow on the pavements, it happened. Charlie Taylor finished the shift one pound and three shillings up on Sheila Redpath. It was going to be his year!

*   *   *

Two nights later, not long after LBJ declared 'war on poverty' in his first State of the Union address, the weather-gods added fog to the Arctic mix. Parts of the South coast hadn't been seen for days; Brighton was all but cut off from the rest of the country (with many in Hove considering this something of a blessing). Downstairs, Charlie Taylor and Sheila Redpath had the heating up full and, with all doors shut, it was nicely toasty. Sheila had been out earlier with DC Mustard. A Methodist minister from Woodville, said to be 'suffering from nervous strain', had gone missing the previous day and now his empty car had turned up at the railway station. No sign of a Minister. The car was sitting in the yard out back.

The uniformed constables had struck a friendly relationship. Charlie, as the more experienced officer, recognised his responsibility to show her the ropes and enable her to benefit from his expertise. He found her chummy enough, keen to please and willing to do her share and on top of that she appeared to enjoy his driving. The only piece of grit in the machine was her facility with cards. He'd thought he'd got on top of that but here he was, down almost a quid! Sheila Redpath was too clever for Charlie but she was too nice a person and too anxious to do well on the Force to exploit her edge. Not much, anyway. She could manage Charlie, no problem, prudently allowing him a win whenever he reached the stage of thinking he never would. Now and again, she thought, let the dog see the bone.

Up in the DS' office, Eddie Mustard was taking a nap, shoes off, feet up on Angela's desk. Shobnall had filched Lennie's newspaper and was reading about the opening of the Train Robbery trial at Buckingham Assizes in Aylesbury. There was widespread speculation that some of the jurors might have been got at. *Be surprising if they hadn't, there's so much money involved.* The front-page article sat alongside a stock-shot of The Dave Clark Five, top of the charts with 'Glad All Over'. They looked like respectable young men. *Dave Clark, I've heard that name before.* He started as Angela's 'phone trilled and Eddie moved seamlessly from dozing to waking, feet to floor, handset to ear. *In that cafe with the Kray twins, Ronnie said they went to their club.* Eddie held out the telephone. "It's Basher."

"Basher. Alan Shobnall here. What's up?"

"He's here." Basher's voice was controlled but was there a tremble there? "Morgan's in the village."

"Exactly where are you, Basher?"

"I'm in the telephone kiosk beside the village green."

"How do you know Morgan is there?"

"The car. It's parked outside the rectory. There's lights on in the church, I think Morgan's in there with the vicar."

*Bullard as well, should have put a watch on the Reverend.* "OK, Basher." He looked pointedly at Eddie, now shod and in his coat. "We'll be there before you know it." Thumbs-up from Eddie, who left the room at the double. "You're too visible in the kiosk. There's a clump of trees at the edge of the green. Take cover there and wait for us."

"Shouldn't I keep an eye on the church?"

*And then you'll take a little look inside, eh?* "No, Basher. Nothing happens until the law gets there and that's us. Stay by the green. We're on our way." He hung up, leaving no room for further protest, and mentally crossed his fingers. *Can't have Basher tangling with Morgan, we could be looking at another corpse.*

By the time Shobnall reached the lobby, a black car, rigged for snow and with Charlie and Eddie already aboard, was revving at the front. Sheila Redpath had the door. "Sir, can I come too, sir. Please?"

Shobnall saw the excitement in her face and he was loth to quash it. *I remember what it feels like.* "I'm sorry, Sheila, we must have someone here and we need to get to Wychnor as fast as we can. It has to be Charlie and you have to hold the fort." He patted her arm. "Your turn will come." He hurried down the steps, tumbled into the back of the car and Charlie moved off smoothly. WPC Redpath watched it accelerate away, relatively slowly for Charlie but, in the conditions, some five or six times as faster than any human being should dare. *He's a big lump of typical male,* she said to herself, *but he can't half handle a motor.*

\* \* \*

# THIRTY-EIGHT

We know what it's like being chauffeured in a hurry by Charlie Taylor and here the maniac was hurling a mechanical tin box on wheels over ice and snow, through banks of rolling fog, lights on full. No need for the bells, they were the only vehicle on the road. Paradoxically, Shobnall was calm. Partly because he sensed the stability of the motor as the chains bit through to the tarmac. Partly because he wasn't sure Basher would obey his instructions or whether, if Morgan was here, the White Horse people would be tagging along. Charlie slowed to walking pace as they neared the village green, doused all but sidelights, pulled up where Shobnall pointed.

He shoved the rear door open as a large figure in anorak and bobble-hat emerged from the knot of trees and ploughed through the snow towards them. *OK, he's behaved so far, half-seven, it'll start getting light soon.* Basher clambered in. "I didn't expect you *that* quickly."

Eddie leaned over from the front seat, smirking. "Our secret weapon, Charlie Taylor. Charlie, this is Basher. He's a pop star."

Basher laughed. "I'll not be having you write my epitaph, Eddie."

"Anything else happened?"

Basher shook his head. "Nothing's moved, no noise."

"Right," said Shobnall. "Me and Eddie are going to walk down to the church. We are officially investigating a case here. We are authorised to barge in. You." He poked Basher in the chest. "Are off to Wychnor House with Charlie."

"Cobblers!" Basher was indignant. "I want Morgan."

Shobnall placed a hand on Basher's shoulder. "I understand, Basher. I'll explain later but there's more going on than you know, a lot more. Eddie and I are putting ourselves on the line by being here and the reason we *are* here is a commitment we gave to look after the vicar and our responsibility for keeping *you* safe. Please play ball. Afterwards.....we'll see. I expect to need you."

Basher was silent. It occurred to Shobnall that the well-built drummer was calculating that Charlie was even better-built and that, if it came to it, the policemen might resort to force. He let out a long breath. "OK. Charlie! While these two play in the snow, why don't you come back for a cup of tea?"

227

Day was seeping into the sky and the streets had been swept. The trek to the rectory was fairly straightforward. Shobnall put Basher out of his mind. *Charlie knows what to do.* He was alert for movement but the village was quiet and he didn't have that 'someone's watching me' sensation. *Doesn't mean they're not behind those curtains.* The rectory was dark but the door was ajar. Eddie went in. Came out, shaking his head.

Basher had been right. Lights on in the church. Inside. No candles; the electric lights high on the walls were on. Someone was speaking in a low tone. As they moved down the aisle, the voice fell silent and two heads turned towards them. Bullard was at the lectern, half leaning, half sprawled across its outsize Bible, a white, fronded page-marker dangling almost to the floor. Shobnall couldn't decipher his expression. *Is he glad to see the cavalry or terrified we've done for him?* The man was trembling, with the cold or fear or both; he was in dressing gown and pyjamas, his feet bare on the stone flags.

Morgan Vetch was sitting insolently on the altar, wearing a long black overcoat and fedora, looking for all the world like an evil spirit overseeing some Walpurgisnacht ceremony. He levered himself lithely to his feet, looked down at them from the raised chancel. "Well, well, well," he drawled. "Our friendly country bobbies." His voice was hard, chiselled from granite.

"What do you want with the vicar, Morgan?"

Vetch's expression was contemptuous. "It's Shobnall, isn't it? Yeah. Shobnall. What's it to you?"

"We need to talk about other matters, Morgan. I'd rather dispense with the Reverend if you don't mind." There were sheets of paper on the altar where Vetch had been sitting. "I assume that's the missing extract from the Diocese's file?" Vetch's eyes flicked back and forth. "We know you removed it and we know why. Tell us, Morgan, did you come here to eliminate the vicar. Like you had young Cox and Gary Stubbs eliminated?" Something had changed in Vetch's face but he wasn't sure what it meant.

"Why don't you ask the vicar if I was about to send him to meet his maker?"

*He's not bothered.* He walked over to Bullard. "Reverend?"

Bullard looked imploringly at Shobnall. "Please. Let me leave this place."

Shobnall stood close. "He dragged you out of bed and into the church. Why? What did he want from you?" There was no answer. Bullard's lips moved in silence. His head dropped to the Bible.

"You're a nuisance, Shobnall." Vetch had moved closer on the raised dais. "A pesky nuisance." The Diocese papers were now in his hand. He tucked them into an inside pocket. "You're a persistent devil, too. I remember you from that night at Wychnor Hall when you faced up to Melinda. Not an easy thing to do." He leaned towards Bullard. "Remember, Reverend. I have this and I know where you live. Now get out!" Bullard raised his head but didn't budge; independent motion was beyond him.

Eddie stepped forward. "I'll take him next door, Alan." He pulled the vicar away from the security of the lectern, supported him as he stumbled down the aisle.

Shobnall kept eye contact with Vetch, listening to Eddie's footsteps and the slap of Bullard's feet until the wooden door opened and swung shut again. "I asked why you dragged the vicar in here, Morgan."

Now it was just the two of them, Vetch seemed to have relaxed a degree although he retained an attitude of menace. He swept a languid arm at the raftered body of the church. "The House of God provides a most conducive atmosphere, I find, for the generation of awe and terror."

"You came here to frighten him into keeping quiet? Because he's terrified of having his past exposed?"

"Got it in one, policeman."

"And not because you were going to guarantee his silence by shutting his mouth permanently?"

Vetch was unmoved. "I'm a businessman, Shobnall. I calibrate risk. I marshall my resources, my labour, capital and intelligence with maximum efficiency. Enough to get the job done, that's my maxim. I have no need to eliminate the vicar and deal with the messiness that would follow. What I know is enough."

"What you know about what?"

"My business, Shobnall, not yours." Vetch sounded assured, the man with an inside tip on the National.

"About how he fixed you up with Melinda."

The composure wobbled. Vetch took a moment. "I may have underestimated you, Shobnall. I shan't repeat the mistake. But yeah, that's what, and I don't care for loose ends that one day might unravel. Quite frankly, I couldn't care less whether the old pervert lives or dies but I see no need for killing." The church door opened and closed again. Eddie rejoined them.

"No," said Shobnall. "And it wouldn't do to dirty your own hands, would it? Where's your number two, Preston?" He could almost hear the wheels spinning as Vetch calculated what the policemen might know.

"He left my employ during our American tour. Claimed he couldn't hack the lifestyle. Personally, I think he'd had a better offer."

"I'd like you to hand over the papers you stole from the Diocese."

"Why should I?"

"Because you know that Bullard will never be brave enough to testify against you and because we don't need any testimony from him to connect you to Melinda." Vetch gave Shobnall a long stare. Reached inside his coat. Handed the sheets to Shobnall. "Thank you. We'll put these back where they belong. Without explanation. The Diocese will be happy enough they are returned."

Vetch was looking like a poker-player  worried about the next card he might be dealt. "What were those 'other matters' you mentioned a while back?"

Shobnall treated him to a confident smile. *My turn for some psychology.* "We don't suffer from awe and fear, Morgan, but it is bloody cold in here, too cold for a friendly chat."

Vetch's thin smile acknowledged the end of skirmishing and the onset of war. "You're right. Why don't we go up to the Hall? Carter will have the heating on." The smile lengthened minimally as he read Shobnall's face. "That's right, my friend. This evening I've learned not to underestimate you. Now you can learn the same about me. Think I'd have waltzed into this hick village without checking what's going on? Come on, my car's outside." He gestured towards Eddie. "I know Shobnall here. What do I call you?"

"My name's Mustard."

A slight pause. "Mustard? You must be keen."

Eddie left a longer pause. Said flatly.  "You know what, Morgan? No-one's ever said that to me before."

\* \* \*

# THIRTY-NINE

Eddie rattled around the limousine's cavernous rear compartment. Shobnall sat up front. He didn't trust the American not to lock them in the back and.....*Do what? Can't see him bumping off a pair of British coppers.* Vetch swung the tank of a vehicle expertly through the village and along the tree-lined track to Wychnor Hall, the Big House seeming to rise as the sky lightened. *I guess Americans are used to big cars.* Vetch halted at the steps. "Let's get one thing straight, Shobnall. You and me will talk, man-to-man. Nobody else. Not Carter, not Mr Keen here.

Shobnall flicked a glance at Eddie, whose expression said 'if need be'. "Otherwise?"

"Otherwise no talk. I get back in my limo and I'm gone. I saw the police car under the trees over there."

"Our driver. He has the muscle to deal with Basher. OK. It's a deal."

Basher and Charlie were, of course, ensconced in the kitchen, seated each side of a roaring fire. Shobnall had been concerned about how this might go but it was fine. Basher was, on the surface at least, all sweetness and light. "Morning Morgan. Surprised to see me again?"

"I knew you were holed up here. I suggested to your new friends that we say hello."

"Oh." Basher looked and sounded disappointed. *The man has many strong qualities but he's out of his depth with a player like Morgan.*

Shobnall still feared Basher might attempt something. "Morgan and I are going into the ballroom for a chat. Eddie's going to keep you company. Any chance of a cuppa?"

"Yep." Basher rose. "Fresh pot brewing, enough for everybody. No milk, no sugar, that right, Morgan?" Vetch ignored him. "Morgan don't take nothing in tea or coffee. He worries one of his friends might slip something nasty in." Vetch the basilisk, tall and implacable. *This isn't going to be easy.*

* * *

The ballroom - scarlet walls, white plasterwork, multi-branched crystal chandelier - was unchanged from his previous visit. The sprung dance-floor, worn and scuffed in places but eminently serviceable, the handful of fancy, velvet-covered chairs on its

232

perimeter. As daybreak filtered through the French windows, the air inside held a misty quality. It wasn't hard to imagine the bustle and swing of a full-scale ball, the windows open to a summer evening's warmth, musicians on the podium on the far side of the room lifting the atmosphere with gaiety while dukes and countesses, gentlemen and ladies of the realm mingled in the margins, accepting a glass of this and a morsel of that, chattering excitedly of glamour and style, of betrothals and bequests, or whispering softly of illicit affairs of the heart.

Not today. The ballroom hosted a duel. No seconds, only the principals, the American and the policeman. As if following some established duelling protocol, the protagonists walked carefully – to avoid slopping tea – onto the podium and took position at either end of the long table. The room was warm. Shobnall hooked his coat over the back of his chair and sat. Vetch switched on the lamp, moved it halfway down the table, went to the windows and pulled on the curtain cord, shutting out the view across the lawns to the lake. The lamp illuminated the table but, beyond, shadows crowded the room. "I hope you don't object to privacy, Shobnall, you never know who might be spying."

*I fancy privacy suits both of us.* "I assumed you wanted to block out the location of Michael Cox's murder."

"Murder?" Vetch sipped at his tea. "I don't recall any official statement suggesting Cox's death was anything other than an accident or suicide."

*Different tack.* "The night we met. You flew to Birmingham and transferred to a helicopter. You had it land at the old Alrewas aerodrome and collect.....Preston." He paused. "Let's call him Cutter. His real name is Terry Carpenter but he's known as Cutter."

Vetch, still in coat and hat, stared down the table. "So Preston had a secret identity? Who'd have thought it? But you're right. Stubbs called me at home. I went directly to the office to sort out travel. I was leaving when Preston.....when Cutter rang and we arranged the pick-up."

Shobnall went on. "He had a key to the house. We have recovered it. We are curious as to how he came by it. Did he steal it or was he given it?" *Which way do you want to jump?*

"Oh, I gave it to him early on. We had three. Stubbs held the others. Once I'd signed the contract, I didn't need to be here. I couldn't spare the time. I left it to.....to Cutter to keep an eye on them."

*Don't over-egg the name-change, Morgan.* "Keeping an eye? Wasn't that Gary Stubbs' job?"

Vetch rapped his mug down, splashing tea onto the table. "OK, OK! I knew Cutter would need to get in a couple of times quietly. He had to get Cox his stuff."

"His stuff?"

"You know what I mean, Shobnall. Your medics must have found him full of coke. It was the only thing that kept him functioning. The kid was a junkie. We daren't leave him with more than a week's supply in case he overdid it. He begged us to keep his habit secret, including from the rest of the group. He was frightened they'd sling him out. Cox was frightened by a lot of things." *Including you and whatever you had on him, I'll bet.* "Stubbs had been around, he likely had his suspicions but he was soft on them all."

*Plausible but how much truth is wrapped in how much deception?* So Cutter went to see Cox to top up his drugs."

Fingers drumming on the table now. "Yes."

*Are you listening, Elizabeth Helm, he had the key in order to enter the building, confirmed!* "What happened?"

The drumming stopped. Vetch sent down a look of extreme malevolence. "Things got out of hand. Cox could be weird, with or without his junk. He could be a real bitch. Cutter has a sadistic streak but he can be thin-skinned. An argument escalated. Cox riled Cutter and he went for the kid. I never asked for detail."

"Morgan, I don't buy that for a moment." The situation felt dangerously intimate; no world existed beyond the two men. "Cutter was a knife-artist, that's how he got his nick-name. If things had, as you put it, got out of hand, Cox would have been chopped and diced. Instead, we have this charade of a suicide."

Vetch had re-assumed his impassive face, spoke in a mock-posh English accent. "I'm awfully sorry, old man, but that's my story." Back to his natural drawl. "I wasn't here, remember. I had to rely on what Cutter told me."

*I'm not getting around his defences.* "Where is Cutter?"

"I already told you. Whatever his name is. He left my employ. He'll be working for someone else, could be in the States, could be here, in London, could be anywhere. The world is shrinking fast these days."

"Morgan!" Shobnall knew he ought to suppress the anger but couldn't. "The Richardsons. Your former associate is a member of one of London's most brutal gangs. Don't let's pretend he's anything other than a vicious criminal." He stood, leaning forward over on the table. "You've been very helpful, Morgan. You've given me enough to put Cutter in the dock for murder. Now I'm thinking about you as accessory."

"Persistent little swine, aren't you?" Vetch, too, was standing and he, too, was venting his anger. While Shobnall's pent-up ire had smouldered and burst out like a roman candle, Vetch's hissed and fizzed with a fierceness than sliced the air. "You think you're so clever but you're overreaching, sonny. You can't touch me."

"Being American doesn't grant you diplomatic immunity, Morgan."

Vetch grinned, a cobra rearing and baring its fangs. "It's nothing to do with my nationality."

"You-" Shobnall stopped dead. The anger dissipated as his brain kicked in and joined up the dots in a different pattern. He dropped back into his seat. "It's you. Isn't it? You're the man on the inside. It's not Cutter inside your outfit, it's *you* inside the bigger set-up." He pressed his hands to his temple.

The tall dark figure looked haughtily down at the crumpled British policeman. "I plead the fifth amendment."

"Not valid in this country." Shobnall's mind skimmed over the evolution of the case, the flood of opinions, suggestions, statements, all that anybody had said. "Gary Stubbs knew the group better than you but you had a different relationship with Cox. You have an eye for weaknesses, you fed his habit, built a dependency. You dug into his past, uncovered things he'd tried to keep secret. Knowledge is power, eh, Morgan? Dependency, power and control. But a special relationship demanded special contact, right? I've wondered why someone would want to kill young Cox. It was nothing to do with drugs, nothing to do with him falling out with Cutter. Cox was closer to you, saw you more often." There was no doubt; Vetch stiffened. "Cox knew something, didn't he? He *saw* something." Shobnall was back on his feet.

Vetch said nothing, his face a mask, eyes on Shobnall.

235

"What could it have been, something that called for his death? Melinda? No. Your being closeted with her in your office late at night would have meant nothing to Cox."

Vetch said nothing, didn't move a muscle, eyes on Shobnall.

"Anything to do with the drugs business wouldn't have registered; Cox was immersed in it. Nothing to do with your management of The Reapers. All he cared about was the music. That and his cocaine and his mother."

Vetch said nothing, eyes on Shobnall, but his hands had tightened into fists.

"No." Shobnall saw light. "He witnessed something he shouldn't have, something you couldn't let pass." *A hit, no question, a tic in his eye.* "He saw you with the people from Operation White Horse. Maybe he knew who they were, maybe not, maybe he had a go at putting two and two together. Or maybe it all passed him by and all he cared about was the junk you fed him. You're a businessman, Morgan, you assess the risk and then consider the efficient deployment of resources."

Slowly, Vetch lowered himself into his chair. He removed his fedora, placed it to one side, rested his forearms on the table and contemplated Shobnall. Resignation was printed on his face. The balance of power was equal once more.

\*   \*   \*

# FORTY

"How did you find out Cox had seen you? Did he say something or did your White Horse friends tip you off? The latter, I'd guess. If you'd found out in time you'd have dealt with it in London. No, the group was already here. White Horse came and said you had a problem. You decided on speed. This is why you had Cutter on loan from the Richardsons, to mop up inconveniences like this.

"I don't suppose he knew what it was about. He's a sadistic villain. It's not in his nature to work things out. You probably bamboozled him with something about the drugs distribution business." *Another hit!* "That's right. I know what you wanted from Melinda. Cutter went in like you told him, quiet and unseen. Make it look like one of those out-of-their-head pop stars overdid things and finished up in the water.

"I have to admit, Morgan, it was smart. In and out by river. We've assembled a bundle of circumstantial evidence but there was one piece of serendipity that helped us. Something you couldn't possibly have played into your risk calculations." He stopped.

Vetch actually smiled. "Come on, Shobnall, you're dying to enlighten me."

Shobnall smiled back. "You're right. I am. Imagine. Early morning, let's say about three o'clock, Cutter is ready to leave Wychnor Hall. Cox is in the lake. The second dinghy is back in the boatshed, wiped. Cox's room has been cleaned. Nobody has seen or heard a thing. Cutter lets himself out, locks the door. Mission accomplished on time. All he has to do is walk back to the Swarbourn and the inflatable and it's plain sailing to Fradley Junction. That boat weighs next to nothing; a man like Cutter can easily lug it over the locks. He'll abandon the boat and walk up to the aerodrome.

"Except it had been raining. The ground was greasy. As he clambers down the river bank, he slips, falls, drops the bottle. It's overgrown down there, it might have gone anywhere. He'll have a torch." Shobnall was half-inventing this as he went on, fancying how it must have been. "He'd have needed one. The rainclouds were obscuring the moon. Walking over the lawn, through the gardens and trees, you'd need a torch. You must have planned it on a map, Morgan, I doubt you ever walked the grounds when you booked Wychnor Hall. There's Cutter, searching among the trees and bushes and leaves and weeds, a regular little forest and it's not just the bottle. He checks his pockets and the key is gone and who knows what else and he has a date with a helicopter and there will be complications if he misses the rendezvous. How's that?"

Vetch wasn't ruffled in the slightest. "I'm impressed, Shobnall. If you've got that far you'll have realised what a fool Cutter turned out to be. The lake was a disaster. He drove up in a van with the boat. To that place with the funny name, Alrewas. All he had to do was get in unseen, help Cox overdose and get out. Stubbs discovers the body, typical pop music affair, two-day wonder, I don't need to worry. Instead, Cox absorbs everything, even the booze, and stays upright so Cutter panics, heads for the boathouse he noticed getting in. He phoned me afterwards."

"Where from?"

"Here. The ballroom." He pointed into a far corner. "See? There's an extension. Nobody'd hear him. I had to improvise. Even then the idiot outdid himself. Climbing ashore at Fradley, he fell in the canal. Can you believe it? The helicopter guy was not amused. Cutter never bothered to mention it was the second time that night he couldn't stand on his own feet."

"He wouldn't, would he? Losing his footing and key pieces of evidence in what might turn out to be a murder case? Nobody else knows, keep your mouth shut, make up a harmless story if needed. Typical villain reasoning."

Vetch stood. "I'm in a jam," he said. He began to circle the room, hugging the shadows beyond the light. "I'm over here in this backwoods of a country, doing a job for my people. It's going well. So far as I am aware, none of the authorities here have wind of it. Then it turns out I'm wrong. It's not down to me. Someone Stateside slips up. I don't know who or how but the Feds are on it and they do what the Feds *never* do. They climb into bed with your buddies in Scotland Yard. Maybe they figure they fought a world war over here, let's fight the drugs war here too."

"The White Horse Operation," Shobnall wanted to be clear.

Vetch returned to his seat, leaned back, as if entering the confessional had dissolved the tension and resentment. "Yup. Those guys tap me on the shoulder and I have to choose between a new occupation as a stool pigeon or becoming a permanent guest of your Queen. Believe me, Shobnall, I wouldn't settle here if I was a free man, let alone as cheap labour sowing mailbags or whatever they do these days in your Victorian prisons. I'm between a rock and a hard place, my people and your White Horse agents. Plus I'm saddled with Cutter and we know what his employers would do if they'd gotten so much as a whiff of treason. While I'm trying to keep all these balls in the air *and* manage a pop group that was intended as cover but now looks like it can take over the world, White Horse drops the bombshell.

"They filmed our meetings. I don't care about that, I'd have done the same in their shoes but when you're the patsy in the middle it doesn't make you feel good. They review the film and one of their guys spots Cox and they check him out and they dump it in my lap. For me, it's a complication too far. I need to snuff it out. I used one of my problems to sort another. You got it right, Cutter was there for the dirty work although he was also the Richardsons' man watching me. He liked to hurt people, you know. Something wrong in his head if you ask me."

"That'll be why he was such a poor businessman."

Vetch laughed, his first genuine laugh. "Yeah, very likely. I tell him he gets to kill someone and any thought of risk or efficiency is forgotten in the excitement of how much bloodletting he might get to do. He had no idea there was a risk that I *did* calculate. I mean, if Cutter had found out *why* I wanted Cox bagged, who do you think would have been in the bacon slicer?"

"With the Richardsons turning the handle."

"They hadn't to know. I paid Cutter a tidy sum to keep it off the collective balance sheet. He had to stay shtum. His bosses wouldn't like him taking money from third parties, not one little bit."

"Cutter must have been a concern. How convenient that he left your employ."

Vetch took it on the chin. "You'll appreciate why I didn't make much of a fuss when he said he was off."

Silence, both reflecting on what had been exposed and what the other was likely to do about it. "Looked at objectively, Morgan," said Shobnall eventually. "It worked out well. You enabled a man who would cut you to pieces if he knew you were playing both sides to take out another who potentially held the power of life and death over you and you managed to leave the assassin open to a murder charge."

Vetch was unfazed. Or didn't care anymore. Shobnall couldn't tell. "You know, Shobnall, I'm real surprised to be talking to you like this. They told me you'd been warned off."

Shobnall nodded slowly, as if recalled to the tenderness of his own situation. "I was. We all were. A warning from high, almost as high as you can get."

"Then why come running out to Wychnor to intercept me? Isn't it your job to do what you're told?"

Shobnall chuckled. "Yes, Morgan, in crude terms, that's how we're organised. It's.....complicated. I'm out here because it's also my job as an officer of the law to look after people. Bullard, for instance. He's led a strange, nomadic life. I suspect he's spent it looking for something and feels let down by his God and everyone downwards because he hasn't found it. All he has left is to live with himself and he isn't finding that much fun. We might think him pathetic but he's simply a human being with nowhere else to go. He has assisted our investigations and we – Eddie and me - gave a commitment to look out for him. I had to honour that commitment. Then there's Basher."

"That big oaf doesn't need protection!"

"Oh, but he does, especially from himself. The first time I saw Basher he was unconscious on a couch upstairs stoned – I think that's the term – on marijuana. I thought he was another of these undisciplined young musicians drunk on fame and money. We're quick to lay stereotypes on people sometimes but there's a lot more to Basher. We've become quite fond of him. No way would I have risked him going up against you and Cutter."

"Do you British policemen go on a psychology course or is this something to do with your genes?"

Shobnall ignored the gibe. "Then there's you, Morgan."

"Me? You came to protect *me*?"

"We were warned that nothing had to happen to you. What might have occurred if we hadn't rushed out here, if we left you and Basher to it? On balance, even without Cutter, I'd have bet on you but I, too, had to consider the risk. Basher might have hurt you, maybe even killed you. How would the White Horse boys react? Especially with the FBI breathing down their necks? I already know how high their reach goes; I daren't test how far they might be able to stretch their revenge. I need to look after you."

"I see."

"There's another irony. The similarity between you and Melinda, battling each other, both spinning too many heavy balls. She took on herself a very final responsibility for finding a way out. You've been manipulating matters in order to, well....."

Vetch snorted. "To keep myself breathing, Shobnall. That's it, pure and simple. Melinda, she was a classy dame, I'll say that. Me? I was in a jam. Hell! I'm still in a jam. I couldn't see the point." He bowed his head, pinched the bridge of his nose for a second or two. *Almost a human gesture.* "To be frank, I don't think I would ever have the courage to take my own life. Melinda. She gave up everything. Why did she do it?"

"I'm sorry, Morgan, I really am, but you're too complicit. Poor Melinda. Like you, she evaluated her options. You were one of the factors, demanding she hand you the transport company on a plate and threatening to reveal her indiscretions. No, you don't have the right to know." He moved on quickly. "Did you help her move the Diamond?"

"Yeah. She let slip what she was up to, appreciated the help. All part of my ingratiation strategy."

"I see. What about Gary Stubbs?"

Vetch reached into his coat pocket and withdrew a slim pewter flask, poured a measure into its cap and threw it down his throat. "I'm not sure why I'm telling you all this, Shobnall."

"Because you're tired of bottling it up. Because I'm a good listener. Because I'm a stranger. Because you know I can't do anything with what you tell me."

"Yeah, all of those, I guess." He held out the flask. "Want a shot?"

"Too early for me, Morgan, thank you. You and Gary didn't see eye to eye."

"True but, like you and Bullard and Carter, there was more to it. Stubbs tried my patience with his incessant questioning, forever implying there was a better way than Morgan's way, his unending demands for the group but he was damned good at his job. I needed him, more as they became so popular. I wouldn't have chosen to lose him. I hired this place because he said the group must have a rest, I even let him have the use of my limo."

"Coming to Wychnor wasn't part of the plan to get close to Melinda?"

"No. I'm something of a regular here. Bullard and I go way back. You know that." Shobnall said nothing. "He'd already connected me to Melinda and I was getting her company into play when she mentioned the place was available just as Stubbs was bleating about a time-out. Stubbs was what you British call a cock-up. I pieced it together later. Stubbs suspected someone was supplying the kid. He kept on probing. Cutter thought the questions were about the death and he got nervous about taking my money. I think this is how it runs. Stubbs calls the office, looking for a meet. Cutter intercepts the call, Stubbs is told I'm in conference but a meeting is possible in some Thames-side bar. When Stubbs arrives, he's met by Cutter and the Richardsons. From what I hear, they took him out on a river boat, fixed a chain around an ankle and dangled him into the propeller. The Richardsons are always looking for entertainment."

"The Richardsons mess things up."

"When my people sent me here, they already had the tie-in with these Richardsons. I had to work with them.

"The White Horse team knew about Cox's murder. They condoned it as a sacrifice for their operation." Vetch nodded. "Did they know about Stubbs?"

"I don't know. It was my nuts they had in the cracker, not Cutter or his cronies. You'll have to ask them."

"Doubt I'll ever get the chance. They don't have anyone on site here?"

Vetch smiled again. "I'm pretty sure not. If they had someone on my tail we'd have known by now." He played with his hat. "You gotta leave me out, Shobnall."

"Maybe." *He's right, I'd lose my job, could get another but Eddie would suffer, George, others,* "No, I'm not going to play games, Morgan. I can't talk officially to anyone about this conversation. If I wanted to be nasty I could leave you with Basher for a while."

Teeth flashed white. *We're getting to be buddies.* "Two of the people you've sworn to protect?"

"Tell me something. Suppose Melinda hadn't committed suicide and the deal was on. Could you have found your way out of this?"

"No question. I travel with a bag of plans. Plan A, Melinda plays ball, the project goes ahead until White Horse and the Feds decide to drop the hammer. I get a new ID, a facelift in your Harley Street and a one-way ticket to South America. Plan B, Melinda refuses, we go looking for an alternative distributor. If we are re-configuring the deal then maybe we lose the Richardsons. Whatever, we carry on. My people see the long game. The Feds will wait and that means White Horse will wait. Ultimately we reach a loop into Plan A."

"But Plan B swings in now. Melinda dead is much the same as Melinda refusing."

"No.  Melinda refusing is entirely legal and takes place privately. Melinda suicide is public. The family tried to keep publicity to a minimum but where it counts, everyone knows. There's too much uncertainty. The instructions from my people are to shut down. Like I say, they play a real long game. Close down, let the dust settle, reassemble as a new project. That's why I'm in Wychnor, closing down, dealing with loose ends."

"You make it sound clinical, very business-like but it's about personal survival, isn't it?"

Vetch grinned again and lamplight panned across his face. Shobnall seemed, for a moment, to see the skull beneath the skin; he shivered. "You think like me, Shobnall. Yeah. Transferring a project is one thing, mothballing is another. Affects my bonus aside from anything else. Truth is, my people are sitting over there in a swanky boardroom discussing how Morgan Vetch has performed and what they should do about me. The organisation hates failure. I may come to think of Cutter and the Richardsons as real nice, friendly guys."

"You think we could be fishing you out of the Thames?

"More likely the Charles River in Boston, Mass."

"You're quite an operator, Morgan. You could have made it in so many ways. How on earth did you get in so deep with.....your people?"

Vetch stood again. Shobnall followed suit. Vetch put his flask back in his pocket, restored his fedora to his head and came down the podium to Shobnall who recognised the sign of finality. "I'll make you a promise, Shobnall. Three months from now, May. If I'm still alive I'll contact you from wherever I am and we'll continue this conversation. Deal?"

"Very well, but I'm still investigating Cox's death. I will interview Cutter when we catch up with him. Formally, we would appreciate it if you would remain in the United

Kingdom until we do. Unofficially, I realise you may need to leave our shores and I hope to hear from you in May. That's pretty much us, isn't it?"

"Uh-huh. You and me, Shobnall, we're so different and yet not different at all. We took opposite decisions once upon a time. There's no going back." He extended a hand. "It's been an unexpectedly interesting morning."

Shobnall stared. He thought about Michael Cox, Gary Stubbs, about Melinda. *What he's done, how we're different, how the cards are dealt and how you play them.* He shook Vetch's hand. The American turned and strode to the windows, slipped between the curtains and was away. Shobnall stood, thinking. After a while, he gathered himself together and made his way towards the kitchen, preparing for the questions from Charlie, Eddie and Basher.

\* \* \*

# FORTY-ONE

"How did young Mustard take it?" Corky wanted to know. "He strikes me as the phlegmatic type."

"Oh, he is," said Shobnall. Early evening. The girls had been feted, fed and put to bed. Now the adults sprawled in the lounge. "He's happy because he thinks we put one over on the White Horse mob, indifferent because he understands that Morgan's untouchable and disappointed because we haven't found Cutter."

"And Basher," asked Elaine. "How did he react to your excluding him?"

"Remarkably well. I think he was glad we prevented him going too far. He believed Vetch's version of what happened to Gary and that calmed him down."

"Will we see him again? Jo is forever asking."

"Oh, I wouldn't be surprised. He says he's become attached to Wychnor Hall. Sounds like he loves the food."

"So where has Vetch gone?" Gordon Crombie was chewing. Since giving up cigarettes he'd turned to gum.

"Back to London. British Railways 'phoned in the next day about a strange vehicle left overnight at the railway station. Looks like he abandoned it. The ticket office recognised his picture."

Crombie removed a wad of gum from his mouth and wrapped it in its silver paper. "Not sure this stuff is the answer. He's making himself hard to find?"

"Yes, he knows that car is like a beacon."

Corky was at the half-open door. "All quiet up there. What are you going to do with the car?"

"Joe Short will give it the once-over then we'll stick it in our yard. The railway boys want it off their premises. It takes up too much space."

"Let me know when you move it."

"Corky! You are not getting a ride in it." Shobnall's firm voice.

"Of course not, my boy, merely an inspection. Technical interest, you see."

"I know you, Corky." He turned back to Crombie. "He'll have tidying to do in London. Hank Walker, the Pinkertons man from the British Museum, called us. One of his agents picked up a story about The Reapers changing management. Morgan seems to have negotiated a deal while the group were doing their shows in New York at the end of December."

Crombie, ever-curious. "No-one we've ever heard of, I presume?"

"It's a corporation headed by somebody called Alan Klein. This would be his first foray into the British music scene but he's big news over there. Accountant, record label owner, music publisher. Based in New Jersey. Hank says he has a reputation as a highly creative financier and as a hard case capable of squeezing blood out of a record company to the benefit of his clients. And himself."

"That's not an entirely attractive portrait," observed Elaine.

"That's what we thought but he sounds like the kind of operator who would speak Morgan's language."

"So," said Crombie. "Vetch is doing a Cheshire cat act, gradually erasing himself from the picture, but he's beyond your grasp anyway. You can't push the case fished out of the Thames, Stubbs, that's out of your jurisdiction. Where's this other chap, the one we're now calling Cutter?"

"I have no idea. I think Morgan knows more than he admitted. I should have pressed him harder. I don't buy this line about Cutter baling out into America. He may have parted company with Morgan but I'd bet on him being in London, the place he knows. He could be back with the Richardsons or he might have his head down if the Cox killing has somehow backfired on him. I've asked Dave Charteris to put the word out."

A sound, a soft moan that might have been 'mummy', floated down the stairs. Elaine was up in a flash and out of the room, leaving three males hovering at the now fully-open door, all thoughts of crime and villains forgotten.

\* \* \*

The man previously known as Preston and now being referred to as Cutter was located faster than anyone had a right to expect. It had been a bitty, unsatisfactory kind of a day. Angela had come good on her threat to take a chunk of leave.

Consequently, Shobnall's work pattern had become erratic; as the only available DS he sought to spread himself as widely as possible, a mixture of days and nights plus a few half-and-halfs thrown in. The DI and Cyril Hendry stepped up to bear some of the load but his irregular hours, he knew, left him more tired and sensitive than normal. On top of everything else, the squadroom atmosphere had become testy. England were busy salvaging a draw in the 3rd Indian test and Bob Saxby was working with one protective hand clamped on his radio, leaving Gideon fiddling with his earpiece for a decent connection to the likes of 'Needles and Pins' and 'Hippy Hippy Shake'. Lennie had taken a day off and was not available to pour oil on troubled transistors. Shobnall stayed in his office as much as possible, staring at the tendrils of fog curling about the window.

Which is where Dave Charteris got through to him. "Dunno if this is the news you've bin wantin', Alan, but we've found Cutter."

Shobnall's spirits rose. "You have? Brilliant, Dave. Where is he?"

"Yeah, well, this bit yer may not be so 'appy about. Right this minute, he's lying in our morgue. 'Fraid I don't know what number cabinet 'e's occupyin'."

"Oh." Shobnall deflated. *All that work for nothing, no justice for Gary Stubbs.*

"Thought that might come as a bit of a dampener, mate, sorry to be the bringer of bad news."

"No, Dave, don't apologise. At least he's not running around free. Where did you find him?"

"Clap'am Common, south of the river. 'Ospital porter from St Thomas' on 'is way 'ome after 'is shift near enough tripped over 'im. When the local boys saw it they called us. Someone 'ad put several bullets in 'im. Wasn't done on the Common, 'e was done someplace else an' dumped. Russ wants to talk to you about it. 'E knows you'll want to see the body."

"Of course but can we hold off? We're a DS short here. It'll be a week at least before I can get down."

"Cutter ain't goin' nowhere. I'll tell 'em to 'old 'im in the fridge till I say. Lemme know when you can make it."

Shobnall sat for some time, reflecting. *I guess that'll be that, our suspect dead, Morgan vanishing, the end of the Wychnor case.* He checked his watch against the clock on the wall. *Eddie should be in by now, better tell him.*

Eddie was at Lennie's desk, leafing through the yesterday's paper lying there. "Catching up with world affairs, Alan. See the Beatles following The Reapers into America. They're already Number One over there. Look at this, Heathrow's never seen anything like it, four thousand to see them off. Strewth! We should send them out to Tanganyika instead of the Royal Marines. What a carry-on! What's the news here?"

Shobnall told him. Eddie's reaction was much the same as Shobnall's had been: disappointment followed by a realistic acceptance of the facts. "Better if we could have finished it off, Alan, but at least he's got what he handed out to Gary Stubbs and we kept Bullard and Basher safe into the bargain. We've done alright in the circumstances."

"When Angela's back, I'll go down for the formalities. You want to come down?" He wasn't sure which way Eddie would go.

Eddie did hesitate, his eyes flicking to the drawer containing his study books, but he looked squarely at his DS. "Yes, I feel I owe it to Gary Stubbs."

"Me too, Eddie. I'll let you know when."

"No word on Morgan?"

"There is something. You're more in touch with the world of pop music. Have you heard anything about The Reapers' management?" He summarised the message from Hank Walker about Alan Klein.

Eddie was nodding as he did so. "I read about that. My pal at Norman's said Klein was supposed to be in London already with his entourage. All part of Morgan's disappearing act, eh?"

"Looks like it, doesn't it? I wonder what the rest of the group think about it."

"Probably won't notice. They're big time now. Album top of the American charts, about to be released here. As long as they're left to write and record and perform and get screamed at, they won't care who's arranging matters for them."

"Hm. Or who's doing what with the money." Shobnall suddenly felt a little bleak inside. *Don't dump it on Eddie.* "At least you and I will remember Gary Stubbs from when it was him doing the arranging."

Eddie eyed his superior officer sympathetically. "Part of the job, isn't it? You try and look after people, take care of the good ones and when they're gone you look after the memories."

*True but how many memories can one person accommodate?* "You're right, Eddie, mustn't get maudlin. Now, I've one more call to make before I leave. Have a quiet night."

\* \* \*

He fished out the business card, studied it for a while, set it beside his diary, dialled the first number; it *was* at the top and it *was* the one recognisable as a British number.

A female voice answered. "Good evening, you have reached the offices of Lord Needwood. My name is Pamela." *She sounds very business-like.*

"Good evening, er, Pamela. My name is Alan Shobnall." He got no further.

"Mr. Shobnall. His lordship told us to expect you. How may I help?"

"I.....I would like to meet with Lord Needwood. I promised him that when I was in a position to do so, I would tell him, er.....what happened to..."

"Mr Shobnall." The voice was lower, more intimate. "We understand that this concerns poor Melinda. Now." Brisk once more. "His lordship will meet with you at Wychnor Hall. He is not in this country at present but we could say Thursday February 13th at 10.00. How would that suit?"

"That would be perfect."

"Excellent. One other thing, Mr Shobnall. His lordship wanted it to be clear that this would be a private conversation." Shobnall chuckled. "Except." She spoke firmly. "He would be pleased if you were accompanied by a colleague, a Mr Mustard. Is there anything else I can help you with at this time?"

"No, that's everything, Pamela, thank you." He wrote the appointment into his diary and laughed aloud. *Well, Eddie Mustard, honest peasant copper, a peer of the realm invites you for a private conversation, Chief Constable not invited.* He didn't feel at all bleak as he hummed his way down the stairs and off home.

\* \* \*

Two days later, their constabulary lot turned sour. Tony Nash and Robin Dixon had clattered down the aircraft steps showing off their Olympic gold medals as Britain's first bobsleigh champions. The Queen Mother had startled the country by being rushed into the King Edward VII Hospital in Marylebone for an emergency appendectomy. And while the nation tuned in to the six o'clock news for the medical update, Dave Charteris 'phoned again.

"Alan, no time for chat." He sounded as if he'd been running. "Get darn 'ere. You an' Eddie. Pronto."

"What? Dave, what's going on?"

"Nah, not over the telephone, juss get darn 'ere. Ain't me talkin'. Russ wants you to drop everyfing. Matter of mutual interest. Urgent. First train in the mornin' if yer can."

He would have trusted Charteris with his life. "OK. I'll fix things. We'll be there but I'll need to get back as soon as."

"Not a problem. This needs handled fast. Me an' Bill will pick you up at St Pancras. An' Alan."

"Yes?"

"This is totally on the qt. Not a word beyond you two."

Shobnall was thoughtful as he replaced the handset. *It's Wychnor, but what?* He went hunting for Eddie Mustard.

*   *   *

# FORTY-TWO

Shobnall spoke with the DI. "I need to see Charteris and his DI, sir." It wasn't much of a conversation. "It can't wait." Largely silences and knowing looks. "Please don't ask, sir." Strangely, George Worthington didn't seem bothered, waved his DS off wherever he needed to go. It was easier for Eddie, who pointed out that he'd be off-duty during the day and at liberty to take a trip; he could kip on the train.

It was a diesel but Shobnall had to admit it provided a smooth ride that enabled Eddie to get some sleep while he stared out of the window at the sunrise and the waking countryside. He hardly saw it. His mind was retracing the case, trying to divine what twist or turn might lie in wait. The longer he brooded, the more concerned he became. As they eased past suburban back gardens, he owned that, yes, he was worried for his colleagues. What he dared not think about were the implications for him and his family.

Charteris was waiting at the barrier, stamping his boots in the cold. He clasped their hands in turn, hurried them to Bill and the car, sitting at the front of the taxi-rank, much to the annoyance of the cabbies. Bill put his foot down but, Shobnall noted, no bells. No-one spoke. There was a tension in the car; it gradually came to him that it wasn't apprehensive, it was conspiratorial. *Dave said to tell no-one, what have they dragged us into?*

He recognised the morgue. *This'll be Cutter.* Bill stayed with the car. Charteris escorted them through the featureless corridors until Shobnall stood again in the large theatre that testified to the scale of violent death in the capital. The harsh white environment, scrubbed and scoured to a brilliant cleanliness as if to deny its purpose. Eddie was clearly taken aback at the seemingly endless row of metal gurneys, some empty, some draped, the two at this end masked by drawn curtains. Something was different. *There's nothing going on, it's deserted.*

"We cleared them out," said a gruff voice. DI 'Russ' Conway, again in dark trench coat but without pipe, had entered behind them. "Didn't want any awkwardness." He moved to stand between them and the gurneys. "You're Mustard?"

"Yes, sir." Eddie was wide-awake.

"Right, lads, we have things to share with you." He led them to the endmost gurney, tugged the curtain aside. A white sheet covered what could only be a body. At a sign from Conway, Charteris whisked the cover away with the controlled flair of a matador. Shobnall and Eddie, on opposite sides, confronted the naked frame of a large

251

male, the upper torso criss-crossed by old scars, the limbs and head decorated with some more recent extra ventilation. Despite the hole between the eyes, there was no doubt who it was or had been.

"Cutter Carpenter," said Eddie. "Or Preston as was. That's our man."

"It is," agreed Conway. "Found, as you know, on Clapham Common a few days ago although not killed there. Plugged in both knees, both elbows and the middle of his forehead. Powder burns indicate close-range firing but we have no bullets, no gun, no idea where the deed was done. What we *do* have is the body of a Richardson soldier dumped on their territory. Somebody was saying 'looky-here'."

"Do you have any suspicions?" Shobnall asked.

Conway rocked on his heels. "We like Reggie Kray for the tap. It's his style. Reggie has a screw loose. He'd have enjoyed immobilising Cutter, probably taunted him. Nutter versus sadist. Nice mix."

"An' if Reggie did the shootin'," added Dave Charteris. "Ronnie will 'ave okayed it."

"Causing us to ask," continued Conway. "Why Ronnie Kray would approve his brother taking out a Richardson soldier. If you had asked us last week what were the odds on gang warfare breaking out in this city, we'd have said it was a very long shot. The Krays and the Richardsons are too focused on milking their own empires. London's still big enough for both. We can't see Ronnie deciding off his own bat to whack Cutter. Yet that's what's coming back to us from the streets."

"Someone asked him to do it," said Eddie. "Someone paid." Conway beamed, like a teacher pleased with the prowess of a student. Shobnall and Eddie looked at each other and Eddie said it. "Morgan Vetch."

Now Conway looked meaningfully at Charteris before responding. "We have been considering that possibility but we haven't been able to come up with a motive."

Shobnall took over. "We can help there. Morgan is preparing to do a bunk. He's closing down his interests, tidying loose ends. Cutter was a loose end." He explained Cutter's extra-curricular role in the disposal of Mick Cox. "Morgan would have seen only one way of guaranteeing Cutter's silence; the permanent solution. What doesn't stack up is flaunting the body. I'd have bet on Morgan asking for it to be lost in a concrete foundation or something. There's plenty of construction work going on down here."

"That figures," said Conway. "It takes some chutzpah to knock off a Richardson. The Krays are probably the only outfit in town who'd take it on. That right, Dave?"

"Spot on, guv, an' if Vetch dangled a wad an' asked the twins to get rid of Cutter, they'd 'ave considered it cowardly to refuse."

"But you're right, Shobnall," resumed Conway. "The deal would have been for discretion. Enter Reggie. He and his goons will have lifted Cutter, taken him somewhere private on their patch and had their fun. This sort of thing excites Reggie and when he gets excited he can lose the plot. He'll have forgotten his manners in the thrill of a little torture and death."

"And stirred up a hornet's nest for you," said Eddie. "It can only escalate."

"Maybe," said Conway. "But then again, maybe not."

*There's something else.* "That's very cryptic, sir."

"No need to be formal here, Shobnall, we're outside rank while we sort this. *Not really but it's a nice gesture.*

"Need to keep an eye on the time, guv." Charteris to Conway.

"Thanks, Dave. Gents, we only have the run of this place for a short while and we have something else to show you. Come." They ducked back out and Conway held back the curtain to the second gurney. They arranged themselves around another draped form. Charteris repeated his matadorial flourish and the four of them looked down at a second naked corpse. Nobody spoke for a while.

* * *

Morgan Vetch was a mess. Shobnall had to force himself to keep his eyes on the corpse. The ear on this side had been hacked to a stump of gristle. The fact that Eddie had closed his eyes suggested he was looking at something similar. He scanned the corpse. *Who on earth could carve a body like this? Like THIS?*

Conway's tone was restrained. "Dave and I have already had one viewing so we know it's no party but you needed to see. You have a *right* to see. I'll run you through the main points. Both ears sliced off. Yes, those are cigarette burns on the chest. Nipples sliced off. If you examine the hands you will see the top joints of all fingers and both thumbs have been snipped off. Our pathologist, who claims to know about these things, suggests they used nail puller pliers; the cuts are very clean. He says the cuts were seared to halt blood-flow. He says this will all have taken quite a time.

"They didn't bother with his toes, likely bored with repetitive snipping. As is patently obvious, they castrated him. Certain body parts not recovered. Let me draw your attention to his ankles. Here. And here." There were visible wounds in each. "Pathologist says eight-inch nails." Conway moved up the body. "Excuse me Mustard." He lifted a hand and rotated it to reveal the palm. Something had been hammered all the way through. "Same in the other hand, take my word for it. Lastly, they slashed his femoral artery in the thigh." He took out a handkerchief and wiped his mouth. "Now. Before any of us throws up, we're heading for my office." He ushered a stunned Shobnall and Mustard through the curtain while Charteris replaced the sheet. "Dave, will you let Bronson in to deal with Vetch? They can have their butchers shop back. Catch us outside."

Conway marched them back to the car, put them in the back and climbed into the front. Bill leaned anxiously over his seat but found that neither was yet ready to meet another's gaze. "Leave them," Conway whispered. They sat for what seemed like an age. Probably not even five minutes. The rear door jerked open and Charteris crammed himself in. "Take us away from all this, Bill," said Conway.

A ten minute journey. In silence. Eddie rolled his window down and leaned into the breeze. At Scotland Yard Conway led, Shobnall and Eddie behind him, Charteris and Bill bringing up the rear. He set a fast pace, up flights of stairs and along corridors that all looked the same, passing uniformed and plain-clothed officers moving sedately about normal police business. A door bearing a plain white plaque: 'Detective Inspector Keith Conway'. A big chair and a big desk, its surface laden with files and paper, in-trays and out-trays and more-trays and other-trays; a meeting table and six chairs beside the windows; an old brown leather couch and a pair of grey filing cabinets on the far side. Conway waved them to the meeting table, Charteris and Shobnall on one side, Bill and Eddie on the other. At the end nearer the couch, a black tray and five glasses. Conway unlatched a window. "I think we could all do with some fresh air, cold as it may be." He moved to one of the filing cabinets. Shobnall inspected the room. All very plain, very functional, very *police*; there would be scores of rooms exactly like this. Except for a set of framed watercolours, small, delicate, peaceful; seascapes, coastal scenes, rural idylls, rolling green hills. Shobnall felt better looking at them.

"We could definitely all do with some of this." Conway poured viscous golden liquid. "Speyside malt, smooth as you like. I suggest you follow my example." He knocked his straight back and waited, expectant. "Bit of a slap in the face for the master distiller but it's the best medicine available." Shobnall felt the heat, the hit and the afterglow. *It's put colour back into Eddie's face, suppose it's doing the same for me.* Conway put another good splash into each glass and sat heavily in the end chair.

"Welcome to an exclusive club, gentlemen, dedicated to maintaining a balance between the pursuit of justice and hanging onto our jobs. I'm afraid that, through no fault of our own, we five are in this together and it is, as Norman Vaughan might say, extremely dodgy. Nobody is going to interrupt us. I've locked the door. Ignore the 'phone. Forget we're in the Yard. We're five blokes discussing matters of shared significance. Alan, Eddie, how're you feeling."

Shobnall had begun to analyse what he'd seen. *Oh my, what an almighty mess.* Eddie was looking to him. "Part of me wants to forget what I saw. I've never, *never* seen anything like that. It's only a week since I talked with Morgan and there he is, what's left of him. I know, he was a heartless criminal. But what kind of.....*thing* could do that to another human being?" He shook his head.

Conway turned to Eddie who, glass in hand, looked him in the eye. "I'm grateful. You didn't try and forewarn us and you had the emergency aftercare ready."

Conway raised his own glass. "Good man. Both of you. Look. Here we are in the capital, eight million souls, financial centre of the world, Buck House, Swinging London and all that sexy crap. We have a dark underbelly you wouldn't believe but even for us that's been an eye-opener. All three of us went white as a sheet, no lie. Bill didn't fancy a second go. You've seen the two corpses and we've talked about Cutter. While we waited for you two we've been thinking about Vetch on the basis of what we know and what the medics tell us.

"As with Cutter, they grabbed him and took him somewhere private. The end of it was a kill but along the way they amused themselves – the cigarette burns, the finger joints, the ears, nipples and.....the rest. Once they got bored, they went to work. They crucified Vetch, nailed him up like, well, like Barabbas; don't want to elevate our man too high. We reckon he was still alive. No idea if he was conscious although I am tempted to think he was. Then they slashed his artery. They probably stood and watched him bleed to death, smoked a cigarette, cleaned their tools, went for a pint."

Eddie took a swig from his glass. Shobnall tried to focus. "When did you find Morgan's body? Where?"

Charteris answered. "Early yesterday mornin'. River Police spotted the body on the bank of the Thames down towards Rainham Marshes. Local DI's an old mate of Russ's an' 'e called us. I mean, you can't see that carnage and not say 'wass goin' on, can yer? Me and Russ went for a gander."

"The local DI is a good friend," confirmed Conway. "We did him a favour, took it off his hands, allowed him to forget he ever saw it. Ask your next question, Alan."

*This man is sharp, in the Old Man's league.* "Is this a reprisal? For Cutter?" Shobnall was recalling Conway's observation that killing Cutter might not imply gang warfare.

Conway looked at him fixedly. "What do *you* think?"

"Morgan is heading for a hidey-hole. He gets the Krays to deal with the Cutter problem. You hear about the Kray involvement from the streets. So, presumably, do the Richardsons?"

It was just Shobnall and Conway. "Way we figure it, Alan."

"They need to respond.  They have to. Someone throws down a gauntlet in their territory, they can't let it pass. "

"We agree absolutely on that."

"But they don't retaliate directly at the Krays." Conway smiled and sipped his whisky. "The streets tell them it was Reggie Kray. This is tricky. They can't afford to get it wrong. They can't move on rumour and suspicion. They need confirmation before they make a move. They go straight for the person taking out the contract on Cutter. They knew."

Conway stared at him. "Impressive."

"The Richardsons working it out?"

"No, you birk. The Richardsons major on violence. Brainpower isn't their forte. You're saying someone gave them a steer."

Shobnall met Conway's gaze. "Only one possibility. Morgan's people. From the moment Melinda committed suicide, the project is off. Draw back, see how the dust settles, have another go. But Morgan is a failure and he knows too much. He's become a liability. It's Morgan's people who tip the Richardsons off that Morgan had Cutter taken out and that they are free to do whatever they like about that. The Richardsons might even see that as a condition of staying in the venture long-term. Sacrifice made,

256

partnership preserved." The room went silent for a while. *And we were warned nothing had to happen to those two.*

Eddie cleared his throat. "The White Horse Operation", he said. "How do we stand with them? Are we in the clear?"

*   *   *

# FORTY-THREE

Conway looked from officer to officer round the table. "That, Eddie, is the question of the day and, quite possibly, of our careers. Let me lay out three givens. First, we absolutely, no question, don't even think about it, *must* tell Operation White Horse about Vetch and hand over the body. Second, we have to do it *fast*. We are the only people who know the identity of the corpse. The Rainham locals don't know. I can say I whisked the body away in order to keep a lid on things. The pathologist doesn't know but he'll be blabbing at his next dinner party. Even pathologists don't often face that degree of inhumanity. At the morgue, only Bronson even knows the body exists and he's with us. Thirdly, before anything else, we need to get our story straight."

Eddie was wary. "We're not going to lie to these people, are we? They have some high-up allies."

"I wasn't thinking of telling porkies," said Conway. "Generally speaking, I prefer the truth although, in this case, I doubt we'd want to tell the *whole* truth."

"Surely." Eddie wasn't happy. "They'll only be a problem for *us* if Vetch is a problem for *them*?"

Conway replied. "Let me put it this way. White Horse *may* have a problem. They definitely have *an issue*. Vetch was in this country putting together a major drugs network and his project is dead. The Feds are the threat. They want the crowd behind Vetch and their route to them was through this country."

"Let's call them what they are, boss." Bill had been quiet. "Organised crime. The Mob."

Conway shrugged. "Whatever the name, Bill, White Horse are no longer in a position to serve them on toast to the Feds. The Americans are not going to be over the moon about that. Fingers will be pointed. Foxholes will be sought. Scapegoats required. The fact that none of this is down to us is neither here nor there."

Shobnall was troubled. "We don't all need to be in their sights. Up to the point we were warned off Vetch, none of us had put a foot wrong. It's me, really, I crossed the line and I dragged Eddie along-"

"I didn't have to be dragged but you're right, Alan, it's us two are in a pickle."

Conway was unperturbed. "White Horse won't see it that way. We've been in it with you ever since you called Dave for information on Vetch. Stubbs brought us right on board 'cos that stank to high heaven. And do I need to remind you who it was wandered the corridors of Scotland Yard with a megaphone searching for something called the White Horse Operation? That's right, yours truly. Since then, we have voluntarily compounded our involvement chasing Vetch and Cutter. Oh, and it's us who are sitting on the bodies right this minute. We." His gesture embraced Charteris and Bill. "Don't have a leg to stand on. Nor are we looking for an out. I think the five of us share the same police values. Including helping our mates in the pursuit of justice." He sat back. "Although we do like having a job."

Shobnall nodded. "We hear you. Thank you. But is it a question of allocating blame? Vetch's project collapsed with Melinda committing suicide. Nobody could have seen that coming."

"Ain't blame," said Charteris. "'S'about who takes the rap. White 'Orse 'ave lost more than this end of things. They've 'ad their mole taken out by London villains. It 'appened 'ere, on White 'Orse's patch."

"So," Eddie ventured. "We need them to understand the Richardsons were tipped off?"

Conway rapped the table. "Yes, Eddie! We do. By Vetch's employers. At the *American* end. If anyone's fouled up, it's the Feds. White Horse are off the hook and so, with a little bit of luck, are we."

"That means we need to give them Cutter," added Shobnall. "The reprisal has to be visible."

Eddie wasn't so sure. "Couldn't we presume The Mob found out that Vetch had been turned? That would be enough for them to have him killed and we can leave Cutter to one side."

"No!" Conway was firm. "We have no grounds for such a presumption. More important, we know from Vetch that White Horse handled his turning. If The Mob were aware of that then it probably came from over here and White Horse are back in the firing line and looking for fall guys. Is it any skin off our nose if we throw in Cutter?"

"Not really," said Shobnall. "We've had a legitimate interest in him for some time and White Horse know that. It was mainly Morgan we were warned off. Not touching Cutter was secondary. However, if we let on why Morgan had him killed it all gets

259

messier. We open up the original Wychnor murder, Cox's drowning. Morgan said White Horse condoned that murder and they'll not be happy if that gets out. It could be hard to control. It might raise difficult questions around how we know so much about what Morgan was doing. We can't say 'Alan talked to him'."

"No question." Again, Conway was decisive. "There can be no mention of your conversation and we do not want to antagonise White Horse by parading their dirty linen. It would be preferable to draw the line at Cutter and Vetch. White Horse aren't displaying top-line policing skills but they'll be checking everything. We need a way of finessing this."

"Suppose," said Shobnall. "A third party volunteered the intelligence that Morgan was after Cutter? It doesn't go back into the Wychnor case, it starts there and then. Say, the Reverend Bullard? They're bound to interview him."

"Would he do that, Alan?" Conway was interested. "Could you persuade him?"

"I think so. Bullard has learned a lot about life and about himself of late. He would see the pragmatic side." *The more I think about this, the more I like it.* "Besides, he owes me an extremely large favour."

Eddie liked the concept. "Would Basher be better, Alan? He's on our side."

"No, Eddie. Morgan went to see Bullard so there is a trail for White Horse to follow. In addition, I think a man of the cloth would be more convincing, especially one who no longer has to worry about blackmail."

"Right, lads." Conway raised both hands for silence. "The story opens with the Reverend approaching you in Burton. Unbeknown to any of us, Vetch has returned to Wychnor to refresh his hold over the vicar. He leaves Bullard with the impression that someone else, someone close to Vetch, is going to be tidied up permanently. I doubt a name is specified."

"No, it's not," said Shobnall. "We infer it. We had Cutter for the Cox murder and Morgan as accessory. Cutter was an obvious loose end for Morgan. White Horse need to know."

Conway resumed. "Good. You call Dave who looks for me. By an amazing coincidence I am at that very moment arranging for a body to be transported from Rainham Marsh. We didn't know it would be Vetch. We assumed they'd have him under surveillance but Alan's right, the information supplied by Bullard suggests White

Horse had not been fully privy to what was going on. No way will they admit they lost him. We clamped down because we saw that was what White Horse would want. The body's under wraps, please take it away. We've played a straight bat throughout. We can only be exonerated. White Horse will keep mum about their own slip-ups and point the finger at a missed trick in the States." He looked thoughtful. "They can point out to the Feds that the way the Mob colluded in getting rid of Vetch leaves the tie-up with the Richardsons in place. The Feds and White Horse should stay on the case." He grinned. "I like it. Do you like it?" They liked it.

"OK. Bill, Dave, take our guests back to St Pancras. Alan, Eddie, thank you for your contribution. Go back home. Draw a neat official line under the first Wychnor death. Prime the vicar and practise your lines. If you need anything from us, shout. I am hot-footing it to our colleagues in Operation White Horse with the expressed hope that we can be of assistance to them.

"I apologise for my earlier statement that we'd not be telling any lies. Obviously, we are. We have the time-honoured excuse that they ain't big lies and we're only telling them to another group of coppers who transparently aren't as smart as they should be. One last thing, gentlemen. This next little while is going to be hard, maybe a fortnight or so but we can hang on to our desks. Behave as normal and hold your nerve."

\* \* \*

Another diesel. *Steam's on the way out, get used to it.* Rolling from under the station canopy, through the city, accelerating into the countryside. *Change isn't necessarily progress.* Eddie had slipped off his shoes and spread his legs on the opposite banquette. "You think Bullard will do it?"

"Yeah, I have a feeling that man will do almost anything for us, up to and including breaking the Ten Commandments."

Eddie smiled tiredly. "Hope so." He slipped lower across the seats. "Think we're in the clear?"

"Can't be sure, Eddie. We've no choice other than to keep faith with Russ and-" He was interrupted by a sudden blast of sound immediately behind them, so loud that he stood and looked over the divider. Three teenagers and a transistor radio. "Please turn that down." The trio looked like they were going to take issue with him so he flashed his card, at which they shamefacedly switched off the radio. As he returned to his seat, he heard the kids exiting their carriage. "Sorry, Eddie."

261

"The Reapers, Alan, that's who they were, listening to. Their last single, 'Shame'" Eddie yawned.

Shobnall mused. "I can't help but feel that Basher is well out of all that."

"I agree. He's a nice bloke. But you were saying?"

"I have as much faith in Russ as I have in George, almost, anyway. I can't put it any stronger. And you know what? We may have another ace up our sleeve." But Eddie had drifted away in to sleep. "Called Needwood."

*   *   *

# FORTY-FOUR

The Reverend Bullard was a piece of cake. They sat with him one evening in a dark, book-lined study, the curtains pulled shut and, chapter by chapter, laid out the story, past, present and hoped-for future. More than anything, Bullard was relieved. "The Lord may chastise me for it but I must be honest. I am glad. The fact that you had removed those papers from his possession has not been enough to extinguish my dread of Vetch. Er, the papers *have* been returned?"

"I took them," said Shobnall. "The Diocese has them secure. You are safe." There seemed no purpose in mentioning a quiet assurance to the Secretary that he need not fret over whatever blot lurked in his own past.

"Gentlemen. I am hugely  in your debt. I shall be happy to begin repayment by doing as you ask. To recap, I have seen nothing of either of you since you were here, Mr Shobnall, at the end of last November, going over some details concerning the night that unfortunate young man drowned. Then, three nights ago, Morgan Vetch knocked at my door. He held certain materials which I would not wish made public. They do not prove me guilty of any offence but they are open to misunderstanding." Bullard's tone was resolute. "If your prediction of a visit comes to pass, I shall refuse to speak further of them. They are relevant only in placing me within Vetch's power. In the course of our conversation, he said.....What would you like him to have said to me?

Eddie read out the form of words he and Shobnall had prepared. "Something like 'think yourself lucky, vicar, you can carry on breathing. Someone who can do me real damage is in line for more final treatment'. We've written it down for you."

Bullard studied his crib. "More final treatment. Yes, I can hear the conversation. Who will come?"

"We don't know. Two, probably.  They'll have warrant cards, like ours. They won't be friendly. They'll be suspicious, doubting everything and going over it time and again. Keep it simple and repetitive. If you'll excuse me saying it, invoke the Lord as often as you like."

"I shall not fail you although I shall seek His forgiveness beforehand." The three men rose. "There is, if I may, one other thing. Mr Shobnall, will you be seeing Lord Needwood again?"

*I know what he wants, we're mutually dependent now.* "That is very possible."

"Might I beseech you to intercede for me? He has been distant. You saw, when he was here, he.....he did not acknowledge me. I once did good service for him and I have been with his family for so long. I cannot bear being cast into the wilderness."

"Reverend, I'm a lowly policeman. I have no idea what value Lord Needwood places on anything I have to say. But yes, I will put in a word." For a moment, Shobnall was afraid the vicar was going to fall and embrace his feet.

\* \* \*

Back at the nick. Eddie still had doubts. "You confident in Bullard?"

"Yes, Eddie, I am. We're his saviours and I think he genuinely wants to help. I've changed my opinion of him. Lennie, Sheila and I all sensed something not right. I think we felt his fear. He'll be an entirely plausible holy man when White Horse come calling."

"Think we'll get interviewed?"

*You're edgier than you're letting on, aren't you?* "If Russ can carry off his end of things and Bullard is convincing, then probably not. I hope not. Obviously, if they're not convinced, we'll get a grilling, although they'll have to come through George. You and I need to stick together, literally. I start a week's nights from tomorrow. I'll get Angela to swap for the week after. Can you manage tonight without me?"

He ducked out of the room as a rolled-up ball of paper sailed towards him. *That's more like it.*

\* \* \*

He felt somewhat equivocal about agreeing another shift-swap with Angela Bracewell, reversing her Christmas argument in favour of a longer stretch. He was pleased with his convincing performance but unhappy at the degree of manipulation. *But it's not really a lie, is it?* He distracted them both by asking about her holiday. She had spent the time skiing in the Austrian Alps. "Never tried it," he admitted.

"Marvellous, Alan, simply marvellous. Strengthens the muscles, improves co-ordination and the food was superb."

"Our breaks need something for the girls."

"Oh, the nursery slopes are packed with kids. They start them young over there. I'm thinking about putting a police team together. I know a DC in Tamworth who skis in France and there must be some in HQ."

Shobnall's attention was already wandering. He'd got what he wanted and his thoughts were of how DI Conway had fared with Operation White Horse.

* * *

The London silence screamed at them. Shobnall considered calling Dave Charteris but, reluctantly, heeded Conway's injunction to behave normally. *If there's anything we need to know about, he'll call us.* Around them, normal life ticked on. One evening, Lennie Morton stayed on for them. "You two are pop music experts," he said, without a trace of sarcasm. "You know The Reapers and their crew. Have a gander at these." He laid down two copies of 'Drowning'. The cover depicted a dark, mournful lake under a lowering grey sky, a forearm and hand extending from the water, fingers spread. Nothing else. "One of these is genuine, one is a fake. Which is which?"

As far as Shobnall could see, they were identical. The obverse of the cover showed the same scene minus the hand. The spines said 'The Reapers', 'Drowning' and the catalogue number. Inside each, a lyric sheet and a grey inner sleeve containing the actual vinyl. To Shobnall, they looked exactly the same aside from a red sticker on Side A of one of the disc labels. Eddie was of like mind. "Lennie, they're the same aside from that sticker."

"No marks, Eddie. That's a reminder to me. The one with the sticker is genuine. The other is a fake." Lennie took back the albums. "If you play the one with the sticker, you hear the current best-selling album. Listen to the other and you get an earful of Andy Stewart and The White Heather Club. Some may prefer that but not anyone who wanted The Reapers."

Eddie was intrigued. "Where did you get them?"

"Normans." Eddie raised both eyebrows. "It's selling like hot cakes, record shops can't get their hands on enough and a bloke who claims to work at a pressing plant lands on your doorstep with a box. Knock me down with a feather but he fishes one out and plays it and it's real. Trouble begins when customers start bringing them back and complaining about 'Donald Where's Your Troosers'."

* * *

On Sunday 9 February, America smashed TV records as 34% of the viewing population tuned in to see The Fab Four on the Ed Sullivan Show. Two days later, their Washington concert unleashed Beatlemania on a continent. In between, Bullard 'phoned. Eddie answered; he and Shobnall leaned together over the handset. "It's OK, Reverend," said Eddie. "We're both listening."

"They came." *Sounds alright, unfussed, normal.* "Two men. One of them was playing at being helpful, asked lots of questions, some of them superficially tricky. The other one was *not* friendly. If you'll excuse my saying so, he struck me as the kind of officer who gives rise to those stories about people taking a tumble down the stairs in police stations."

"No idea what you mean, sir," laughed Eddie. "How long did it take?"

"They were here nigh on two hours."

"They really strung it out, by the sound of it," said Shobnall. *Bullard seems very comfortable with all this.*

"They kept going over and over the same ground from different angles. I could see the friendly one was trying to trip me up while the other one would sit back and come in with a sudden challenge to my veracity. I followed your guidance, stuck to a simple story and, er, invoked His witness where appropriate."

"What did they say about Morgan?" Eddie prodded.

"Apart from interminably picking over my recent meeting, they wanted to know if I'd heard from him since. I said no and that I had not expected further contact because he knew I dare not cross him. They kept wanting every word you said to me. I patted all those deliveries back down the pitch. I hope I didn't overdo it, we had been at it for some time by then and I was a little fed up."

"You once told us you were good at reading people," said Shobnall. "Do you think they were convinced?"

Bullard's voice quickened. "I believe so. I don't want to sound conceited but I am a well-educated individual and my calling necessarily keeps my brain supple. I do not think my inquisitors were accustomed to dealing with such an adversary. They appeared seriously deficient in the skills of interviewing. I presume they will be reporting to a superior and I would expect them to describe an ageing rustic cleric with an unfortunate stain on his history who had touched the very fringe of whatever affair they are engaged in." Shobnall eased away from the telephone, nodded to Eddie.

"We'll know for sure before too long. Thank you, Reverend, we'll be in touch when we can." Eddie hung up, shook his head. "Dear me, Alan, 'appeared deficient in the skills of interviewing'. I wish Conway and Chateris could have heard that."

*   *   *

# FORTY-FIVE

No news. Not a dickey-bird. Each successive day stretched out like a life sentence. By February 13$^t$, Shobnall was worrying about Eddie. *He's more and more unhappy, wonder if it's the silence or the prospect of shaking hands with aristocracy.* The day arrived in a full palette of greys, banks of light and dark cloud hanging low over the countryside, strands of mist clinging to the bare trees along the A38. At least the rain had stopped. The track from the village to the Hall had been constructed by engineers who understood drainage but it was muddier than usual and spattered with puddles. *I'll have to clean the car it but that can wait, if I'm out of a job I'll have time on my hands.* Another vehicle was already parked at the Hall. Shobnall drew up alongside. Eddie whistled. "I've never seen one up close." A steel-grey Silver Cloud. "Whitewall tyres and all."

"More brown than white, Eddie. Mud shows no favours. You ready?"

Eddie didn't react. Then he turned to Shobnall. "Actually, Alan, I think I'll wait here if it's all the same to you."

Shobnall didn't push. "Whatever, Eddie. It's no big deal given what's hanging over us – but don't you touch the Roller!" He clapped his colleague, his friend, on the shoulder and left the car.

He knocked. Somehow, this morning, it didn't seem right to walk right in. *Did I ever return those keys? Where are they?* The door was opened by a tall young woman in a gray two-piece with an elaborate flounce at the neck. The outfit, in subtle but unmistakable terms, said 'very expensive'. "Mr Shobnall, please come in. His Grace is in the kitchen." *Of course he's in the kitchen.* Lord Needwood and Albert Haynes were at the long table, ledgers open in front of them. *Glad they've got the fire going.*

Needwood walked over and shook his hand. "Thank you for coming, Alan. This is Pauline, my assistant and, for today, my chauffeuse. Albert you already know." Haynes smiled and, without another word, departed with the girl. *Under instruction.* Needwood shifted position so that they shared a corner of the table rather than facing one another across a solid barrier. "Now, what do you have to tell me?"

Shobnall shuffled his thoughts. "I'll work through from the beginning. Melinda is negotiating with two governments. With India, to agree the assignment to Britain of assets whose ownership has been up in the air since independence. In exchange for this, you will return the Needwood Diamond to India. With Britain, seeking permission for you to return to the country of your birth, the price for your returning the Diamond and securing the assets. Everyone wins. The two governments and you. Excuse my repeating all this."

"Tell the story howsoever you wish, my boy. I am all ears."

"The negotiations are not straightforward. There are hiccups. Everyone is guarding their position. But they progress. Melinda thinks a deal can be done with a little more time. She asks you to extend your deadline. You agree. Melinda is not telling you everything at this point. She is already under pressure from another direction. During the negotiations Melinda has faced an old friend, a Crown Prince and member of the Indian Government. They enjoy.....a dalliance."

"No need for euphemisms, Alan."

"Sorry, sir. They start an affair or maybe renew a previous relationship. It makes no difference. Unwise in the circumstances. It needn't have become a problem as long as they were discreet but it could have ruptured the deal if it had become public. The Prince is, after all, married into the Indian Prime Minister's family.

"We have another, rogue strand, one with long roots in time and geography. It centres on the people behind The Reapers, the pop group who stayed here last year. One of them drowned in the lake. These people weren't primarily interested in the music business. They took over the group as cover for something else. Pop music is *the* new business to be in. Swinging London, Beatlemania and all that. The music goes hand in hand with vast amounts of money and with sex and all manner of drugs which means even more money. We are only beginning to see how much money.

"It's the drugs. The people controlling the narcotics trade are mainly in America, although I am told there is a strong connection to Italy. They want to move into Britain. This country is in the vanguard of the pop industry and offers a lucrative market. Besides, if they can establish a bridgehead here it's only a hop and a skip to Western Europe and Scandinavia. We have an unholy tie-up between The Mob and one of London's ugliest criminal gangs. The Mob sends one of their operatives to organise a distribution network."

Needwood was taking in every word. "And this operative effectively takes over this pop group. I see. He understands business and its techniques."

"This operative is a complex and devious individual. Clever, a man of vision and resolute leadership, possessed of considerable charm when he chooses but, at the end of the day, a villain and a nasty villain at that. He has a talent for nosing out people's dark secrets and using the knowledge to manipulate them. He is a master blackmailer.

269

"As far as the narcotics are concerned, supply is assured, agents are available. Distribution is the issue. The Mob aren't interested in a single city; they deal in nations." Shobnall saw Needwood adding two and two and making four. "That's right. They plan to subvert a legitimate network. TransUK Haulage looked ideal, especially since your shares had been transferred to Melinda. She effectively controlled the company. She became his target and history provided him with a way in.

"He knew Bullard from 1950s Boston. He was instrumental in what went awry for the vicar there and it was easy for him to get his hands on incriminating material. He leaned on Bullard for an introduction and Melinda found herself engaged in a different set of negotiations. I have no idea what the arrangement was to have been – a takeover, a back seat, some form of control. The only people who could tell us are dead. There is still no crisis. It is a private discussion, albeit it must have unsettled Melinda. I would imagine it was some time before the real nature of what was on the table became clear to her. And yet, all other things being equal, she could have rebuffed the approach, maybe threatened to blow the whistle. He would have looked elsewhere. She didn't." Shobnall could feel the intensity of Needwood's attention.

"The affair?"

"Precisely. He uncovers the affair with the Prince. It doesn't take him long to discover why the Prince is in London, what Melinda is doing and how powerful a card he now holds. He threatens to play it. Melinda has to choose between getting in deep with The Mob – and that has been described to me as joining a club you can never leave – or seeing the deal over the Diamond founder, leaving her father unable to come home." *Is that a tear in his eye?* "The pressure must have been unbearable. My suspicion is that when she asked for the extension of the deadline, she was already facing that dilemma, bottling it up. I think she was worried about losing the Indian delegation. She replaced my colleagues with the Presidential Guard in an effort to bolster their confidence."

Needwood made no bones about it, produced a handkerchief, wiped his eyes. "The pressure burst." Silence. The two men turned away from each other, both stared at the fire, seeking diversion in the flickering flames. "Can you tell me his name?" Needwood asked.

"Please, sir, the stakes are too high for me and my colleagues. Melinda kyboshed everything. She caused the project to fall apart. There are *other* things I shouldn't know about." Shobnall found Needwood's stare intimidating. "He knew his employers would punish his failure. He set about closing down and vanishing."

270

"Was he successful?"

Shobnall shook his head, looked into Needwood's eyes. "He's dead."

It was as if Needwood pressed a switch; his focus remained but its heat lessened. "Alan, I am grateful. I am thankful for what you have felt able to share with me and I respect where you have felt you must draw a line. You are, however, forgetting one thing." Shobnall froze. "I own this house. I do!" He'd seen Shobnall's mouth opening. "You were about to remind me that it is owned by Melinda or by her estate. I may tell you the transfer documents included clauses to the effect that if anything happened to her within a certain period then ownership reverted to me. As it now has. My lawyers are very expensive but they are very careful on my behalf." He paused. "I own this house. I know who has used it. I know who signed the contracts." *Ah, the ledgers he and Haynes were examining.* "We shall not name him."

*Careful, Shobnall.* "Thank you."

"Who killed the boy in the lake?"

*He knows I think that was a murder.* "It doesn't matter." He sighed. "For what it's worth, the man I believe murdered young Cox is also dead. That case is done."

The two men sat for a while, the only sound the crackling of the logs in the grate. Needwood broke the pause. "It should not be that a child goes before the parent but it is in my philosophy of life to rejoice in what I had rather than to lament what I have lost. I am a peer of the realm, a successful businessman, one of the richest men in Europe." He made a moue. "I say that to myself every so often as a reminder of how insignificant it all is. None of it matters as much as my daughter. That said, due largely to those things that don't matter, I am close to influential and powerful people."

"I never doubted that, sir." *What does he know? Who?*

"I am aware you were warned away from the pursuit of.....your prime suspects, shall we say?"

*Oh bugger, underestimated his connections, one of the first things the DI warned me about.* "I was. We were."

Lord Needwood was composed. "You disobeyed. Not whomever you mean by 'we'. *You* Alan, *you* disobeyed."

*No point lying.* "I don't see it like that."

271

"How do you see it?"

*How did I get into a scrap like this?* "Bullard and the man who's been staying here lately - Carter, he was in The Reapers – had helped us with the investigation. One or both of them might have been harmed. I couldn't allow that. Alternatively, Carter might have hurt.....the person we were warned off. That could have rebounded on me and on colleagues."

Needwood processed it. "I see. I would imagine that, for some of you, nerves are fraying."

"You're not kidding, sir. Eddie Mustard's especially."

"Ah yes, your lieutenant. I had hoped to thank him. He declined?"

"Those nerves. He's fraying in the car outside. A last-minute decision on his part."

Needwood smiled. "And now your case is concluded. Nothing else to do bar the written reports?"

"Nothing formal. I promised to debrief the Crown Prince."

Needwood stood. "Let *me* speak with the Crown Prince. He sent me a touching letter. Most kind. I wrote back but should like to meet him."

"I think he would appreciate that and I need to keep a low profile for the time being. I wonder also, sir, if I could ask you to speak with the Reverend Bullard. The man is aware of the mistakes he has made but his help has been invaluable to us. He feels alienated. Would you consider.....?"

"Of course. As I am sure you know, my family and the Reverend have a long, tangled relationship." His brow creased. "It was petty of me to cut him. I should have borne in mind his past good service. He and I are too close to the end for such disharmony. Alan, you are assiduous in seeking favours for others and not for yourself, despite the – shall we say – awkward position you occupy." He had opened a door but Shobnall made no move to enter. "Keep hold of my card. It will remain the case that any of those numbers will be ready to help should you call. The Carillion will remain available to you and yours whenever you should indulge us by enjoying our facilities. And Alan! I have friends at court, as they say. If a situation becomes too stressed, I would be pleased to help."

Shobnall swallowed. *Don't know quite how to respond to that.* "What about you, sir? And the Diamond?"

"Me? Did I not say?" Needwood's eyes twinkled. "Of course I didn't. Nothing has yet been made public. My boy, I would never trust a government minister but let no-one say that our modern administrators are totally devoid of compassion. All parties, British and Indian, to the negotiations around the Diamond were distraught at Melinda's death. An agreement has since been reached. The Diamond will stay for the final weeks of the British Museum exhibition; the Indian delegation will then carry it home. The assets which have been hovering in an Anglo-Indian limbo are being assigned to their British claimants. Although." He beamed – and Shobnall glimpsed what made Needwood and Mr Salt such buddies. "I would rather you kept this under your hat since I have a reputation for toughness in business. I can't afford to parade as some sort of left-wing softie. I have instructed my lawyers to arrange for the Needwood plantation to be transferred to the ownership of the workers in whatever form of co-operative Indian legislation permits."

"That's a noble gesture, sir."

"They need it more than me. India is a nation of huge potential but also widespread poverty. Our Empire sucked too much strength from the country's sinews. It will become great again but it will take them time. One plantation won't tilt the scales but every little helps. Lastly, I am pleased to say – and if Melinda is listening, wherever she may be, I hope she will feel redeemed – that I may come home with legally-binding if entirely confidential protection from an avaricious Treasury."

Shobnall reconfigured things. *It all worked out for you in the end, everybody won, except.....* He rose and faced Needwood. "Sir, do you think....." *I don't know how to put this or even if I should.* "You know your daughter best but is it possible, do you think that –"

Lord Needwood raised a hand and sighed. Not an *'I wish you hadn't mentioned that'* sigh, more of an *'I thought you might ask'* one. "That Melinda had devised a final plan? That she had concluded, in the circumstances, that killing herself was the only way of satisfying all parties and delivering for her father?"

*Oh dear.*" Yes, sir, that is what I was wondering."

Needwood was reflective. "We will never know, Alan. Was my daughter uncontrollably pitched over the edge by the pressures? Or did she deliberately weigh the pros and cons and calculate how the various parties would react? Did she see the choice between disaster or her death? The manner of her departure, her return to

Wychnor, does not suggest to me a woman out of control but I cannot be sure. It goes to show, my boy, that no matter how deeply you love a person, you can never know them as well as you would wish. It is a lesson that we only learn too late."

*How sad.* "But surely, sir, the love is so much more important than the knowledge?"

Needwood raised his eyebrows. "There speaks a father. You are right, of course. When all is said and done, love is all there is."

Shobnall was thinking about his kin. *Elaine, Jo and Alice, Helen and James, Neil and his family. My mum and dad.* "It's all we need, sir. If only it was all we *wanted*." They stood quiet for a moment. Shobnall cleared his throat. "Will you, er, come back here, to Wychnor?"

"At one stage I considered it. This was home for Melinda and me during her early childhood. The place holds fond memories but my present wife prefers London and is conducting a string of interior designers around one of our Belgravia properties. We are keeping this house and the estate. We will not abandon the people who live and work here. I am having the attic cleared. I have selected one or two mementoes but the rest can go. Pauline and Albert have been upstairs compiling an inventory. They should be done by now and we must be off. I have time to stop off at the rectory and repair relations. Then we have a date at Bruntons Brewery where the owner has promised a tour and lunch. Did Reuben ever tell you I once tried to buy his little kingdom?"

Shobnall chuckling in recollection. "Yes, he did. He made it sound like the Clash of the Titans."

Needwood laughing. "Our first meeting. Please don't tell Reuben I said this but I met my business match. Thankfully, we became firm friends. I must go, Alan, but I cannot allow your Mustard to evade me entirely.

\* \* \*

Eddie was dozing in the Anglia, the consequence of fatigue, not a symptom of unconcern, knees against the dashboard. He missed the party emerging from the house, Haynes and Pauline moving to the Silver Cloud, Pauline opening doors, Haynes stowing a cardboard box in the boot before returning to the foot of the steps. Needwood marched across the gravel and tapped on the Anglia window.

Shobnall made out the horror on Eddie's face, the door opening, Eddie almost falling out of the vehicle. *If Eddie had a cloth cap handy he'd be twisting it in his hands, a bare-headed peasant.* He couldn't hear what was said but he saw Eddie's expression clear, Needwood extend a hand, the shake, Needwood turn and head for the Rolls, salute Haynes and climb in. Pauline closed the doors. Not a sound but the Rolls, without seeming to disturb the gravel, floated away like a phantom over the drive, through the trees and out of sight.

\* \* \*

"Jesus, Alan! I'm woken up by Lord Needwood grinning at me!"

"Yes, I saw that. What did he say?"

"He said 'Eddie, I'd like to thank you for all you've done'. Then he told me he'd be there if we needed help. Did he mean that?"

"Yes, Eddie, I believe he did. Hang on a moment." He walked over to Haynes. "How are you, Albert?" Haynes was looking at him differently.

"I'm well, thank you, Mr Shobnall. We all are. Lord Needwood has restored Wychnor to an even keel."

"I'm glad to hear that. Listen. I had hoped to have a word with Basher but there's no sign of him."

Haynes was taken aback. "He didn't speak to you? Mr Shobnall, he's gone. The big lug's gone."

Shobnall deflated. "Without saying goodbye? That's not like him."

"It's bad, Mr Shobnall. He's taken Mrs Farlowe with him. I'm having the devil's own job finding a replacement."

\* \* \*

# FORTY-SIX

London and Scotland Yard might as well have ceased to exist. Their thoughts explored only three scenarios – bad, worse and worst. Shobnall brooded; he kept wishing the 'phone would ring and when it did wished it hadn't. Eddie was looking peaky, like a man not getting a full day's sleep. Part of Shobnall thought he should have a word with the DI. *He must know something's up but he's not saying anything, there's nothing he could do anyway, no, we agreed, the five of us, leave George out of it.* Hunched, he stalked along the corridor.

Nobody else was in yet. Eddie Mustard was clearing up. "Eddie. That's two weeks and two days and not a peep. I may need to swap some more shifts. What do you think's happening?"

"Don't ask me, Alan. It's doing my head in. I feel like staying in bed with the blankets over my head until someone tells me either I'm in the clear or I can get down to the labour exchange."

"Don't!" Shobnall grimaced. "I keep telling myself no news is good news but the longer this goes on the less convincing I sound." He walked to the window. The white sky presaged snow. "The Met Office is promising blizzards. The County will shut down again and everything will take longer. All we need."

Eddie had borrowed Saxby's radio and a female voice warbled in the background; 'anyone who had a heart, tum-tum'. "What on earth are you listening to, Eddie? The BBC aren't pumping out pop music dawn to dusk now, are they?"

"No," said Eddie. "That's pirate radio, Radio Caroline. They've set up a transmitter on a ship, thumbing their noses at Auntie. These are test transmissions."

"The BBC aren't going to like that."

"Nothing anybody can do. The ship's anchored in international waters. Good move, if you ask me. The BBC is too old-fashioned. From what I've heard so far, the Caroline people are going to teach the stuffed shirts a thing or two.

"You do manage to keep yourself well-informed on the music scene."

"Huh!" Eddie made a face. "Maybe Norman's will employ me if I need a job. Wouldn't be so convenient for studying but beggars can't be choosers."

"It would play havoc with your breakfasts, too."

He hung on into the day shift. Cyril Hendry had called up to say the DI had been delayed but would appreciate a word with him before he left. He chatted with Angela but she was off to a meeting at the Town Hall about the arrangements for the forthcoming local elections. She took Sheila Redpath. *You'll find that stimulating, Sheila.* He tried to address his admin but couldn't concentrate. *Somebody must have decided something.* By mid-morning he was becoming irritated. He made a cup of tea and phoned Elaine so she didn't worry. The clock on the wall moved close to 11.00. *Come on, George!*

And in walked the DI, as if everything was as it should be. "Morning, sir." The DI said nothing, made himself comfortable at Angela's desk and looked at Shobnall with a benign expression on his face. *OK, he's not here to tick me off about anything.* They sat in silence for a minute. Two. *He's waiting for something, someone.* Three minutes.

Shobnall's telephone exploded. Well, it sounded more like an explosion than a ring. He jumped, reached for the handset, looked at the DI. Who raised a finger to his lips. Shobnall kept his eyes on Worthington. "Alan Shobnall." It was Dave Charteris.

"Alan! Thank Gawd I caught yer. Mate, are yer on yer Jack Jones?"

Eyes focused on the Old Man. *This is what he was waiting for.* "Yes, Dave, I am, where've you been, what's happening?"

"'Ang on, 'ang on, what I'm callin' about."

"Sorry, Dave, you can imagine....." *Does George know everything?*

"Course I can, mate. Lissen. I juss 'ad a call from Russ. Dunno where 'e is, I ain't seen 'im for a couple of days, 'e's art an' abart wiv 'is ear to the ground, know what I mean. Any road, he called juss now, told me to tell Bill and pass the message to you as soon as."

"What message, Dave? Come on!"

"Sorry, sorry, I'm too busy learnin' to breathe proper again. We are in the clear. White 'Orse ain't interested."

Shobnall sank back in his chair, eyes still on the DI. He was certain his heart-rate had just gone sky-high and immediately dropped to two beats above dormant. "What else did he say?"

"Nuffinck. Said 'e 'ad more but 'e'd sit down wiv me an' Bill tomorrow. 'E juss said pass the 'eadline on. Normal service resumed. End of message, Alan, now I gotta go find Bill. When I know more I'll call yer."

Shobnall put the 'phone down in slow motion. The DI's benign expression hadn't shifted but he became aware that his own face was sporting an idiotic grin. He removed it. At last, the DI spoke. "Come with me, Alan." Downstairs, through the rear exit into the yard and the DI's Riley and away down the A38. Shobnall's nervous system was cleansing itself of a fortnight's accumulated stress; he could almost feel the grit dislodging and washing away. The DI ventured a few more words. "Sometimes I find it's not necessary to say things out loud." The car slowed and Shobnall knew exactly where they were headed.

The sky was overcast, the air muggy, but green was breaking out all over, the chestnut was covered in blossom  and Wychnor Hall was in stately mode, the tall windows clear, the ivy shading into purple. Once again, a car sat on the drive. A large police black, dark blue light on the roof. *A London reg, now who can that be?* The DI led the way around the side of the Hall to the lawns beside the lake. *I had a feeling they were closer than they let on.*

* * *

DI 'Russ' Conway was standing by the boatshed, a camera on a leather strap around his neck, consulting a light meter. "A trifle dark but it'll do. Dave spoken to you?" Shobnall nodded. "Good. I'll be filling him and Bill in first thing tomorrow. Pints of relief all round." He snapped the light meter cover shut, put it in a pocket. "I'd heard so much about this place, I wanted to see it for myself. Persuaded the Estate Manager to show me inside." He stared at Shobnall. "Including the ballroom. Must have been interesting, chatting in there. I've not got long but I particularly wanted a word. Why don't we rest our bones on that bench?" Shobnall and Conway sat. Worthington chose to remain two or three yards away, positioning himself as an observer. *Or a witness. Or a guardian. I can't quite get the dynamics.* "Alan. You, we, have a complete bill of health. I can't say we've been exonerated or acquitted because we've never been suspected or accused. Everything's been archived."

"You mean, Operation White Horse?"

"There is no Operation White Horse. It might never have existed. The team of six officers, a DI, two DSs and three DCs. Disbanded. Visit their offices today and you'll find Road Safety people; ask 'em where White Horse have gone and they look blank. The overseeing Super has decided to take early retirement with enhanced benefits. An offer he couldn't afford to reject."

"Where have they gone?"

"That's the thing. Not back to their normal posts and not redeployed elsewhere in the Met. No. It seems the powers-that-be didn't want to lose their accumulated knowledge and expertise around the drugs business. They are all on indefinite secondment to Interpol's Narcotics Task Force. With immediate effect. Beautiful place, Paris. You been, Alan?" Shobnall shook his head. "Dave's been, obviously, loved it. Generous remuneration and expenses. Accommodation overlooking the Seine. Travel to exotic places. South Italy, for starters. Seems four of them were so taken with it they've gone with wives or girlfriends."

"A sort of promotion, then?" It didn't sound a bad deal to Shobnall.

"You could look at it that way. Even if it's the only option being dangled." A break in the clouds took Conway's attention and he checked the light meter. "Hm, not much brighter. It does look unusual, doesn't it, George?"

Worthington had his pipe going. "I already said, Russ, I've never come across an operation being parcelled up like this. I contacted an old pal at Interpol, Inspector Hans Jager." *I remember that name from the Bruntons case.* "The remarkable thing is this Task Force didn't exist until a week or so ago and no-one seemed to know how it suddenly came into being. Aside from an overseeing Interpol Inspector who happens to be on extended sick leave, the only staff are the former White Horse officers." *I don't like the sound of this.*

Conway turned back to Shobnall. "Alan, tomorrow I will be recounting this to Dave and Bill. They'll get the same story even though I may use different words here and there. What matters to them and your mate, Eddie, is that they are in the clear. No recriminations, no repercussions, nothing on the record. However." He stood and looked down at Shobnall. "It is in some ways hard to explain."

Shobnall stood and faced him. *I can see what's coming.* "What do you mean, sir?"

"It looks very much as if someone high-up, *very* high-up, someone with influence that reaches across international borders had things fixed in such a way that Operation White Horse vanished. Morgan Vetch never came to the Met's attention. Cutter

Carpenter is an unsolved gangland slaying, Gary Stubbs an accidental drowning. You were never warned off for the simple reason that there never was anything to keep you away from. The whole thing has been fixed. Extremely well fixed, if you ask me. I have made enquiries and been shown more brick walls than you've had hot dinners." A short silence ensued, during which Conway looked expectantly at Shobnall. Worthington didn't seem to be looking at anyone or anything in particular. "I was wondering, Alan, if you might be in a position to cast any light on how this might have come about?"

*Dive straight in, Shobnall.* "You're wondering about Lord Needwood, sir." Conway didn't react. "This isn't normal for me. He's the only Duke I've ever met and then only because I was the one who found his daughter. I never asked him to intervene in any way."

"You're sure about that." Suddenly, Conway's voice was steelier. "If I had Lord Needwood here and placed a Bible in his hand, he would bear you out?"

"Yes, sir, he would. I never asked. I never agreed to anything."

Conway looked towards the lake. His voice returned to normal. "I needed to know, Alan." He reached out a hand and they shook. "I know you like my people. My job means looking after them. I have to guard against all manner of outside influences. Thank you for your understanding and tolerance."

They walked Conway to his car, waited for a few more photographs, waved him off. As the sound of his car faded, the DI tapped out his pipe on the wall by the entrance steps. "I wouldn't be surprised, Alan, if he makes Commissioner of the Met one day. He's a great copper and, in my estimation, a good man. That would be an adventurous combination for the top man. He was, of course, looking after his own position and prospects as well as his people." He paused. "I assume Needwood did offer to use his connections?"

"Someone told me, sir, you don't always have to say everything out loud."

The DI chuckled. "Just so. I keep forgetting how fast you young people learn. Let's head back. On the way we'll wake up young Mustard and put him out of his misery. Say farewell to Wychnor Hall."

*       *       *

# FORTY-SEVEN

Early March. Air as bracing as Skegness. The Beatles, having subjugated America, came home and spun 'Can't Buy Me Love' directly to Number One. In the pop stakes, they now had real competition. That Reapers' long-player, 'Drowning', refused to budge from the top of the album charts. The taxman rubbed his hands. The future was exciting, especially for the young. It wasn't going brilliantly for everyone. Neil Shobnall and his colleagues at the British Motor Corporation were struggling with the strikes spreading like a rash through the car industry. Letters to The Times lamented the growing power of the unions.

Overall, though, the mood was positive. The Government announced record exports, including exports of records. Shobnall and Eddie Mustard were prone to whistle in the corridor at any time of day or night. Betty had taken to regaling the station with songs from the hit parade while she scrubbed and polished; fortunately, Agnes' croaky accompaniment was muffled by the perpetual fag. More than one Wychnor parishioner, uplifted by another barnstorming Sunday sermon, remarked on how the Reverend Bullard 'seemed to have got his second wind these days'. Albert Haynes was happy. He had a successor to the redoubtable Mrs Farlowe – not quite up to her standard, maybe, but more than competent (and another widow) – while His Grace had authorised a major refurbishment programme. Lavinia Salt, Hilary Henderson and Elaine Shobnall bid *adieu* to winter with a trip to The Odeon and 'The Crimson Pirate' with Burt Lancaster mightily buckling his swash (or swashing his buckle; even Lavinia wasn't certain). 'I Love the Little Things' took second spot at the Eurovision Song Contest. Many questioned whether Matt Monro's ballad reflected where British pop music was taking the world.

Ian Jessop was invited to an exclusive cocktail event in Whitehall. He had little time for the drinks and nibbles and even less for most of his fellow-guests but he knew an apology when he saw one and was appeased. So much so that he told George Worthington about it. And, when the Shobnalls were invited to the Worthingtons' home for dinner, George told Alan and Elaine. He did so while he and Esmée insistently coaxed the young man through the unexpurgated version. Almost unexpurgated, that is; George wasn't convinced the lad had divulged everything about the conversations with Lord Needwood.

It was the day after that excursion when Elaine accosted her husband as he prepared to leave for work. "I took your other work suit to the cleaners and found these in a pocket. I didn't recognise them." She passed him a ring with two keys, a Yale and one that might have unlocked a prison cell in the Tower of London's dungeon.

"I meant to look for those. Wychnor Hall. I took them from Albert Haynes the day I found Melinda's body."

"Well," said Elaine. "You better return them."

*  *  *

He drove out at lunchtime. The Hall was closed up but the sawmill foreman directed him to Haynes relaxing on the bench in front of his cottage, an empty plate beside him. The same tweed jacket. *He must have a wardrobe stuffed with them.* Haynes was in mellow mood, insisting on Shobnall taking a cup of tea. It was very pleasant; the sun was warming up and the view was tranquil beyond measure. "It's the cows," said Haynes. "Grazing, ruminating, being bovine. You can't but feel good." The two men sat contentedly as Haynes outlined Lord Needwood's plans for the Hall and for the estate until Shobnall decided he really had to make a move. He did remember to return the keys.

He stopped off at the Big House. He didn't feel like moving from the Elysian peace of Haynes and his cows straight to the police station. The building was waking from hibernation, spreading out its reddening cloak under the stimuli of sun and spring. He ambled over the lawn and past the orchard, its trees in bud, the route Cutter had used that night. Round to the lawns at the rear. The turf had been re-laid and the wooden bench shifted to the lakeside. He tried it. Another peaceful scene. The sawmill was silent but the buzzard was abroad. The lake was full of blue sky. A pair of swans moved serenely into view from behind the boathouse, rippling the surface minutely. *Swans instead of cows, Albert.* It was one of those moments when Nature seemed about to reveal her soul.

Which is why he heard the car so clearly. It didn't sound like the basic version of the internal combustion engine he had in the Anglia, nor was it the sophisticated murmur of Needwood's Silver Cloud. A suppressed, throaty roar, a big cat warning off a rival. *Down the track from the village.* The crunch on gravel proved him right. The roar stilled. He swivelled on the bench, looked back at the corner of the building. A woman appeared, a youngish woman in jeans and a high-necked fluffy blue pullover with a black slash running from one shoulder. *Could be a Heather Wilson creation.* The slash matched the hair, trimmed to shoulder length, framing the face. *She looks very 'with it' as they say.* She smiled, turned to someone. "He's here."

A mad thought struck him. *Surely not.* A man joined her, a large man, long hair, dressed in black. A familiar figure who put an arm around the woman and propelled her towards Shobnall. "Alan! You alright?"

Shobnall shook his head. "You rascal. You abandoned us." He and Basher hugged.

"Yeah, sorry, my impulsive side. Albert tipped me off Lord Thing was visiting. He didn't say it but I had the impression he didn't see me and his lordiness mixing." *I wouldn't be so sure about that, my friend.* "'Scuse me, where are my manners? This is Sue. This is my good friend, Alan Shobnall, a most unusual policeman."

The woman, Sue, smiled again. "Bob has spoken about you a lot."

Shobnall was caught on the hop – *Bob?* - and said without thinking, "Haynes told me you'd, er, I mean....."

Basher creased up. "Aye. He would have done. This is Sue Farlowe."

Shobnall didn't know what to say. Until he realised they were laughing at him and he saw the hilarious side of things. Sue Farlowe put a hand on his arm. "Did Albert lead you to believe Mrs Farlowe was a retired old biddy?"

"If you don't mind my saying so, you don't look like most people's idea of a widow."

That set them off again. "Oh, I'm no widow. Don't tell Albert. He's an angel really. I made that up to get the position. Albert's quite conservative and, for him, a widower made me more respectable. I wouldn't be surprised if my replacement isn't also a widow." She laughed. "I've never been married."

"But you will be," said Basher.

"Bob!" She tugged at his arm. "We'll see."

Basher gazed fondly at her but spoke to Shobnall. "Alan, don't you start calling me Bob. Alright, we're *planning* on getting married but Sue's making me wait."

*They look very right together.* "Congratulations. How did you know I was here?"

"I wanted the ending. I follow The Reapers. Klein in meant Morgan out. I figured you'd know what happened and we wanted to give the new motor a blast. We called in at your nick. No sign of Eddie but a helpful geezer name of Lennie said I might find you up here. So did Morgan get away with it?"

Sue Farlowe demonstrated a sense of discretion that raised her further in Shobnall's estimation. "I'll wait in the car, Bob. Alan, lovely to meet you. I expect to see you again." Another warm smile.

A thought struck Shobnall. "Sue!" She turned. "When you were catering for The Reapers here, did you have to wear anything special?"

She made a face. "Goodness! That get-up! Albert said it was part of the arrangement. When I was in the Hall, I had to wear this black thing, sort of overalls. Didn't fit me properly and irritated my skin. Stupid really. When I was in they were all asleep. Only person I regularly saw awake was poor Gary, although." She glanced at Basher. "I did bump into the drummer. Why?"

"Nothing important. I'm a stickler for dotting i's and crossing t's, that's all."

Shobnall and Basher watched her go. "You're falling on your feet, Basher." Shobnall turned, stared out over the lake but he was seeing Morgan's corpse on the slab. "No. Is the answer. He didn't get away with it. Neither did Cutter. The people who managed to get away with something were me and Eddie." They sat on the bench while Shobnall ran through the final stages of the case. When he'd finished, the two men watched the swans as they up-ended for some bottom-feeding.

"Morgan knew the risks," said Basher.

"He knew he'd never make it but he had to try. There. You have as much of the story as you need. Put the book on a shelf and get on with life. With Sue."

"Yeah." Basher ran his hands through his hair. "With 'Drowning' going double gold, it doesn't seem to matter how much the taxman takes, my account keeps adding noughts. I've made a small fortune but I know I'm well out of it. The pop music industry eats people. Me and Sue are going into business. We've bought a small hotel on The Wirral, outside Liverpool. We're doing it up. Sue's going to manage it, run the kitchen, I'll swan about looking important and – don't give me that look! – *not* drinking the profits. I'm planning some jazz nights with a little combo I'm putting together. 'The Carter's Arms'. Like that? I've had the cards printed. Here. Take one for Eddie. Sorry I've missed him. You'll be welcome anytime. Bring the family, those little girls. They've got rhythm, you know, 'specially Josephine." He stuck out a hand.

Shobnall gripped it. "We might just do that. Jo keeps asking after you."

"Little angels. Give Basher's love to them both."

They made their way to the front. Shobnall's sardine can of an Anglia sat beside a striking, glossy black machine; beautifully-engineered sleek lines, a racing bonnet, the hood down, gracefulness personified. Sue was in the passenger seat. "Basher! Is that a car or a missile?"

"Lovely, ain't it? Jaguar E-type. It'll do 150 mph blah blah blah. That Italian bloke, Ferrari, he says it's the most bella car ever." He paused. "Gary would have liked it. Gary was into motors." He lowered his voice. "What about Gary? They do him and all?"

That was difficult. "Yes, Basher. They did. But it isn't going public."

"Don't matter. Public or private. Long as I know. Gary was OK. He looked after us. He looked after Mick's mum." His face screwed up. "Shame there's always casualties."

The Jaguar treated him to a throaty roar as it bit into the dirt track and then Sue's waving arm was lost to sight. *There was a uniform in the bag, I doubt Haynes knew what else, that look in his eyes was no more than a tiny triumph.* He considered letting Haynes know ace-detective Shobnall was on top of every detail. *What for? He's a decent bloke, an angel, Sue said, allow him his sense of victory.*

\* \* \*

The man had been casing the stall for a couple of hours, moving around inside the market, having a cuppa in the tiny cafe with a good view. This bloke on the stall selling haberdashery and personal items looked perfect; middle-aged, a tad overweight, not too alert, the air of a fool who'd jump at something for nothing. The man had a nose for the mix of greed and gullibility that blunted the force of reason. He and his associate needed to diversify. The bottles were a solid earner but you had to be careful. He'd several crates in the van but he'd probably saturated Burton. The records had been a doddle but getting hold of the covers had been lucky. They couldn't bank on that with any regularity. Time to try out some silken luxury. He'd fetched a box from the van.

The stallholder didn't ever do much – lean over a newspaper, fiddle with a Derby County tie, exchange a word with the tall guy at the next stall, the one selling models, Airfix and all that, he had a bit of a Yorkshire accent and his patter never went beyond cricket. The man eased into his spiel – wholesaling blah, top of the range exclusives blah, pure silk ladies' stockings from France blah, giveaway price blah blah, last one, shame to take back to the warehouse blah blah blah! He saw that dull gleam well up in the eye sockets and did his sleight-of-hand, apparently plucking a packet at random

285

and slitting it open. The stallholder leant across, his hand over the man's, no, not here, come round the back and let's have a feel of them, at that price I can't let them pass by if they're as good as you say. The man could have written the script for the nincompoop.

He sidled between the stalls, the dupe helpfully holding the canvas aside. He was ready to clinch things. If these worked they would be a valuable second line. As he dragged the box through the gap, he heard the stallholder call to his neighbour, the Yorkshireman, "Hey, Bob, come and have a look at these, you might be interested in a pair for the missus." The man almost licked his lips.

*   *   *

## FORTY-EIGHT

Imagine one of those invigorating days when it suddenly seems that spring has taken control. There may be patches in the garden where the earth has not yet lost its frozen edge but green shoots and leaves are everywhere, the cattle are grazing outdoors again and the Corporation flower-beds are sprouting orange and purple crocuses, the emerald stems of early daffodils. People tire of skulking indoors and want to step outside and *feel* the world. On such a day, the Shobnall family went on an expedition.

They met Corky and Lavinia outside The Swan at Fradley Junction and promenaded along the southerly reach of the Trent & Mersey. The girls gambolled delightedly. Lavinia looked distinctively Russian in a long grey coat with a fur collar; on her head a violet creation that Shobnall thought might still be alive. Corky gaily swung a knobbly walking stick. They paused at Middle Lock, where Josephine required her father to explain how the mechanism worked. Four years had passed since he first sailed along here. *Wonder where Joshua and Spike are, that pair of oddballs should fit right into the sixties, rebellious and idiosyncratic.* Alice began to dawdle so Corky lifted her onto his shoulder and they turned back. Josephine, her energy and curiosity unquenchable, continuing to demand what this or that in the hedgerow was called or to essay conversation with mallards paddling by.

It was early afternoon when they regained the Junction. Music wafted out of the pub: *'I'll buy you a diamond ring my friend, if it makes you feel alright'*. A boat exited the lock and headed northwards. "I want to go on the water." Josephine was emphatic. "I want to be a sailor."

"You must be careful on the water, my dear," said Lavinia.

"It's safe here, Aunt Lavinia," replied the child. "It's not wild like the sea."

"Would you like to go on a barge like that?" Elaine asked.

Josephine treated her mother to an expression that wasn't scornful but did suggest that mummy knew nothing. "It's not a barge. Daddy said. It's a narrowboat." Her parents swapped glances. "I want to go on *that* one." A launch eased from the Coventry into the basin, its hull decked out in white and navy, a low-slung orange superstructure. Shobnall waved. The man at the wheel spoke over his shoulder, a second figure rose from the stern and the boat changed course towards them, exposing the 'POLICE' bow plate..

Fred brought the boat neatly to the bank. "Shobnalls ahoy!" He cried.

"All aboard for the skylark," rumbled Vern. "Trips down the river for well-behaved young sailors."

"And older mariners," added Fred. "This must be Josephine and Alice." The latter, deciding she was no longer weary, squirmed from Corky's grasp, took her sister's hand as they stared, goggle-eyed, at the launch. "Nothing much doing today," explained Fred. "We're helping out the Transport Commission boys, running an eye over the locks and wharves. Fancy a little voyage?"

Josephine knew what she wanted. "Mr. Fred, Aunt Lavinia says we need to be careful on the water."

"Your aunt is wise, little one," said Fred. Vern looked smitten. "We'll take good care of you."

"Mummy. Daddy." Josephine looked up at her parents. "Can we? *Please* can we?"

They couldn't refuse. Shobnall whispered to Elaine "You all go. I want to pop into the workshop and say hello to a couple of old friends"

Jo insisted on a place in the cockpit; Fred upturned a crate for her so she could reach the wheel. Vern, Alice clasped to his chest, positioned himself alongside. Elaine, Corky and Lavinia disposed themselves in the stern and sat back, ready for the pantomime. Shobnall watched as the launch swung in a lazy arc and headed back down the Coventry, shrieks of delight audible even after the craft had passed from view around the first bend.

*     *     *

"Evenin' Alan."

Startled, he whipped round. "Ernest! Ernie!"

"Evening, Mr Shobnall," said Ernie, the younger and taller, carrying both carpenter's bags. "We was leaving early and saw you loading up the boat."

"Aye," said Ernest. "We've a birthday tea but we couldn't leave without saying howdy. Them your nippers?"

"Yes, Josephine and Alice. An unscheduled boat trip. I was going to call in and see how you were."

"Bonny-looking kids," said Ernest. "That older one'll have Fred an' Vern eating out of her hand."

"Ah! You've met Fred and Vern?"

"Oh aye," confirmed Ernest. "They came to pick up that inflatable we found. You get that business sorted?"

"All sorted, Ernest, reports written." *A small white lie.*

"Hey, dad," interrupted Ernie. "Getting right crowded here. Look who's turned up." He pointed across the canal to where a shiny black Humber had swung in beside Corky's Triumph Herald. Mr Salt emerged. He didn't bother with the bridge but nimbly negotiated the nearest lock gate.

"Evenin' Mr Salt," said Ernest.

"Hello Reuben," said Shobnall. "I see you know everyone."

"Oh yes." Mr Salt shook each one by the hand. "When one has need of a skilled carpenter, anyone in the County who knows anything comes to Ernest and Ernie. Finished your apprenticeship yet, Ernie?

Ernie grinned but it was his father who responded. "Another couple of years should do it."

Mr Salt laughed. "Ernest, you've been saying that since the first time we met."

Ernie had been instructed, it transpired, to have his father at the birthday tea on the dot. "Mother said to stop him gabbing over-long." Farewells taken, the Waterhouses trudged off along the path. Shobnall and Mr Salt watched them go, Ernest still talking.

"Best chippies in Staffordshire." Mr Salt's was authoritative. "Don't mention it to Ernest but I'm not sure that Ernie isn't the more precise these days. Ernest's touch is not quite what it was. The passage of time, I fear. However, I was expecting to find more than a solitary you."

"The others are taking a little trip on the canal, courtesy of Fred and Vern, the police divers."

Mr Salt's eyes widened. "Ah! You have spoken of them. They were at Wychnor, I believe. Talking of which, Billy Needwood came for lunch after he met you. He told me all about it. I must say, Alan, considering that we are somewhat out in the sticks here, you do manage to become embroiled in some intriguing adventures."

*I hope Lord Needwood didn't tell him everything.* "I'm not sure that's how I see them, Reuben."

"I'm sure you don't. Your perspective is utterly different. You need an amanuensis, a faithful recorder of your exploits. A Dr Watson to your Holmes."

"Reuben." Shobnall's tone was admonishing. "You read too many of those detective novels. Wychnor could have been the end of my career as a policeman. Leave me in oblivion. It's less stressful." He caught a very un-Salt-like expression flitting across the brewer's face. *I think that's what Elaine would call 'a puckish grin'.* "Stop winding me up!" He punched Mr Salt playfully on the upper arm.

Mr Salt chortled and changed the subject. "That looks like our pleasure cruiser returning."

The two men re-crossed the canal to the bank by The Swan and waited on the launch's approach. "Lavinia and Corky are doing an amazing job as god-parents, Reuben. They do seem to be getting on very well."

"You've noticed?" Mr Salt smiled contentedly. "*I* have been thinking so." *Am I coming to think like Reuben Salt? And would that be any bad thing?* "I do so want my sister to be happy."

The Josephine-Fred combination manoeuvred the launch alongside the bank. Shobnall strode forward to help with mooring and disembarkation, anxious to return his family safely to dry land, thankful to his friends for looking after them. The girls were ecstatic. "Daddy!" Josephine shrieked. "I helped Fred steer the ship!"

Alice was reluctant to leave Vern's grasp. "Uncle Vern," she gurgled.

\* \* \*

Mr Salt, who had unobtrusively retired to lean against the side of his Humber, folded his arms and let the scene unfold. *Those children are delightful.* He rooted around in the special pockets of his jacket to ensure he was armed with carnation stems and coins, should magic be required although, from the look of it, matters nautical had trumped conjuring this afternoon. The helmsman, that would be Fred

Bull, clearly entranced. The large chap, Vern, equally adoring. Lavinia, resting in the stern, hand-in-hand with Rupert Cork. Mr Salt had done a little detecting of his own; by all accounts, the man was a decent all-round good egg. *What might be in prospect here, I wonder?* He was not given to wishes but he made one now.

Billy Needwood had plainly not revealed all but from what he had been prepared to say, the Wychnor case had been a nightmare. Alan obviously appreciated all too well how dicey his situation had been. Billy had made it clear there was to be no mention of his own words in highly-placed ears. Mr Salt was happy with that since it served his friends well. Out here in the provinces, he thought, one might expect an easier life. *Except these days it is all connected. Communications are shrinking distance, accelerating time. London disseminates wealth but it also incubates disease. Swinging London, The Beatles, all those other groups. They say The Beatles are moving into film! It's all bright colours and catchy tunes and lauded as our desirable future but there's a darkness beneath the glitter. You can't have one without the other. What of those other children, Pauline Reade and John Kilbride, for whom the Manchester constabulary are combing the moors? They will tread no shining path.*

He sighed as Shobnall handed his wife ashore and gave her a peck on the cheek. *That's twice young Shobnall has handled an exceptionally complicated and perilous case. Suppose I was his Dr Watson, what title would I give my manuscript? 'The Wychnor Murder'? Too prosaic.* Mr Salt's bed-time reading was Ross Macdonald's 'The Zebra-Striped Hearse'; titles mattered. *'Death and the Maiden'? No, hard to cast Melinda, God rest her soul, as a maiden while the Schubert reference would be lost on today's pop-obsessed public. 'The Needwood Diamond'? The gem was the catalyst with which Billy set things in motion. The hardest of natural materials, resistant to nearly all impurities, the Diamond has survived everything, the treason and the tragedy, and is being restored to its rightful home. Yes, 'The Case of The Needwood Diamond'. That is how I shall remember it.*

Fred and Vern had cast off and were heading for the dry-dock where their Land Rover and trailer waited. Corky and Lavinia were standing close, speaking quietly. He would wait until Lavinia was ready. The Shobnalls were at the Anglia. Alan settling his children in the car. Opening the passenger door for Elaine, ensuring her skirt was clear of the door. Pausing at the driver's door, looking around, seeking Mr Salt. Who raised an arm in salute. Watched the Anglia rattle back up the track. *I fancy he will rise high. He was, after all born on a Thursday and 'Thursday's child has far to go'.*

\* \* \*

# IT'S OVER

June was eventful, full of ups and downs, of harbingers for a better world and disquieting messages from a grim future. The kind of conjunctions beloved of newspaper astrologists as they plot a horoscope in which *something* is bound to fall out in line with their prediction. Thirty-year sentences were handed down to seven of the defendants in the Great Train Robbery trial. The train driver remained in hospital. The Burton police forced entry to a warehouse on the outskirts of Swadlincote and seized printing equipment, carboys of cheap alcohol, hundreds of glass bottles and bales of nylon stocking 'seconds'; a detective constable threw copies of The Reapers' 'Drowning' LP into a dustbin. Cyril Hendry, slotting mail into pigeon-holes, left Shobnall a small package, a foot square and a couple of inches deep, brown paper and string, Essex postmark. It felt padded. Shobnall noticed a similar parcel in Eddie's slot.

British pop continued its conquest of the globe. 'House of Lies', the latest single from The Reapers, soared to the top of the charts here and, shortly after, in America and a score of other countries. The group's appearance on 'Top Of The Pops' provoked a near-riot in the studio and brought inflamed demands from Mary Whitehouse of the 'Clean-Up TV' pressure group for the head or, failing that, the resignation of the Director-General of the BBC. The final test against Australia, at Nottingham, ended in a draw. Much to Bob Saxby's Yorkshire delight, a young batsman named Geoffrey Boycott debuted with 48 runs in the first innings.

Shobnall took his package to the DS' office, stripped off string and paper. The contents were protected by some semi-transparent rubbery plastic impregnated with tiny bubbles of air. Inside was a framed watercolour, from the same family as those hanging in DI Conway's Scotland Yard office. He took it to the window, studied it. The Aberdeen typhoid outbreak topped 300 cases. Tins of corned beef were recalled across the nation; butchers reported a fall in sales; clinical experts wondered what would happen if some totally new disease appeared and ripped through the country. Nelson Mandela delivered his 'I am prepared to die' speech at the Rivonia trial in South Africa. The Melody Maker's northern correspondent gave a four-star review of a gig by a new jazz outfit, The Bob Carter Quintet.

*He's changed the weather, it wasn't like that when he was there.* Wychnor Hall. The Big House. *He must have researched what it looks like.* A summer's day, blue sky, crisp surfaces. The now-familiar building dressed it its late-summer burgundy ivy. *Amazingly detailed for something so small.* There were no figures but Conway had cunningly positioned a two-wheel farm cart resting on its shafts to one side. *Makes the scene more soporific, hotter.* Even the gravel looked warm and crunchy. The old chestnut's intrusion at the edge was like a nod from an old friend. In the lower right

292

corner, in tiny script, 'KC'. He turned it over. Strung, ready to hang. A label in the same script: 'Wychnor Hall, 1964. In the clear.' *It's not going on the wall here, that's for the wall at home.*

Those inveterate film-goers, Lavinia Salt, Elaine Shobnall and Hilary Henderson, visited the Gaumont for a choc-ice and the attraction of multiple Peter Sellers in 'Dr Strangelove or How I Learned to Stop Worrying and Love the Bomb'. They laughed a lot during the first reel but by the journey home the mood was sombre; Lavinia was musing on what Corky must have seen at Nagasaki. Thunderstorms swept the South of England and the Vatican condemned the use of the contraceptive pill for women. Twelve year-old Keith Bennett, from Fallowfield in Manchester, last seen on his way to his grandmother's house, became the third child, after Pauline Reade and John Kilbride, to go missing from the area. Police were said to be combing Saddleworth Moor. Shobnall heard that news item on the radio as he tapped a nail into the lounge wall for his new picture. He recalled Lennie Morton's words. Here in 1964 Swinging Britain. Where you never had it so good. Dark appetites lusted for innocent food. Something rotten was abroad. And hungry.

\* \* \*

Printed in Great Britain
by Amazon